BRIAN S. LEON

CHAOS UNBOUND

THE METIS FILES: BOOK TWO

Chaos Unbound
The Metis Files™
Copyright © 2016 by Brian S. Leon. All rights reserved.
First Edition: February 2017

ISBN-13: 978-1-940215-83-9
ISBN-10: 1-940215-83-8

Red Adept Publishing, LLC
104 Bugenfield Court
Garner, NC 27529
http://RedAdeptPublishing.com/

Cover and Formatting: Streetlight Graphics

It is said that if you know your enemies and know yourself,
you will not be imperiled in a hundred battles;
if you do not know your enemies but do know yourself,
you will win one and lose one;
if you do not know your enemies nor yourself,
you will be imperiled in every single battle.

—**The Art of War**, Sun Tzu

CHAPTER 1

San Diego, September 2011

SELKIES. THIRTY-FIVE MILES OFFSHORE IN the Pacific Ocean, and I'm dodging freakin' selkies in my fishing boat. It's like they're seagulls, and I'm dropping French fries at the beach. Man, do they screw up the fishing. Worse, when they appear, bad things tend to follow. *And it's just my luck.* Of all fae to show up randomly, it had to be *these* shape-shifters — the kind that could transform into seals and even into sea lions, which scare the crap out of the fish. Every pile of floating kelp we'd fished around so far had one of these fairies under it. Every kelp except the paddy right in front of the boat.

"Captain Dore, look! Another seal," the woman said, reaching for her camera.

And that selkie made it a perfect five for five.

I couldn't help but hang my head. My clients — a simple Midwestern family of Mom, Dad, and Teenage Son — considered it endearing to see a seal poke its head up from inside the kelp, but *I* could see their true bulbous heads, seaweed-like hair, and pudgy gray-green humanoid forms. Their giant, shiny-black eyes fixed on me as if they knew exactly who I was.

The creepy shape-shifters were part of the Unseelie Court — fairies that are decidedly unfriendly to humans — and the fact that we kept encountering them was starting to unnerve me. Encountering one in the Pacific was rare. In fact, I couldn't recall one off Southern California since an entire tribe of them showed up around Catalina Island in the 1980s. That appearance had led to a spate of unidentified *submerged* object and alien sightings, not to mention a few mysterious plane crashes around the island and a heap of sunken boats.

"Hey, what's that big fin?" the father asked, pointing at the rapidly approaching triangular object sticking out of the water and heading straight at the paddy from the opposite side.

"Shark," I said with a sudden smile. "Damn big one, too. Great white, from the looks of it. Rare for us down here in San Diego."

"Oh, swim, seal! Swim!" the mom said as all hell broke loose around the paddy.

"Wow, really," the kid said. "It's like a real *National Geographic* moment." He whipped out his phone to video the event.

I was the only one on the boat rooting for the shark. If they'd known what that shark was really chasing, they probably would have thought it was more like a *National Enquirer* moment.

Knowing the selkie-shark conflict would ruin the fishing within a mile of that paddy, I pushed farther out, always on the lookout for signs of life *other* than selkies. As long as we could avoid them, we found lots of small football-sized yellowfin tuna while we trolled, and I'd even managed to convince the anglers to release the little guys, in hopes of finding bigger ones. The small fish kept me blissfully busy until we made it back to the dock at around four in the afternoon—so busy, in fact, that I forgot about how screwy the presence of selkies was until I realized my buddy Ned was storming down the dock toward my boat as I pulled in.

As usual, Ned was dressed in a Hawaiian shirt with colors usually reserved for Las Vegas neon. The fact that he resembled a derelict version of Santa Claus usually drew people's attention. It was either that or the fact that he always smelled like beer-soaked seaweed washed up on a beach. *It could be worse given that Ned was in fact the Titan God of the Sea, Nereus, in self-imposed exile.*

As I secured the boat to the dock, my cell phone, stashed inside my captain's bag within the console, chirped the unique ring my buddy Geek had helped me assign to Sarah Wright. I felt guilty for avoiding her over the past two weeks. Despite scrambling to reach the annoying device before the call went to voice mail, I wasn't quick enough. I tossed the phone on the console, thoroughly disgusted with my wishy-washy-ness regarding our relationship—or whatever we had. I was pretty sure we both wanted to take things to the next level, but I was conflicted about what that would mean for both of us since my situation wasn't exactly normal.

I'll call her back as soon as I can. I sighed, watching my three clients stumble off the boat, trying to adjust to sea legs on land after a full day on the water. They chatted excitedly about sharks and sea lions as they went. Ned stood down the dock, waiting, staring intently at me with his hands on his hips and one flip-flop-clad foot tapping away. The trio barely managed to get past him before he charged the boat.

"Diomedes, dude, glad to see you made it back okay." Ned's shoulders dropped a bit as he exhaled heavily. "Now get yer ass off the damn boat and back onto land." He dipped his head slightly and glared over his sunglasses at me, his brow deeply furrowed.

I stopped taking rods out of the rod racks under the gunwales and stared back at him. Something had him on edge, and *that* was saying something. Normally, he made people on Prozac appear edgy. In over a thousand years, I'd never seen him like this before.

"Now, dude. Now!" he said, raising his voice and gesticulating wildly.

The myriad of seagulls and pelicans gathered around the boat awaiting leftover bait and fish carcasses took off in a sudden deafening and chaotic commotion.

"Whoa. Relax, Ned. What's got your panties in a bunch?" I said, getting back to my after-charter chores. "Sheesh. Besides, I think the dad left a few beers if you want them."

Normally, Ned's first question to me would have involved the possible presence of abandoned beer. Instead, he fixed me with a withering stare. His hands were back on his hips, and his foot again tapped on the dock. When we'd first met a few thousand years before, he'd naturally emanated an aura of power. Though he'd since willingly given up most of his other-dimensional essence, the preternatural blue glow was now visible.

"Dude, which part of 'now' ain't you understandin'?" He spoke through a clenched jaw and pointed at the dock forcefully, like a parent demanding a child's immediate presence. Over his sunglasses, his eyes darted everywhere, keeping watch around us.

"Okay, okay," I said, eyeing my fish-slimed gear and all the sardine scales and scuff marks marring the deck. "Who's gonna clean all this up? You know if I let it sit, it'll be even harder to clean later."

"I'll take care of it," Ned replied. "Just get yer ass off the water. Right. Now."

"Fine." I kicked at my rods like a petulant child. "Let me get my damn gear bag, and I'll leave."

I grabbed my captain's bag and stormed down the dock in a huff, glaring at Ned. I didn't even bother to take off my grungy gray rubber fishing bibs. He avoided making eye contact as I passed him, which only pissed me off more. Instead, his eyes continued to dart around the marina. *Whatever.*

I got to my truck, threw my gear bag in the bed, then stripped off the rubber bibs. While hopping around on one leg like an idiot, trying to get the bibs off over my deck boots, I worked myself up from a huff to a tizzy. *Who the hell did he think he was ordering me around like that? Athena?* Throwing my bibs into the bed with the rest, I glanced over my shoulder, toward the dock.

Just as I was about to get into my truck, a more pressing question hit me: *Why?* Ned actually yelled at me. In over two millennia, I had never even witnessed him raise his voice. *What'd I do to him?*

I instantly felt like I owed him an apology, without even knowing what I'd done. I headed back down to the dock.

As I approached the top of the gangway, Ned was in a heated discussion with something in the water on the other side of the dock from my boat. I couldn't get a clear view of who or what Ned was talking with, or hear what was being said. The only things evident were the loud and freakish sea-lion-like barks and Ned's wild and very uncharacteristic gesticulations. Instinctively, I searched for something to use as a weapon—a boat hook was leaning against the fence next to the gate down to the dock.

Then a putty-colored round female head covered in thick yellow-green hair popped up just above the dock and peered directly at me. Ned noticed me, as well, and all at once, the creature disappeared below the water's surface, creating a wake that tossed the floating dock and rocked the boats tied up nearby. She was definitely one of the selkies I had encountered earlier offshore.

I stopped dead in my tracks. Ned shook his head and stomped toward me, which couldn't have been easy in flip-flops. His eyes were ablaze—literally. His awakened aura pulsed from white to blue like a lightning storm.

I shrugged and raised my eyebrows as his gaze fell on me. The temperature began to drop, and the water around the dock changed from a drab green to black and turned rough, as if it were about to boil. The disturbance bounced the moored boats against their bumpers and the dock, and the rigging on the sailboats began to clang. Even the remaining birds evacuated — only noiselessly.

"Boy, who did you piss off this time?" he said *at* me more than *to* me in a voice that reverberated through my skull. It wasn't loud, but it was insistent in its tone.

"I... um... I, ah... what?" I asked, vapor trailing from my mouth in the cool air.

I couldn't recall having done anything to anybody since chasing down that witch, Medea, a few months back, and as far as I knew, everyone I could have pissed off doing that was dead.

Ned continued up the ramp from the dock toward me, somehow appearing larger than normal. His face, especially his eyes, darkened. "Don't play games with me. You got selkies chasin' yer ass all over the Pacific, and they had to travel around the world to get here to do it. Nytrocyon herself is here to find you." He pointed back down toward my boat. "She says Mab wants you. Says you killed Lord Indronivay."

"Nytrocyon, ruler of the selkies? Seriously?" My teeth started to chatter, and my jaw muscles clenched in the frigid air. "Wait... she said I killed *who*? Lord Indronivay, Mab's warmaster? Are you kidding me? Why the hell would I have killed that uptight, belligerent asshole?"

I'd never even met him, but his reputation as a jerk was legendary. Even as a Guardian and protector of humanity, I knew him only through stories that suggested he was a giant at nearly eight feet tall and was about as friendly as a shark with a toothache. All I really knew about him was that he personally ran every major war and military campaign Queen Mab of the Unseelie Court had waged for tens of thousands of years. *Hell, the guy might have charged into battle against Queen Titania of the Seelie Court on the back of a triceratops.*

"You're sayin' Nytrocyon is lying?" Ned's voice boomed through my head, shaking me back to attention.

I shrugged again. "Now why the hell would I do something like that? Honestly?"

Ned's shoulders dropped slightly, and his pulsing aura faded.

5

Though his face brightened and his bushy beard and mustache split, revealing his white teeth in a broad smile, the rest of him remained rigid. "Good. I didn't think you were dumb enough to attack a member of one of the fairy royal courts. That'd be grounds for war. Only problem is then, dude" — he slowly slipped back into his normal relaxed and carefree persona — "you gotta ask yerself one question: why does *she* think you did?"

CHAPTER 2

COULDN'T FATHOM WHY SOMEONE WOULD think I'd killed one of Queen Mab's retinue. While no one in my world would doubt the action if I actually *had* killed the guy during a war, they also should know I would never do such a thing without clear reason or cause.

I finally realized I had been clenching my jaw so hard that my teeth hurt. I crossed my arms. "Did they say how I killed him?"

"Naw, man. Just that the Unseelie Court has offered a bounty on yer head for the death of Lord Indronivay. But if you didn't do it, someone tried to make it appear like you did."

"A bounty? How much?" I asked.

"If it came from Mab and Nytrocyon herself is here, it ain't money, boy. She's got to be offerin' a personal favor."

"A favor from Mab? Yikes. But why me?" I'd had plenty of run-ins with all kinds of fae from both courts, not to mention hundreds of other types of Parans and Old Ones. It's been my job to protect humanity from all kinds of creatures and beings for nearly three and a half thousand years. *But not once was I ever pre-emptive, let alone unprovoked. I only respond to threats.* Anything else would be interpreted as an act of war by most of the nonhuman races of our world—especially the fae and the Unseelie Court.

"You got bigger problems right now than figgerin' out why you, dude. You got Unseelie bounty hunters lookin' fer you. If I was you, I'd get rollin' and fast, man."

"No kidding. Look, I need your help—"

He threw his hands up, palms out. "Nah, man. No can do. You know I can't get involved here. I'm neutral—beyond neutral. I'm nobody anymore, and I wanna stay that way. I mean, I might nudge the ocean conditions a little here and there, maybe get some free suds from fishermen and surfers, but you know I can't interfere with something like this. I've worked hard not to have any enemies anymore."

"You're kidding me, right? After all the crap we've been through? And now you can't get involved?" I said hoarsely, on the verge of shouting.

I'd known Ned since I saved him from a boatload of fishermen several thousand years ago. Sure, he'd never actually interceded in anything I did before, but he was always there to help a little if the situation called for it.

"I need to know more about the situation, and you can at least get information without getting involved, can't you, you —" I was about to throw in a nasty epithet but thought better of it.

"Get to yer car now, dude. Move it. I'll do whatever I can," he said, ripping his sunglasses off his face. His eyes narrowed as they tracked past me, out toward the parking area at the top of the boat ramp off to his right.

A massive shaggy green-furred dog sniffed the air in the middle of the parking lot on the other side of the tackle shop about two hundred feet away. It was a Cu Sith, a barrow hound of the Unseelie Court, and it was nearly the size of my truck. Thankfully, it appeared to be overwhelmed by the scents of low tide, rotting fish, and bird crap.

I shot Ned a quick wide-eyed glance and slowly but deliberately started toward my truck, fumbling for my keys. I briefly lost sight of the hound as I crossed behind the tackle shop, but the dog loosed three loud wails that had the intensity of sonic booms, shattering most of the windows around the showroom of the neighboring boat dealership.

His beard flowing over his shoulder, Ned walked with long strides in the direction of the Cu Sith. He waved me on without making eye contact, urging me to keep moving. Almost instantly, the smell of rotting seaweed overwhelmed me. The fetid odor was rife with the watery smell of vegetation mixed with putrefying meat.

I gagged but continued walking quickly toward my truck while Ned distracted it. My primary concern was getting away from whatever might be controlling the fairy dog while I was unarmed and ill prepared. Once I reached my truck, I could see Ned standing at the top of the boat ramp. Hands on hips, he watched the barrow hound try to relocate my scent amid the rotting seaweed smell that

Ned produced. Screams erupted from the tackle shop as well as the hotel across the marina, followed by the sounds of glass shattering and something tossing around heavy objects on cement. As the hound swung its enormous head along the ground, occasionally lifting its nose to sniff the air, a second Cu Sith, just as large, bounded into the lot through the hotel's outdoor restaurant as people scrambled in every direction.

I got to my truck and took off down Ingraham Street toward my house without paying attention to the traffic lights. My home wasn't the safest place, but at least there, I had weapons and armor to defend myself. I wasn't worried about leaving Ned with those hounds. They weren't after him. I kept glancing in my rearview mirrors to see if I was being followed but saw nothing other than cars behind me by the time I got to the bridge over the San Diego River less than a mile down the road.

That was when I hit sudden traffic. Nothing was moving. Traffic around three or four in the afternoon on Point Loma was bad, but I had never seen anything *this* bad before. People were starting to get out of their cars to see what was going on. The traffic lights up ahead were out, but I didn't see any accidents or hear any sirens. In fact, I wasn't hearing *any* noises other than the cars around me—not even jets at the downtown airport on the other side of Point Loma.

I switched on the radio and found out that the electricity had gone out in some parts of San Diego for some unknown reason, and lucky me, I just happened to be in one of those parts. *Of all freakin' days for the power to go out in San Diego.*

I opened my door and stood on the running board to get a better view, turning to check behind me in case the hounds had picked up my scent. The only smell was the riverbanks below me, during the falling tide. I still couldn't see the hounds, but it didn't appear as if I was going anywhere in my truck any time soon. I sat back in the cab and listened to the radio while trying to think up a plan. I kept getting hung up on why someone would think I killed Lord Indronivay, but I couldn't afford to dwell on it. I needed to be in motion. Somehow.

The radio began reporting that the blackouts covered a far larger area than originally estimated. Callers were reporting in from around San Diego County that they were also without power. *Holy crap. I got a bounty on my head from the Unseelie Court, and I'm stuck in traffic in the biggest blackout San Diego has ever seen.*

Three loud barks from someplace behind me shattered the relative silence like a barrage of artillery fire. I, along with hundreds of stranded motorists, was a sitting duck, and I was putting everybody around me in mortal danger with no way to defend them. Everyone I could see searched around to see what had caused the noise. People stuck in traffic near me asked if they were explosions, and that was followed quickly by the supposition that the whole blackout was probably the result of a terrorist attack. That led to people frantically honking their horns and shouting, while others began pulling out onto the road's shoulder in an attempt to move, gumming up the traffic even more. I reached for my cell phone, hoping to check the map for traffic, and it dawned on me that I had left it on the console of my boat. *Perfect.* Even so, I could only imagine that cell phone reception was crappy, too, as everyone in the entire city tried desperately to contact someone else. The only thing I could think to do was keep moving so that the Cu Sith would focus on tracking me rather than all the innocent people stuck in their way. *But how?*

Over the growing confusion, I heard a motorcycle making its way up the street through the stopped cars behind me. *Bingo.* I was going to feel really bad about what I was about to do for a while, but I figured being well adjusted and an otherwise reasonably upstanding guy, I would get over it.

Thanks to a crazy driver on my left trying to create a third lane down the middle of a two-lane street, the motorcyclist would have to pass my truck to the right, along the narrow shoulder. I scooted through my truck's cab to the passenger side and threw open the door as the motorcyclist approached. He was dressed in that bizarre computer-generated blue camouflage the Navy used and was driving a blue Aprilla RSV 1000 R motorcycle that cost as much as my truck — something I knew thanks to my vehicle-crazy friend, Duma. The rider slid to a stop, turning the bike almost completely sideways without dumping it.

As the driver began gesturing and reaching to take his helmet off so he could scream at me face-to-face, I grabbed the handrail above my passenger door and threw my legs out at the rider as hard as I could. The maneuver caught him square in the chest and totally off guard. The person went flying over the side of the bridge, and the bike fell to rest partially against my truck door. I hopped on it, backed it up, and reached out to close my door before glancing over the side of the bridge. It was only a few yards over the San Diego River, and the rider, probably on his way to report to duty down on Point Loma, had landed in the slow-moving water at low tide. He was already dragging himself ashore on the muddy banks. *Boy, am I gonna feel bad. At some point. If I live long enough.*

I gunned the bike and took off up the shoulder, trying to put as much distance between me and the Cu Sith as I could. I was trying to formulate my next move and not crash at the same time, and I was only doing one with any real success. Weaving through stopped vehicles mostly by pushing the bike along with my legs, I made it to the Interstate 5/8 interchange without dumping the bike or hitting anyone. There was no way I would make it to my house through some of the most crowded streets and neighborhoods in San Diego. So my pathetic plan revolved around the fact that my only weapon was the fishermen's multi-tool I still happened to have in my pocket. I hoped I could draw the creatures and whatever controlled them away from the heavily populated areas. *At least if their handler has beer, I'll be able to open their bottles for them.*

Trying to head east to the less densely populated areas of San Diego, I followed the flow of traffic the best I could, eventually merging onto the 163 North. The only sign of the hounds was steady but distant barking.

Then everything completely bogged down. Three lanes of traffic had been expanded to anywhere between six and eight cars wide, and multiple cars were pulled onto both shoulders, blocking the road completely. One vehicle in the mess clearly had mechanical issues, and several other drivers had stopped to help the waylaid motorist. *Bully for good Samaritans. Don't these people realize I need to move?*

I decided to take the next off-ramp and get onto surface streets. To avoid becoming further mired in the stalled traffic on the ramp, I tried to hop the median, but my attempt at Evel Knieveling the bump didn't work out too well. I hit the divider so squarely that I couldn't stop the front wheel from cutting hard to the left, jerking the handlebar and throttle from my grasp as the bike went one way and I went another.

CHAPTER 3

THE DUMP WASN'T EVEN SPECTACULAR. I flew up and off. The bike bounced over, then I landed hard on my butt. The bike wobbled off a short distance, where it fell under a brown delivery truck.

I picked myself up, trying to recover any dignity I might find scattered among the ice plants along the way, while the delivery guy jumped out to see what had happened.

"You okay?" he asked, eyes wide as he stared at the motorcycle under the back of his truck. I didn't know what was hanging him up more — me crashing a motorcycle into his truck while dressed as if I'd just walked off a boat or the blackout thing.

"Yeah, I'm fine, but the bike is shot," I said, brushing at the dirt on my rear.

Realizing that the only thing really injured was my pride, I quickly forgot about the delivery guy and the growing crowd of looky-loos and surveyed my surroundings to figure out where to go now that my daredevil days were behind me. Not only did I have some nasty members of the Unseelie Court on my ass, but my ass *actually* hurt, too.

Several of the gathered motorists began to approach me, asking questions, while others examined the bike. I power-walked toward an industrial area at the end of the off ramp while shouts erupted from the gawkers behind me. I needed to get out of there before somebody whipped out a camera phone if they hadn't already.

I crossed the street, darting around the stopped vehicles, and rounded a few of the buildings, leaving the wrecked bike and gathered mob behind. I had to be careful not to run so fast that I drew any more attention to myself. As I reached the far side of the buildings, I could see the edge of a large construction site a bit farther up the street. It was a multi-story apartment complex still in the early stages of framing. I headed directly toward the site, hoping to find a temporary hiding place and maybe a weapon or two.

I checked my watch as I approached the massive dirt lot dominated by two separate cement and stick-frame structures. It was a little after five in the afternoon, which meant that what normally should have taken fifteen minutes had taken over an hour. Part of me was relieved that I hadn't seen or even heard the Cu Sith in a while, but that meant those things were running amok through San Diego somewhere. Thankfully, the construction site appeared entirely empty of people, most likely due to the blackout. A line of cars blocked the streets along both the north and south sides of the site, making it impossible to hop the fence from either street without being seen. Along the property's west side was a parking lot crowded with vehicles trying to merge onto the already-jammed streets, but the east side butted against several large condominium complexes.

I jogged down the sidewalk toward the condos to a walking entrance into the complex and found it much more secluded than the street and practically mazelike. I continued around several more buildings, running along the fence line to make sure no one would see me jump it. The last thing I needed was police chasing me, too.

As I walked among the earthy green and tan condos, I could hear people chatting and laughing nearby, probably using the blackout as an excuse to gather with neighbors and empty their currently thawing freezers onto grills. While I didn't see any of the gatherings around the buildings I was between, as I continued farther along, the smells of barbequing meat carrying through the early-evening air made my stomach growl. I made a habit of not eating while out on a charter, so I hadn't eaten anything since dinner last night.

Over the sounds of my now-awakened stomach, I heard a radio somewhere broadcasting the opening game of the football season. *Dammit. I completely forgot about that.* My original plans for the evening involved my being ensconced in my leather chair, with a bag of cheese puffs, watching the game. Clearly, that wasn't going to happen.

I fought through the disappointment and hunger like the warrior I am and made it to the six-foot-high chain-link fence that separated the construction from the complex. Some sort of heavy green cloth used to prevent construction debris from blowing off the site covered the fence. Since I couldn't see through it, I grabbed the top rail and pulled myself up to check if the coast was clear then vaulted over. The soles of my stupid rubber deck boots landed hard and flat on the compacted dirt, and I crouched, cursing the pain in my feet under my breath. Grinding my teeth, I crept to the edge of the nearest building under construction.

The site was huge for Southern California, easily seven hundred feet long between the bordering streets and half as wide. It was dominated by a sea of concrete forming a massive, enclosed underground parking garage that spanned almost the entire length of the lot. The structure also formed the foundation for two distinct sets of wooden framework buildings. I had jumped the fence at a spot between the two skeletal buildings. The nearest entrance into the subterranean parking levels was less than ten yards to my left.

With only the occasional and faint sounds of barks from the Cu Sith, I figured I was safe in the structure for the moment. *Woefully unarmed, but safe.* I needed a weapon. Searching in the darkness for anything I could swing, I found a few stray pieces of rebar lying around — as good a weapon as any when you don't have a real one. Rebar in hand, I made my way across the skeletal structure and took in my surroundings. In the odd darkness of the blackout, the evening air was eerily still and quiet. There were no sounds of cars on the nearby highway or jet noise from the Marine Corp Air Station to the north. Nothing. I knew the Cu Sith would still be searching for me, and not at least hearing them — at any distance — was unnerving.

In the failing light, I thought I noticed movement on the top of a fifty-foot-tall mound of fill dirt next to a big dump truck parked at the plateau a hundred fifty feet away. It could have easily been birds or rabbits, but I decided not to take any chances. Members of the Unseelie Court chasing me — they thrived in the cold, dark places of the world.

I tried to remind myself that not all fae were that bad and that some members of the Seelie, or Light Fae, had proven helpful to me over the years. When it came to the fae, though, I would have loved to have my Peri friend, Duma, and his brother, Abraxos, around to help. But I'd left my cell phone on my boat, and I didn't have any other way to contact them or anyone else, so I went back to staring at the area where I was sure I detected movement, pissed at my stupidity.

I watched so intently for the next few minutes, I thought my eyes would pop out of my head. But just before I gave up, ready to chalk my sighting up to what we call "happy eyes" in fishing, I saw it again. Something was definitely down there, only now it was *underneath* a front-end loader on the same hill of dirt. Then something else moved near the dump truck's wheel again. Whatever *they* were, they were human sized — too small to be the Cu Sith. Unfortunately, in the fairy world, size has no correlation to dangerousness. Something the size of a rat could rip my head off as easily as something the size of an elephant could.

The pair of shadowy figures creeping around the heavy machinery finally crossed into the open. After thirty-two hundred some odd years, I'd witnessed a lot of things, but I had no idea what I was seeing. They were around seven feet tall, solidly built, and covered in shaggy dark fur or hair. The first thing that popped into my head was Bigfoot, but these things were much more compact, and their stubby arms ended in hands — for lack of a better term — that bore four massive claws that Wolverine would have envied.

It was a moonless night, and the lack of power to the area made it even darker, but as the creatures faced each other, I could see a massive set of tusks protruding upward from what I could only guess was a mouth. They paused for a second, then one took a few steps, bent over, and began burrowing at the edge of the dirt mound. It quickly disappeared into the ground. The other creature began to scrabble down the side of the mound on two legs in a gangly loping manner that demonstrated dexterity but not grace. Whatever they were, they were apparently not completely comfortable walking upright.

My hands tightened around the piece of rebar as I scanned the area for an easy exit. The place was a warren rife with dead ends, pitfalls, and stacks of wood and sheetrock, while the fences were across open ground. Even if I made it out of there, I was still on foot. I was going to have to make a stand.

Sneaking through the unfinished interior, around piles of construction materials and debris within the superstructure, I made my way over to the base of an I-beam that connected the building to the one next to it. I tried to keep an eye on the one creature still above ground, but I lost sight of it once the furry thing made it to the cement foundation almost directly below me. I leaned out and noticed it was hunched over right under my position, its head tilted up in my direction. I jerked back, bumping into a pile of wood and cut sheetrock. The impact jarred a large box of nails on top of the pile and knocked it to the wooden subfloor with a hollow metallic clatter that echoed forever through the empty belly of the structure. A quick rasping growl emanated from below. *Good job, Mr. Stealthy.*

My concern for my clumsy mistake was short-lived. As I chided myself, it dawned on me that the shaggy beasts were likely fae, and no fairy, Unseelie or otherwise, could tolerate iron or even an alloy of iron, including steel. Nails are steel. Rebar is steel. And it would all burn them—not like acid, but instead like a base chemical: Their skin blisters and then sloughs off, causing intense, freezing pain. *I'm standing in what amounts to a fairy House of Horrors. Hot damn!*

I grabbed the remaining box of nails and my rebar and decided to go on the offensive.

"Hey, Shaggy!" I screamed. The sound echoed through the wooden structure. "You lookin' for me? 'Cause I'm right here!"

Suddenly, the floor began to shake. Wood snapped below me like a rifle shot, then the floor began to tilt. The creature had to be using those massive claws to rip apart the wooden structure below me. *Sonofabitch.*

I jumped farther back into the construction to more stable footing, dropping the nails, but I managed to hang onto the heavy piece of rebar as I landed on my side. The floor that I'd occupied collapsed, bringing with it the floor above. Within the din, I could hear the nails and other metallic objects fall, raining down below, followed by an ear-splitting bellow of pure agony.

"Eat cold steel, furball!" I shouted as I got to my feet.

I could hear the thing shifting under the rubble, along with labored breathing mixed with an occasional gurgle. I carefully crept over to the edge of the structure that collapsed, rebar in hand, and peered over the edge. Not much was visible, but the plywood flooring formed a sort of slide down to the first floor, and I decided to risk the splinters. From the lower level, I jumped to a clear spot on the cement and whirled around to face the woodpile and the creature I assumed was trapped within it.

There was no longer any movement coming from the pile, but I could still hear the wheezing and gurgling from under the debris. In the darkness, I couldn't see anything through the rubble. Part of me

16

wanted to see what the hell the thing was up close, but the rational part wanted to get underway again since I had no idea where the other one was. I hopped down to the ground along the west side of the building. The site office trailer was about a hundred feet away, with a car parked in front of it. I waited silently for a moment, just in case the other creature was still around, but nothing moved.

Hunched over with the rebar at the ready, I loped over to the car, intending to steal it. The owner of the car was nowhere to be found. Something about that was wrong. I couldn't believe that the noise that thing made bringing down two floors of wood, metal, and who knew what else wouldn't have roused a security guard from the middle of even the deepest sleep.

As I worked my way toward the driver's door of the beat-up old Chevette, something dark and shiny in the scant ambient light on the ground in front of it caught my eye. And that's when the smell hit me — a sweet metallic odor mixed with the slight tang of sewage. Unfortunately, I'd smelled it often enough in my long life to recognize it instantly — a disemboweled body.

I used my free hand to cover my mouth and nose in a pathetic attempt to stifle some of the smell. Once I got all the way around the car, I discovered the body — or bodies. There was simply too much carnage to belong to only one person. Finding the vehicle unlocked, I opened the door and switched on the car's headlights. The illuminated scene was straight out of a Hollywood slasher movie. The two security guards had been totally ripped to pieces. They were little more than a big mound of ground beef with the random piece of gray or black cloth and bone sticking out of it. While I stared at the bloodbath, shaking my head, knowing that their deaths were partly my fault, one of the torsos began to wiggle a little.

My first reaction was that the guy was still alive, but that was *not* possible. I shifted the rebar in my hands then decided it might be more prudent to get in the car and get the hell out of there. I kept glancing at the quivering mass while I fumbled through the vehicle's interior, trying to find the keys. I checked the overstuffed glove box, above the visor, in the armrest, along the grungy, disgusting floor, and anywhere else I could think of — because I had no earthly clue how to hotwire a vehicle. After a few moments, I realized the keys were more than likely on one of the two bodies. *Talk about a disgusting egg hunt.* The gruesome task made me think about heading back to the condos next door to ask for help, but the sight of the two mutilated guards reinforced my instincts to draw everything chasing me *away* from humanity.

So I started to poke around the horrific mess with the length of rebar. The first thing I jabbed was the quivering torso. Just as I touched it, an explosion of carnage burst from the ground underneath it. The surprise, more than the force, caused me to stagger back into the hood of the car. The car lights illuminated the other fur-covered clawed beast, its long black fur matted and caked with blood and gore.

"You're coming with us," the creature said in impossibly perfect diction through a mouth like an angry red gash flanked by two enormous tusks and cutter teeth that were big enough to come from a five-hundred-pound Russian boar. I couldn't see any eyes on its shaggy stump of a head.

"Not a chance," I replied, getting my feet back under me. I held the rebar in front of me with both hands like a staff rather than a sword. "Besides, if by 'us,' you mean you and that other furball you came with, you probably ought to know that he might be a little flatter than you remember." I jerked my head back in the direction of the collapse without taking my eyes off the creature.

"My Queen prefers you alive, Diomedes, but she will still reward me if you are dead." The creature's wide mouth became even wider, in a grotesque attempt at a grin. Stepping to its right, it started to circle, crouching as it progressed.

I turned to keep myself as square to the beast as I could. For some reason — maybe the rebar — it kept its distance, bobbing slightly from side to side as it hunched, its arms down at its sides. Its long, curved claws dragged in the dirt.

"Back off and let me go, or this is gonna get ugly," I said. "And tell Mab whatever she thinks I did, I didn't. Um, why does she think I did it?"

The creature made a throaty, gurgling laugh, then it lunged. I stepped backward and dodged to my left, narrowly avoiding its reach. I quickly sprang forward, driving the rebar hard across the monster's chest, sending it staggering backward and eliciting a howl of pain as the steel touched its skin. Recoiling, the creature doubled over, hissing and drooling on the ground. I pressed the attack, swinging the rebar around overhead to my left, to bring it down in an arc like a club. Thanks to the combination of the awkward weapon and the creature's incredible speed and agility, it landed a glancing blow, sending shockwaves through my arms and jarring my teeth as the rebar hit the ground.

The beast backhanded me while I was off balance, striking me across my right shoulder and upper back, knocking me to one knee. I used the momentum to tuck into a roll that brought me along the shaggy fae's right side. As I got to my knees, I thrust the rebar upward into the creature's gut. It screeched a piercing, high-pitched shriek and brought one of its clawed hands down sharply across the rod, cutting the rebar cleanly in half with another howl. The reduction in weight and length threw me off balance enough to cause me to tip forward.

I managed to catch myself with one hand before I pulled a full face-plant while the creature hobbled off into the darkness faster than I expected, groaning as it wrenched the steel bar from its abdomen. Honestly, using iron against a fairy was almost cheating, but I was in a pinch. *Besides, all's fair in war.*

CHAPTER 4

I SCRAMBLED BACK TO THE BLOODY scene and began carefully but quickly poking at anything pocket-like, desperate to find the car keys. By the time I found them, I probably looked like one of the unfortunate extras in a Dario Argento movie. So be it. I had bigger problems to deal with.

I hopped in the Chevette and floored it. Fortunately, the traffic on the roads had significantly cleared up. Reports on the radio were saying that the blackout extended from Riverside County to Ensenada and as far east as Arizona, but they still had no idea what had caused it or how long it would be before power was restored. The DJs were laughing about crazy reports of two large green wolves running wild through Mission Valley, and no one could identify the source of the numerous and destructive sonic booms. Fortunately, it sounded like the fairy glamour the Cu Sith emanated hid their true monstrous forms from innocent bystanders. I hadn't perceived so much as a whimper from them in a while, but they would eventually find my scent. The only way to truly lose them would be by traveling through the Telluric Pathways.

An entire contingent of Mab's hunters was probably waiting at my house, and armed only with a chunk of rebar, I would be a fool to head there. So I just drove with the sole objective of remaining on the run for as long as I could. I was a little surprised Athena, my benefactor and the source of my inhuman strength and speed, hadn't stepped in to help me, but the more I considered it, the more her indifference made sense. She would have assisted if she could. She was likely trying to negotiate and resolve the mess before things got out of hand, maybe trying to buy me time. For the moment, I was on my own.

I flipped through radio stations, trying to find the football game,

20

and it didn't take me long to discover the Chargers were losing. *Today is not turning out well for me.*

After meandering around several unnervingly quiet and dark neighborhoods, I found myself on an onramp for Highway 52, which was completely deserted, and decided to head east, hoping to find some open ground. I almost made it up the big hill at the edge of Mission Trails Park before the car began sputtering like water dumped into hot oil and spewing steam from under the hood. The car finally came to a stop, and I actually had to let the piece of junk roll backward downhill to get it to the side of the road.

Marine Corp Air Station Miramar took up all the land on the north side of the highway, while a state park occupied the land to the south with the nearest neighborhoods a few miles ahead or behind. I didn't expect to encounter anyone, given the blackout. It was as good a place as any to hide, so I stayed in the car. At least if anything found me on the side of the highway, it was out of the way. I was surprised by how different things were without power. The vast majority of my life has been spent without any sort of electricity, yet I still couldn't avoid the sense of utter isolation in the darkness even though I was only a few miles from several major shopping malls and neighborhoods.

I didn't even know if Athena could help me out of a mess with the Unseelie Court. The whole situation reminded me of how tired I was, running and hiding for the past few hours with no good plan of action and no real idea why I was running. I knew Mab *supposedly* wanted me for murdering her Warmaster, but I didn't know why she believed *I* had done it. Clearly, I was going to have to figure out what had really happened and do it quietly and damn fast, before any other Unseelie uglies got a shot at me. And I needed to keep any confrontations as far away from people as possible, not only so they wouldn't see it, but to protect them from becoming collateral damage. I had no idea if it was even possible—or even worthwhile—to plead directly to Mab. The fae system of justice always struck me as a kangaroo court—if a man wasn't guilty, he wouldn't be there. Besides, if someone was framing me, I had to know who and why. That was the only way to end this mess without dying.

The next thing I knew, I woke up startled, blinded by the glare of a flashlight as someone tapped on the window. It was still dark, and while I shielded my eyes with one hand, I rolled the window down a bit. It dawned on me that I was driving a stolen car covered in the owner's blood, but at the moment, blinded by a flashlight, I couldn't even tell if the guy tapping on the window was human or not.

"You okay, buddy?" a voice asked from the other side of the window. "You're covered in blood... are you hurt?"

"Ah, I'm fine," I replied, trying to sound coherent. "Just bumped my head."

The window knocker lowered the flashlight beam, and I began to get enough vision back that flashing blue lights became evident in my rearview mirror. Either I was being abducted by aliens, or this was a cop.

"You okay to step out of the car for me, Mister, or should I call an ambulance for you?" the voice behind the light asked.

"No, no, I'm okay. I can get out."

This is going to be fun. At least it's not aliens. I opened the car door slowly, trying to get a sense of the situation. One officer stood behind the door I was climbing out of while another stood at the car's trunk, his hand on the gun at his hip.

"You have any ID, sir?" the officer asked loudly but politely, acting as if I might be drunk.

Oh well, what the hell?

"Ah, I think I left it at the bar." I patted my pockets then stumbled a bit, finally leaning on the open car door for support, playing into his suspicions.

"What's your name? Sir, can you tell me your name?" the cop asked as I bobbed and swiveled my head in every direction.

"It's... um... it's... Frank." I retched as if I were about to vomit. "'Scuse me. I think Immona be sick—" I began wobbling quickly around the back of the car, past the other cop, toward the side of the road.

The cop at the rear of the car backed up a few steps, avoiding my awkward gait. Once along the side of the road, I fell to my knees and began to heave. The cops kept their lights on me, but they also kept their distance. One of them said something to the other, then one of the lights trailed off as its owner headed back to their cruiser. I doubted the car had been reported stolen yet since its owner was dead, but I also knew that me being covered in blood in an undamaged car was suspicious.

While I continued to fake-vomit, I tried to make out the terrain in front of me. It wasn't great—all rocky hills covered in scrub brush with little cover. The familiar glow in the sky to the southwest, over what was undoubtedly downtown San Diego, told me the power must be back on. Silhouetted against the light noise, something on a hill about five hundred yards off caught my attention. I tried to focus on the area without staring directly at it, trying to pick up the movement rather than detail. I could only make out a large dark shape, crouched near the top of the hillock. From its size, I guessed it was either one of the Cu Sith from earlier or a grizzly bear—and unfortunately, grizzlies had been extinct in California for about a century.

Oh boy.

"Hey, Mister, did you hear what I said?" the cop behind me asked. "Why are you covered in blood?"

I had two options. I could let the cops arrest me then deal with that mess, assuming the Cu Sith wouldn't rip them to shreds first, or I could make a break for it and deal with the Cu Sith on my own, probably saving the cops a gruesome death. I've seen firsthand what the hounds were capable of, and I wouldn't have wished that on my worst enemy. And since I'm supposed to protect humanity and all, I didn't really have much of a choice.

I bolted upright and faced the officer standing behind me. He was holding his flashlight about shoulder level, shining it at my chest, but his other hand was resting on his gun. His partner was sitting in the passenger side of the cruiser on the radio with the door open fifteen feet to my left.

"I strongly suggest you and your partner get into your car and leave, quickly," I said in a calm, even tone.

"What?"

"I said I strongly suggest you and your partner leave. Now," I replied.

"Sir, I don't know what you're talking about, but maybe it's best if you put your hands behind your head and get down on your knees. You've been hurt, and you're clearly intoxicated. For your own safety, we're going to bring you in for the night."

His hand moved toward his handcuffs, and I could see his partner climbing out of the car, pointing a Taser at me from between the car door and the windshield. The Cu Sith disappeared in the dark valley below.

I wasn't sure what the safest play was, but it had nothing to do with keeping my back to a Cu Sith. Facing a Taser wasn't giving me warm fuzzies, either.

The cop pulled out his handcuffs and began cautiously making his way closer to me. Then a sharp thunderclap echoed from the hills behind me, startling the hell out of the two cops. In the blink of any eye, I stepped to the right and behind the cop with the handcuffs, grabbed him by the collar of his shirt with my right hand, and pulled his gun with my left. Lifting him so that only his toes touched the ground, I used the dangling cop to shield myself from his partner's Taser. I really didn't like doing it, but at the moment, it really did seem like the best way to save their lives.

My sudden action caused the Taser-wielding cop to fire, hitting his partner square in the chest. When the guy went rigid, I didn't so much drop him as let him go. Gravity did the rest. I fired well over the other cop's head, causing him to duck behind his door, but the Cu Sith responded to the noise with an eerie baying howl that was answered by three booming short barks from another not-so-distant place.

That makes the pair of them. Shit.

I couldn't miss the enormous fairy hound across the hilly field bounding in our direction at frightening speed, but I didn't see the other one yet. I grabbed the cop who'd been Tased, threw him over one shoulder, then ran around to the driver's side of the police car. I dumped the limp cop into the back, slammed the door, and climbed into the driver's seat, still holding the cop's gun in my right hand. I went to start the engine, and the other cop knelt down at the passenger-side door with his service revolver aimed at me.

"Stop!" he said, stammering. "I'll shoot!"

A thundering bark rattled the car and nearly broke the windows. I reached across the car's interior, grabbed his wrist, and tried to pull him into the car. He smacked his head hard on the vertical riser between the front and rear doors, knocking himself unconscious, and I had to drag him into the car by his shirt. I floored it as the first Cu Sith made it to the road less than fifty feet behind us. The open doors slammed shut as the tires squealed on the pavement.

It took the police cruiser about four seconds to get up to sixty miles an hour, but the damn fairy dog was already at full speed—which was apparently much faster than sixty. The giant dog came along the passenger side of the car and slammed into us, nearly causing me to lose control. The impact shattered the passenger-side windows and lifted the car slightly, but thanks to the police car's beefy transmission, the collision actually jarred the one-ton dog, causing it to veer away. I kept the accelerator floored and, aiming the gun over the unconscious cop, took a bead on the hound's flank as it closed in. I fired through the shattered window until the gun clicked empty. I had five shots left after the one I fired to scare the cop. But the lead in the bullets, though not a ferric metal, caused the giant dog to nosedive and cartwheel off the shoulder of the road as it howled in pain. The .38 rounds wouldn't do much long-term damage to the hound. Neither would the crash, even at high speed. I checked the rearview mirror, which was empty at the moment, but I knew the other hound wasn't far behind. At least I had time to put more distance between us.

CHAPTER 5

MADE IT ABOUT TEN MILES, well into the town of Lakeside, before I pulled over in a fast-food restaurant parking lot. After giving the cops a cursory check, I left them. Both were still unconscious but breathing, which was good enough for me. I grabbed a cell phone and a baton, thinking I could call Duma and Ab as soon as I got somewhere I could lie low.

I was a few miles from Lake Jennings, and I could hide out there until dawn. Things might be a bit easier in the daylight. While I expected the lake to be empty early in the day, I hoped that a city full of people getting back to their usual business would slow my pursuers down and allow me to get back on the run and maybe hook up with Ab and Duma. The normal fae disdain for human interaction hadn't really helped me so far, but it was all I had going for me at the moment. The simple fact that fairies were actively chasing me through heavily populated areas just underlined the urgency of the situation. To make matters worse, all I had to defend myself was a wooden baton, and I was pretty sure the police would soon be searching for someone with my description, if they weren't already. All in all, I was screwed.

Walking to the park, I made my way along the lakeshore until I found a secluded spot away from the largely empty campground to hunker down and make my phone call. I chose an area that was both isolated and offered the most cover along the northern edge, and tried to think transparent thoughts. I quickly found out the phone was passcode protected. The only thing I could do was dial 9-1-1, and I was likely already wanted by the police. I tossed the phone into the water. Wired and disgusted, I found myself wondering what the bass bite was like as the sky started to lighten off to my east. While I

26

watched the water's smooth, still surface for signs of feeding fish, the ground began to rumble.

The slight movement quickly became intense enough to cause the water to ripple. While Southern California certainly has its share of minor earthquakes, the disturbance was too localized to be a natural phenomenon. *Things just keep getting better and better.*

I scanned the area. Ten yards up the hill from me, an odd upwelling of dirt erupted like water bubbling from a spring. I contemplated running but decided I would end up far too exposed along the water's edge. So I hunkered down, waited, and watched as two huge clawed hands broke the surface, followed by a familiar shaggy black-furred creature. I readied my wooden baton and prepared to hit the thing first—and hard.

Before it could completely pull itself free from its burrow, I circled around behind it. For a moment, I watched as its stumpy head rose out of the dirt and it noisily sniffed the air, trying to gain my scent. *The damned thing probably tracked me across the city by the metallic smell of the blood of the security guards.* As it crouched, I could see that part of its side was matted and caked with dirt, leading me to believe this was the same creature I'd impaled last night. Then something else occurred to me: maybe being a creature of earth, it was one of the fae that couldn't tolerate water, either.

I charged and hit the creature in its lower back with the baton braced across my forearm. The tackle would have made Lawrence Taylor jealous. It probably would have broken the back of any normal being. Luckily, I managed to catch it off guard, and it was injured. I was hoping to knock it off balance and maybe drive it toward the lake, but I hit it hard enough that we both fell and rolled right down to the water's edge. I got to my feet first and began to circle in behind it again. The last thing I wanted was to face those claws unarmored, with only a wooden baton—especially since they'd sliced through rebar.

The beast took a few seconds to regain its footing, jerking away from the water as if it had accidentally gotten too close to a fire. Before it could gain its composure, I hit it again, lowering my shoulder and shoving as hard as I could toward the lake. The creature's footing gave way, and we both tumbled into the water.

And all hell broke loose.

The creature began thrashing and howling like a cat in a bath—if the cat were the size of a tiger. Flailing, the beast nailed me across my left shoulder, knocking me back up onto the bank, and I dropped the baton. The panicked creature continued to writhe so violently that it kept getting deeper and deeper, and the howls became wilder and wilder. Luckily, no one was around. I couldn't help but watch—partly in amazement—as I picked myself up. I had never seen a fairy with water issues actually come into contact with water before, and I had no idea what would happen. Much to my horror, it seemed to be melting as chunks of black fur began sloughing off. All at once, I felt appalled and guilty, wishing I had some sort of real weapon to end its misery.

I'm not sure how long I sat staring, mesmerized while sickened with myself and the scene. Mercifully, the howling and thrashing ended, leaving several floating mats of black fur in the shallow water. While he was a foe and I have no qualms about killing those that take up arms against me or any human with intent to inflict harm, there was no honor in letting a being suffer to its death. Despite my predicament, I felt as though I'd been gut-punched.

"Stay where you are," said a strong, clear woman's voice from behind me. It was familiar, and the tone instantly sent shivers up my spine. "Get on your knees and place your hands behind your head."

I sighed heavily but didn't move. An arrow pierced the ground next to my butt so deeply that it left only the fletching above ground.

"I will not ask a second time, Diomedes. You have killed Her Majesty's Bugganes and wounded *my* favorite hound. I am within my rights to ask restitution in the form of your life, but the Queen requires you to stand trial. Now, on your knees."

Yep. I recognized the attitude that went with the voice, and the comment about *her* hounds confirmed it.

"Hello, Belphoebe. It's been a while," I said, glancing back over my shoulder at her.

While I might have overpowered her, I would never have been able to move fast enough to engage her directly or even run away. And there was no chance of persuading her I was innocent. Of course they would send her after me. She was my counterpart for the Unseelie Court, holding a title equivalent to duchess. Like almost all female fae, she was devastatingly gorgeous, and she knew it. Like most of the members of the fairy courts, she was a true Sidhe, the progenitor race of all fae, and during the Great Schism millennia ago, she'd chosen to follow Mab rather than Titania. I was screwed. And she *knew* I knew it.

"Still twelfth in line to the throne?" I figured she could have shot me any time she wanted, so she really did want me alive.

Standing nearly a hundred and fifty feet away, she nocked an arrow and drew down on me. I knew from experience that she was deadly accurate with her bow at over a hundred yards. I cringed slightly, mostly inwardly, so she couldn't tell I was cringing, preparing for an arrow to the back. She was a first-class predator, and I didn't want to show her my fear. If I did show any weakness and somehow survived this mess, she would throw it back in my face for centuries to come. *Those are the injuries you really want to avoid.*

"Still killing the sick and infirmed for kicks?" I asked.

"Still an arrogant ass?" She walked closer, still aiming at me. Her long auburn hair was trussed into a tight braid over one shoulder, and her red eyes were ablaze in the morning light.

"No more than you—"

She fired, and the arrow hit me in a glancing blow in the outer bicep, but the impact still caused me to twist slightly. It happened so fast, I didn't really feel it. Until after.

"Owwww," I said, trying not to reveal that it had caught me off guard or that, even though it was clearly a flesh wound, it really hurt. I turned my head away from her defiantly, taking a few deep, steadying breaths.

"Her Majesty wants you alive," she said, the disdain evident in her tone. "Your condition upon delivery is *entirely* up to me."

While no creature could hear well enough to hear her footfalls—not even across loose gravel—I *did* hear the telltale stretching noise of her drawing the bow, closer and just to the right behind me.

"I suggest you kneel, Diomedes, because I can easily make it so that you can never stand unaided again."

I could almost *hear* the smile on her face. I watched her as she approached cautiously. A copse of trees stood on either side of us, with the water at my back. The trees to my left were bigger than the ones to my right and offered more protection, but I would never make it before she fired. My options were limited to stupid or none.

"So..." I said, trying to stall. "How's Amoret?"

Belphoebe's twin sister was a sore spot, and I intended to use the fact that they were complete opposites to annoy her into making a mistake. Where Belphoebe was belligerent, her sister was exasperatingly pleasant—and a member of the *Seelie* Court, to boot. It was the only hot button I could think to push at the moment.

Surprisingly, it worked, too. Belphoebe lowered the bow a fraction of an inch, and I bolted for the larger trees to my left. I dove behind the largest tree as something flew past my butt.

"Aw, come on, Pheebs, you're ruining my good fishing pants," I shouted, crouching behind a tree. Rather than poking my head out, I used the reflection in the water behind us to track her movement. *The last thing I needed was a new part in my hair.*

She continued to advance while she pulled out another arrow. Before she nocked it, however, I watched her reflection dip the broadhead tip into a small horn container she wore on her belt. *Doubt that's a painkiller.*

"I will give you one more chance to give yourself up with honor," she said.

"Never of my own free will. There is no honor in it, Pheebs. Would you surrender if you were in my position?"

"I suppose not," she said, closing to within twenty feet.

I had nowhere to go without exposing myself to her. "I guess we're at an impasse then."

"Not necessarily," she said.

I heard the odd squeak of her drawing back the bow, followed by a resounding *thuup*. Almost simultaneously, I felt the arrow hit the tree, then something poked me in the ribs where I leaned against the trunk.

Sonofabitch. Definitely not painkiller.

CHAPTER 6

WOKE UP IN PITCH DARKNESS, but I could hear water drips and occasional tapping sounds coming from somewhere near my feet. The only thing I could smell was myself—fishy, sweaty, and generally rank. I sat up slowly, feeling around, trying to gain some sense of my location. I felt some sort of rock wall to my left, and I could sit up without trouble, but searing pain in my butt, shoulder, and upper back reminded me what had happened. Reaching around to my upper back, I found some sort of dressing over the wound where Belphoebe's arrow had jabbed me through the tree. The entire area was tender and sore but otherwise okay. That was the worst of my injuries, except the one to my pride.

I'm not sure how much time actually passed, but it wasn't the first time I'd been held prisoner in a dank hole. Darkness is one thing, but pitch-black is something else entirely. It's disconcerting, unnerving, and just plain annoying. I knew that, eventually, the blackness would turn cold—even if it really wasn't—then I would lose all sense of balance. Sounds eventually become magnified, and every noise or vibration is interpreted as a threat. The mind falls apart. And it happens fast.

I also knew that's why I was being kept this way. My captors wanted to soften me up, and though I'd been in similar situations before, it never got easier. The last time was during the Basque Witch Trials in Logroño, Spain in 1609. I was imprisoned for trying to free several of the benevolent witches that had been offered up by truly nasty ones. As with my imprisonment then, I tried to focus on building a mental picture of the hole I was in, and that meant I needed to feel around to get to know my surroundings. I found I could stand up and walk from wall to wall without smacking my head, and my outstretched hands couldn't touch the ceiling. The room was about three paces by three paces, or roughly eighty square feet. The walls were featureless and smooth, hard stone, except along one wall, where I thought I found a seam or crack.

At first, I hoped the anomaly might outline a door, but it became less distinct the more I explored it. As I followed the fissure from the floor, up the wall, across a short span, and back down to the floor again, it became clear the seam wasn't much of a joint because neither air, nor light passed through it. I couldn't blow through it, either, and I found no sign of any kind of hinges. It was also small — maybe three feet by three feet — but its surface was completely different from the rest of the cell. Oddly, the small section was somehow warmer and felt like hard, highly polished wood.

I pushed on it with all my strength, which actually caused it to flex a bit. Doing so, however, elicited a low, guttural groan from the surrounding wall that sounded as though I'd disturbed a sleeping animal.

Great. Just great. What kind of fairy hell am I in?

To make sure I wasn't hallucinating, I pushed on it again. In response, the whole cell quavered, though nothing cracked or collapsed, and I had to drop to my hands and knees to keep from falling in the dark.

Screw it.

I backed up the few steps it took to cross the cell to the wall opposite and charged the small section of wall with every ounce of strength remaining in me. To my surprise, the area gave, absorbing the impact completely without making a sound. Even stranger, as hard as I hit it, I didn't even feel the impact. It was like running into a wall of gelatin. Then it sprang back and flung me into the opposite wall like a rag doll, making me hit my head hard enough that I blacked out.

At some point, I woke up with someone standing above me wreathed by a dim light, their features completely masked by the darkness.

"Did you have a nice rest, Diomedes?"

I hoped Belphoebe's echoing voice emanated from the figure standing over me rather than from places as yet unseen.

"Ugh," I replied, propping myself up on my elbows.

Even though the light was faint, I had to shield my eyes with one hand and squint to focus. The little that I could make out showed that

I was right about the room's dimensions. I could not see the ceiling at all—it simply disappeared into darkness above. Across from me, the section of wall I'd bounced off actually did resemble light-colored wood, but its highly polished surface kept shifting patterns in the dim light. Of course, it could have been my aching head swimming, too.

I slowly pulled myself up to a seated position and rubbed my pounding head and the sizable knot that had formed above my ear. "You wouldn't happen to have any aspirin, would you, Pheebs?" I asked, my voice cracking from a dry mouth.

"No. Like I said, my lady asked only that I bring you in alive. She did not specify your condition," she said with a smug lilt to her voice.

"When I get out of here, you and I are going to have words," I said, continuing to rub my head. "And by words, I mean I'm going to kick your ass." That got me thinking about escaping. When the door opened for her to leave, I might have a tiny window of opportunity. Pheebs was under the assumption I was cowed and maybe too injured to try, so she wouldn't expect it.

She sniggered and shifted so that the light was no longer coming from behind her, and I could see she was dressed in the customary courtly armor I'd seen her wear for solemn occasions. It consisted of the long, formal dark-blue surcoat worn by a Lady of the Royal Court, except—befitting her role as Guardian of the Unseelie Court—hers was armored with fist-sized translucent black scales. Her ornate cuirass was covered in the same scales as her skirt. She appeared to be unarmed. *Even better for an escape attempt.*

Like all Sidhe and many fae, she bore no scars, which might lead someone to think she had never seen real combat, but I have seen her so bloodied from fighting on one rare occasion where we fought together that it would have meant death to a lesser creature. She was fearless in battle, and equally as ruthless. She had no concept of compassion or forgiveness; that indifference was typical of the Sidhe since they lacked almost all human emotions. In fact, she'd once told me she regarded me as a kindred spirit, but that my weakness was I allowed myself to *feel*.

"So you never answered me... how's Amoret?" I asked, trying to get a rise out of her while I waited for the right moment to make a move.

She kicked me hard for my effort—right in the side of my chest.

And to make matters worse, the scales covering her damned long skirt had cut my cheek. I tried to roll with the kick, but I had nowhere to go, so I ended up curled into a ball, desperately trying to suck air into my lungs.

As I sat there, forcing myself to inhale, the odd, small section of wall shifted then evaporated into a much larger door-sized opening. Belphoebe turned to leave, and I saw my opportunity. Biting back the pain, I scrambled to my feet as quickly as I could and charged her, but my efforts were clumsy and way too slow. Before I could hit her, she stepped aside and brought a heavily armored forearm down across the back of my neck. I dropped like a lead weight, but I'd made it far enough out of the cell to see that the space beyond the door was an unending, dimly lit hallway of brown rock. Pheebs dragged me back into the cell by one foot.

"I'd have been disappointed if you didn't at least try," she said as I fought to gather my wits. "Get some rest, Diomedes. Your trial will begin soon."

"Eat shit," I said through clenched teeth.

She left the room, the doorway closed up, then the dim light in my cell faded to pitch-black again.

CHAPTER 7

EVEN IF I HAD ESCAPED the cell, I had no idea where I would have gone. But like Pheebs said, I had to try. I wallowed in the darkness for some time before I decided I needed to focus on something to keep from going crazy. Belphoebe had said my *trial* would be soon, but to an immortal creature, time was irrelevant, so who knew what that meant. If I went batty in the meantime, my delirium would only make it easier for them to convict me of killing Indronivay.

Convict me.

I laughed to myself. I had no idea what kind of legal system, if any, the fairies had—especially the Unseelie Court. For all I knew, I'd already been convicted and was awaiting the sentence. Again, I hoped that Athena was diligently working on some diplomatic way to free me. I did know that punishment consisted of one thing—death. To be fair, though, the fae could be quite creative in that respect. They might simply chop off my head, feed me to Cu Sith or some other creatures, draw and quarter me, administer the Blood Eagle, or flay me. Then my stomach growled. Maybe they were going to starve me to death. *That would really suck.*

Thinking about that crap is just another path down the loony trail. My Survival, Evasion, Resistance and Escape training as a SEAL wouldn't help me much in this fae abyss, but centuries of training and experience fighting the creatures would. I lay back and began to relax, focusing on every part of my body and imagining it was loose, free, and comfortable. Predictably, with an achy head, chest, butt, shoulder, and back, the process took time. *What else do I have to do, though?*

My mind wandered back to June of 1673. It was dark, and the fighting during the initial push across the moat and into the stone ravelin that protected the entrance to the walled city of Maastricht during the Dutch War was horrendous and bloody. My garrison of Gray Musketeers had barely managed to clear a demi-lune fortification right inside the city, where the thirty of us who had survived were holed up for the moment. I kept watch while our scant force regrouped and tended to our injured. Our legendary captain-lieutenant, Charles Ogier de Batz de Castlemore the Comte d'Artagnan, as well as every other man there was fighting for political reasons that were beyond me. My sole concern was the Marquis Jacques de Fariaux, Baron de Mande, governor of Maastricht and leader of the Dutch and Spanish forces within. Stories suggested he was more than human, and I witnessed the result of his supernatural reputation during our push as the mere mention of his presence in the Dutch ranks caused French soldiers—elite musketeers—to flee, leading to the slaughter of many of our ranks. It was my job to remove any nonhuman influences— good, bad, or indifferent—from human conflicts.

We didn't have much time before the Spanish auxiliary employed by the Dutch gathered for another assault, and we would likely not survive it—especially with so many of our small force whispering that they had seen bullets bounce off the baron and that he was immortal. They were terrified, and even the great d'Artagnan himself couldn't rally them.

My one glimpse of the baron during our siege had convinced me that he was no mortal man. Bullets bounced off him as if he were heavily armored, though he wore only a tunic. I also recognized the foul, greasy brown-black energy that he radiated as indicative of the living dead. I had encountered similar creatures a few decades earlier in the Thirty Years War, and I suspected that, like those monsters, the baron was a Fext. I had no idea what changed them or how, but I knew the condition would spread and that only glass bullets would kill them. And I was armed with special Dvergar-made crystal bullets for my flintlock.

I watched from inside the main entrance to the large crescent-shaped stone fortification while the Spanish forces formed ranks surrounding us. Instinctively, I began checking over my flintlock, until the stares from my fellow musketeers distracted me. I was used to funny looks from most of my comrades, because I was a mercenary and a loner. My odd weaponry underlined the fact I was foreign. Ignoring their stares and scorn, I went back to watching out for the baron. I didn't care about their opinions, or their war, only about killing the Fext.

Our men were all but defeated as they sat quietly in the dark stillness of the stone structure. I doubted they could even hear the forces amassing outside. There was no way I could rely on them helping me make another push if the baron showed himself. They were exhausted and scared, and we were trapped well away from the rest of our troops, who were across the moat outside the wall. They wouldn't last the night unless I did something.

Finally, the baron strode into view among the Spanish soldiers, swaggering around as if already victorious. I glanced back over the barely lit faces of the musketeers and their wary eyes, pulled my swords, and screamed as I charged out the entrance of the demi-lune. In the pale torchlight around the Spanish troops, I could see the whites of eyes grow among the first few ranks as I bolted across the open street between us. They were so surprised that not a Spaniard moved until I was more than halfway across. Before the first riflemen readied their weapons, I tore through the first rank of pikemen, causing men to clumsily retreat around me. Behind me, across the street, d'Artagnan led the small band of remaining musketeers out of the demi-lune in a wild assault. My crazy idea served to rally our men behind me as they drew rapiers and pistols and charged screaming across the square, while it appeared I advanced into certain but heroic death.

They're on their own now. My goal is the baron. I approached too fast for most of the Spanish and Dutch musketeers to aim at me effectively, and I pushed through the soldiers, bulling my way through many of them as they tried to pull swords or pistols. Most gawked in amazement as I shoved my way through their ranks.

Eyeing me with concern, the baron began to quickly fall back into the city. There was no way he had any idea who or what I was, but he clearly identified me as a threat. As I charged forward, I could see fear develop in the faces of the Dutch and Spanish garrison around me as they recognized that their commander—a man they regularly witnessed inspire fear in their enemies, one they assumed could not be killed—was fleeing for his life. I pushed farther through the Dutch and Spanish ranks and into the city streets beyond after the baron. Meanwhile behind me, the telltale volleys from the Gray Musketeers echoed through the stone streets and fortifications as they began an offensive.

Chasing after the baron, I returned one sword to its sheath on my back and pulled my flintlock. With a single-shot pistol, I might only get one good opportunity, and I needed to be close before I fired to make sure I hit him.

For the better part of an hour, I tracked down the Fext within the city while a new battle raged at the city's entrance. The sun began to rise, brightening up the narrow cobbled streets. Following the Fext wasn't hard, because it was so heavily perfumed to cover the smell of its decay. I knew I was close long before I found it cowering in the corner of a pigsty in an alleyway behind a butcher's shop—the pigs taking refuge as far away from it as they could get.

As soon as he saw me, the creature threw his pistol and sword into the mud. "*Ik overgeven, ik overgeven,*" he said, holding his hands up in surrender. "I am the governor of Maastricht and an officer in the Dutch Army. You cannot kill me. I surrender. Just do not kill me."

He may have been a nobleman at one time, deserving of such genteel treatment, but the thing had long ago ceased being a man, noble or otherwise. It was a coward and a monster that had no place among men.

I shot it in the head from less than ten feet away. The skull shattered like a dust-filled pot, and the body shrank in upon itself. As its skin blackened, the baron became unrecognizable as anything but the rotted corpse it should have been for years.

Making my way back through the small town, I was struck by how quiet it was. There were no sounds of musket fire or fighting. The musketeers had either been wiped out, or by some miracle, had prevailed. By the time I made it back to the demi-lune, dozens of blue-jacketed men were wandering the streets—English soldiers from the Duke of Monmouth's regiment. Louis XIV's ally had aided our garrison and ended the assault. The bluejackets ignored me as I made my way through the battle-stained streets littered with scores of injured or dead Spanish, Dutch, and English soldiers. The instant I spied one of the surviving men of my garrison, I smiled wearily.

"I'm surprised you came back, traitor," said the musketeer, fixing me with a reproachful and unrelenting stare. "He's back," he said, turning to shout over his shoulder at the entrance to the demi-lune.

Instantly, several more musketeers filed out of the fortification, one covered in blood that was clearly not his own. "Arrest that man this instant," said the bloody man — a second lieutenant, like me.

Three musketeers and two bluejackets, including a captain in the English regiment, approached me with their pistols drawn. For a moment, I contemplated attempting to flee then decided the only way to do that would be to kill many of these men.

"I'm no traitor," I said as the men shoved me toward the demi-lune and ignored me.

"We'll keep him here until French reinforcements arrive," the second lieutenant said.

Inside the fortification, brightly lit by oil lamps and torches, lay the lifeless body of Captain-Lieutenant Comte d'Artagnan in a pool of his own blood.

By the end of the day, instead of being welcomed as a hero for charging the enemy's front lines and rallying our troops, I was in the prison in Maastricht, held as a traitor responsible for abandoning my post, leading to the death of our Captain-Lieutenant. I waited for military activity around the city to slow for a week then made my escape before they brought me up on formal charges and shot me as a traitor.

I would never see my duty the same way ever again. While my time with the Musketeers was far from the last time I enlisted in mortal militaries or militias, I vowed never to actively pursue rogue nonhuman elements *overtly* while serving. That was the first time I fully understood that what I did was best kept as far from mortal eyes as possible. At first, I told myself it was to protect them, but truthfully, it was to keep them from interfering. The majority of mundane humans were not prepared to deal with my world.

That was also the first time I was wrongfully imprisoned. I realized then that there was no way to get justice by staying a prisoner or even standing trial under those circumstances. My only chance to clear my name, or even survive, was to escape. The only problem was that my newest captors weren't the simple humans who'd imprisoned me in 1673.

CHAPTER 8

A T SOME POINT, I ALLOWED myself to fall asleep. I wasn't sure when I woke up or even how long I was out. I was still in control of my faculties, but I had no concept of time at all. I doubted I'd slept long because all of my aches and pains still ached and pained. Sleeping on the cold, hard stone floor had added a stiff back and neck to the mix. I knew I needed to develop a routine if I wanted to stay sane.

I forced myself to get up and begin some light calisthenics in order to get moving and focus on something. It felt good to get the blood flowing again and knock the chill off, and the activity actually lessened some of my stiffness. It did nothing for my smell, however. I began physically running through hand-to-hand attacks and defenses, almost like a form or kata in martial arts, only I did them slowly and deliberately, like Tai Chi, focusing on each movement. It forced me to maintain my balance in the darkness.

In between my physical routines, I focused on fighting techniques and tactics as a mental exercise, imagining a maneuver then its counter. I deliberately and painstakingly went through every fighting style I knew, armed and unarmed, then went through battlefield troop tactics. Then I went through my own battles and various fights and considered how I might have done them differently. Most importantly, I worked on different scenarios for escaping.

I repeated this routine sixteen times, each time I woke up, driving myself into gear. In the event the opportunity to escape came up, I continued to explore my cell, running my hands over every part of the floor and walls I could reach, familiarizing myself with my confines. In addition, it helped me fight the suffocating effects of sensory deprivation. To my surprise, I discovered a small indentation in the wall near the door, at about waist level, barely deep enough for my

40

hand. The bottom of the little divot actually formed a bowl that was always filled with water and allowed me just enough room to scoop a handful when I needed it.

Every so often, the door would open a bit along the bottom, and a small, heavy wooden bowl would slide in, filled with a cold, pasty substance that had almost no flavor and a texture like grits. I took my chances eating it. I kept a close count on the number of times they fed me, using it as a sort of clock. Despite my routine, the interval between feedings felt almost random, but I couldn't be sure. After a dozen feedings, I began to watch for any sign of who or what fed me, but I never perceived anything more than a shadow. On one occasion, I tried to ram my feeding dish under the opening to prop it open, but the wooden bowl shattered like glass as the small gap closed on it without hindrance. The image of the smashed bowl kept me from jamming my hands under it. Still, I kept the larger, sharper pieces of the destroyed bowl as weapons, just in case the opportunity ever arose.

I chose one corner for my bathroom, but mercifully, the seemingly living cell always absorbed or somehow eliminated the waste as well as the odor. I was struck by the contradiction. From time immemorial, humans have allowed prisoners to wallow in their own filth. Apparently, the fae didn't mind driving a prisoner crazy, but they at least kept their captives clean while breaking their minds.

As I lay down to rest, I began counting as high as I could, reciting memorized verses of literature, or singing, each time in a different language and sometimes at the top of my lungs. No matter how loudly I screamed, the odd chamber dulled the sound. I also thought about Department of Homeland Security Agent Sarah Wright—and her gray eyes. A lot. I still was hesitant about our relationship for about a million reasons, but none was more prevalent than the fact that she was a mundane. The more I thought about her, the more I worried she might eventually realize I was missing somehow and do something stupid like search for me. She was definitely capable for a human, but a mundane stood no chance against an entire fae court. She had no chance of standing with them, either.

Despite my routines, visions began to assault me. The faces of all the friends and comrades I'd lost over the centuries, many whose names I could no longer remember, crept in from the darkness. They woke me more and more, until my sleep became fitful, at best. Finally, after I'd finished my waking exercises for the twenty-eighth time, the doorway opened, revealing a humanoid shape cast in shadow. I had been in blackness so long that even the dim light from outside the cell hurt my eyes, so I turned my back to the doorway, ducked my head, and shielded my eyes with my arm. I palmed a shard of the splintered wooden bowl in each hand. I assumed the figure would be Belphoebe, but I was wrong.

"On your knees," said a harsh but clear, deep male voice devoid of any discernible accent. I had to give it to fairies. They all spoke with perfect elocution and diction.

I glanced over my shoulder, still shading my eyes, hoping to get an idea of who or what had entered the cell, but it was all a painful blur. "Make me," I replied without thinking. I was hit along the back of the legs, bringing me to one knee. *Note to self: If I survive this, I might have to work on that brain-mouth filter thing. On second thought, fuck the filter. Resist.*

"Bet you won't do that again," I said through clenched jaws. I was goading him to let them know they hadn't broken me yet. Realizing I still couldn't see well enough to make an effective break for it, I needed a better idea of my surroundings before taking off. If I got one shot at it, I needed to make it count.

He hit me again — in the lower back, sending shooting pain down both legs.

"Ha! You missed my legs." I exhaled loudly through my nose, trying to control the pain.

I braced for another blow, but all that came was a derisive laugh that was more like a pig's snort. On the positive side, my eyes had adjusted to the dim light enough that I could make out two blurry, dark, and slender humanoid shapes at the door, but the process of trying to focus led to an instant headache. I closed my eyes and ducked my head. *Patience. Wait for the right time to attack.*

I focused on listening. In addition to the two at the door, at least one other creature was in the cell with me — the one who'd whacked me like I was a baseball at batting practice. Fae move so silently, they're impossible to hear even when dancing on eggshells while wearing jingle bells, but I was sure that Babe Ruth was still standing to my left, behind me.

For the briefest of moments, I contemplated attacking Babe Ruth. I might as well go down swinging, but some part of me wanted to know why they thought I killed Indronivay.

"What's the deal, Slugger?" I asked, still feeling the pain in my legs and back. "Don't I get a phone call or something?"

My comment elicited a series of grunts and scoffs, with a surprising one coming from behind me to my right. There were at least *two* fae in there with me—that made four total. There was no way I could fight my way out of the cell half-blind against four of them. *I need to be patient.* A smell like rancid meat marinated in bird crap wafted across my nose and made my eyes water. *One of the two beings flanking me is either an ogre or the zombie version of Big Bird.*

"They're ready for him," said a different masculine voice from behind me, to my right. *Zombie Big Bird.*

Ready for me? I squeezed my hands around the wooden shards so hard I could feel the splintered edges bite into my palms. I made the decision right there that if the opportunity to run never came, then I was going to do as much damage as possible before I went down. *They would never be ready for me.*

"On your feet," Babe Ruth said from my left, followed by a quick poke in the shoulder from something blunt.

"Down, up, make up your fucking mind already." I hesitated to stand, so I expected him to hit me again. Instead, something grabbed my right arm in a solid, viselike grip and lifted me off the floor as if I weighed nothing. The grip was only painful because I was being lifted by it, not because it crushed my arm. And whatever lifted me was definitely the source of the lovely new smell. *Has to be an ogre.*

"Why do all you ogres stink so badly?" I asked.

The response was a belch, followed by a breath blown my way. Rotted fish wrapped in used diapers smelled like daisies by comparison. If I'd had anything in my stomach, I would have vomited. Instead, I retched, which brought a deep chuckle from above my right shoulder. *Way above.*

I finally gained my composure as they pulled me around to face the door and shoved me forward. I stumbled but managed to get my feet back under me. I risked trying to open my eyes again. Everything was still out of focus, but the ambient light was faint enough that the pain wasn't searing into my brain anymore.

From what I could tell through half-squinted eyes, another tall, thin guard was waiting in the hall, dressed in black like the other two at the door. That made no less than five: three black-clad figures in front and the two ogres behind. The three lanky figures led me down a clean, featureless corridor wide enough for them to walk abreast. My vision began to become clearer as we walked. The smooth walls, floor, and ceiling of the corridor, awash in a soft amber light, were a dull, earthy tan. I couldn't identify the origin of the flat illumination. My vanguard were bald-headed, dressed in long black greatcoats, and carrying poleaxes—Dreaichbard, elite royal guards of the Unseelie Court. The guard accepted only those of Sidhe ancestry, so there was no way the ogres behind me would be part of that unit.

The only noise in the hall came from me scuffling along, trying not to bounce off the walls or fall while I shielded my eyes, desperate to conceal the wooden shivs I hid in my hands. I couldn't even hear my babysitters breathing or their clothing rubbing. I watched for anything that suggested a way to escape. I began counting to myself to see how long we walked, but I never observed any doors or side passages—it was one long, monotonous tunnel.

Based on my counting, we walked for at least *eight minutes* without turning or changing directions before we stopped at a dead end. The middle guard nodded his naked head, while the remaining two stood at arms. Then the wall melted away like ice under hot water, revealing a darkened space beyond. As soon as the opening was big enough for him to pass through, the lead guard entered, then the opening melted closed again.

"Cool trick," I mumbled, mostly to myself, blinking and rubbing at my eyes with the back of my fists.

The statement earned me a smack on the back of the head. "You are better off not speaking until you are addressed, human," said the ogre on my right, spreading his stinky breath.

My eyes watered, and I couldn't help scrunching up my face. I gasped and waved my closed hand in front of my face. It never failed to strike me that such a disgusting creature could speak so eloquently.

"You know, we got these things called breath mints—" Like the last time, the smack wasn't meant to hurt, only annoy, and it shut me up for a second.

"Just saying. Because your breath smells like ass."

The next was much harder, and it caused me to flinch a bit.

"I mean *rotten, moldy* ass—" I said then prepared for the blow.

A solid shot to the ribs behind my right arm knocked the breath out of me, dropped me to my knees, and probably cracked a few ribs, too. While I was down, trying to suck air back into my lungs, I took a few seconds to take in my surroundings. In addition to the two Sidhe guards in front of me, only two stood behind me, dressed much more simply than the ones in front. The ogre on my right carried a cudgel the size of a small tree. The other creature on my left was smaller but every bit as heinous as the ogre. I stayed down on my knees as long as I could.

"Get up," the big ogre muttered, clearly trying to keep his voice down. He kicked me lightly to reinforce his point.

Resist. I repositioned slightly as if to stand, but as I got to one knee, I shifted—quite painfully—to my right. With every ounce of strength I had, I drove my elbow into the big ogre's groin, ready to jump forward at the two Dreaichbard with my wooden shivs when they attacked. But they didn't.

The sound that erupted from the rank creature's quivering lips probably drove every dog within a thousand miles crazy. He collapsed in a heap next to me with a resonant thud, straining to breathe as he curled into a ball. His cudgel slammed to the ground next to him. I could feel the sneer form on my face as I contemplated grabbing the heavy wooden weapon while I braced myself for a beating that never came.

Before I could get to my feet, a sonorous bellow came from the front of the group. "*Stop!*"

I lifted my head to see the dead end had once again opened—an imposing figure dressed in elaborately decorated gold and dark-blue robes stood in the gap, with his pale left hand extended. The two guards in front of me remained frozen, each with his weapon at port arms.

The imperious being in the doorway lowered his outstretched hand, and the upright ogre behind me snapped back into position. Toilet Breath remained in a fetal position behind me. I struggled back to my feet, wincing at the pain in my chest. The gray-skinned dignitary in the blue robe had to be some sort of Sidhe.

The pair of guards in front of me parted, and a prod to my bruised ribs shoved me forward. I entered a massive, dimly lit cavern. My first assumption was that the place had been hewn by hand, like the hallway and my cell. Once I was fully inside, it became clear that the expansive cavern was a formal gathering place. Rows of benches, like giant steps, cut out of most of the cavern's walls, extended at least halfway to the ceiling—and at the moment, the seats were occupied by dozens of beings, all focused on me.

All of the seats faced a large stagelike area with three shallow alcoves set into the wall behind it. These recessed areas emitted the only light in the colossal space. At the center of the stage, three hooded figures sat at a huge wooden desk. Light from behind silhouetted the figures, but the central figure emanated waves of dark power like heat radiating from asphalt in summer. Not the most powerful Paran I'd ever seen, but still pretty damn strong, whoever it was.

The two Dreaichbard escorted me to the center of the chamber, where they left me standing beside the ornately dressed gray fairy. Clearly, they didn't consider me much of a threat at the moment, because I remained unshackled, the shivs still hidden in my hands. My two guards flanked the stage while the remaining one behind me retreated. A low din began to arise from the gathered crowd, but there was very little movement from them. It was unnerving, actually.

My curiosity took over. I slowly surveyed the spectators, but details were impossible to make out in the low light. With the doorway I came through closed again, the room had no identifiable entrances or exits. And like my cell, the cavern had no visible ceiling. Staring up was like peering into a void, and it made me slightly dizzy.

This has to be one of the sanctuaries of the Unseelie Court. All of a sudden, the middle of the three hooded figures pounded something on the great desk with booming cracks that echoed through the chamber like artillery fire. The light brightened and dimmed with each rap. The murmuring ceased instantly, and I could feel all eyes shift from me to the figures on the raised platform in front of me.

The individual sitting to the left—the smallest one—stood and pulled back the hood. It was Belphoebe. *At least I know someone at this party.*

She began to speak in the formal language of the Court—a complex and ancient tongue that I did not and would never understand. Before I could protest, the gray fairy next to me began translating.

"Before us stands Diomedes, Son of Tydeus, and one of, and perhaps the greatest of, Humanity's champions," he said. "And he has killed Warmaster Indronivay without provocation and, concordant with his race, in barbarous and cowardly fashion."

The crowd erupted in a deafening roar.

"I did no such thing!" I shouted at the top of my lungs, but the cacophonous cheer drowned me out.

Belphoebe allowed the peanut gallery to continue its grumbling for some time before she finally raised her hands to quiet them, and even then, it took several more seconds.

Should I wait for a chance to defend myself, remaining respectful of the Unseelie Court, or should I take matters into my own hands, attack the first being I can reach, and end it all right now? Frankly, I wasn't much good at waiting when my life was in the balance.

"Diomedes's actions against fae of both Courts are well known to us all, but his dealings with Queen Mab's subjects are notoriously brutal," she said as the translator continued.

"What proof do you have that I killed Indronivay?" I screamed.

My outburst caused another round of shrieks, and quite a few individuals rose from their seats. The translator took several steps away from me, either in surprise or to get out of the line of fire.

The roar died instantly as the middle of the three figures at the desk rose. Even Belphoebe bowed her head in deference to the gaunt robed figure standing next to her. The pulsing aura of dark energy that surrounded the figure began to coalesce into an imposing shadow.

"You misunderstand, human," said the calm but resolute female voice from inside the hood. She spoke in clear, precise English and practically spat out the word *human* as though it tasted sour. Gold and silver embroidery along her dark-blue robe glinted in the glow of the room as she stood.

I had no idea who this was, though I was pretty sure it wasn't Mab. A mere human would never be important enough for her to appear in person. And, from what I'd been told, Mab's presence would be almost blinding, given my gift of seeing beings in their true form. Mab, like her counterpart Titania of the Seelie Court, was pure power and energy. As I understood it, only a select few had ever actually seen either queen in person. All I knew for sure was whoever *that* was commanded serious respect.

"You are not being tried for this crime," the figure said.

Not tried? Then why am I here?

"You have been brought here so that Queen Mab's justice may be served upon you for your transgressions against her and her subjects. You are *guilty* of this heinous and craven act against Her Majesty's Warmaster." She sat back down.

Ask a stupid question...

"With respect to this gathering, don't I get a chance to defend myself? How do you *know* it was me?" I asked. On a calculated risk, I took a few sudden steps toward the three seated figures in outrage, and all at once, every single being in the venue stood. Everyone *except* the middle figure at the desk. The sudden motion of the crowd stopped me in my tracks. *At least now I know I'll probably be dead before I make it halfway to any one of these beings if I attack.*

"There is *no* defense for what you've done," Belphoebe replied.

"But I *didn't* kill him. I swear on my honor," I said. "What proof do you have that it was *me*?"

At that moment, all attention but mine shifted to my right. The murmuring increased yet again, until I finally glanced around to see what was going on. An opening had appeared at the top of the bench seats far to my right, and two figures dressed in luminous emerald-green and gold robes were gracefully descending the broad, steplike seats to floor level. One was male, and one female. Both were quite tall. They radiated a warm glowing light that highlighted them like an otherworldly spotlight, and everyone they passed gave them room to do so comfortably.

I recognized them both: Lord Elegast and Lady Amoret of the Seelie Court. Like Belphoebe, Elegast was the champion of his court and my counterpart among the fae. Lady Amoret was his consort—and Belphoebe's sister.

Elegast and I had a passable relationship. We had worked together harmoniously on numerous occasions—the last time was over sixty years ago. In the past, he was known among humans as the Fairy Knight and had even fought for and helped Charlemagne. At seven feet tall, he positively exuded charm from every inch as he strode confidently in the midst of his Unseelie brethren, throwing back his robes to uncover his brilliant yellow-and-white surcoat over a bloodred leather hauberk. His shoulder-length blond hair brushed back from the sharp features of his face as he crossed the floor.

Amoret was easily as attractive, and like her sister, she was about my height, although her hair was golden blond. Under her dark-green outer robe, she wore a yellow dress of such fine material, it appeared weightless and sparkled as she glided next to Elegast. If he was power, then she was grace, and it was hard to tell which of the pair everyone was paying more attention to. Even I found myself mesmerized by their appearance.

They stopped several yards away. Elegast winked at me then faced the three seated figures. *Was that wink supposed to reassure me or condemn me?* My mind raced back to our last encounter.

The memory made me cringe. It was March of 1942 in Saint-Nazaire, France, during World War II. I was fighting with the British as part of the No. 2 Commando unit, and Elegast was working with the resistance. He helped the surviving four members of my unit and me escape to Spain, but not before one of my men shot the big fairy when he surprised us. It was a hectic and messy few minutes while I pried the lead bullet from his chest, covered in a light-purple ooze. Thankfully, humans and fairies didn't always share similar anatomy in regard to our blood, hearts, or even the number of them. The lead had hurt him more than the impact itself. *Could he still be holding a grudge? No. No way. But...*

"Forgive my intrusion upon these proceedings, Duchess Nicnevin, but Queen Titania sends her warmest regards." Elegast dipped into a low and flamboyant bow. "And she wishes to make her interests in this matter known."

Amoret curtsied deeply next to him, tipping her head slightly as she did so.

Nicnevin. That explains a lot. I shouldn't have been surprised that *she* was the central figure. After all, she was one of Mab's closest advisors and her proctor. And if that was indeed the case, then we were all fortunate she still had her hood up. Rumors were that she was not blessed with the typical fae condition of perfect features. In fact, if she walked into a cornfield, the crows would bring back the corn they'd stolen *last* year. But she was *extremely* powerful in her own right, capable of throwing around enough energy to light up a town. She certainly was not on Mab's level, but few creatures of Earth were. But I couldn't fathom why in the hell Titania was interested in my mess.

Nicnevin stood and bowed in acceptance of Elegast's presence.

"Of course we welcome Titania's huntsman," Nicnevin said, shifting awkwardly as she sat back down. "But, pray tell, what interest does she have with these proceedings?"

"Please forgive the intrusion, but my liege begs that you would allow me to elucidate her interests in these matters," Elegast said, his head slightly bowed in respect as he addressed the duchess. With great flair, he spun around and presented his hand to Amoret in archaic fashion. She took it, and he escorted her to the nearest seat in the gallery, forcing several Unseelie fairies to move to accommodate her. Compared to the Unseelie fairies around her, she positively glowed. Again with exaggerated aplomb, Elegast returned to stand at my right hand, glancing at me with a grimace on his face before turning to address Duchess Nicnevin.

"In matters pertaining to Diomedes and his attack on Queen Mab's Warmaster, Lord Indronivay..." he said then mumbled, "the prick..." ever so softly out of the side of his mouth before continuing again. "Her Highness Queen Titania wishes to add that he has also attacked and killed Duke Goibniu, Her Majesty's most favored bladesmith."

Again, the murmuring around the chamber flew into a full-blown roar, and my jaw dropped to the floor. "What the fu..." was all I could manage. My heart all but stopped, my mind reeled, and Elegast just glanced at me and winked once more. I wanted to attack him right there, but I was too surprised to do anything but stand there like an idiot.

Nicnevin began pounding on the desk, trying so hard to regain control that black bolts of energy flew out from under her hand. To her right, Belphoebe had the most evil grin on her face as our eyes met.

I'm screwed. Big time.

"Duchess!" Elegast screamed over the growing outrage. "Duchess! Please!"

"*Quiet!*" Nicnevin roared, rattling the walls and floor. It was damned scary.

"Lord Elegast, are you saying that this... human... is also

responsible for a death in the Royal Court of Queen Titania, as well?" she asked.

"Bullshit!" I screamed at the top of my lungs.

"Indeed. And my liege asks a small show of goodwill between the courts and requests that I might have a brief moment alone with this..." He glared at me in almost comedic disgust. "Pusillanimous caitiff." Then he winked at me yet again.

What the fuck is going on?

"Time... alone?" she asked. "Why?"

"Queen Titania acknowledges that this human is Mab's prisoner, and we ask not that he be surrendered to us, only that we may execute some small measure of punishment for our loss before you carry out your sentence. It is a matter of honor to Her Majesty." He made the statement readily, as if it'd been rehearsed.

Nicnevin sat utterly motionless. I could only imagine the political implications the situation had for the two courts. The peace between them was always tenuous, and I doubted that Nicnevin wanted to start open war again. Sure, Elegast's unannounced presence might have been in poor form, but I couldn't imagine that such a simple request would be denied.

But then what the hell am I thinking? A few minutes alone with Elegast so he can beat the snot out of me before Nicnevin finishes me off in some way only she and a few demons in hell could imagine? They think I killed Goibniu, too? I didn't even know he existed. Sure, I knew she had a smith, but it could have been Santa Claus for all I knew. *Fuck this.* If I was about to die, I was going to take at least one of these fairy clowns with me.

I couldn't help but gaze back and forth from Elegast to Nicnevin, confused and dumbfounded at their statements, as I shifted the shivs in my hands, ready to attack Elegast and whoever else I could reach before they ripped me apart. I knew my name had been used as a sort of boogeyman among Parans for centuries, but I'd never been accused of something I hadn't *actually* done. And all of what I had done was honorable, face-to-face and for very specific reasons. I had *never* attacked a fae of either court unprovoked. I wanted to on any number of occasions, but I always managed to restrain myself. *Until now.*

But an instant before I attacked, something in the rational part of my brain raised an alarm. *Don't commit the crime for which you are being blamed.* The balance between humans and Parans was too delicate for selfish and rash actions, particularly between humans and the Unseelie Court. *Humans are the damned reason there are two courts to begin with.* The Unseelie fairies wanted to commit wholesale genocide. Not that the Seelie Fae wanted to protect humans; they had simply concluded it was better to leave people to their own devices. And I'd been accused of doing something that could upset the entire balance. *And I didn't even do it.* At least I didn't *remember* doing it.

My skin went cold, and the hair stood up on the back of my neck. Was it possible that someone or some*thing* had manipulated me into assassinating two members of the fairy courts without me knowing? It wasn't impossible. Highly improbable, but not impossible. It would take immense power far beyond all but a very few humans — and most fae, for that matter. But I couldn't recall any missing periods of time.

I tried to figure out who would stand to gain from such strife. I didn't get far before Nicnevin's voice cut in. "I will admit I am reluctant to grant the request made by your Queen, Lord Elegast, but in the interest of maintaining... *peaceful*... relations between the Courts, I will allow it — on one condition."

"May I first express my appreciation for your willingness to hear my liege's request in this matter and, might I add, for receiving me with such... graciousness," Elegast said, again flamboyant in his gestures.

Man, do I hate politics. The obvious contempt on both sides was palpable.

"Very well, then," she said. "Anything you wish to do must be done here and with an observer appointed by me."

"My lady, I understand your reticence in this matter, but I would prefer to conduct my queen's business privately. Queen Titania is more than willing to trust Queen Mab's proctor to carry out her punishment as she sees fit, without benefit of a witness on my queen's part. I will not kill him, and I will add that I will leave him in healthy enough condition that your punishments, whatever they may be, will not be diminished in their efficacy."

Well, that sure makes me feel better about Elegast showing up. And I really did hate being talked about as if I weren't actually standing right there.

Suddenly, my concerns about starting an unfounded war didn't strike me as a very big deal anymore. I was going to die for something I didn't do, and I had no way out. For a second, I considered waiting until I was alone with Elegast to attack, knowing my odds of surviving would increase only slightly, but some part of me wanted all of the fae who'd gathered there to see what I was made of — that the human spirit would not be broken, even in the face of certain death. I let the wooden shivs slide a bit, until the points protruded just past my fingers. Then I attacked Elegast, slashing at his flank with my left hand, but he must have known the attack was coming. He simply sidestepped it, throwing me off balance. Before I could right myself, Elegast brought both arms down across my back with a hollow thud that knocked the breath from my lungs. I fell flat on the ground, and both shivs skidded from my limp hands as I blacked out.

CHAPTER 9

I WOKE UP IN A HAZE, with everything progressing in slow motion. The two ogres, including the one I had dropped back in the passageway, were dragging me by the arms down a featureless corridor, probably the one we'd traveled before. All at once, time sped back up, and an involuntary shudder went through my body. My attack had failed, and they had apparently reached some sort of agreement.

The big ogre wore a nasty shit-eating grin full of crooked, broken teeth.

"Ah, you've finally awoken," Elegast said from behind me. "Let him walk."

The ogres both grunted. I tried to focus on the walls, searching again for anything—*anything at all*—that I could use to get out or at least take one of the fucking ogres with me before I went. *Why not— they couldn't kill me any deader than dead.* My captors pulled me up to get my feet under me so that I could walk rather than be dragged, and I jerked my arms away in defiance.

"I got it, you turd blossoms. I'm up." I straightened my ruined fishing shirt with my bloody hands and started walking behind them, wondering if I could hit an ogre in the neck hard enough to break it.

After a few yards, a hand grabbed my shoulder. It startled me at first, but while firm, the grip wasn't rough.

"Slow it down, Diomedes," Elegast whispered hoarsely.

I slowed to match his pace as he kept a hand on my shoulder. The ogres maintained their steady gait, progressing down the passage slightly faster than we were.

"Trust me. I'm going to get you out of here, but it's not going to be easy. Just go with me on this," Elegast said once the ogres were ten yards ahead.

I nodded ever so slightly, and my heart raced with relief. He barely tapped his fingers on my shoulder reassuringly. He hadn't killed me back in the chamber when I attacked him, so presumably, I could trust him.

After an indeterminable amount of time spent walking down the hall illuminated by the eerie light that had no discernible origin, the ogres stopped, and a hole opened in the wall across from them. When we caught up a few seconds later, Elegast shoved me through hard enough that I lost my footing and bounced off the far wall, landing hard on my butt, sending a shockwave of pain through every injury I'd sustained over the past few weeks. I could hear the cracked laughter from the ogres outside the door. I was disoriented, sore, and hungry, but I resolved that if I ever got my hands around the big foul-breathed creature's throat, it would take a crowbar to pry my fingers loose.

Wincing, I sat there on the floor with my arm over my knees until Elegast grabbed my shoulder, only this time much rougher. With a viselike grip, he practically picked me up off the floor. I scrambled to get my feet under me and relieve the pain of his grasp. Once I was up, he shoved me at the back wall. This time, I caught myself and turned to face them.

I may or may not have been in the same cell from before, but it appeared identical. The opening into the cell was gone, and the big ogre stood against the far wall, grinning like an idiot, while his companion stood in another corner, with Elegast a few feet in front of me. Again, the fairy knight winked then placed his hand on the pommel of a dagger at his waist.

Faster than the blink of an eye, he closed the distance between us and grabbed my right shoulder and pulled me close, forcing my hand toward his dagger. I may have been a little fuzzy on what day it was, but the primal part of my brain instantly understood his intention. I grabbed for the dagger, and he caught me with his left arm and shoved me backward.

Already on unsteady legs, I tripped, but not before my fingers closed around the knife's grip. I tucked the long, delicate blade along my forearm as Elegast grabbed my shoulder again then threw me across the room — right at the smaller ogre.

The creature didn't have time to act before I hit him. The impact itself wasn't forceful enough to cause injury, but the ogre certainly wasn't expecting it. By the time I bounced off and hit the ground, the guard had regained his balance and bent over to pick me up. I rose up to meet him with every ounce of my remaining strength, thrusting the fairy-made stone blade into the flabby skin under his jaws. Pushing with both hands, I drove the ogre back upright, embedding the knife deep in the creature's skull. His eyes rolled to white, I pulled the knife free from his jaw, and he tumbled backward against the wall, making a slight gurgling noise as he fell.

The big ogre stepped forward, cudgel in hand. He stopped to stare down at his fallen companion, and I lunged, driving the blade into his shoulder hard enough to snap the stone blade. The ogre roared and took a wild swing at me with the heavy wooden club. Even in my current exhausted state, I was fast enough to avoid the blow, but too worn out to counter as quickly as I wanted. Still, I stepped in, pinning his arm across his body, and hammered my fist into the toothy mouth, breaking off a protruding canine. I continued to pound until he pushed me back, slightly dazed while taking an awkward and weak backhanded swing. I stepped close enough in that I caught the arm then brought my forearm down on his elbow with a satisfying snap. Again, the ogre screamed. The heavy cudgel fell from his broken arm, and the ogre slumped forward, drooling thick ropes of black blood from ruined lips.

Catching my breath, I picked up the cudgel with both hands and swung at the ogre's head, feeling the skull crack. The brute slumped to the ground, and I dropped the heavy wooden weapon. I bent over, with my hands on my knees, to catch my breath, too worn out to feel as vindicated as I'd hoped. Tension slipped from Elegast's shoulders, and the wrinkles on his forehead melted away as he relaxed somewhat.

"We don't have much time," he said in a hushed voice.

"What the fuck is going on here?" I asked.

"Someone killed that insufferable ass Indronivay using a high-powered rifle at nearly a third of a league." He took a deep breath. "Goibniu was killed by a smaller firearm at what you call 'point-blank' range. Both courts are convinced these attacks were carried out by a human, because of the weapons involved. Since the skill level that was displayed in not only the shots but also the infiltration suggests not only human, but *super* human, and given that your reputation among the fae is less than favorable, the assumption is that no one *but* you could have accomplished these attacks against such powerful fae. I have scant bits of intelligence that point elsewhere, but I cannot convince anyone in Titania's retinue to look beyond *you*. I also have reliable information that suggests recent human unrest in the Middle East has had, how should I say... help... from nonhuman sources and that several human leaders are also in imminent danger. The whole thing threatens to cause massive strife across all races unless the real culprit can be stopped."

I didn't know what to say, but Elegast's expression was telling — he pressed his lips into a tight, deep frown. He actually appeared haggard. Even more striking was the concern evident in his eyes under his heavily furrowed brow. If guns were used to perpetrate the attacks, then that ruled out almost all Fae. *Almost.* And if the courts concluded that the attacks were beyond a mundane human, then that left very few possibilities, with me right at the top of the list. *But I didn't do it.*

"*You've* got to stop whoever it is. But first" — he peered down at the dead ogres — "we need to get you out of here."

"I'm up for that part. Why can't you —"

He cut me off with a wave. "You know fae don't care to be involved with human concerns. Moreover, your death at the hands of fae under these circumstances would cause an uproar among those humans 'in the know.' And..." He lowered his head and exhaled heavily. "Because I'm going to be very injured."

I jerked upright.

"For you to escape, it's going to have to appear as if you overpowered me and then used me to escape. You're going to have to make it very convincing. *Very.* Do you understand?"

I didn't know what to say to severely injuring the guy who had offered to save my life. I understood his line of reasoning, but that didn't make it easier to swallow. Still, he was right. While human groups like the Guardians, the Hermetic Order of the Golden Dawn, Pugnus Dei, the Odin Brotherhood, and others familiar with Parans and Old Ones might try to wage war, they didn't have the strength to take on either fae court, even collectively. Moreover, fae generally weren't willing to expose themselves to humanity, either, which was why open war between the races had never occurred before. My execution, along with the death of human leaders and fae royalty, all ostensibly at the hands of opposing factions, might give them all reason to try.

"No, there has—"

Elegast held up his hand. "This is our only option, and we don't have time to argue."

I finally nodded. "Look, I don't even know where I am or how long I've been here."

"Poveglia. For about thirty days, as far as we can tell. Someone is waiting above to help you off the island. Andunail sent them for you," he said, closing his eyes and cringing. "Now hit me."

In my haze, it took me a second to piece together everything he'd said. Poveglia was an Italian island, off the coast of Venice. It was considered to be one of the most haunted locations in the world. Every human attempt to inhabit it has been met with disaster, and for good reason: the island had long been a stronghold of the Unseelie Court, and its powerful and very nasty genius loci, or prevailing spirit, didn't need a physical form to cause issues for creatures within its realm. Like the Unseelie, the genius loci despised humans, and it worked for Queen Mab. She has used the island since long before my time, and I doubted she had plans to give it up anytime soon.

I rolled my shoulders and squeezed my fists, trying to loosen up or maybe even delay what I was about to do to Elegast—to a friend. Maybe an alternative idea would pop into my addled brain.

But why was the name Andunail familiar? Andunail... wait, that's what fae call Athena. Given her mindset since our days together at Troy over three thousand years ago, she would not have chosen to interfere directly—even for me. But I knew there was no way she would abandon me. Considering what Elegast had told me about what else was happening in the world, at least I knew why she hadn't acted.

Because of the damned genius loci, the Unseelie would know I was escaping almost instantly, and they would know exactly where I was. Fear crept into my mind, but I pushed it away. *I would rather die trying to get out of here than die on my knees. Especially for something I did not do.*

Elegast opened one eye and arched an eyebrow high on his forehead as he noted my slow comprehension of the gravity of the situation. "We must act with haste. Now," he said through clenched teeth. "Hit me!"

I was weary and nowhere near ready. But I had no choice. And no time.

Elegast opened his mouth. "I said —"

I laid into him. Despite being exhausted and sore, I had to make the beating realistic. To make things worse, I also needed him alive *and* awake. Among Elegast's many unique abilities was opening any lock, door, or portal simply by asking. *But he has to be able to ask.* That wasn't his only trick, but it was the one I would need most.

Elegast fought back, though halfheartedly. Less than that actually, because Elegast at half speed was one of the deadliest beings I knew. I tried desperately not to think as I kicked and punched him until he finally sagged beaten to the ground and peered at me through swollen eyes. Holding up his hand to stop me, he nodded slowly. I was numb, but some part of my will forced me to act.

Grabbing Elegast, I threw one of his arms over my shoulder and dragged him to the wall where I guessed the doorway was.

"Open it," I said.

Somewhere down the long hallway behind us I could hear the clatter of weapons and shouting echoing toward us. *My head start was damn short.*

"Craich," said Elegast, in a cracked voice, pronouncing the Sidhe word for "open" through swollen and bloody lips.

The opening in the wall appeared, and I dragged Elegast out.

"To the right," Elegast said. "All the way down to the end..." and his head dropped.

I could tell he was still alive, but he was out of it for right now. Meanwhile I shuffled as fast as I could, given my condition and the fact I was dragging a three-hundred-pound fairy. I could feel the passage come to life — which was an understatement. The walls, the floor, and even the rocks reacted to my presence, turning soft under my feet and shifting as I stepped, making me dizzy. The light began to pulse from inside the walls at rapid intervals as if the genius loci had set off an alarm. I could only imagine it was like being in the middle of a rave while stoned. I kept my legs churning, placing one foot in front of the other as fast as I could manage, until I hit another dead end. The entire passage began to tremble. I laid Elegast down and gently tried to wake him. In desperation, I finally slapped him.

He gazed up at me through slits in his swollen face, and I could barely see his eyes shift back and forth as he recognized where we were. "You realize I'll have to come after you now, too. You better find this guy before we find you." He coughed and spit a gobbet of purple goo onto the floor. "Craich," he said as loudly as he could manage then passed out again.

At first, nothing happened. Then one wall fell away, forming into a stairway. I gently laid Elegast down and stumbled upward.

CHAPTER 10

THE STAIRS ENDED IN A white hospital-like tiled room in a seriously dilapidated building with no roof and only the moon for light. All around me, the air buzzed with electricity, and I could feel a malevolent presence surrounding me, coming up out of the ground. While I couldn't see it clearly, I could feel the energy reach for me like a plant, trying to entangle my legs and arms. I kept trudging forward on weary legs.

In the moonlight, as I tried to navigate the building, I could tell the decrepit structure was definitely a hospital that had been abandoned for years. Twice, I nearly fell as I tripped over mounds of broken tile, plaster, and unidentifiable metal objects. The indistinct tendrils of void-black energy crept everywhere along the walls and floors, heading me off. For the moment, there were no signs of anything following me, but after beating and then carrying Elegast, I couldn't move fast enough to avoid the tendrils of energy. They began to grab at my feet and ensnare me. Dread and despair overwhelmed me. My mind began to wander, and I could barely focus on my surroundings, let alone which way I was headed. My eyes blurred, and I was unsure if I was hearing things behind me or not. All I could think about was how tired and hungry I was until I finally stopped in the middle of a room and sank heavily to my hands and knees, breathing raggedly. The dark energy crept up my body, holding me tightly. The feelings of hunger, misery, and exhaustion increased until something in my head told me it was hopeless—that it was okay to give in and stop.

What?

The sensation sent a cold shiver up my spine to a place in my brain that could not comprehend the message. My obligation to humanity and my sense of duty formed the core of my being and drove me. *Give up?* No. *Stop?* Never. I would die first.

Anger started to rise in my chest, and the despair began to recede. Some feral part of me growled, refusing to give in, as I tried to stand again, straining with waning strength against the shadowy energy that held me. *Resist.*

"D, get your ass up and get moving…" said a familiar voice from somewhere in the darkness.

I didn't know if I was imagining things or not. I blinked hard and searched for the source but couldn't locate it. I continued to struggle, getting to one knee.

"You know I can't carry your ass, and Ab ain't here to help me, so get up and get moving… *now!*" said the voice in the darkness.

Ab? Did the voice mean my friend Abraxos? Suddenly, another cold surge of adrenaline began pumping through my body, and my heart sped up.

"Duma? Is that you?" I asked.

"Yeah, man, now get your ass *up.* Up the stairs to your left. The fucking spirit of this place won't let me any closer, and we gotta move, and in case I hadn't said it enough, I mean *now!*" he shouted. "Bad guys are right behind you."

Scuffling and shuffling noises closed in from almost every direction. A fully armed legion of fae would hardly make more noise than a few birds, so smack in the middle of an Unseelie stronghold, I really didn't want to know what was creating the sounds.

Through my haze, I saw the stairs. Visions of every combat instructor I've ever had—from my father thirty-two hundred years ago, to my SEAL instructors through BUD/S most recently—all screaming to get up flooded through my mind, but it was a vision of the intense, unyielding warrior-aspect of Athena's countenance standing silently over me that drove me. *She would never allow me to flinch. Resist.* I willed myself to my feet, pulling myself slowly free from the black tentacles of energy until I could walk. I drove myself toward the stairs—and collapsed as I hit the first step.

"Good enough, I guess. Now hold your breath if you can, 'cause this is gonna be a little noxious," Duma said. The hollow rattling of a tin can tumbling across the tile floor behind me was followed by a dull whump then the sound of gas escaping. An acrid smell hit me as I sensed my body rise an instant before everything went black again.

***

I smelled fish cooking then heard the sounds of a kitchen and someone screaming in an Asian dialect. I didn't feel depressed anymore, though I was still so exhausted I couldn't focus my eyes, and my limbs weighed thousands of pounds each. Then the smell made my stomach growl and twist involuntarily with an intense hunger that made me retch.

"Get up, you lazy pile of pink flesh," Duma said, followed by the sensation of being grabbed and lifted under my arms as I was dragged to my feet. "We gotta move, man. Let's go," he said with a pained grunt as I was pulled up faster than I could stand on my own.

"I fucking hate this place," Duma said.

I suddenly began to run, stumbling along as I was dragged by my arm. My eyes focused only long enough for me to see flowing shoulder-length hair so pale, it was almost white. I should have known I could count on Duma when my ass was in a sling. I would die defending my Peri friends, despite the fact that the relationship has caused me grief over the years. We'd fought side by side for centuries for no other reason than that I asked for their help. I owed my life to them on more occasions than I could count, and I'd saved them many times, as well. Apparently, it was Duma's turn to save me.

At some point, I drifted back through the murky haze of consciousness and discovered I wasn't moving. I was assaulted all at once by the combined smells of pungent spices, gamey animals, fish, garbage, sewage, stale water, cooking oils, wet asphalt, and cigarette smoke. I shook my head, fought for balance, and forced myself to stand on my own. I rubbed at my eyes. Artificial lights, though not bright, pierced my eyes, and I squeezed them shut again. In the brief moment I had them open, I'd seen I was either in a back alley of Chinatown somewhere or actually in some Asian country.

I shielded my eyes with my hand and forced them open again. Colors, shapes, and lights began to coalesce into identifiable objects. Ducks hung from racks by their bent necks, and live chickens were stacked in crates on one side of us. Crates packed with ice and loaded with fish and sea creatures of all manner lined another side. Duma was to my right, in front of me, arms crossed across his chest and one eyebrow arched as he watched me.

"Aw... there you go. Is ums all better now?" he said. "D, come on, man, we gotta go. Just stay on my six whatever you do," he said.

I nodded, and he took off down the alley at a brisk trot. I fell in step behind him, tired but elated to be out of the dungeon and off that island. He waved a hand, and the fabric of the space in front of him parted like a rip in a curtain. He headed into the tear, picking up speed. I followed, shielding my eyes and stumbling along as best I could.

CHAPTER 11

DUMA HAD OPENED A PORTAL into the Telluric Pathways, but we were covering ground so rapidly that I couldn't focus long enough to tell where we were. I had absolutely no idea where we were going. I could have sworn we traveled through Paris, Chicago, and Moscow, guessing mostly by scent, but we passed through far more places I couldn't identify in the few seconds we spent there. Some were tropical, some bitterly cold, and while a few felt desolate, the majority gave off the almost claustrophobic and frenetic feel of large urban settings. No beings were more adept at using that energy of the ley lines as a pathway than fae.

In my stupor, I marveled at the fae's innate understanding of the Ways. They see them as plainly as I see highways, and like a highway, the lines apparently had signs that told them where they were and where they were headed, too.

We moved nonstop for at least half an hour. Duma kept making sure I was right behind him, rolling his head exaggeratedly, and sighing heavily *every time* he did so. While I was normally much stronger than he was, he'd always been faster. Not significantly, but enough. Right then, I was like a kid trying to keep up with Usain Bolt.

Finally, Duma stopped and dragged his hand down in front of him. All at once, I could hear automobile traffic, voices, and construction, along with smells of smog, coffee, and aged wet stone as the Ways parted. We emerged in a cobblestoned alleyway in an old, damp but urban area. The usual city noises were remarkably light, and the alley was surprisingly clean. The surrounding buildings were short but abutted one another, and the architecture was an old combination of stone, plaster, and wood, so it had to be European.

"Where are we?" I asked, breathing hard, barely able to stand. I slumped down along one wall to rest.

"Zurich. Wait here and don't move. They aren't far behind us."

Duma glanced around furtively before taking off down the alley toward a cross street.

I must have fallen asleep, but it couldn't have been for long. The low, throaty rumble of a massive engine startled me awake. When I opened my eyes, I saw a brilliant-red Aston Martin One-77 in front of me. The growling engine vibrated in my head.

The door on the opposite side of the car from me opened, and Duma stuck his head out. "Get in. And don't scratch the car. Move!"

As he said it, three figures in long dark coats jumped down from a gabled roof down the alley, landing a hundred yards behind the car. I slammed the car door shut, and Duma floored it, causing the tires to squeal on the wet stones as the engine roared to a finely tuned crescendo. I watched in the side-view mirror as our pursuers kept pace with us until Duma pulled out of the alley, skidding onto a main road, where he furiously began to work the shift paddles behind the steering wheel until the speedometer hit one hundred miles an hour. Other cars and buildings whipped past so fast on the narrow street that it made me dizzy, forcing me to close my eyes.

Duma tossed a pair of sunglasses into my lap then merged onto a highway, expertly weaving through slower traffic until the speedometer hit two hundred. The car's sleek light-gray-and-black interior caught my attention. It was more impressive than the inside of my house back on Point Loma. Hell, it was nicer than most houses. I bet it cost more than some, too. The leather used for the seats was probably worth more than my boat, and the rich smell pleasantly overwhelmed the car's interior.

For a few minutes, I tried to pay attention to where we were. I watched as expansive green hilly fields and valleys interspersed with ancient small towns whipped past with a massive snow-capped mountain range in the distance, but I finally gave up the fight to stay alert and passed out. The next thing I knew, Duma was helping me out of the car. He mentioned something about Vienna, but mostly, I heard, "Blah, blah, blah..."

***

I woke up on a futon in a darkened room with an IV in my arm and a splitting headache. To make matters worse, I was wearing a diaper. On the floor next to the mattress were two bottles of water and a jug of aspirin. I partook of both.

Despite being alive for a few thousand years and kicking serious ass of some of the most bizarre creatures imaginable, removing an IV needle freaked me out. Needles and shots didn't bother me, but I could never watch—the idea of removing the damned thing from my own arm gave me the heebie-jeebies. I did finally get it out, but I nearly bit my tongue off twice in the process.

The only things in the bare cement-walled room were the futon, a chair, and a dresser. A long, thin steel sconce by the single door provided the small amount of ambient light. A pair of sweatpants hung on the back of the chair. I pulled off the diaper, horrified at what I might find, mercifully to find it clean, then put on the pants. Oddly, as I tested my limbs, my hands hurt far worse than anything else. The bruises, scrapes, and cuts were stark on my knuckles. They weren't swollen anymore, but they were stiff, and flexing my fingers hurt. I could only imagine how Elegast felt.

Whoever tried to frame me was dangerous enough that Elegast voluntarily submitted to me beating him to a pulp to help me escape from his opposing court. *Whoever it was would pay for Elegast's honor. And for what they did to me.*

I opened the door to the room and was hit all at once by the smell of something cooking, and a flood of bright artificial light instantly made me dizzy then nauseated. I swallowed hard then squinted, following my nose down the cement-walled hallway toward a larger room. It had the distinctly austere feel of an ultra-modern Asian apartment, though none of the decorations reflected that. In fact, the décor was elegantly simple. The spartan furnishings—a couch, two chairs, and three tables—were a combination of wood and various kinds of stone. Though the room was brightly lit, there were no windows. To my left, noises and voices were emanating from a room that was also the source of the food smells.

"Look who finally woke up," Duma said, coming up the hallway from behind me. "You want something to eat?"

I reacted a little too quickly and had to catch myself on the back of a chair to keep from falling. The ridiculously attractive fairy was dressed in *tailored* coral-colored sweats, undoubtedly chosen to accentuate his alabaster hair and skin. They were silk, too. Not the stuff I wore.

He passed and waited for me at the doorway, holding a pair of sunglasses. I snatched the glasses from him and entered. The room was a kitchen and informal dining area, and an Asian woman dressed in a short robe stood at the stove. Another petite Asian woman, dressed similarly, was setting the table.

"Good morning," they said in unison, in heavily accented English.

"Uh, good morning," I replied.

Speaking Japanese, Duma broke into a full dialogue with them. They laughed and nodded as he pointed at me. Finally, he sat down at the table.

He motioned to one of the seats. "Sit down before you fall down, D."

"Where are we?" I sat and put on the sunglasses.

"A safe place. We're in Tokyo. One of my secure hideouts near Golden Gai. What would you like to eat? Eggs? Bacon? It's all fresh." He gestured at the stove, and the woman standing next to it bowed her head a little.

"Yeah, eggs and bacon would be great. Scrambled's fine," I said. "Secure? Are you sure?" I asked Duma.

He smiled at me, though it was the sort of polite smile reserved for someone who was clearly a moron. "From humans, pretty damn. From fae, absolutely. We're in the most populated city in the world, and this building is in the middle of one of the busiest markets on Earth, open all day, every day. We're surrounded by a sea of humanity. No fae would ever come here unless the circumstances were dire."

"Trust me, *dire* would require a major improvement," I said.

"What's going on, D? All I got was a note from you saying to get your gear bags and meet you where I did. Poveglia is bad enough, but then you showed up half-dead, to boot—"

"I didn't send you a..." Then it dawned on me. "Athena. This is a really long story, so just deal with it." I brought Duma as up-to-date as I could.

"Whoa, now that's a serious conspiracy," Duma said when I'd finished the tale. "You really think someone is trying to start a war between humans and fae? But why? Humans, by and large, don't know about us. Crap, they are more willing to buy into *aliens*. Hell, half of fae sightings are chalked up to aliens as it is, so how do you expect humans to suddenly believe enough to wage war? Fae against fae, no problem, but fae and human? Not likely, D. You sure it's not just open season on you?"

"What's the point of framing me? Besides, Elegast says he doesn't buy the assertion that I killed Goibniu. He had information that led him to think it was someone else. He said the Seelie Court suspected me because of the *way* it was done. But I didn't do it. Elegast said I needed to find out who did."

"Yeah, Elegast. Now there's a self-righteous windbag." Duma sneered.

I rolled my eyes.

"Again, I gotta ask why. It's definitely a crazy time. Hell, only a few days back, the Iranians tried to kill the Saudi Arabian ambassador to the US. Of course they deny it, but since they approached me about doing it, don't trust them. And, man, is there some crazy crap going on in North Africa. Gaddafi's offering mercenaries a boatload of cash, but he's so batshit crazy that Ab and I won't even touch it. And for *me* to say that, you know it has to be nuts. But that's all human shit."

"*What?* How long have I been out? Where's your TV?" I got up, taking stock of the apartment.

"TV? Seriously? And it's the middle of October, according to your calendar," Duma said, following me into the other room.

"Hey, if Elegast is right, then there are going to be assassination attempts against human leaders and all kinds of political unrest." I suddenly felt completely overwhelmed by the implications of my predicament. "He also mentioned that the uprising going on in Egypt and the rebellion against Gaddafi's regime might have been driven by whoever killed Goibniu and Indronivay. Maybe you're right. A full-scale human-fae war might be farfetched, but all-out war, human against human and fae against fae, *wouldn't* be as much. But who would stand to benefit from this kind of conflict? I need to contact Athena."

"Aren't you, you know, like mentally connected to her?" Duma asked.

"Yeah, but to save my sanity and allow me some semblance of still being my own person, she stays out of my head as much as possible."

"Well, then we have a problem. I am shut off from the outside world here, D. This is a safe house. I can have a runner get you a cell phone if you want, but you can't use it in here," Duma said.

"Fine, get me a cell phone. I need to have her check into who or what would benefit from this kind of widespread chaos. It sounds like the kind of crap that witch Medea was up to when we killed her. Regardless, I *need* to find out who tried to frame me. And I am going to start with where they say I killed these two fae courtiers."

"D, I thought you only needed help to disappear for a while. I didn't sign on to go against both fae courts. Been there, done that," he said, waving me off.

"I can't just disappear. You know me better than that." I fixed Duma with a hard stare. "It's my *duty* to be violent in the face of monsters so that humanity can go on unaware."

"No kidding," he said. "You are always the right man in the wrong place. But even your Shakespeare wrote, 'Caution is preferable to rash bravery.'"

"Wow, Shakespeare? Really? I didn't know you could read."

"Funny, D. Actually, I was part of the theatre troupe that first performed *King Henry the Fourth*. It was his first back in 1590. But that's beside the point."

"I'm not asking you to help me track down whoever killed these guys. I understand Peris like you and Ab are despised by both fae courts. And I appreciate your help getting me off Poveglia, but I *am* going to find out who's behind this," I said, pointing in short jabs at the floor.

Duma stared at me, his brow heavily knitted, before letting his head loll back, hands on his hips. "Ah, hell, I've seen that look in your eyes before. Belphoebe and Elegast will track your ass down inside of two days if I don't help you." Duma smiled crookedly. "If you need me, I'm there. Ab's busy, though."

"He's not in North Africa right now, is he?" I asked, almost afraid to hear the answer. Duma and his brother ran world-class human mercenaries around the world, and the last thing I needed was Ab to be unwittingly involved in this whole mishigas.

"Ah, no. He's... elsewhere. Best you don't know where."

"Good. Now where's my gear you said you had? And get me that phone."

Time to get to business.

CHAPTER 12

ATE PLATE AFTER PLATE OF eggs, bacon, steamed rice, gloppy rice porridge, fish, miso soup, pickled vegetables, bread, yogurt, and green tea. I probably could have eaten more, but according to the cook, I'd pretty much cleaned out the kitchen. Meanwhile, Duma's other housekeeper spent about an hour picking me up two prepaid burner cell phones. While I waited impatiently for her to return, I went through the things Duma had brought for me from my home.

He'd managed to get my main gear bag and one other equipment duffel. It was actually an impressive feat because I kept them in my load-out room, which was essentially a metal vault protected by two biometric locks. I forced myself to check the gear and not dwell on what was probably left of my bedroom. *He was helping me out.*

My main gear bag contained my battle dress fatigues and other gear, holsters, guns, bladed weapons, and my cuirass, currently sewed into a Blackhawk Omega Elite vest. This equipment was my security blanket and had been the virtual embodiment of humanity's safeguard for over three thousand years now. My swords and my cuirass, forged by Hephaestus himself, were a gift from Athena. The cuirass was unbreakable and had saved my life more times than I could count, probably countless times I was unaware of, as well. The swords were old-school Kopis-style blades that were the height of favor before I became immortal. They were sharp enough that, with sufficient force, they could penetrate and cut through anything. I'd driven them through the armor on an M1A2-Abrams Main Battle Tank *and* taken the heads off trolls just as easily.

While the idea of swords and armor made me feel old and a little archaic, they were necessary in the world I lived in. Most Parans I'd encountered were undeniably old-fashioned and followed a strict code of honor. Guns and bombs didn't fit into their world, where combat was often still one-on-one and hand-to-hand. Then there were those creatures that bullets simply didn't affect much.

Once I took inventory of my main bag and checked my weapons, I went through the second. It contained climbing and rappelling gear. *Great.* At least I was covered if I needed a few hundred feet of rope. *At least it isn't the bag filled with my dirty laundry.*

A short time after I inventoried my gear, Duma's housekeeper returned with the phones. The first thing I had to do was contact Athena. I walked outside and up several flights of stairs to the roof. I forwarded a coded sequence to a secure phone number she used only for our communications — and only when necessary. I waited for her reply to confirm it was her responding. It was paranoid, but better safe than sorry in this situation. Once I received confirmation, I sent a short message letting her know I was going after whoever was behind these attacks and asking her to get me any intel she could dig up on the assassinations and who was left after Medea that might benefit from such wide-scale chaos.

My guess was that her focus was already on any trouble brewing in North Africa, working to find a peaceful solution via her front, the Metis Foundation. If Elegast was correct about some nonhuman involvement, she would normally have sent me in to remove the interloper. But if Elegast *was* correct, then my situation and all of that stuff was connected *somehow*, and my direct involvement could cause further issues in brokering any peaceful solutions. Either way, I was going to have to do this as quickly and quietly as possible. I didn't know how Athena would get me the information. I never did, but she would get it to me — wherever I was.

I made a second call: Agent Sarah Wright of the Department of Homeland Security. I was hoping she might be able to help me with any known assassins capable of pulling off attacks like the ones for which I'd been framed. For a plain-old vanilla mortal who'd been dragged into my world during my fight with Medea about a year ago, she'd managed to hold up better than most would have. I was so focused on what I was about to do that I almost forgot about our awkward personal situation.

Her phone rang twice before she answered. That didn't give me enough time to contemplate the complexity of our relationship or the fact that I had been sort of deliberately avoiding her for a few weeks before my stint at Fairy State Correctional. So almost two months had passed since we'd last talked.

"Agent Wright," she said in a clipped but professional response.

"Hey, um, it's me," I said, trying not to stammer.

I'd never been good with relationships that don't involve me cracking skulls. And a romantic relationship with a mortal wasn't fair to either of us. We'd *almost* talked about it but left things largely unsaid the last time we were together. It hurt to think about because I really did like her.

"'Me' who?" she replied.

"Steve, I mean Diomedes," I said, beginning to sweat. I could hear Duma snickering behind me, listening, no doubt, as intently as he could.

"Oh, the number came up blocked," she replied.

"Sorry about that. It's a burner," I said. "How are you?" Despite the urgency, I thought maybe trying to be social was a good way to go since it had been a while.

"Busy. Is that why you finally called? To see how I was?" she asked.

"Well, not the only reason I called." My mind reeled for the right things to say. I finally sighed. "But I do need your help with something."

"Hold on." She talked to someone while she tried to muffle the call. It barely took a few seconds, but with each passing moment, I felt like a bigger ass for calling to ask for her help.

"How odd," she said, returning to our conversation. "I just got a large file from the Metis Foundation, marked *Operation Fugitive*. Anything to do with you?"

"Um, yeah, actually. I'm sorry I didn't call sooner, but right now is not the time to do this. I *really* need your help."

"Of course. I told you I wanted to help when I could," she replied. That was a small relief.

"I've been accused of killing members of both fairy courts," I said. "And I just escaped from the Unseelie Fae after almost a month of imprisonment. I have reason to believe that someone or some*thing* is trying to frame me."

"Wow, okay." Her concern was evident even over the phone.

"It gets worse," I said. "Whoever is doing this may be working to further incite unrest in North Africa. Probably elsewhere, too."

As I spoke, I could hear her flipping through pages, presumably perusing the file she'd received from Athena.

"I need anything you might have pertaining to where these assassinations took place and cross that with any intelligence you can get on known assassins capable of carrying them out," I said.

"Yeah, we don't usually keep databases of information about fairies," Sarah said.

"I'm not entirely sure it *was* a fairy who did this," I said. "Warmaster Lord Indronivay was Mab's General, and Goibniu was Titania's chief bladesmith. Apparently, one was shot with a high-powered rifle at a very long distance—over a *thousand* yards. The other was shot point-blank."

"I didn't think fairies used firearms."

"They don't," I replied. "That's my point. It could be a human doing this. But to pull off that shot on Indronivay, they'd have to be good and very likely someone DHS might watch out for."

"I can check into it, but it might take me some time," Sarah said. "Where did the assassinations take place?"

As we spoke, I couldn't help but think about our kiss on the side of Mount Alvand after we had taken out Medea about ten months back. I still had a few loose teeth from when she'd punched me, too, but the memory of both made me smile.

"No clue. I don't know where Indronivay or Goibniu lived, let alone where they were shot," I said. "I know that's not much help, especially since they were fae—"

"Wait," she said. "According to the info in this folder, Indronivay had a stronghold in the Ural Mountains. Seriously? A *stronghold*?"

"Yeah, probably. He was an effete snob and a very anachronistic fruitcake. Where exactly?"

"Kholat Syakhl, well north of Ivdel in the Sverdlovsk Oblast. *In Russia*. Holy crap, that's near where the Dyatlov Pass Incident happened back in the fifties," she said, the excitement evident in her tone.

"Yeah, that makes sense. Those hikers probably got too close for comfort if they were near his place, and that's why they all died in such mysterious ways," I said. "The Russians covered it up before I could get there to investigate. I thought it might be Russian military testing, but that certainly makes more sense. What about Goibniu?"

"Oh, much nicer. Vanuatu. Mount Gharat on Gaua." She whistled. "Jeeze, it's an *active* volcano."

"That figures. Seriously, I need any info you can find on a possible shooter, and Athena might be able to help more, but I need that info. The quicker, the better."

"I'll do my best... take care of yourself."

"Thanks, I'll try. Duma's with me. And I'll be in touch." After an awkward moment of silence, I hung up. *I'm an asshole.*

I could hear Duma stifling laughter behind me. He was trying so hard not to laugh that he was actually crying. I smacked him in the back of the head as I walked past him, heading back downstairs.

He burst out in a rolling laugh. "Have you ever actually *been* involved with a woman before?" he asked, breathing heavily and trying to regain his composure.

"Shut up. We got bigger things to worry about," I said, trying to convince myself as well as Duma that the situation with Sarah didn't bother me.

"Yeah, bigger than you might think. You said that Indronivay was taken out with a rifle at long range, right? And I'm guessing that, like you, even the good Agent Wright thinks that fairies don't use firearms," he said as we walked back into his apartment.

"Yeah, so?" I said, irritated by his obtuse leading statement.

"Think, dummy." He pulled a gun on me from behind his back.

My first instinct was to close the distance between us and disarm him, but my body wasn't up for full speed yet. Instead, I lurched clumsily to my right and nearly tripped over a rug. For a moment, I couldn't even think, and my heart began to race until the goofy expression on Duma's face stopped me. His mocking my confusion eased the sudden tension and cleared my head.

"Ha ha, funny guy." I had completely forgotten that the outcast Anseelie fairies had no qualms about using modern human weapons or even metals even though it still burned them if they did so unprotected. "I forgot that some of you aren't so rigid in your thinking about guns. But wait..." I sat down. "The only Anseelie I've ever met are you and Ab. How many are there left like you guys?"

"None as far as I know." He put the gun down on a table. "We're the last of the Peri, except a few crazy distant... relations." Duma spread his hands, palms up for effect, but before I could ask the obvious question—which I didn't even want to know the answer to—he continued. "But there are *other* races that could still have survivors." He bared his teeth in a perceptive grin. "I *know* you weren't thinking Ab and I had something to do with this mess."

"Me? Nah," I said, almost ashamed it *had* occurred to me. "But how in the hell do we go about trying to track down fae that may or may not exist when they have successfully avoided every other fae for millennia?"

"Oh, it may be worse than that," Duma said, his face suddenly becoming slack. "I think I know who our number-one suspect might be, and you ain't gonna like it."

"I already don't like it, so just tell me. No, let me guess: Lady Gaga?"

"Ha! No, but she could easily be a half-breed. She's cool enough to be part one of us," he said. "Actually, I don't have a real name. It's more of a boogeyman-type story. But it fits."

"A legend? Seriously?" I threw up my hands before getting back on my feet. "I got both fairy courts chasing me and the world as we know it possibly on the brink of war, and you have a bedtime story?"

"I know, I know, but listen." He rolled his hand dismissively at me. "There is a race called the Blud, and as bad as the Peri reputation was, Blud were much worse. We look very similar, but they were master manipulators, constantly misleading humans and other fairies into situations they couldn't escape from. They were instrumental in the schism that split the fae into the two fairy courts, but one individual in particular was far worse than the rest of us. And he was different. We call him the *Hanner Brid*, which means 'half breed,' because he is rumored to be a half-Blud, half-Succubus cambion."

"A cambion? You mean like Merlin?" I asked.

"Well, yeah, except Merlin had a human mother and an Incubus father. *This* guy was supposed to be a real monster: manipulative, greedy, paranoid, and bloodthirsty. I mean bloodthirsty in a way that makes Countess Erzabet Bathory come off as squeamish," he said, referring to the notorious sixteenth century Hungarian cannibal who was actually a Strigoi vampire. "Over the centuries, rumors would pop up about his involvement in some death or issue. Things like the

Roanoke Colony or the Lake Anjikuni Village and the disappearance of Percy Fawcett. The last thing I know attributed to him was Hoffa."

I actually laughed at the last one. "Seriously? Where do the rumors come from, and how come neither Athena or I are familiar with them?"

"They come from the same place as all rumors," Duma said, holding up his hands. "You hear things. Some wacked-out old fae, a crazy survivor story—the usual. As far as why you and Athena never heard about him, I don't know. You always say you still see stuff all the time that you've never seen before. And Athena only *plays* at being a deity; she's not omniscient, D."

"Yeah, but if a fairy were involved in something like the disappearance of the Roanoke Colony, I would have known about it. That kind of stuff is my job, Duma." I shook my head vigorously.

"There's a lot of stuff that goes on that *you* don't know about. D, you're only one man. You can't know everything that goes on between fairies and humans. Hell, you don't even know everything that goes on among you humans." His laugh was without mirth. "And *all* rumors have a kernel of truth to them."

"So you're saying that you think this cambion is real and that he's the assassin." Frustrated, I pounded on the arm of the chair with my fist.

"No, I'm saying it *could* be him. Whoever *him* is," Duma replied. "Call it a working hypothesis. But whoever it is, we ain't gonna catch 'em sittin' on our asses. And ease up on the furniture, man."

He was right. At least we had a suspect. And a couple of crime scenes to start on.

CHAPTER 13

DUMA TOOK LESS THAN TEN minutes to gather his weapons and gear. We left the safe house in the early evening, and things in the market down below were jammed and bustling with shoppers like ants swarming a discarded piece of candy. We stepped out of the stairwell onto the least crowded street around the building. The mass of humanity was nearly overwhelming. People on the narrow side street were jostling elbow-to-elbow, walking in every direction, avoiding collisions with each other as if they were on a track that guided them. The paper lanterns, signs, multicolored banners and curtains, and the glaring neon would have given Vegas a run for its money, but the smells were otherworldly. They were strong and entirely unique though not unpleasant—a mix of seafood, fresh and cooked meats, gas and oil, smoke, and even cement. It blended with spices of all kinds, pungent herbs, and things I couldn't place at all, making my stomach growl. At least the pain in my eyes was finally lessening. I put on sunglasses, pulled a baseball cap low over my eyes, hunched a bit, then waded into the flow of people. Duma, a hoodie covering his blond hair, oozed in effortlessly behind me. We towered over most of the people around us.

"We need to get to Shinjuku Station," Duma shouted, pointing ahead of us. "Left at the end of this street and straight on. From there, get on the first bus to Kawaguchiko Station near Mount Fuji."

I nodded once, and we split up as I walked along the crowded street. I made it through the alley-like streets and down the gray stone walkway. While crossing the massive six-lane Yasukuni Dori, I got that weird feeling in the pit of my stomach that usually meant I was being followed. I crossed the street with a mass of other people, feeling like a giant among them. *Following me in this crowd would be easy, even for a blind man.*

I could see the narrow street I was supposed to take continuing ahead, but traffic was a mess at the intersection. Bikes, motorcycles, scooters, and cars of all sizes jammed the street from sidewalk to sidewalk, and the eerie glow of neon and vehicle headlights made it hard to focus on anything, let alone see someone deliberately trying to hide or follow me.

Suddenly, a substantial commotion behind me caused everything to devolve into a snarling mess — an accident in the middle of the teeming intersection. Cars screeched to a halt while motorcyclists and bicyclists tried to avoid being crushed. Car horns, random screams, and shouts of irritation from people backed up by the chaos added to the tumult, which all emanated from a spot on the other side of the street. While everyone was focused on the source of the mess, I took advantage of the mayhem and kept moving.

The buildings and streets were the same monotonous color of gray cement, only broken up by the lively colored canopies and signs for the never-ending restaurants and shops. While the buildings were rarely above three or four stories in this district, they were so close together, they gave the impression of being far taller. The side streets were barely wide enough for a single car, or in most cases, delivery trucks, but all of them were crowded with people, making me feel far more claustrophobic than any neighborhood in Manhattan, even at lunchtime.

I made it through the seemingly endless warren without further incident and actually managed, despite the language barrier and heavy construction, to get a ticket on the next bus for Kawaguchiko Station. It was late, but buses left twice an hour twenty-four hours a day, and I discovered the trip took a little less than three hours.

To make sure I wasn't being followed, I waited until the last possible second to board the bus. While I had no idea how he would make it to Mount Fuji, I didn't expect to see Duma on board. In fact, I perceived nothing but mundane humans, mostly staring at me with piercing glares because I was holding everything up. Trying to appear smaller, I quickly found an open seat and flopped down heavily with a sigh. *If only these people knew who I was and what I did for them, maybe then they'd be less aggravated by my strange behavior.*

Even surrounded by mundanes I still felt exposed. My gear bag and all my weapons, except one of my tanto knives tucked along my belt at the back of my pants, were stowed under the bus. I would have to make do with the knowledge that other than being a tall *gaijin*, I more or less resembled a simple tourist headed for a hike on Mount Fuji.

I rested my head against the back of the seat and watched some crazy game show on a small TV screen mounted above me. The next few hours were uneventful, and I slept on and off until the bus pulled in to the station at the foot of Mount Fuji. I collected my bag and walked around the station, trying not to seem like a big lost foreign idiot. I did, however, take a moment to remove the Sig Sauer from my bag and place it inside my belt on my hip. I couldn't stop myself from searching faces, watching shadows, and paying attention to any odd behavior while I waited for Duma. The role reversal of being the chasee instead of the chaser had me completely out of sorts.

Kawaguchiko Station struck me as bizarre. It reminded me of a cross between a traditional Japanese temple and a European ski chalet while the immediate area around it reminded me of a train station in any small town. Directly across the street were a small hotel, a few small shops, and restaurants. In the distance, even in the dark, the imposing silhouette of the snowcapped Mount Fuji was impossible to miss. I stood on the darkened edge of the stoop outside of the bright floodlit front entrance of the bus-and-train depot for about fifteen minutes, until another tall person approached me out of the darkness from alongside the building. Instinctively, my hand traveled to the gun inside my jacket, but a glimpse of the pale hair made me relax.

"How did you get here?" I asked.

"How do you think? Did you expect me to take public transportation?" he asked.

I threw my hand into the air. "Why the hell did I have to then?"

"I needed to see if anything followed you," he said, walking past me.

"And?" I said, quickly catching up to him.

"And we had a tail. A Kitsune, but I got rid of him," Duma said, watching around us alertly.

"Did your taking care of it have anything to do with the mess in the street back in Tokyo?"

Duma stopped and gave me a half smile.

"Figured as much." I shook my head, worried who might have gotten hurt in the process.

"Let's go. We need to get into Aokigahara and make our jump." Duma headed off toward the far corner of the dimly lit parking lot next to the station. "It's only twelve miles from here, and the Sea of Trees is a Nexus point in the Ways. Once we jump from there it'll be nearly impossible to tell where we've gone," Duma said.

Given that it was late, most of the bus passengers had already left for hotels or gotten rides, leaving the station largely deserted until the next bus or train arrived. Without hesitation—and much to my surprise—Duma quickly smashed a window on a small older-model sedan, opened the door, and hotwired it. I didn't have time to be angry with him for stealing the car—we were in a hurry. Duma cursed the small four-cylinder vehicle under his breath continually as we drove through a largely residential neighborhood until we got to Highway 707. Merging onto the highway, Duma began screaming at the small car's lack of power in a bizarre language that sounded like a cross between German and some African clicking-dialect with a heavy lisp. After a few miles and a lot of cursing at the car, we got back onto some side roads and passed a country club of some kind and drove until the road dead-ended.

We abandoned the car on the side of the road, well away from the park entrances and trails, and hoofed it straight into the surrounding forest, and then geared up inside the tree line. The forest was incredibly dense with thick stands of cypress, fir, oak, and maple trees, made even more forbidding by a nearly impenetrable secondary growth. It was nearly impossible to see more than a few yards ahead. Duma was securing the last of his knives while I put my guns into their holsters on my hip and vest. Unfortunately, I didn't have any more ammunition, nor did I have a larger primary weapon—a fact I was mumbling to myself when Duma, regrettably, overheard me.

"What did you say?" he said, his voice rising in tone.

"Nothing, I just wish you would have grabbed the *other* gear bag in my closet and not the one with my rappelling equipment, that's all," I said, trying to sound grateful.

"Dude," Duma said, pulling the glove off his right hand and shoving it at me. "You see this? These are the remnants of the burns I got *days* ago from the stupid metal buckles on that fucking duffle bag you keep your crap in. I wasn't about to open the damn things to see what was inside. I grabbed two of them and got out."

"Sorry. I know, thanks," I said. "I'm just feeling a bit out of sorts having to rely on someone else like this."

"And let's not forget I had to pull your ass out of fucking Poveglia, D. Poh-fucking-veglia. That's a damn Unseelie stronghold, in case you forgot. So suck it up, and let's get going," he said, putting his glove back on and then chucking me in the shoulder harder than he needed. "Oh, and by the way, that Kitsune I shoved into traffic earlier? He was a scout for a *Boryokuda* called *Hyakki Yako*," Duma said, heading deeper into the forest.

"A barracuda named Hacky-Yacky?"

He stopped and glowered at me, which I could easily see on his pale face, even in the darkness. "There's obviously a bounty on your head, and I guess these guys are trying to claim it. Their name means 'Demon Nightmarchers,' and their leader is an Oni named Dai-rin."

Great, now a Hackysack group run by a vicious Japanese ogre was chasing me. *Crap.* "Oh goody. Well, I guess I'd be insulted if they just sent the Boy Scouts," I replied.

"Stick close to me as we enter. This place is loaded with *Yurei*," Duma said.

The *Yurei*, or ghosts, were visible almost immediately upon entering the woods — these were the "suicide woods" after all, where countless Japanese people went to kill themselves. The forest is dense and spooky enough, but all the spirits that dwelled here raised the freaky bar to a whole new level of disturbing. Fortunately, most of the apparitions were little more than wisps of human forms, defeated in life and now timid in death. They were reluctant to come out from their hiding spots. Others were curious, but they all kept their distance as we passed.

We didn't cover ground as fast as I expected, because even Duma had a hard time navigating in this place. As a nexus for the Ways, he explained it was like Grand Central Terminal at rush hour *all the time*. Even I could see hints of the massive amounts of energy from the Ways in the area. It was like peering through the heat coming off a fire. We had to stop while he got his bearings quite a few times. It was during one of these stops that I noticed we were being followed by something a little more corporeal than a ghost.

I tapped Duma on the shoulder, and he ignored me, frustrated about not easily finding his way. I drew my swords, backed up in front of him to block his view, then pointed in the direction of our pursuer. It barely registered on Duma's face. He was in another world, or so I thought.

Duma's right hand blurred into motion, a slight breeze brushed past my face, then I heard a soft impact and a gurgle from behind me. Duma was fiercely focused, his white eyes bright in the dim light of the dense dank forest. The edges of his mouth barely ticked up into a smile, and he tipped his head in three directions: Behind me, to his right, and behind him to his left. I crouched low, watching behind Duma for signs of movement.

Seeing nothing, I shook my head. He lifted his face faintly upward, indicating they were coming from above.

I placed my back to the tree nearest me and renewed my watch. Something caught my attention again off to my right. Almost simultaneously, Duma took off frighteningly fast, though what made his action truly scary was the total lack of sound he made as he went. It was easy to see why human witnesses imagined Peri could fly.

From overhead, through a break in the canopy, I could see several large, thin, almost gangly birds circling and initially reached for the Glock on my hip. Then I hesitated because I was only seeing shadows and glimpses of them, and I was worried the noise would draw additional attention to us.

While I watched the shadows above, something approached quickly from my right. Whatever it was wasn't particularly stealthy in its run, but it didn't sound particularly large either. The dense forest kept it hidden from me until the last second, when a creature about the size of a big dog jumped at me from the darkness. The creature barely hit my shoulder as I ducked to my left and rolled into a defensive position. It landed a few yards up the path in a crouch, chittering wildly like a squirrel.

The bizarre creature had the head of a monkey and a heavy doglike body with stout legs. What really caught my attention was that its tail was a snake that ended with a large fanged head.

I stayed in my defensive posture on one knee, one sword up across my body and the other at the ready down by my side. The creature bowed like a dog at play and began screeching and growling at me while the snake bobbed over the top of it. I feinted right, and the creature lunged after my juke. I attacked immediately, but the snake tail remained stretched out behind it. When I reached to stab the beast, the tail struck. It forced me to jerk awkwardly back in front of the creature to avoid being bitten, but not before I slashed at the snake with my left sword, severing its head.

I ended up on my back while the beast bounded off a short distance, chittering wildly again as its now-headless tail flailed wildly, spraying a dark liquid I guessed to be blood everywhere. I got back to my feet and squared off against it. Again, the thing dropped its head and held its ground. I sprang at it, stomping the ground in front of me, trying to get it to react. But it remained at the edge of my reach, snapping and swatting back as I jabbed. Its paws were massive, far too large for a creature this size, and they resembled a large cat's foot, complete with wickedly curved claws.

Tired of useless sparring, I finally dropped the swords to my sides and took a step forward, anticipating the creature would attack like a cat or a dog and leap at me.

It sprang at me, easily covering the few yards between us. I dodged to my right, turning slightly into it, slapped it farther to the side with my left hand, and stabbed it hard with my right. I hit it mid-body and tore a gaping wound through its chest and abdomen before I wrenched the sword free. The bizarre creature hit the ground with a wet thump, one leg still twitching. I walked over to its prone form and neatly severed its head, causing the creature to go completely still at once. As it died, its body dissolved into a wispy black cloud that dissipated around me.

Before I could recompose myself, one of the gangly birds — stork-like in appearance — landed on the ground in front of me with a peal of thunder as it touched down. *That was an eerie coincidence.* In the accompanying flash of lightning, it transformed into a human form, cloaked in a long reddish robe. Its nose remained abnormally large and beak-like, but it didn't even acknowledge I was there at first. It had a samurai's katana on its narrow, belted waist. This thing had to be a Tengu, which also happen to be expert swordsmen. I quickly glanced around trying to locate Duma but couldn't.

Rather than wait to see what it was about to do, I advanced, thrusting with one hand while keeping the other ready to parry if necessary. The Tengu managed, albeit barely, to sidestep my advance, drew its sword, and attempted to bring the blade down on my head in a downward blow, but I met the swing with my off-hand sword and deflected the blade. I easily outweighed the creature by a third, so I had that in my favor. From its attack, I knew it was fast, but I didn't know how fast.

I set my feet while the Tengu kept his sword out in front of him, pointed at my throat. It watched me with large birdlike eyes set in a narrow and very angular human face atop a very skinny neck, trying to assess weaknesses and strengths. I had longer arms, but my Kopis blades were much shorter than his katana, so neither of us had the advantage on reach. They all used Kenjutsu, the traditional Japanese sword-fighting style. I had studied the form, but I had also studied almost every other form of sword fighting, as well. I regularly bastardized all of them as necessary, making my style highly eclectic and less predictable. For a Tengu to take human form, it had to be old, which meant experienced. I quickly made the assumption that the Tengu's responses would be predictable, but even though I was pretty sure I knew what it would do, that didn't mean I'd be quick enough to defend it.

I decided it was time to shake things up and see what fell out. Rather than continue the circling dance we began, I stepped forward, directly at the Tengu. In the blink of an eye, it batted at my left sword and then lunged forward in an attempt to slash at the side of my chest. I purposely let the blow glance off my cuirass and followed his strike upward with my right hand, keeping my blade under his, driving it up and out, barely missing my neck and chin. The creature was nowhere near as strong as I was, so I could easily direct the blade's momentum. This left his entire right side vulnerable. I brought my left hand through in a level swing that nearly cut the delicate human form in half at its waist.

As my blade cleared the creature's chest, several more Tengu landed behind me, but this time only one of them transformed into human form as thunder rolled off in the distance and lightning flashed. *These guys have a helluva soundtrack.* I didn't have time for this. So in true Indiana Jones fashion, I impaled one sword into the ground, pulled the Glock off my hip, and put two rounds into each of the birdlike creatures, dropping them instantly. Unfortunately, the report of the gun ripped through the dense forest and echoed as if we were in a canyon, but that was *my* soundtrack.

I returned my gun to the drop holster at my hip and reached down to get my sword, when a sound like a derailed freight train barreling through the forest to my right drew my full attention.

A massive red-skinned creature wielding a huge club extended fully over its head emerged out of the darkness of the forest. This had to be the Oni Duma mentioned with the hackysack thing. It was big, brutish, and ogre-like, though, like most Oni, oddly put together. This freak show had three eyes and a nice pair of horns protruding from its forehead and fangs so large that walruses would be jealous.

The Oni charged wildly, throwing itself off balance in its attack, which made it easy to jump out of the way. I landed off to the left of the creature as it brought the massive iron club down with a thud that I could feel through the ground a few yards away. His club, a spiked kanabo, was easily twelve feet long, and the blow was so fierce that the head of the club ended up buried several feet into the soft earth, making it difficult for the big red beast to free it. I took the opportunity to hack the truncheon just below the Oni's hands, severing its shaft and leaving its head buried while Red Hot fell back on his ass. Like all ogres, Oni aren't known for their mental acumen, and this one wasn't proving any different.

"Stay down or die. Your choice, Red Hot," I said, holding both swords loosely at my sides.

The slightest rustle came from behind me, and I shifted around, raising my left sword defensively. I kept my right sword pointed out in front of me.

It was Duma, kukri knives in hand, dripping a dark liquid from both curved blades.

Before I turned back to the ogre, the Oni shot up and tackled me like some deranged football player, screaming as it ran. The stunning blow hurt and took my breath away as he squeezed me briefly before suddenly letting go. It hurt worse when the big dumb red thing staggered and then fell, landing on me. Oddly, though, it simply stared at me with its three dull eyes as it lay there on top of me with a twisted grin on its overcrowded mouth. Then it started to drool black blood all over me, its head dropped, and the weight suddenly felt as though it had increased tenfold, smashing me. Luckily, my cuirass kept the dead weight from literally crushing me.

"Get this damned thing off of me," I said, sputtering.

"How?" Duma replied. "*I* can't lift it. It's gotta weigh six hundred pounds."

"Help me roll it off..." I said, grunting and trying to rock so I could use the creature's weight to shift it.

Normally, I could have lifted the bloody red blob by myself, but given my recent vacation at Club Fae, it took more effort to roll the Oni than I expected. It didn't help that Duma only stood there.

"Thanks," I said, finally getting back to my feet, realizing my sword had impaled it through its chest when it tackled me.

"What? Wait, you really wanted me to help?" Duma asked, his eyebrows tented on his forehead. "I figured you had it." Helping me up, I could see him eyeing the dead creatures around us. "Wow, Tengu, huh? And an Oni." He grimaced and jerked a bit when he recognized the ogre.

"Yeah. I also killed this freaky dog-thing," I said, stretching and still trying to recover from being hammered by the Oni as I pulled my sword free from its torso. "Head of a monkey, body of a dog with huge catlike paws. Oh, and a *snake* for a tail. Freaky. Some kind of weird chimera."

"Nue," Duma replied matter-of-factly. "It dissolved into a black cloud when you killed it, right?"

"Ah, yeah," I said.

"A Nue." Duma held out his hands as if it were common knowledge and I were an idiot.

"Whatever. Let's just go," I replied.

"No kidding. Especially after you fired those shots and alerted every blabbermouth *Yurei* within a mile to our presence," Duma said, taking off at a trot. "Oh, and the Oni there was the head of *Hyakki Yako's,* Dai-Rin's, little brother."

And the hits just keep on coming...

CHAPTER 14

WE LANDED OUR JUMP THROUGH the Ways into a cold, marshy field on the edge of an old-growth forest. It was the middle of the night, but the moonlight revealed several small mountain ranges along the skyline in the very near distance with one snowy peak off to the southwest. In the pale moonlight, I could see a break in the ridge leading to the summit directly to the south of it. The peak was around a mile high, though luckily, we were still too early for the first real snows of the season. There was nothing moving in the darkness.

"That pass should be Dyatlov, I think you call it," Duma said, pointing at the break in the ridge. "And that peak is Kholat Syakhl."

"So where is Indronivay's place?"

"Dunno," Duma replied. "Never been here before."

"Well, if his place is supposed to be up there," I said, pointing at the tallest peak, "I gotta believe he'd pick the most inaccessible face, and a place that afforded him controlled access."

"Yeah, but he'd also want easy access to this point, here," Duma said, hooking a thumb back at the portal through the Ways we came through. "It's the only way in or out, except on foot or by dogsled in the winter."

"If I really was the shooter, I might use that opening in the Ways as well. And so would a rogue fae," I said. "But if I were a mundane human, I probably wouldn't have access to it. I'd have to come in some other way. Thinking from a purely human perspective, I'd have hiked in on foot from another direction."

"Yeah, but you'd have to cover miles through this crap," Duma said, using his chin to point at the swamp we were standing in.

"Precisely, and probably not something Indronivay would ever expect. I'll bet you anything that those hikers back in the '50s were

88

making for Dyatlov Pass and got too close. They probably encountered Indronivay or some of his goons by accident," I said. "Plus, Elegast said the shot was from almost a mile away. There's no way I'll be able to determine a good sniper's roost unless we get up there," I said, ripping up a tuft of marsh grass and tossing it. "Dammit. I'll still probably need satellite images, binos or a spotting scope, a rangefinder... hell, a GPS at the least."

Duma started laughing. "I swear. How did you humans ever survive and manage to cross oceans before computers?"

He was right. I've been around since navigation involved stars and we determined time of day by the sun's angle in the sky, and I was whining about not having a GPS. I had to laugh at myself. "Okay, okay... point taken. Let's work with what we've got," I said. "We need to find Indronivay's stronghold on that peak and reverse-engineer the situation."

For the sake of safety and speed, we waited at the edge of the forest until first light before beginning our trek across the swamp toward the peak. At one point before dawn, several creatures that sounded like wolves bayed back and forth, though they were clearly some distance away. Knowing Indronivay's reputation, he could have employed wolves or some other creatures as watchdogs, which meant Duma and I had to remain alert as we covered the open ground to the foot of the mountain. Fortunately, we encountered nothing of consequence along the way and were able to travel efficiently even over the marshy ground.

The hike up the mountain slowed our progress considerably. Though it was only a few linear miles, the terrain was uneven and entirely uphill, though not a particularly complicated ascent. Plus, I really wanted to take my time as we went so that I could check for clues and stuff. My problem was that I was a great soldier and not a great detective.

Because I was still not operating at one hundred percent and checking everything that struck me as out of place, the climb took us a grueling four hours. We could have easily made the climb in under a half hour, even at altitude. Every time I stopped to examine something, Duma would grumble to himself. To make matters worse, I found nothing suspicious. I didn't really expect to find anything, but since my life and who knows what else was on the line, I wasn't about to half-ass anything.

When we finally got to the peak, nearly four thousand feet of elevation, the view was surprising. This was the highest point for miles and afforded an unobstructed view in every direction. It wasn't much of a mountain by Rockies or Alps standards, but it was still impressive.

I had little doubt that Indronivay's stronghold would be *inside* this mountain rather than a structure on it. Even hidden by glamours, hikers, skiers, and even planes, helicopters, or satellites might stumble across an exposed structure up here. Glamours wouldn't impede *me* from seeing it if it were here, anyway. From our vantage point, we could see all of the surrounding area, but I still couldn't figure out where on this rock the entrances to Indronivay's place would have been. The southwestern and southeastern faces of this peak were much steeper and precarious, leading farther into the range. A second ridge split the north face, but the northeast face was gently sloping. I highly doubted someone like Indronivay would create an entrance on any of the easily accessible slopes. The northwestern face, however, was sheer and forbidding. Finally, something caught my eye as I surveyed the most difficult approaches again: a recent, but slight, rockslide beginning underneath an inaccessible ledge below our position. Nothing else we had seen so far on this mountain was as remotely disturbed as this was.

"Down there," I said, pointing to it. "That rockslide. You think it's possible that's where Indronivay fell when he got shot?"

"More likely than anything else we've come across so far," he replied. "It's hard to tell from up here, but even I would need climbing gear to get down there, unless there's a path we aren't seeing somewhere."

Duma was right. It was too dangerous to get to free-climbing, but the more I stared at it, the more I was convinced the slide wasn't natural. After about thirty minutes of gazing at the slope below us, using the slide's origin as the rough target area, I noticed a potential sniper's roost on a third smaller ridge well below us, running north by northwest from where we stood. Even better, it appeared to be about the right distance from the summit, too—assuming that Indronivay wasn't a mountain goat and there really was an entrance up here somewhere.

"Got it," I said to Duma, pointing toward the spot. "If that rock slide was Indronivay, then of everything I can see, that's not only the best spot, it's the *only* spot, unless the sniper was a spider. At least one entrance has to be somewhere on the rock face below us."

We began our slow, precarious trek down to the ridge along the northwest face and then out along a northward-branching crest that eventually sloped down to the valley below, into a river. So far, we had seen no signs of life, except some deer on the far edges of the marsh. The closer we got to the spot I'd identified, the more it became clear that it was damn near inaccessible. Duma had no trouble working his way over the rocky terrain, and if I weren't stronger and more agile than a normal man, I never would have made it without serious climbing gear and a monumental effort. Not to mention days to make the climb. The ridge, the one we'd crossed from the peak, and a smaller ridge extending northward from the peak itself formed a box canyon of sorts, creating a howling vortex of wind within. The last few hundred yards were so treacherous that the distance took us nearly two hours to traverse, mostly because I was tentative without climbing gear. All I could think about was the other bag Duma had brought for me and I'd oh-so-wisely left behind. *Idiot.* I hadn't expected to be scaling the side of a mountain.

Once we reached the potential roost, the view back toward the peak below revealed several openings in the sheer rock face. They were like optical illusions — invisible from all but the right angle. I could see the entrances to at least *six* different caverns. *Bingo!* That made this spot ideal, except for the swirling wind and the treacherous terrain.

The distance to the nearest cavern had to be at least seven hundred yards, while the one above the rockslide was around a thousand. To make a shot up toward the peak of Kholat through the howling winds would have been a monumentally difficult task. I was good, but I wasn't entirely sure I could make the shot, even given the right gear. I was pretty sure my buddy Frigate, one of the best snipers the Navy SEALs had ever seen, could pull it off, but he would have needed at least two people, maybe three, to make the ascent with his gear. That narrowed the list of possible shooters down to maybe half a dozen guys in the world, and they *all* would have needed help.

Unless Duma was right and the assassin wasn't human at all. That was the disturbing part.

I could see no signs that anyone had ever been on this ledge before. *None.* And a pair of men, even experts, couldn't completely cover their tracks on the side of a mountain. It was too warm for fresh snow to have fallen over the past few months, and I saw no evidence of recent rock falls from climbing activity, like I left behind. If the shooter was human, he was not only better than me, but neater, too. All ego aside—that wasn't likely.

"Whatever did this wasn't human," I said finally. "There's just no way."

"Are you sure? Maybe it was a Spec Ops team," Duma asked, throwing rocks off the ledge out of obvious boredom.

"Exactly why I say it wasn't a human action. I know those groups; I was part of them for years. I did stuff exactly like this with them, and even the best would have left some evidence behind. Crap, even the most sophisticated intelligence agency operatives would have left some indication that someone was here. They probably could have covered up the shooting, but they couldn't have wiped the environment this clean. It's like we're the first ones ever to step foot here, and you saw how difficult it was for me to get here."

"So either this isn't the sniper's hole, or now you're saying you believe my boogeyman story?" Duma said with amusement.

"I'm starting to, yeah." The idea made me shudder.

After searching the small ledge in earnest for an hour, Duma and I began the arduous trek back down the mountain. It wasn't as demanding for Duma as it was for me, and I kept imagining how hard it would have been for a normal human to make the climb with a rifle, spotting scope, and provisions, even with climbing gear. Whoever killed Indronivay was definitely not human.

We'd made it to the bottom of the ridge and begun heading for a small river when a harsh, high-pitched bark split the air. Intensified by the surrounding rock walls, the sound nearly forced us both to our knees as we covered our ears. The reverberation only served to prolong my deafness, but being temporarily unable to hear over the ringing in my ears didn't bother me half as much as finding out what might have made the noise. It sounded vaguely like the howls we'd heard when we arrived, only much more intense and a whole lot closer. Cu Sith calls were devastating up close, but the bark was a far more focused, piercing, and guttural howl. I regained most of my composure and was just recovering my sense of hearing when the same distant baying rang out almost like a response to the deafening screech.

Duma grabbed my shoulder and shouted something I couldn't make out, but he was pointing back toward the portal we'd used to get here. I nodded, and we both took off running. Duma didn't slow down for me. He had a thing about dogs that stemmed from the circumstances surrounding our first meeting and my subsequent saving of him and his brother from Cu Sith.

The ringing in my ears started to die down as I ran, but our gate to the Ways was easily another few miles out, and it was all open, albeit swampy, ground in front of us. Against my better judgement, I decided to break a cardinal rule about retreating during a firefight: don't stop to check your six until you're under cover. I glanced back to see a sleek dark-gray doglike animal about the size of an elk barreling toward me like a freight train less than a few hundred yards out across the swamp. In front of me, Duma zigzagged through the tall grass as fast as he could run. Less than a hundred yards ahead, he was still a long way from the jump point. As fast as the gray thing was, if I didn't do something stupid — and do it quickly — neither of us would make it.

I made a hard left turn and headed for the little river, hoping the thing would follow me. Call it luck, either good or bad, but it locked on to me — and managed to catch up quickly when it extended a massive pair of wings and took flight. *Wings!*

I had no idea how shallow the river was, but I hoped that I could use the geography to my advantage or that it would at least allow me to do something other than run like a chicken with its head cut off.

The river was little more than a creek at this point of the season, but its steep banks offered a large enough drop that I could take cover as the screeching thing flew over. I had one chance.

I dove toward the creek, tucking into a roll right before I hit the icy water, and came up on the other side in a crouch. Before I could take another breath, the winged creature sailed over the narrow riverbed, traveling far too fast to stop. Up close, I could see it was a winged wolf—a really freaking big one. For the moment, I was too preoccupied to see what Duma was doing.

I pulled my swords and stayed crouched along the creek's edge. On the bank above me, the beast bayed then huffed loudly. I could hear it sniffing, so I knew it was close. I eased up to my feet and slowly stepped back into the stream until the ice-cold water reached mid-calf. Then I whistled as if I were calling a family dog.

Instantly, the giant winged wolf—easily three times the size of a normal wolf, with the wingspan of a small plane—saw me and let out a growl that rumbled in my chest twenty yards away. Folding the massive feathered gray-black wings back along its body, the creature ran forward a few yards then jumped, lunging with its massive jaws agape.

Unfortunately, the wolf attacked so quickly, I didn't think I would get a clean shot off with my sidearms, and with its size, I didn't know if a nine-millimeter or even a .45 caliber bullet would do much anyway. Normally, in a dog attack, my first reaction would be to present my arm for it to bite, then grapple with it. This thing was too big for that type of tactic. Instead, I presented my right sword as if it were my arm then dodged to my right to get out of the way of the leaping fur-and-feather freight train.

The creature's massive jaws grabbed at the blade as I ducked out of the way, and the momentum jerked the sword from my hand—but not before the sword almost severed the dog's head in half at the jaw, causing it to stumble into a skid that took it into the marshy grass on the other side of the riverbank.

I jumped up and chased it, stabbing it with my remaining blade between its immense shoulders without seeing if it was already dead or not. I didn't want it to suffer needlessly. Only the pommel was visible, sticking out under its ear. I pulled the sword free from the creature's mangled maw.

While I was trying to figure out what the thing was, movement in the periphery of my vision caught my attention. Another wolf-thing was flying in low across the marsh, directly toward Duma, who was wildly gesturing for me to do something. Even over the several hundred yards between us I could see the wavy outline of the slit in the fabric of the normal world. The Telluric Pathways shimmered behind him. The wolf-thing was coming from the forest line well to the north, so it still had a few miles to go. Although, at the speed it was flying, it wouldn't take long to cover the distance.

I tried to determine where I would most likely intercept the creature if I took off at full speed then ran for that spot. I wouldn't make it all the way to Duma — the creature was too fast. But I couldn't think of anything else to do. Hitting it would be like a car T-boning a semi. Sure, the truck driver would know he'd been hit, but the car would be crushed in the process. *So be it.*

Suddenly, Duma angled straight toward me, drawing the creature into a head-on collision course with me. I stopped dead and ducked into the thigh-high grass, hoping that Duma would run right past me with the creature in hot pursuit, too focused on Duma to bother with me.

Duma shot past me, running slowly and crazily, arms flailing, screaming like a lunatic. At first, I didn't know if he'd lost his mind or if he had a plan as dumb as mine.

"Remember, I don't have to be faster than that dog, just faster than you..." he screamed as he passed me.

Twenty yards out, the flying dog shot straight up then tucked its wings. It went into a dive like a falcon, aiming straight at Duma on a course that would lead it right over my spot. As it approached, I stood up and braced myself, swinging one sword in a wide overhead arc that traveled through the thing, almost cutting it in half nose to tail. The impact knocked me on my ass and into a backward roll. The dog's momentum carried its bulk another fifty feet before it finally came to a rest in massive bloody mess in the grass.

I walked over to the remains and noticed a smelly, matted tangle of fur over its right shoulder, under its birdlike wing. Kneeling, I poked at the crusty mess and found two large inflamed and puckered wounds surrounded by crusty scabs. The injuries had the telltale wrinkle of bullet wounds, only much bigger than most standard hunting-rifle rounds. Indronivay was shot by a sniper at a very long distance, which would have required a substantial round, and as good as his shooter was, I doubted he could have gotten across the marsh and through the mountain pass without dealing with the winged dogs, too.

Hoping to find out exactly what had done the damage, I cut open the injured area with one of my knives.

"Nasty. Simargls. Man, I hate dogs, with or without wings, but not enough to mutilate them once they're dead, D," Duma said, walking up behind me. "And this one is pretty damned dead."

"It was shot before I killed it. The wounds aren't recent and might coincide with Indronivay's death," I said, digging at the holes until I found something. "This thing's shoulder blade stopped the round from penetrating farther, but the wound was festering. Hmmm. That's interesting..." The bullet was huge, and it appeared to have been made from some exotic alloy. It was barely deformed from the impact.

"Well, yeah, I guess, if you find winged dogs interesting," Duma replied.

"Not the dog. This." I held up the bullet. "Looks like a .338 Lapua Magnum round—a highly specialized bullet used for serious anti-personnel sniper work."

"I'm familiar, dipstick. That round appears a little different than a standard .338 LP, though. Never seen one quite like it," Duma said.

I forgot sometimes that despite being fae, Duma and his brother were intimately familiar with *all* weapons. "Sorry, fairy boy, but yeah, I was thinking the same thing. It actually held its shape pretty well. It's definitely made from a unique alloy and likely wildcatted, which means it might come from a unique weapon." I smiled at Duma while I pocketed the bullet. *That would be what a proper detective calls a clue.*

"Damned tough animal. Even a few ounces of metal in its side didn't hurt it much," Duma said in both awe and disgust, kicking at a paw the size of a catcher's mitt. "By the way, *that* wasn't infection. That's its body trying to excrete the metal round combined with the simargl gnawing the wounds to try to get at them itself. Fae don't get infections or disease. Bacteria specialize in the dominant life-form on this planet—namely mammals. Anyway, now it's dead. Let's go before we find out if Indronivay had cats that breathe fire, too."

I stood there staring, bloody knife in hand, focusing on the deafening silence around us. I wondered what the hell everything had come to over the past few weeks and how much worse it was going to get if I didn't find the assassin fast. The bullet was unique, and its manufacture would have required a highly skilled *human* armorer. I knew Sarah could help with information about who might have made it. With luck, I would find another lead at Goibniu's place. Tracking down an assassin who was trying to frame someone else was one thing, but if Duma was right, ferreting out a myth like the Hanner Brid was something else altogether.

CHAPTER 15

I KNEW OUR PATH OUT OF Russia would be purposely circuitous, making it difficult for anyone to track us, but I was still surprised when we walked out of the Ways into an arid, hot red-tinted desert at the foot of a massive mesa. We jumped from the Ural Mountains to Ayers Rock in Australia, which was also apparently a Nexus point for the Ways. That made sense. The way the Aborigines talked about the place, which they called Uluru, and described Songlines matched up pretty well with the Telluric Pathways.

After Ayers Rock, we passed through cold and forbidding mountain terrain, followed by another desert, a back alley in some big city, a jungle, a swamp, another alleyway, then someplace tropical. We couldn't have walked more than half a mile in the process, though.

"Where are we now?" I took in the lush green foliage so thick that I couldn't see the sky above or more than a few yards in any direction.

"Welcome to Vanuatu. The island of Gaua, to be specific," Duma replied. "That was where Goibniu's forge was, right?"

"Yeah, Sarah told me the information she got from the Metis Foundation only said Goibniu was killed somewhere in his smithy in the volcano on this island."

As we walked through the dense tropical growth, my Maglite fell out of my vest and landed on my boot with a thunk. That was when I realized that my tactical vest over my cuirass was pretty much shredded. Ballistic nylon and Kevlar were great against bullets, but they sucked against blades. Checking what was left of my gear, I found that somewhere between getting slashed in Japan and playing tag with the flying dog, I'd managed to lose one magazine and all my loose ammo. On the upside, my knives were still in place, and I still had my Maglite.

"Just great," I said, swatting at the heavy elephant-ear leaves in my path like an overtired child. "I've got three spare mags, and that's it. I fired four rounds from the Glock, and the other still has a full magazine. That sucks."

"You're just gonna have to make 'em count, I guess," Duma replied.

We were headed for the highest point on the island, a lonely, smoldering peak called Mount Gharat. After about forty minutes of shoving through vines and undergrowth that would have given Tarzan fits, we came to the edge of a large village composed of thirty small structures, most of wood and thatch alongside a few constructed of corrugated metal. All the buildings surrounded a larger low open-sided structure covered by thatch. My first instinct was to avoid it, but something was off.

There were no fires burning, no food cooking, no people working, no dogs running around, no kids screaming or playing. Nothing. Against Duma's protestations, I got closer. At the edge of the village, the stench of death and decay hit us. I drew my Glock and entered the clearing cautiously.

Bodies were everywhere. Dozens of them. Most were hacked apart and otherwise destroyed so badly that their features were unrecognizable. Those bodies still intact were badly decomposed, and all of them were covered with flies, maggots, and other insects. The stains of dried blood covered nearly every surface of the village, from the ground to the houses. There were men, women, and children among dogs and chickens. Even the valuable pigs were in the carnage. Most of the people, including the children, had some form of bloody weapon near them, from knives, axes, and machetes to shovels, hoes, and even sticks. My breath caught in my chest as I tried to make sense of the grisly scene. There were no footprints around the edges of the village or any other signs that suggested a neighboring village or foreign group had invaded. It was as if they had all simply attacked one another until everybody was dead.

Everything was still, and there were no sounds beyond the overwhelming buzzing of flies. Then a whimpering cry rose from behind one of the small A-shaped huts on the edge of the village. I glanced at Duma, who pulled his two kukri knives. Then we each headed in different directions around the hut.

On the other side of the structure, Duma and I both saw the woman at the same time. She was emaciated, dressed in a bloody, tattered skirt and a cartoon-character T-shirt. Dragging a blood-encrusted machete in one hand and a mangled severed arm in the other, she was oblivious even as we came into her field of view. Her eyes were wide but unfocused, and her dark, dirty skin was tight and gaunt over her bones. She could have been young, but her condition made her appear ancient. She kept mumbling incoherently until Duma approached. Her dead eyes suddenly opened impossibly wider as she saw his face, and she began screaming and swinging the machete wildly at him. I tackled her from behind, knocking the machete and the severed arm from her weakened grasp. She struggled so violently that I was afraid I would hurt her if I kept restraining her, so I let her go. She shot off into the jungle, screaming unintelligibly.

"What the hell happened here, and *what* was that all about?" I asked Duma, not really expecting an answer.

Duma's expression was scarily somber. "I don't know," he said then heaved a heavy sigh. "I think she believed I was a threat, maybe a spirit or something—pale skin and hair and all. She called me *Mosigsig* and said *I* made them turn on each other."

"What? Why would she think you're the trickster spirit?"

"I'm telling you: it all fits. I'll bet you *anything* these people killed each other. That's how Bluds work," he said, shaking his head.

With the toe of my boot, I poked at the severed arm the woman had dropped. I grimaced. It looked as though it had been chewed on.

"Blud have the ability to confuse, mislead, and trick people. Stories say this guy used to turn families against themselves for fun. Blud are not nice guys, not even by Peri standards—and we have low standards. But the Hanner Brid..." Duma loosed a low whistle.

Duma's expression was as grim as I'd ever seen. It wasn't fear— I'd never seen him afraid of anything. Instead, he was intense, and he absently spun his knives anxiously. He might be right about the cambion, but until I had further evidence, I couldn't rule out any possibility.

"Okay, sure. But we have no real idea what happened here. Don't start jumping at shadows on me now," I said, trying not to sound too condescending.

Part of me was starting to buy into Duma's theory. And his reaction gave me the willies — especially if the Hanner Brid was capable of making a village full of people kill each other. Possibly just for fun.

"Let's keep moving," I said, trying to push the ghastly sight of the slaughter out of my mind and focus on searching Goibniu's place.

Whoever did this needs to die.

Duma was edgy the rest of the hike into the caldera, overreacting to almost every unusual noise. And in a tropical jungle, those were numerous. Still, we managed to make good time and reach the rim before nightfall. We headed toward the lake at its base, keeping an eye out for any lava tubes that might have been an entrance to Goibniu's forge. Other than birds and the occasional wild pig, we encountered no life.

Having fished these islands many times over the years, I knew the caldera of Mount Gharat was atypical. Three-quarters of it was underwater, forming Lake Letas, but our path, approaching from the southwest, led us straight up to the peak. Thankfully, Gharat was not a lava producer like the volcanos in Hawaii, though it had spewed ash as recently as a few years before.

Lava tubes and old flows pockmarked the northeastern side of the peak inside the caldera overlooking the lake, like some sort of surreal moonscape, especially in the dark. Surprisingly, the inside of the crater was mostly covered in dense foliage, like the rest of the island. Lake Letas was massive, easily several miles across, but its hot, somewhat-acidic water was almost devoid of life.

As we explored the caldera, every lava tube we encountered billowed plumes of steam. I couldn't imagine anything living inside a boiling-hot furnace, fae bladesmith or not. The more we explored, the more it seemed like we were on a wild-goose chase with no hope of finding a reasonable entrance.

"Okay, if you were Goibniu, which of these tubes would you hide down?" I asked Duma.

"If I were Goibniu, I'd be a tall, big-nosed, bald Sidhe who reeked of sulfur. All these holes would work for me," he said. "You know he was a master of obsidian blades? Best in the world, hands down. They say he could make his own obsidian. All I know is that he could cut the rock so it was as durable as steel."

"That's nice," I said, stopping at the top of the next large lava tube. "And if that's the case, then we're going to have to start heading into some of these things. We'll split up and go every other one. I'll take this one, you take the next. Then I'll take the next, and so on. If you find something, wait outside the mouth till you see me. Break a branch off a bush or something to lay at the mouth once you've been down a tube so we know where each other is, okay?"

"Works for me. What if we encounter something?" he asked.

"Use your judgment—or the opposite, in your case. Try *not* to kill anything unless it attacks you. At least *try* to talk with it *first*," I replied.

"Gotcha," Duma said as he walked around me and toward another tube. "Talk first; stab later. See you on the other side."

I had no idea how long these lava tubes were—for all I knew, they stretched all the way down to the beach, miles away. But the fact that they were almost all steaming meant they still had some sort of access to the active magma chamber below. As I entered the first one, I wouldn't have been the least bit surprised to find the very gates of Hades themselves at the end of it. The dry air had to be close to a hundred and fifty degrees inside the tube.

The next four tubes I ventured down all ended in cracks and fissures less than a hundred feet down. From the branches left in front of every other tube, I could tell Duma was having no luck, either. In fact, it wasn't until midnight that I emerged to see Duma sitting at the mouth of another tube a short distance away, a smoldering pile of something unidentifiable at his feet.

As I approached, he held his finger over his mouth. I pointed at the steaming mass at his feet, and he kicked at it gently. Once I got closer, I could see it was a broad lizard-like creature about four feet long, with heavy scales and a wide, flat head. It wasn't a lizard, but a salamander—a fire elemental—but its presence in a volcano wasn't exactly surprising.

Duma waved me away from the entrance of the tube and began whispering. "It's crawling with 'em. Kinda freaky, really, but it's the kind of thing Goibniu would have kept as pets. Also, I heard some talking. Sounded like Gnomes. Probably Goibniu's underlings."

"Wait here," I told him then ran down to the next tube. I walked carefully inside and slowly worked my way fifty yards down until I began to hear soft sounds like steam escaping, only at different pitches—the *voices* Duma had mentioned. From what I could hear, it couldn't have been more than two or three creatures. A few yards farther down the tube, I came to a series of cracks where the wispy voices came through more clearly. I couldn't understand them, but they had to originate from somewhere close by.

I peered through the cracks and counted four tiny but stocky bearded humanoid creatures, each no more than eighteen inches tall, in an adjacent lava tube. They were dark skinned and filthy, covered in sweat and ash. Each wore only a cap and apron made from some scaly animal hide, likely salamander. They all had tiny welder's goggles draped around their necks. None of them had any tools or weapons. They were definitely gnomes.

The four gnomes waddled out of my limited line of sight, chatting in their vaporous voices, and I quickly ducked up the tube and back toward Duma, eager to get to cooler air.

"Yep, gnomes. At least four," I said quietly. "Probably a lot more down there."

"More than likely, but they're not really tough. We can take 'em, easy," Duma said, mocking a soccer-style kick.

I grimaced at him. "Are you crazy? I'm trying to clear my name of murder, not add a legit charge to it."

"Sorry, D, just an idea. What's your plan then? We're going to need to lure them up here, though. Goibniu's forge is too far down that tube. The heat would bake your human lungs after ten minutes down there."

"Good point. Still, it'd be nice to poke around down there."

"Why?" he asked. "You think you'd find fingerprints? Maybe footprints? No human would survive long enough to have killed this guy down there. And if it was fae—the Hanner Brid, say—then you won't find crap anyway."

Duma was right. Everything pointed to a nonhuman killer, whether it was his boogeyman or not. Still, I wanted to know what the gnomes knew about the event.

"Okay, we need to grab one of the gnomes—*quietly*—and then ask a few questions. And then let it go. *Alive and unharmed*, got it?"

Duma sneered. "Gotcha. Did you have a *plan* for your plan, genius? Or are we winging it?"

"Actually, I do," I replied, glaring back at him. "If I remember right, you always carry gold pieces on you. How many do you have?"

"A handful in case I need to grease a wheel or two. Why?" he asked.

"Gnomes are drawn to precious objects taken from the ground, right? Jewels, pure gold, silver, and the like, right? So, we're going to leave a trail of gold for them to follow right back into these bushes, where we'll grab one of them so we can chat."

Duma stifled a laugh. "Oh, okay. You sure you don't want to put a coin under an old box propped up by a twig with a string tied to it, Elmer Fudd?"

"Only if this doesn't work. Gimme the gold, wiseass," I said, holding out my hand. "And be *vewy, vewy* quiet."

Duma sighed heavily then reluctantly fished the coin purse from inside his jacket.

I laid out a short trail from the mouth of the tube off into the bushes. We were going to have to be fast. Gnomes could travel *through* earth as easily as humans walked on it. Once Duma and I were set, I flipped one final coin, which landed in front of the tube with a clear metallic ring. I hoped it would draw the gnomes like moths to a flame.

It took a few minutes, probably because they were being understandably cautious, but the first grungy gnome emerged with wide eyes fixed on the golden coins. He ushered the others to follow his lead, and five more appeared behind him. The group fumbled with each other, fighting over the gold. It was like watching piranha feeding. They had no idea of our presence until it was too late. Duma and I both quickly snatched a gnome in each hand. The two on the ground instantly burrowed into the rock and dirt beneath them.

For such little creatures, they put up a big stink. Their soft, screechy language hid their ability to shriek like three-year-old girls.

"Calm down," I said, raising my voice in as restrained a fashion as I could. "We aren't going to hurt you, I swear on my honor as a Guardian. All I want is to talk."

That shut them up briefly while they dangled from our hands, but they quickly began chattering to each other like long-lost friends recently reunited. They pointed at Duma, screeching, then kicked at us. Duma laughed as he listened, until all at once, his face contorted into a vicious scowl, his teeth bared in a snarl. He screamed at them in their hissy language.

"Duma," I said, bellowing loud enough to echo off the rock walls around us. "What did they say?"

"They think I'm going to kill them off the way *my kind* killed Goibniu," he said, breathing heavily and grimacing wildly.

"They think a Peri killed Goibniu?" I asked.

"Well, not necessarily a Peri, exactly, but one of my traitorous kind," he said, sarcastically jiggling his head side to side.

"What does that mean?"

"It means I'm gonna squish their sweaty little asses." He glared at the two gnomes he held as if contemplating bashing them together.

When they began to struggle wildly, I tried to change the subject. "No, no, no, you're not. Calm down, Duma. We need their help. I need to find out who killed Goibniu. I've been accused of the crime, but I didn't do it," I told the gnomes I held.

Since all fae spoke and understood every form of communication fluently, choosing not to speak in the language being used was an insult. These little guys began collectively mumbling something in their own language, then one of them rambled on for a full minute without stopping. Though I got the feeling they were *attempting* to annoy me, I tried not to be offended. I wasn't sure why, but my experience has been that the smaller the fae, the more irritating they were. At my limits, I glowered at Duma for a moment then raised my eyebrows. He lolled his head, sighed, then began to translate.

"They found your statement ridiculous. They know it was not a human that killed Goibniu, but Mab's guard ignored them because the smith was killed with a human weapon — a firearm of some type. A small one. The bullet casings were proof enough for the guards. The assassin shot Goibniu at close range while he worked at his forge, though the weapon made almost no noise. The killer was dressed as human soldiers sometimes do, with a mask covering his face, yada yada yada... but they claim he was definitely one of the traitorous fae." Duma's nostrils flared, and his breathing becoming deep and deliberate as he translated while the little guy yammered on. "What? Like me? Why, you little turd, I ought to —"

"Whoa, Duma, let them go, before you do something I regret," I said, stepping directly in front of him.

"Definitely not human?" I asked the two I still held, as Duma half-dropped and half-threw the two he held. They tunneled into the ground and disappeared in seconds. The pair I held blinked their big, dark, watery eyes slowly in defiance.

"I know you understand me. I'm only trying to find the being that killed Goibniu, and I need your help," I said to them.

They glanced at each other and continued to blink exaggeratedly. I was beginning to feel like an idiot.

Duma finally said something to them in their own language that caused the expressions on their tiny faces to change instantly from one of willful defiance to abject fear. Both gnomes began talking at once — in English. Duma was smiling broadly.

"Whoa, whoa, one at a time," I said then turned to Duma. "What did you tell them?"

"The traitor said that our master was killed by the Half Breed and that he would be back for us if we did not cooperate," said one of the gnomes. "Is that true, Guardian?"

"What? Wait... half breed?" I asked.

"The *Hanner Brid*," Duma replied. "I told you, he scares the crap outta all fae."

"Oh, right." I shifted my attention back to the gnomes. "I am trying to stop this Hanner Brid. If he's as twisted as you believe, he very well could come back for you, but I doubt it. He has a larger agenda. But with your help, I can stop him, or I will die trying. I so swear on my honor."

The gnomes watched each other silently, then one finally spoke. "We will tell you what we know of that day, but we ask something from you."

Nothing ever comes for free with fairies. "What?" I asked.

"We wish to examine your armaments, the ones made by Mae'r gof Anrhydeddu," said the other gnome.

"He means the one you called Hephaestus. Your swords and cuirass," Duma said, rolling his hand around at the wrist. "Oh, come *on*! We don't have time for this crap. Tell us, or we'll pop your tiny heads off."

"Duma, be quiet," I growled. "If they want to see my swords and cuirass, fine, but they must tell us what they know first." I'm not sure what I was hoping to find out, but anything, including distinctive mannerisms or traits, could prove helpful for Sarah in tying him to other crimes.

The gnomes exchanged glances, then one began to talk. They didn't reveal much that Duma hadn't already translated earlier, but they did say they still had the bullet casings. That confused me a bit. No serious hit man would ever leave casings behind—unless it was on purpose.

While I contemplated the reasons why I might do something like that, I rammed my swords into the volcanic stone at my feet so the gnomes could see them but not steal them. Dozens of the little folk popped out of the ground like mushrooms and began to stare and gawk at them. Eventually, a gnome appeared from the mouth of the tube, pushing a small wheelbarrow with four casings in it.

I grabbed the small brass cylinders and examined them. I recognized them immediately—.22 caliber long rifle. Normally used in a rifle rather than a handgun, the rounds were useless for killing a person unless the shooter was right next to the victim. This caliber did have one major advantage though: it was one of a few subsonic rounds that worked effectively with a silencer.

Things were starting to add up: the rifle shot requiring a highly skilled sniper in Russia, an extremely specialized small-caliber weapon fired covertly at point-blank range with brass, conveniently left behind, and a killer dressed like a soldier. It all pointed to a human perpetrator attacking the fae. Then there were the issues of the sniper firing from a virtually inaccessible roost and enduring the heat of a furnace, all without leaving much of a trail—both almost impossible for a mundane human. Factoring in that the killer was so brazen and adept, I could see why they thought it was me. No other human Guardian I knew of could have done this, either. If it wasn't me, then the killer wasn't a human at all. The Hanner Brid, boogeyman or not, jumped to the top of the list of my prime suspects.

"Where is the breastplate?" asked one of the gnomes from somewhere in the crowd of tiny fae gathered around my swords.

I thumped my chest so they could hear the metallic *thunk*. I pushed aside some of the torn ballistic nylon of the tactical vest to reveal a small portion of the cuirass underneath. The revelation elicited more gasps from the tiny mob. After a few minutes of obsessive fawning, I pocketed the four casings and located Duma, who was down near the lake's edge, throwing rocks.

"I've held up my end of the bargain. Is that everything you can tell me?" I asked.

They all stared at each other for a few seconds before one of them spoke. "The assassin was skilled, moved without sound through our corridors, and was unaffected by the heat. These things suggest he was of our kith. But he used the human weapon brazenly, which implies he is a dishonorable wretch of a being. We have given you the alloy castoffs he left behind. That is all we know." The gnomes nodded almost in unison.

"Well then, we should get going," I said, shouting so that Duma could hear me, then returned my swords to their sheaths on my back.

The gnomes let out a collective sound reminiscent of an asthmatic trying to breathe.

"Thank you for your help. I will do my best to find and punish the one responsible for the death of your master, Goibniu," I said to the group. I waved at Duma to follow then headed back up the caldera the way we'd come.

Cries of protest arose from the gnomes behind us as Duma caught up and we broke into a sprint, running as fast as we could back to our door through the Ways. Along the way, I began thinking about our next move.

"Somehow, I need to get these bullet casings and the round I found in the simargl to Sarah for analysis," I said to Duma as we ran. "If it turns out that .338 round's makeup is unique and maybe even wildcatted, then that's all highly specialized and not the easiest thing to do unless you know how. If we can find out who might make that kind of ammunition, then we might be able to find out who had them made."

CHAPTER 16

BECAUSE OF THE MASSIVE TIME change, it was morning the day after we left Gaua when we emerged from the Ways into an empty parking structure that stank of exhaust fumes, oil, and concrete. Duma was quick to point out that we were outside of Union Station in DC.

I got my cell phone out, but before I turned it back on, I began to worry about involving Sarah. I was concerned they might come after her to try to find me, or worse, punish her for helping me. Not to mention that it wasn't fair of me to use her.

"What's hanging you up? Call her already, would ya?" Duma shook his head. "Isn't time of the essence or something?"

There was a message on the phone from Sarah, but I didn't listen to it since I was about to call her. She picked up on the third ring.

"Hey, just got back into range," I said when she answered.

"Did you get my message?"

"Yeah, but only right before I called. I haven't listened. I needed to call you anyway. I need another favor. It's a big one."

"Well, you need to get scarce. There's a Department of Justice/FBI/DHS bulletin out for a person who fits your exact description for ties to known terrorist groups. I can't help you much on tracking any shooters down directly, and I shouldn't even be talking with you. You're in *deep*," she said softly, but I could hear the concern in her voice.

"Oh, okay. I probably shouldn't tell you that I'm down the street then." I was joking, but I also wanted to see if she might be excited at the prospect of seeing me.

"Are you crazy?" she replied.

Not what I was hoping for. "Meet me in the parking garage at Union Station. Fourth floor, northeast corner in thirty minutes," I said.

"Make it forty-five," she replied then hung up.

***

I gave Duma my weapons and my vest, then he made himself scarce without my asking. I knew he would be close and, knowing him, probably eavesdrop, too.

The moment she exited the elevator, my heart started to race, and I suddenly became sick to my stomach. I didn't know if it was excitement or fear. Maybe both. She looked like she had on the day we'd first met at the Met bombing over a year ago—all business. She wore sunglasses and had her shoulder-length dark-brown hair pulled back in a ponytail. Her dark suit matched the unmistakable grim expression on her face. As soon as she recognized me, I turned to gaze out over the traffic on First Street.

She walked up next to me and watched the traffic without saying anything for several long minutes. I had no idea what to say.

"Looks like you got yourself into a deep pile of shit." She pushed her sunglasses onto her head, and I could see the gray of her eyes was the color of storm clouds.

"You have no idea," I replied, staring at the ground. "Look, I really need you to run some ballistics tests on some bullets I found. A .338 Lapua Magnum round, likely modified for longer range, and some .22 LR rounds. Both come from the assassin I'm after—I'm sure of it. A custom .338 LM round can't be very common, and finding the manufacturer might lead me to the person they were made for." I held the bullets out for her. She was in a tough position, but I was hoping she could still help somehow.

"I can try, but if they get flagged, I'm not sure what I'd say to cover. A non-standard .338 Lapua Magnum is pretty uncommon. However, the .22 LR is not. Heck, even the Boy Scouts use them for merit badges," she said quietly, reaching out to take them. "Obviously, I'm not checking for prints."

"No." I still couldn't bring myself to make eye contact. "Listen, if you can help, great, but don't get yourself in hot water for this. I need to know anything you can tell me about them. I need a direction, because right now, I'm stumped."

"I'll do what I can. Be careful, Diomedes, please," she said. "But given that you're wanted, I should probably go now."

The obvious concern in her voice got to me a bit and distracted me for a second while I pondered the what-ifs. *This isn't the time to think about things like that.* And that was one of many reasons I told myself I didn't do relationships.

"Yeah, I'll be in touch," I said quickly and stoically as my voice got husky. I watched her head back to the elevators, and once again, I felt like an asshole and an idiot.

The fact that my description was linked to some sort of terrorist activity to alert human authorities didn't surprise, or even bother, me. In fact, I'd expected it. The fae avoid mainstream human society, which encompasses most of the modern world, but it wouldn't be the first time they used humans as their eyes and ears or even to unwittingly help them do their dirty work.

I pulled out my phone to make another call. On the second ring, the line disconnected, and I got the intense, almost shocking tingle along my spine that accompanied Athena showing up unannounced.

"Contacting me isn't wise, Diomedes, and you know it." Athena emerged from a preternaturally dark corner across from me. Her brilliant-red hair and the spark of her electric-blue eyes stood out in the fluorescent wash of the bunker-like space.

"I know, but I think I'm actually being framed by a cambion Blud fae-Succubus assassin bent on creating major chaos. I know it all sounds crazy, but you're the only one I know who *might* be able to point me in the right direction. I gotta find this guy, and not only for my sake."

"Hmmm. Blud *and* Succubus. There used to be stories of an extremist half-breed among the fae, but I've heard nothing of him in decades, except stories."

"Not helpful. I've become privy to all kinds of tales about this creature in the last couple of days, and trust me when I tell you fae are scared of him, rumor or not. There is a real possibility that he might even be involved in furthering the unrest in North Africa and probably elsewhere. And I'm pretty sure we ran across some of his sickening handiwork on Gaua." I folded my arms across my chest. "He may have influenced the massacre of an entire village."

"Yes, those are the kind of unsubstantiated rumors I'm familiar with." Athena's eyes flashed. "This half-breed has been blamed for all kinds of things by the fae community, but there has never been any *real* evidence."

"I can tell you that Elegast believes it but won't admit it to anyone else. The gnomes at Goibniu's forge said the assassin was one of the traitorous fae, though Mab doesn't want to hear it, and I can guarantee you that who or whatever took the shot at Indronivay was inhumanly capable. It all points to someone like this so-called rumor framing me and trying to cause unrest among all the races. The only problem is I don't know why." I shook my head.

"You may be more right than you know. A Magus from the Hermetic Order of the Golden Dawn was killed two nights hence with a stone-bladed weapon. It points distinctly to a fae perpetrator, and the order assumed it was in retaliation for *your* alleged actions against the courts. For the moment, I have contained the situation with them, but they are clamoring for retribution nonetheless," she said, her eyes beginning to spark like a failing circuit breaker.

"There was also a massacre within the Odin Brotherhood. It carried all the hallmarks of the Unseelie huntress Belphoebe, using Cu Sith to run the victims down and then finishing them off with arrows. The brotherhood is too weak to retaliate now, but perhaps more frighteningly, there are rumors of a death of a Gnosticus of the Fraternitas Saturni as well as an attempt on a Brother Apostle of Pugnus Dei. Since both groups are distrustful of me, I hold no sway with them. Neither of those groups is talking, however, so I have no idea of their current intentions. Additionally, Strigoi covens throughout Europe and even Therianthropes, particularly the Kurtadam Lycanthrope pack, may have been attacked, as well, though those groups are always at war with some race or other."

I sighed heavily, feeling not simply old but ancient. This was the first time I could *ever* recall that much crap going on all at the same time — it had to be related. I could only think of one reason for creating such widespread conflict, and it bothered me to my core.

"It sounds like Medea's crazy endgame of unleashing chaos on the world, but she's dead. Frankly, an underground war among witches, wizards, monster hunters, and all the various Paran races wouldn't raise much concern among mainstream humanity except in obscure chat rooms on the Internet," I said, pointing at the ground to emphasize my point. "But... doing all that plus escalating political instability in already-unstable regions would. I asked Sarah to help me with some unique ballistics this assassin used. You've got to try to calm everyone down before something breaks loose and we end up with wars between and among every race, group, and creature on this planet, and I gotta find this asshole. And we need to do all that *fast*."

"Indeed. I will do what I can," Athena replied. "I'm sorry about dragging Agent Wright back into your world, but it is wiser for us to work through her than for us to communicate directly. She is a simple mortal and probably off the fae radar because of it. As always, I will inform you of any relevant developments whenever possible."

An intense shock of cold built in my chest and then climbed up my back and neck as she walked back into the darkened corner. When the shadows lifted, Athena was gone.

CHAPTER 17

"SO WHY DIDN'T MISS HIGH and Mighty come to save your sorry ass?" Duma asked, stepping out from behind a minivan. "And who the hell drives these things?" He glared at the squat vehicle as if it were gum on the bottom of his shoe.

"She won't confront anyone directly like that," I said. "That kind of thing is usually my specialty."

"Look where that's gotten you." He snickered.

I glanced down at the phone then at the tattered remains of my vest Duma carried over one shoulder. I knew he hadn't meant it as an insult, but to some extent, he was right. Such was my life. But so be it. If not me, then who? And better me than someone less prepared.

"So then, what do we do next?" He leaned against the sedan next to me, folding his arms.

"No clue." I shook my head, pointing at my vest. "I need to change out my gear and grab some more ammo. Beyond that, I'm open to suggestions."

"That's not much of a plan, my friend," he replied with a derisive snort. "But if that's the next step, then my nearest weapons cache is in Atlanta."

We made the jump to a park on the west side of Atlanta then walked to a rather upscale warehouse surrounded by a ten-foot-high chain-link fence topped with razor wire in a subdued old neighborhood along a set of railroad tracks. The lock on the gate was some sort of digital keypad that paled in complexity to the one at the office door. Two oversized garage bay doors took up the rest of the front façade of the aluminum-siding-clad building. The inside was one contiguous space taken up by half a dozen cars under covers, a row of five-foot-tall mechanic's tool chests against one wall, and a pair of hydraulic car lifts in the center. As the ballasts for the fluorescent lighting popped to life, I could see the place was spotless.

"Yeah, I don't need a car. I need weapons." I turned, trying to locate the stores of weapons I knew he'd have around somewhere.

Duma glared at me as he walked over to one of the giant red tool chests, opened the top drawer, and reached in. A loud metallic *thunk* echoed through the garage, and the metal grate underneath one of the hydraulic lifts popped open at one end. An electronic whirring noise began increasing in volume, and the metal grate began to rise on one end, revealing the entrance to an underground space.

"Oh ye of little faith." He smiled.

I took my time locating what I wanted from Duma's stores. I needed to add a few things and replenish what I'd lost, destroyed, or used. I replaced the vest over my cuirass then gathered up ammunition for my sidearms. I grabbed an FN SCAR-H Mk 17 Mod 0 assault rifle, a flash suppressor, and six twenty-round magazines for the weapon. I was loading for bear.

I took a few minutes to strip all my firearms and do a quick check to make sure they functioned properly, but somewhere in the back of my head during the mindless process, I kept going back to the idea of the half-breed. *Half Blud, half Succubus.* There had to be some way to use that.

That's when the light bulb in my head went off: Succubi were descendants of the fallen angel Na'amah, sister of Lilith, the primordial Strigoi. And I knew a few people that really knew fallen angels and their demon brethren. Thankfully, one of them was a Guardian, like me, only much younger. His name was Ditaolane, or Deeta, the avatar for Uhlanga, known to me as Artemis. And for the last fifty years, Deeta had specialized in hunting fallen creatures. If anyone knew how to find the half-breed, it was him. All I had to do was find him—and that, I could do.

"Duma!" I shouted from the underground bunker. "Where are you?"

"France. Where the hell do you think I am? What's up?" he shouted back.

"Find a modern world map and get me your scrying pendulum, fast," I said.

A few minutes later, Duma climbed down the stairs, unfolding a recent world map. I laid it on a worktable while he dangled a black crystal hanging from an intricately carved chain made of bone in front of me. It was stronger than it appeared, and unless examined closely, it was impossible to tell the chain was even bone. I ripped a small piece off the corner of the map, hurriedly scribbled something onto the scrap, wrapped it around the black stone, and secured it with a rubber band that was lying on the table.

Duma's mouth dropped open, and his eyebrows climbed high on his forehead. He stared at me like that for what felt like an eternity.

"What?" I asked, frowning at him.

"Humans," he replied, shaking his head. "First, that's a black diamond, and you smeared your greasy human fingerprints all over it. Second" — he held up my rubber-band-secured mess, pointing at it and scowling — "are you kidding me?"

"Duma, we're in a hurry..." I said.

"Pendulum scrying don't know from hurry. Besides, you rush a miracle man, you get rotten miracles," he said, imitating Billy Crystal from *The Princess Bride*. "The energy you put into the ritual helps make the ritual. You put fakakta energy into this thing, and you'll be searching for this person on the moon."

"Duma —"

"Back off, dipstick. Let me do this right," he said, holding up his other hand to stop me. "Is the person's name on this piece of paper?"

"Yes," I replied, rolling my eyes and sighing heavily. *I knew he was right.*

"Full and complete name, the way they spell it?" Duma asked, eyebrows raised and his voice soft, as if he were speaking to a child.

"Of course. I'm not a total idiot."

My statement earned me a reproachful glower. He shooed me back a few steps then undid my haphazard preparation. He carefully cleaned the black stone while I flattened the paper scrap with the name on it and folded it three times. After wrapping the folded paper smoothly around the diamond — which had to be close to eighty carats — he took a small piece of twine from the workstation and tied it around the paper, securing it to the diamond. The pendulum suspended over the map, he began the tedious process of entering a trancelike state.

The process always amazed and bored me at the same time. For those who could use magic — or more accurately, manipulate ambient energy — scrying required an effort of will to harness energy to make a link between the object in hand and what's being searched for. To help focus that energy, I used conjuring circles, rituals, or ritual objects. Fae, on the other hand, were so intrinsically bound to the Earth and its energies that for them, it was like logging on to the Internet. Their focus, or so Duma and Ab have told me, helped them weed through the mass of energy they get bombarded with when they tap into it. *It just takes too damn long.*

I had long ago resigned myself to the fact that for me, scrying was nothing short of a miracle to pull off. Not only did I lack the patience, but the energy I was best at focusing came from rage, which was not useful for delicate work like scrying. I had to fight not to check my watch every few seconds. I wondered about Deeta. He was a good kid, but I hadn't seen him in a few years. Not since his inexperience in dealing with the Hermetic Order of the Golden Dawn almost landed him on their shit list. Thankfully, he still owed me for that one, and I was about to cash it in.

Once the pendulum came to a complete and utter stop several long minutes later, he opened his eyes again. I knew he was just getting started, though. Few creatures could hold so still that it was positively creepy. He continued his statue imitation for a full five minutes more before the pendulum began to waver as if being pulled. It moved slowly but steadily from the southeastern part of the United States, where we were, across the Atlantic toward the Mediterranean. Eventually, it settled in Libya. I took a step closer to see the precise location when Duma blinked rapidly and looked down. The stone's point was resting on the city of Sirte.

"That was ridiculously tough," he said, dropping the chain and rubbing his face with his hands. "I don't get it, but it was hard to pinpoint his energy."

"Yeah, Guardians, we're a slippery bunch. What can I tell you?"

He reached down to grab the scrying stone, and I caught his hand and took the paper off the stone with my free hand. "Nope," I said, wadding the paper and shoving it in my mouth. I trusted Duma with *my* life, but I had no right to give someone else's information to him. And a Guardian's true name would be worth an untold fortune.

"Gross," Duma said. "Well, at least tell me who we're trying to find."

"Ditaolane, a fellow Guardian who specializes in demon hunting."

"Gotcha. This the guy you call Deeta who almost got himself blown up by an Adeptus Exemptus of the Hermetic Order?" he asked as he put away his scrying pendulum.

"Yep. Now, what's the fastest way to Sirte in Libya?"

CHAPTER 18

DUMA AND I WERE ON our way back to the entrance to the Ways when I began to think about Deeta. One of few remaining Guardians, he was the youngest. I'd first encountered him in 1961 during the Angolan War of Independence, right after he had become a Guardian. He was chasing an Abiku that was killing children orphaned by the ongoing rebellion against the Portuguese as they fought against forced labor in cotton fields. I was after a Mbwiri that had possessed the brutal Portuguese warden of São Paulo Prison. We'd ended up helping each other and become fast friends.

I found out sometime later that Ditaolane's mother had survived a demon attack on her village when she was pregnant with him by hiding in a dung pile. His Basuto tribe in Lesotho said it was the reason he could sense demons and evil spirits even before he became a Guardian. The goddess Uhlanga chose him because he always chose to defend those who couldn't fight for themselves, despite the fact he wasn't the biggest or strongest kid around. I anticipated seeing him again, even if it was under such dire conditions.

Our passage through the Ways took us three jumps, but as we approached our final destination, I could feel the temperature rise, as well as a nearly overwhelming sensation of anarchy, fear, anger, and confusion. We exited into the middle of Martyr's Square in the center of Sirte amid what I could only describe as a redneck parade on the first day of hunting season. I hadn't been there since my days with the Teams almost twenty years ago. The atmosphere was so tumultuous that no one even noticed us walk out of thin air. Among the war-ravaged and devastated buildings and rubble around the edge of the park were throngs of armed men dressed in everything from jungle camouflage to T-shirts, all firing every kind of gun imaginable in random directions, including straight up. They were gathered around a variety of technicals—pickup trucks they had converted into makeshift mobile weapons platforms mounted with heavy machine guns, rocket launchers, and even howitzers.

Watching these would-be soldiers made up of citizens tired of Gaddafi's dictatorship, I began to realize that they were mostly firing west, toward the Old City. Most of the whitewashed multistory apartment buildings still standing around the park were little more than shells, missing outer walls or half destroyed. Many were effectively piles of rubble. Every wall still intact was riddled with bullet holes from heavy machine-gun fire. Not a single structure within view had escaped damage. Thankfully, it was clear that noncombatant civilians had abandoned the area.

I pulled my assault rifle around into a low ready position and waved my hand in a quick chopping motion across the park, indicating the completely out-of-place Assembly building that resembled the Space Mountain ride at Disneyland. Remarkably, the odd structure was largely undamaged. I had no idea where in Sirte to find Deeta, but as a Guardian, he would be where the action was heaviest. I wished I had his uncanny ability to follow any creature over any surface.

Duma and I began leap-frogging down side streets that were less congested, taking cover among the rubble and burned-out vehicles. The farther west we went, the closer we got to the center of the action. In case things weren't bad enough already, the streets in the Old City were flooded to about knee deep. Trying to reassess our heading, we sheltered in a blown-out building during a lull in the almost-random artillery and mortar fire.

"We gotta get someplace high. I need to get a lay of the land," I said to Duma as a particularly heavy barrage obliterated a building next to us.

Duma pointed at a five-story building past another small park that was little more than ruins. Unfortunately, the sounds of gunfire were also more consistent from that direction.

"Let's go, flat out. Roof of that building," I said. "Southwest corner. Move!"

Duma took off, and I followed. There were no doors or windows left on the first floor—only gaping holes. In a blur, Duma headed straight through one and up the stairs, bounding over a dead rebel soldier partially covered by rubble. As I reached the doorway, the artillery started up again, impacting something beyond the building. The bombardment was so haphazard that most deaths probably came by accident rather than design.

I made it almost to the roof without a problem, only to find Duma hunkered inside the access way to the roof, holding a finger over his lips. He held up two fingers and gestured toward the door and then to the left.

He pulled two wicked thin-bladed dirks from his bandolier and gave me an impish grin. I grabbed his arm and shook my head. I pulled one knife from his hand and spun it over so the pommel faced up. His grin faded to confusion then utter disappointment. *I swear, you can take the fae out of the wilderness, but you can't take the wilderness out of the fae.* I slapped him lightly on the side of the face, and he took off out the door. A few seconds later, I kicked the door open, rifle at the ready, and Duma was kneeling over two prone rebel soldiers. Putting his dirks away, he eyed me as I walked up.

"They'll live," he said, frowning.

I crouched as I approached the side of the roof. Poking my head up enough to see, I spotted rebel snipers on half a dozen of the surrounding rooftops. Below, the bodies of half a dozen rebels and at least that many uniformed soldiers lay where they'd fallen in the streets and inside blown-out buildings. I continued scanning the city for spots of particularly intense fighting. One area definitely stood out a few blocks south of our position, right on the edge of town.

"That's where we need to be." I pointed in the direction of the heaviest artillery barrages.

"What's with you always running toward crap that's being destroyed? I swear..." He shook his head.

"If Deeta's here, then whatever he's chasing is likely to be there, too. It's a Guardian thing. If there's a pile of shit somewhere, you can bet we'll be knee deep in it." I laughed. "Listen, one group is lined up along the main road there to the east, while the other group is holed up over there near those buildings to the west. This road below us is a no-man's land that runs right between them," I said, pointing at the partially flooded street that ran from where we were, almost due south through the city.

As I spoke, a rocket-propelled grenade took down part of a building a few blocks down our intended path, followed by a sustained volley of heavy gunfire in the same area. Duma glared at me. I smiled in return then squat-walked back to the stairs.

Still partially obscured by smoke and dust from the rocket's impact, things were much more claustrophobic down the abandoned, flooded street from ground level. That dust would help keep us concealed as we ran, but it also kept us from seeing potential threats clearly. I'd traversed similar situations on numerous occasions as a SEAL, but not having to hold back or worry about my teammates somehow made the situation seem less dangerous. I didn't even have to say anything, and Duma was off, heading down the street in a red-and-black blur. I tried to do my best imitation, but my instinct to stop at good cover proved hard to overcome.

By the time I made it halfway down the street, another RPG hammered the building that had just been hit, and I was less than thirty yards beyond it. The concussion knocked me flat on my stomach in the flooded street as I got pelted with rocks, bits of mortar, and stucco. Instinctively, I curled up and covered my head until the rain of debris stopped. Luckily, I was at the outside edge of the most dangerous part of the blast radius. Before I could uncover my head, someone grabbed my vest and started pulling me up. I couldn't hear anything over the ringing in my ears, but it was Duma trying to urge me along.

For a moment, everything moved in slow motion as I tried to understand what he was yelling. Then something hit me hard in the lower back, knocking me off balance. Then Duma ducked as large-caliber bullets tore gaping holes into the wall to our right. Adrenaline kicked in, and the world sped up again. I dove for cover inside the closest doorway, and Duma lurched around the corner as heavy machine-gun fire raked the building. Somebody clearly believed we were the opposition.

I poked my head out long enough to see four men pushing a battered black pickup truck with a heavy chain gun mounted in the bed backward into the flooded street. The technical's gunner was aiming at our position. They were easily a hundred fifty yards away, which put them in range of my SCAR and us well within range of that chain gun. Given that the fighters were hardly soldiers and that their vehicle didn't even appear to run, I surmised that if I fired in their direction, they would run for cover and give us enough time to leave the area. For added insurance, wounding the gunner would buy us even more time.

"Duma!" I shouted, "Move now! Go! Go! Go!" I stepped out from the doorway, dropped to one knee, and took aim at the truck. Then I fired several bursts into its already-beat-up flank.

The pushers scattered, but the gunner hunkered behind the gun's armored plates, leaving only his lower body exposed. I took careful aim, exhaled, and squeezed the trigger. Several rounds hit the gunner, and he dropped into the bed of the truck. I doubted I'd hit the guy anywhere vital, but it was enough to stop their advance for a few seconds. I fired a few more shots into the truck's tailgate to empty the magazine, then I ejected and replaced it and started running again. I made it to the corner of the next building, where Duma reached out and jerked me into cover behind a burned-out car with the partially charred body of a rebel, no more than a teenager, inside.

"What the hell—" I spat, but he clamped his hand over my mouth.

In the sudden and stark relative quiet of the side street, I could hear the sound of a heavy diesel engine and the unmistakable squeak of tank treads on concrete. My shoulders sank.

"Some idea you had, Wile E.," Duma whispered.

More than likely, the tank was on its way to meet the technical we'd just encountered, and its driver had no idea we were even present. I had little doubt, however, that like the guys around the technical, they would fire at us on sight. I stuck my head out around the burnt-out car's bumper to get an idea of how far out the tank was, just as an RPG from a nearby rooftop slammed into the side of the tank's turret. The resulting massive explosion was far out of proportion for the grenade alone. The old Soviet-made T-55 had to have upgraded explosive reactive armor, because the impact did little more than rock the tank, leaving it fully operational. The vehicle began rotating the main gun in the direction of the attack, leaving Duma and me temporarily clear.

"Let's go." I slapped Duma on the back to get him moving before I continued running.

Rather than taking off at full speed, Duma kept pace with me as we leap-frogged from cover to cover down the street for another block, racing toward the heavier fighting while watching for any sign of Deeta. At the end of the next block, we encountered five more technicals moving into position to take on two tanks farther down in a straight-on street fight. At least thirty armed militiamen surrounded and took cover around the battered improvised fighting platforms, while it appeared the tanks were on their own. Three of the technicals were outfitted with chain guns like the one we'd encountered earlier. Another had a multiple-rocket launcher, and the last carried a 105mm howitzer. To make matters crazier, the technicals were so close together that if one went up, it could easily take two others with it. The entire situation was tactically insane and made no sense. *Even inexperienced civilians should be smarter than this.*

Without warning, the multiple-rocket launcher fired first, sending six shells downrange in quick succession, though none came even remotely close to the tanks. The instant the smoke cleared, heavy machine-gun fire erupted from both ends of the street, tearing chunks of concrete up from buildings and the street itself. Men were preparing the howitzer to fire when a figure launched from a rooftop next to the trucks and landed on a roof across a narrow alleyway, easily covering twenty feet in the air. Milliseconds later, a dark-skinned figure in a white kaross followed, wielding a long, thin spear and holding an oval shield. I backhanded Duma's shoulder, pointed at the rooftop the two figures had jumped from, then took off across the street to follow.

"On the rooftops! Focus on the guy being chased. The other one's got to be Deeta. Let's help him," I shouted as Duma caught up to me.

Duma veered off to the other side of the street, jumped, then vaulted himself onto a second-floor balcony in a single fluid motion. Being less of a showoff, I crashed inelegantly through a partially closed door and charged up the stairs to the roof of the building. Stopping only long enough to locate the runners, I found them bounding across rooftops several hundred yards away, with the chaser falling steadily behind. The figure being chased ran with Duma's speed and fluid ease, easily covering thirty to forty feet at a leap because of his momentum. Though I couldn't see him well while running, something about the chased figure's visage struck me as odd.

I ran after the figure I guessed was Deeta and was catching up fast. Ditaolane had his patron's prowess as a hunter, and like me, he had greater-than-normal human endurance, strength, and speed but not to the same extent that I did. He was extremely strong for his build and probably a little faster than a world-record sprinter. I didn't know if the figure Deeta was after was as fast as Duma, but even

I couldn't keep up with the Peri for more than a few dozen yards, and I could never catch him if he had a head start. Deeta rapidly lost ground on the guy he was chasing, and I was catching up to Deeta just as quickly.

As I jumped rooftops, I glimpsed Duma's blur a few buildings over, making a beeline for the target, not gaining as much as cutting the angle to close the distance. Behind us, the tanks and trucks thundered away at each other, loudly enough that I didn't hear the report of the sniper's rifle even after it tore into the wall below the roof ledge as I jumped to the next building. Surprised, I landed in a roll and stayed prone. Lying still, I could hear random sniper fire from several directions, and it wasn't aimed only at me.

I popped my head up long enough to get a bead on one sniper three rooftops to my left while the target figure dived for cover. A few buildings to my right, Duma ducked behind a structure on the roof he occupied as a bullet tore into it. Only Deeta kept racing along undaunted.

I counted enough different rifle reports to infer there were enough snipers to keep us all pinned down. The heavy fighting and explosions behind us — especially the chain guns — kept me from hearing the sniper rifle reports very well. The monotonous *chuk-chuk-chuk-chuk-chuk* made directional hearing nearly impossible. I tried visually to follow the trajectories of the impacts back to where the gunmen were hiding, but my position kept me from seeing all but the one I'd already identified well to my left.

Frustrated, I was getting ready to risk shifting for a better view when a chunk of masonry exploded near my head and showered me with sand and rocks. I dropped back down, but the fact that the shot had hit where it had meant that at least one sniper repositioned to get a better shot at me. I lizard-crawled over to the far wall and quickly poked my head up in the direction the shot had come from, immediately identifying the shooter two rooftops over. I raised my SCAR over the short wall while remaining on my back. I fired randomly in the sniper's direction, hoping he would duck long enough for me to get into an offensive position. The gamble paid off.

While the shooter took cover, I scrambled to my knees, using the low wall for support, and took aim at the sniper's gun protruding from his hiding spot. Once the sniper rose back to his position behind his rifle less than eighty yards out, I fired a short burst, hitting him several times and knocking him down. Behind me, Deeta, still several buildings away from his target, kept running as multiple bullets tore into the structures around him—the snipers began focusing on him since he was the only available target.

I ran toward him as fast as I could, firing the SCAR in uncontrolled bursts in the directions I guessed the snipers might be, attempting to buy him time. I cleared two more buildings while, off to my right, Duma dispatched another sniper. I didn't stop even when a shot rang out to my left, less than fifty feet away, startling me. Without slowing, I brought the SCAR to bear on the sniper's position and sent a sustained burst into his nest, killing him. That was when I realized he wasn't aiming at me. Skidding to a stop, I noticed Deeta stumbling across the roof into a face-plant.

"Deeta!" I screamed. "Stay down. Help's coming."

I began running again for Deeta and noticed the figure he was chasing—now back on his feet—was doubling back on him. Only he was much closer.

I sprinted as fast as I could, still too far and running too fast to use my weapon effectively, when Duma screamed from my right. "I got 'em, D. Get the guy in the bedsheet!"

The figure closing in on Deeta's position was simply too fast and too close. I watched as Deeta clambered back to his feet, using his spear to prop himself up. His once-stark-white kaross was stained crimson. The other figure reached the rooftop opposite Deeta and slowed, glancing first toward Duma—closing at frightening speed—then at me. The figure was still too far for me to see details, but I could tell he wore a balaclava, along with other modern tactical gear. Something still bugged me about the unusual brown pulsating energy he radiated—it definitely wasn't human, and it was unlike any Paran's I had ever seen. As he eyed me, he pulled a delicate pistol with a long barrel out from a holster under his left arm and aimed it at Deeta.

"Don't do it!" I screamed, coming to an abrupt stop in an attempt to slow my heart rate and control my breathing enough to make a quick shot with my SCAR.

To put him down for sure, I would have to hit him in the head, but from a standing position, with my heart pounding and several hundred yards between us, there was no way. I hoped that seeing me ready to fire would cause the guy to panic and run. I also hoped that being outnumbered might spook him. Instead, the guy calmly pulled another gun from behind his back and aimed in Duma's direction. The second gun was a hand-cannon — something like a Desert Eagle .50 AE because it was the size of a handheld howitzer.

Duma made it to the roof of the building on the gunman's left and ducked behind a small structure. With Duma out of his line of sight, the gunman aimed the hand-cannon at me. I had no doubt that thing had the power to hit me, but I also knew that his best shot at this range was center mass, and I was covered for that. I began walking forward, slowly, keeping a tight bead on the masked figure as I crossed the roof. Duma, two buildings to my right, spun his kukri knives in each hand.

"Stop where you are and do not pursue me," the figure said in a crisp and clear tone, without even breathing heavily.

His crazy aura pulsed once like a flash of lightning within a cloud, and as he spoke, my entire head vibrated as if someone had put a tuning fork to my skull. The sensation stopped me momentarily and forced me to shake my head to clear it.

"Diomedes, we should leave this guy alone," Duma shouted from his position under cover.

"Duma, stay where you are. I got this," I replied, once again focused and back on target.

"Yeah, but he asked us to leave him alone," Duma shouted back, his face a mask of intensity.

What the hell is he on about?

"Ah, *the* Diomedes." The gunman's voice carried over the battle behind us. "And so we meet. No hard feelings, I hope? You are simply a convenient scapegoat."

I kept progressing slowly. His scapegoat. *This guy? The Hanner Brid?* While I was concerned about Deeta, the notion suddenly occurred to me that if I could keep this guy talking, I might be able to stall him long enough to get in position for a reasonable shot and end the whole mess right there. "So you're the one who framed me?"

He canted his head slightly. "Take another step, and I will kill *two* Guardians at once." His voice never wavered.

All of a sudden, Deeta, who had been using his spear as a crutch, shifted and heaved the thin spear straight at the gunman. The throw was weak and obvious, allowing the masked figure plenty of time to duck to his left as the spear flew past, barely nicking his thigh. The gunman appeared to do nothing in response, but Deeta jerked then fell lifelessly to the roof.

Screaming, I opened fire, emptying the clip at the gunman. His body spasmed as several of my bullets hit him. Not only did he not go down, but he also managed to fire back with the large handgun. His shots were surprisingly well aimed for snap shots fired under duress, and I caught several in my lower abdomen. They thumped into my cuirass like a line drive, causing me to twist away. I dropped to one knee, ejected the spent magazine, inserted another, and began firing again—but the guy was already running again. After a few steps, he jumped off the roof, and I lost sight of him. I ran and jumped across to the adjacent roof to help Deeta, screaming for Duma to chase the guy down, but the Peri never moved.

By the time I reached Deeta, he was barely conscious. A Basuto warrior by birth, Deeta was dressed in the traditional style of his people, wearing a white toga-like kaross and no shoes. Though the kaross was apparently backed by a Kevlar weave, the garment left most of his upper chest unprotected. Two bullet holes in the exposed flesh on the left side of his chest were both gushing dark-red blood, and he had a gaping wound through his upper left shoulder. He was bleeding too much, and I tried to compress the smaller holes with a strip of his kaross.

Ditaolane was tall, nearly six feet two, but he weighed no more than a buck eighty soaking wet, and his dark skin—usually the color of very dark chocolate—was pallid. His thin body was more gaunt than usual. His wood-and-hide shield lay at his feet. I'd liked the kid the first time I met him, but he was too naive, maybe because of where he'd grown up. Good or bad, my perception of him was as more of an activist than a warrior, though his fighting skills had definitely improved over the years.

"Deeta, it's me, Diomedes. Just lay still. We'll get you help. You'll be okay," I lied then shouted for Duma.

Deeta's eyes stared into the middle distance, and I knew he didn't have long. The revelation that I'd just encountered the assassin I was after, combined with Deeta dying in my arms, made me howl with rage.

"Deeta, who was that?" I didn't really expect a response, but I wasn't sure what else to do, except make sure he knew he wasn't alone. Again, I screamed for Duma.

"The spear..." Deeta said in a barely audible whisper, trying to reach for his weapon but unable to muster the strength. "Get my spear. Blood..."

"I will, Deeta, lay still." An icy shock in my skull that was characteristic of the presence of one of the Old Ones—one I hadn't sensed in a long time—jarred me.

I glanced over my shoulder to see Artemis dressed in an orange kaross with a brightly colored blanket of the kind made by Basuto women draped over her shoulders. To Ditaolane, she was Uhlanga, the Goddess of the Marsh. She wore her long sandy hair in a single braid draped over one shoulder, and her normally brilliant-blue eyes were as gray as wet cement. The rest of her face was an unreadable mask as she knelt next to Deeta. There was nothing we could do to save him.

Deeta was dead within minutes. In my long life, I had witnessed that same moment for many fine men, too many times. I felt helpless each time, and it was a weakness I hated. And it pissed me off. That bastard had killed a fellow Guardian and friend. He was causing massive problems in both human and nonhuman realms, and he was trying to frame me. When I caught up to him, he would be lucky if I only killed him.

CHAPTER 19

ARTEMIS AND I SAT SILENTLY next to Deeta for several long minutes while the sounds of war roared in the background. Buildings were being blown apart, and the echo of artillery and gunfire hung in the air all around us. I didn't want to leave him there, but I really wasn't in a position to do anything about it. And Artemis remained annoyingly silent. Our relationship had been rocky since she'd chosen to fight with her brother Apollo for the Trojans and snatched away Aeneas before I could kill him. But in that moment on that rooftop, I was willing to let bygones be bygones if she would only say something.

Thankfully, Duma broke the painful silence by showing up with Deeta's spear. He had a sheepish expression, and he wouldn't make eye contact with me. "Um... I went after that guy. All I found over there was this." He held out the spear.

I glared at him, unable to understand why he'd failed to react. Artemis stood and gently took the spear from him. She faced me, her forehead wrinkled and her eyes sad. The edges of her mouth twisted down ever so faintly.

"Perhaps you can find a use for this," she said, presenting the long, thin weapon to me.

"I'm honored, but no. You know I am the keeper of the Pelian Spear, and I don't use it often as it is." I bowed my head.

I stood out of respect for Artemis and her offer, and my eyes traveled to the spear's leaflike blade. It was covered with an oily, yellowish goo that resembled pus. And then I connected the dots. *Spear... blood.* That was what Deeta had said before he died. It wasn't just a dying warrior wanting his weapon—he'd known there would be blood on it. With that, we could track the bastard. I knew the kid carried a special amulet of divining bones that helped him locate demons, but he'd apparently had other tricks up his sleeve, as well.

Eyeing Artemis, I gripped the spear tightly. I could feel the grin widen across my cheeks. She smiled back at me as I took the spear and held it out to Duma. I was so charged up that we could track the jackwagon that I'd forgotten—for a moment—that he had abandoned me when I needed his help.

"I need you to use this blood to track that son of a bitch," I said to Duma, angling the blade toward him so he could see the yellow liquid. "Can you do that?" It wasn't the time or the place to lay into him for his inactivity.

"Of course, but it will only work for about forty-eight hours, and it'll get harder as the blood degrades," he said, taking the spear, his eyes suddenly wide. "I'll get right on it."

Artemis had taken the blanket from her shoulders and wrapped Deeta's upper body with it, covering his head. "I'll take care of him and see that he gets the burial he deserves," she said, her eyes still dark and her expression unreadable. "I do not think I shall find another to take his place."

"Don't give up on us humans," I replied. "He was good, but I'll guarantee there are others out there with his skills and determination. None will ever replace Ditaolane, but there are those that can continue his work."

She smiled at me, but there was no warmth in the expression. "Perhaps you are right, but I have become weary of this world and its growing cynicism. I am not sure I have it left in me to choose another."

She picked up Deeta's shield, laid it on his chest, then retrieved the spear from Duma, who was already hard at work, scrying for the gunman's current location. Artemis returned to Deeta's side and knelt beside him, tucking the spear under his arm. She placed her hands on Deeta, and they both simply disappeared. No flash. No sound. They simply vanished, leaving no sign they'd ever been there. Not even Deeta's blood. Deeta was the first Guardian I had ever seen die. Just because I didn't age and had survived far longer than any of my predecessors, that didn't mean I couldn't die as easily.

After a moment, I walked over to Duma, who was kneeling over the map we'd brought from his warehouse in Atlanta. He had his finger on Seville, in the southwestern part of Spain.

Duma and I headed back to Martyr's Square as fast as we could go, avoiding as much of the fighting as possible. We made it through the Ways to Seville without much more than a word spoken between us. Duma continued to act sheepish, and I was still pissed about Deeta's death and the Hanner Brid. I was furious with Duma—about the whole damn situation. I knew better than to think that some action on Duma's part might have changed what happened back on that rooftop, but that didn't lessen my anger toward him. In the hundreds of years I'd known and worked with him, he'd never frozen up. I didn't get it—and *that* bothered me more than the rest of it. Deeta was a good man who had served humanity well, but he was dead. Duma, on the other hand, was still alive, and another bout of cement foot might get him killed, or worse, get me killed. *Once we get this son of a bitch, Duma and I are going to have it out.*

We emerged from the Ways into a large, open parklike area surrounded by palm trees and covered by more dirt than grass. Rooftops and multistory apartment buildings rose above the scrubby trees and palms in almost every direction, but based on the ambient engine sounds, car horns, and road noise, I could tell that a major highway ran somewhere close by.

"We need to find a local map if we intend to keep up with this guy, D. Fast," Duma said, still unwilling to make eye contact with me.

I hadn't been in Seville in centuries. I still remembered when it was a Roman outpost called Hispalis founded by a predecessor, Heracles. It had changed more than a little bit since then.

"I know where we are. There's a gas station on the other side of those buildings. They should have a street map for us to track him locally." Duma pointed at a high-rise to the north.

"Let's go."

Thankfully, there weren't many people walking around the late-afternoon sunshine yet, though street traffic was heavier than I preferred—especially since I was armed to the teeth. My militant appearance combined with the events of the last few hours kept me on edge as we ran down alleyways and behind buildings, trying to remain as inconspicuous as possible. The few people we did encounter simply ducked their heads, sped up, and gave us a wide berth.

We were making good time along one alley when Duma stopped, placed a hand on my shoulder to stop me as I passed, and met my gaze. "D, I'm sorry I froze up back there." It was a few long seconds before he continued. "I... I'm not sure what happened."

"We don't have time for this—"

"D, wait. You don't understand. I. Don't. Know. What. Happened. The guy said stop, so I needed to stop. I can't explain it. I'm not making excuses. I'm trying to apologize. I let you down, and your friend got killed. I'm sorry."

I held his gaze as he talked. He was as contrite as I've ever seen him, which was saying a lot. Emotions were a stretch for fae, but for a Peri, it must have been serious gymnastics. They usually don't even understand them enough to fake them. Apparently, though, they are either learnable or contagious over time, because Duma's apology was sincere.

"He was a Guardian and a friend, but I didn't know him as well as I should have. I hadn't even seen him in years." I placed my hand on his shoulder. "My greatest concern back there was that your inaction would get either you or me killed. This guy we're after—that guy back there in Libya—is dangerous, and we're going to have to be all-go, no-quit to catch his ass before he kills someone else. I *need* to know you've got my back, Duma."

"I'm telling you, D, my actions were entirely involuntary," he replied, his eyebrows raised and his head cocked. "I *had* to stop. I don't get it. I've never felt anything like that before."

"You're saying this guy pulled some sort of Jedi mind trick on you?" Then I remembered the odd aura flash and the buzzing sensation in my head when the Hanner Brid had said to stop. "Didn't you say that Blud had the ability to confuse and mislead people?"

"Yeah, that's their thing, but normally, it wouldn't affect another fae so strongly," he replied.

"But if the stories are true, he's also half *Succubus*, right? They are also master manipulators, and who knows what kinds of abilities *that* might give him, even as a half-breed?"

"Maybe. It would explain a lot. But why didn't it affect you?" Duma asked.

"I'm guessing it's because of my ability to see through glamours and mental tricks. I sensed something on that roof, but I was able to fight through it. Come on—we gotta get that map." The fact that it may not have been voluntary inaction on Duma's part went a long way toward forgiving him. "You think you can ignore him if he tries it again? The last thing I need is for you to turn on me when we catch up to him."

"Maybe," he replied. "I don't know. His request sounded damn reasonable at the time. I guess it depends on what he asks me to do."

I didn't like his answer, but I needed his help. There was no way I could track the Hanner Brid and avoid both fae courts at the same time. I was going to have to risk it.

A few blocks later, in the alley behind the gas station, I pulled off my vest and cuirass and went into the store to find a map. Using Duma's credit card, I also grabbed bottled water and three local maps, just in case. Frankly, since the art of scrying was tantamount to complex thaumaturgy in my book, I didn't know what exactly Duma might need. I contemplated buying food, too, but greasy gas station food, even in Spain, wasn't going to cut it.

"Why can't we use a GPS?" I asked Duma as I handed him the maps and a bottle of water.

"Not really sure, actually." He opened his bottle and took a big drink. "Never tried it, but somehow, I doubt electronics and harnessing and refocusing specific energy will go together. I'm all up for trying it, just not right now."

I pulled my gear back on then sat on the hood of a rusty car in the alley behind the gas station while Duma spread the map out on the ground and conducted his ritual for scrying. It took an agonizing ten or twelve minutes.

"Got 'im," Duma said through a big, toothy smile. "I should have known. He's a few blocks away, and I know the place. You're not gonna like it, though."

"What do you mean I'm not gonna like it?" I asked, sliding off the car. "And what I like or dislike is irrelevant right now."

Duma snorted as he gathered his things, and we left as quickly as was prudent. "This place we're headed is kinda like a flophouse," Duma said as we walked down an alleyway that led us into a warren of industrial buildings and warehouses. "It's mostly frequented by runaways and derelicts of all races," he replied, waving his hands around. "Not to mention the occasional *fugitive*."

I knew him well enough to know he wasn't telling me the whole story. "So?"

"So... *you*" — he hooked his thumb at me — "probably won't be welcome there."

I didn't know how to respond to that statement. It actually ticked me off a little. As a human, I tended to think of this world as mine, especially within a human community as old as Seville. And I was a Guardian, a protector of humanity, which meant I went anywhere I needed to go. Besides, I had no problem ignoring beings, even fugitive ones, as long as they weren't causing trouble for humans.

And then I realized the structures around us had changed. None of the buildings had windows, and the area was barren of life — even rats. Oddest of all, it was *clean*. There wasn't so much as a random scrap of paper or plastic on the ground, and the walls were all devoid of graffiti of any kind. The deeper we traveled into the maze of alleys, the more evident it became that the path had been specifically designed that way. Becoming more vigilant as we walked, I noticed subtle glamours over side passages, likely meant to obscure emergency exits or back entrances. The occasional shadowy figure quickly melded into darker recesses and corners. Not once since we'd entered, however, had I heard even the slightest sound — not even traffic on the nearby major highway.

"How much farther?" I asked in a hoarse whisper.

"Shush, and stay behind me," he replied out of the corner of his mouth. "And whatever you do, don't pull a weapon. And if we get in, don't go all Guardian-y on me. You got me?"

I didn't know what bothered me more: the fact that Duma expected I would go all Guardian-y — whatever that meant — or the fact that we were about to walk into an unfamiliar place populated by potentially dangerous miscreants. Either way, I didn't like it. I especially didn't like that Duma wanted to go into this den of outcasts and fugitives without so much as a nail file drawn. I left my swords sheathed and my guns holstered, but my fists were cocked.

I followed Duma up to a massive metal door that could have been taken from a nuclear silo, except it had one of those stupid slots that slides open so the guy inside can scowl out menacingly and ask for the secret password. The entire building was shrouded in a cloak of magic — more accurately *magics*. Plural. The hair on the back of my neck stood on end, my skin became clammy, and I couldn't stop rubbing the fingers of my right hand together.

Duma knocked a few times, but nothing happened.

"Try—"

Duma flashed me a withering glare over his shoulder with his stark-white eyes wide and his lips drawn into a tight, thin line.

I stood there, hands on hips, staring at the ground.

After another few minutes of standing around in utter silence, I was about to say something about knocking again, when Duma quickly waved his hand at me, trying to get me to step out of view. I did. Reluctantly.

Eventually, after yet another few minutes, the little slot in the door slid open with a sharp *snick*. Duma lifted his head ever so slightly to peer into the slot.

"Who's the human?" asked a thick, gravelly voice.

"He's with me," Duma replied. "I'll vouch for him."

The slot closed, and we remained standing there for another few minutes. I folded my arms across my chest and hung my head with an audible sigh. With nothing better to do, I kicked at loose stones on the ground.

Finally, a loud metallic *clunk* came from within the substantial door, followed by a rattling sound. Then the door slid open enough to prove it was no longer sealed. Duma glanced at me with his eyebrows raised then grabbed the handle. Pulling with all his might, he swung the heavy door open with the high-pitched screech of metal grinding on metal. After about two feet, it stopped solidly. The gap was only big enough to allow a single person to pass through at a time, and I followed Duma into an area shrouded in a heavy, damp black mist that blocked all light from entering.

Whatever was shrouding the space wasn't a glamour or magic, because I would have been able to see through those. Even the sunlight failed to penetrate more than a few inches into the murk, but I could make out some sort of indistinct magical aura to our right as we entered. Once we were both inside, the heavy outer door squealed shut again, followed by the same combination of rattling and clanging that had accompanied its opening—only louder. Once sealed in, we were in pitch darkness, save for the coursing magical aura I perceived through the gloom—which I assumed was some sort of protection enchantment. Suddenly, I found myself back in the blackness of the cell on Poveglia, and I had to fight to shut down the panic rising in me. Thankfully, the dank miasma began to fade after the last clunk from the outer door.

As the mist cleared, I realized we were standing in a small entryway facing a single door. To our right, in the fading murk, stood a powerful but squat figure about my height. He didn't possess the magical power I perceived, but was *composed* of it. Before I could think twice about the odd figure or determine its disposition toward us, the interior door opened, and Duma stepped through it without hesitation. I followed, curious about what I would find now that I was down the rabbit hole.

CHAPTER 20

THE ODD MAGICAL FIGURE STAYED inside the entryway as Duma and I passed through the door into a large, open warehouse. The bulk of the humid, dimly lit space was one giant open room with tables, benches, chairs, and beat-up old couches that formed a common area right out of a medieval fraternity house. Old, dark wood walls, hidden behind piles of garbage in some spots, lined the edge of the common area. Darkened hallways and closed doors alternated along the wall in areas not taken up by the garbage piles. All in all, the place was dingy and smelled like the large-mammal house at a zoo. Musty wood, candle wax, and the acrid odor of a well-used gym all combined with the cloying aroma of rotting garbage. The only light came from hundreds of candles. They were stuck in candelabras, chandeliers, and wall sconces, while some randomly sat on tables. It was a disgusting firetrap. *I feel cozy all over.*

At first, the room appeared empty, then I sensed movement from all around us. I followed Duma toward the center of the room, a location that made me *very* uncomfortable. As a rule, a soldier recons an unknown area from the periphery first, not only to avoid getting caught in an indefensible position, but also to find alternate means of egress. We were putting ourselves center stage. My hand instinctively wandered toward the holster on my vest, but Duma slapped it away, surprising me.

In the second it took me to recompose myself, two humanoid figures stepped out of the darkness from opposite sides of the room. One was gigantic and would have given Duma's enormous brother, Abraxos, an inferiority complex. The other was slender but moved with fluid ease and a greater presence than the tall but slim build suggested. The slender figure kept to the shadows along the wall to our right, while the two-legged mountain lumbered out into an area to our left lit by a chandelier covered in drippy candles.

The gigantic creature's face was grotesque. The skin on the planet-sized bald head was a grayish green and was covered in boils or warts, or both. Its mouth was misshapen and lopsided, with one large lower canine protruding from thick lips. The small, dark eyes, however, were alert and showed signs of curiosity and intelligence as it eyed me in particular. The thick, ropy muscles in its arms, chest, and neck twitched constantly as they tensed and relaxed, but luckily, the creature had no weapons that I could see. Not that it would need any with the logs it had for arms.

While I sized up Snaggletooth, several more figures appeared at the edges of my peripheral vision—which made me do a double take.

"What brings you here, Duma?" the figure asked in a smooth voice deep enough to suggest it was male.

I focused on the newcomers. Three figures, including the one who had addressed Duma by name, stood in front of us at the far reaches of the room. The speaker was close to my height and dressed in ratty clothes that were probably salvaged from a garbage can. A hoodie pulled over his head hid his face. The two flanking him looked every bit as grungy, but the one to his right was taller and lankier, while the other had a similar build to the first. No one appeared to be armed, nor did I perceive any signs of magic or glamours from them. Still, it was clear that none of them was human.

"And who did you bring with you?" the hooded figure asked, taking a few steps toward us.

"Don't worry; he's with me." Duma crossed his arms over his chest as he faced the speaker. "We're looking for someone."

"Are you now?" Grungy replied, matching Duma's stance. "Who, may I ask, are you seeking?"

Duma strode purposefully toward Grungy, stopped less than a foot away from him, then leaned in to close the distance even farther. "I think you know, Gracen," Duma said in a whisper that managed to carry through the open space. "Tell us where the Hanner Brid is, and we'll collect him and leave."

Of course Duma would know this guy.

"The Hanner Brid?" Gracen laughed, leaning away from him. "Seriously? I thought you stopped believing in the boogeyman when we were children, Duma." He took a step back and placed his hands behind him. The two figures flanking Gracen let out phlegmy cackles.

Reading fae was difficult, so I didn't know what to make of their reactions. If they had been fae of either court, they could twist the truth, but they couldn't lie. Duma had said these guys were outcasts, though, and that could mean they were Anseelie—neither Dark nor Light Fae. That would mean they had no issues with lying.

The slender figure to the right fully emerged from the shadows. "Besides, many of us here *are* hanner brid," said a distinctly female voice.

Snaggletooth let out a snort.

"*The* Hanner Brid, not half-breeds in general," Duma replied, dismissing her comment with a wave of his hand. "He's here."

"There are only those you see, Duma," Gracen said. "So unless one of us is the Demon Fae and doesn't know it, I suggest you and your friend leave the way you came."

Gracen turned his head in my direction, though I still couldn't see much of his face under the hood. Short of fishing, my patience stretched about as far as one of those little rubber bands dentists used for braces. Since I'd pushed my limits about as far as I could while waiting outside for the door to open, I was about to break.

"Maybe one of you is..." I examined my hands then adjusted the thin leather strips I wore instead of gloves. I could feel everyone's attention shifting to me as I spoke. "If this... Demon Fae, as you called it, is here and you are hiding him, I suggest you bring him forth before I have to search for him." I didn't want to take them all on in a fight, but given that they were outcasts who preferred to hide, I doubted they would offer up much resistance if it came to it.

Duma stepped in front of me and frowned, his brow heavily furrowed and his teeth bared slightly. "D, don't—" he said, the muscles along his jawline twitching.

"Duma, enough." I shoved past him toward Gracen. "I mean these beings no harm, but we've wasted enough time, and I will dismantle this place if I need to in order to find the bastard. There are far more lives on the line than those here."

I came to a stop so close to Gracen that I could finally see into the hood and smell his breath. It was rank. The face, on the other hand, was pale and shared the same fine features as Duma's and Ab's.

Gracen had to be a Peri, though something was different about his eyes and his nose. I stared into his pinkish-white eyes for a long few seconds, hoping to let him know I was neither afraid nor bluffing, and I could tell his nose was aquiline rather than straight and perfect like Duma's. No one moved until Duma put his hand on my shoulder. I kept my gaze on Gracen for a few more seconds before turning.

"D," Duma said, "you can't do that, not here. Give me a minute. I'm asking you to trust me on this."

"Ah, this human barbarian must be the Guardian, Diomedes," Gracen said behind me, "*N'est-ce pas?* I knew you traveled in questionable company, Duma, but why would you choose to help this... *butcher?*"

I reached for my gun. If Duma hadn't been faster than I was, I would have drawn it, too. With one hand still on my wrist, he grabbed my vest with the other and shoved me back a few steps. That couldn't have been easy for him physically since I was far stronger. Ignoring him, I continued to glower back over Duma's shoulder at Gracen, until Duma put his face right in mine.

"Duma, let me go," I said. "The prick called me a butcher. I do not kill wantonly."

"No, *no*, he didn't, Diomedes." Duma pushed me back another step then let me go. He remained right in front of me. "He called you '*bruchad*,'" Duma said, pronouncing the word slowly and distinctly. "It's the term Peris use for humans. Now. Back. Off. I'm telling you if you want to find out anything here, *back off*." He placed his open hand in the middle of my chest.

"You know there is a sizable bounty on your head, Guardian." Gracen smiled. "More than just money."

I eyed Gracen. I wasn't sure if I believed Duma about what Gracen had called me, but he was right—ripping the place apart wasn't going to help anything. Readjusting my vest, I trudged over to a rickety wooden table, pulled out a beat-up old chair from it, and sat down heavily. Several of the beings around me exhaled audibly, and a few shoulders sank noticeably as everyone started to move again.

Duma walked back to Gracen, and they began speaking very quietly in the same mellifluous language Duma used with his brother, but I did not understand. Meanwhile, I watched as the slender female figure from the shadows walked forward and threw herself onto the couch with a dramatic flourish that made her appear to float down rather than fall. Out from the shadows, she was devastatingly beautiful — and that was through a filter of partial darkness. She knew it, too.

She wore her blond hair very short and was dressed like a refugee from a corny medieval movie — thigh-high leather boots, an oversized shirt loosely secured at her neck by a thin leather cord, and leather bracers on her wrists. She crossed her long, lean legs at the ankles as she threw them up on a nearby chair and flashed me the barest hint of a grin. All at once, the entire structure began to tremble as Snaggletooth approached. The female glanced past me and barely shook her head, and the monstrous creature stopped. Its twisted mouth opened a little to reveal several broken teeth, then the creature let out a heavy breath that resembled a bull sneezing and averted its eyes.

Duma and Gracen continued to talk. Gracen kept his arms crossed and stared at the ground, constantly shifting his weight from one foot to the other. *He's afraid.* I sat as patiently as I could, breathing audibly through my nose, drumming my fingers on my knee, while keeping a watchful eye on everyone in the room.

"My, my, we're uptight, aren't we?" the woman asked.

I growled in response. She took her legs down, got up, stepped to the end of the couch closest to me, and sat back down and crossed her legs again, all in a single fluid movement. As she shifted, I could hear Snaggletooth grumble and feel him take a slight step forward. Again, she raised her eyebrows and tilted her head, stopping the massive creature instantly.

"I've never seen a Guardian before," she said, practically purring.

I tried to focus on Duma's conversation, but the woman was at the edge of my line of sight. I growled again, but she leaned forward, elbows on her knees, staring at me.

"They are an endangered species," a male voice said from somewhere near the building's entrance.

The entire atmosphere suddenly became electric. I recognized the voice at once from the rooftop back in Sirte. Duma and Gracen's quiet but heated conversation stopped instantly, and everyone faced the speaker, wearing expressions of genuine surprise. *Either they really didn't know this guy was here, or they didn't expect him to reveal himself.* I bolted upright, knocking my chair back as I spun to face him, my right hand resting on my chest, just above the gun on my vest.

The woman hopped up and vaulted back to keep the full length of the couch between her and the mystery man. The action was so graceful and dexterous that it was like watching her in slow motion. Snaggletooth took a few heavy steps forward, as well. The three figures near Duma, including Gracen, all spread their feet and dropped their arms to their sides. *Clearly, none of them knew this guy was here before now.*

"Did you really think I wouldn't find you?" I said.

He let out a short, derisive laugh then strolled out from the shadows, leaving only his face still obscured, though I could see a golden glint in his eyes as he stared back at me. His odd brownish aura made even less sense up close: It resembled the aura of an Old One but was stunted somehow. The energy was less intense and almost parasitic, as if it were feeding off him. I could feel the tension growing in the room as his aura pulsed rhythmically. Something was about to happen, even without the cool showdown music. *It's times like this I wish I could whistle better.*

He was still dressed in the desert camo fatigues and body armor, and from the neck down, he resembled almost any modern special-ops operator or private military contractor. He even had a keffiyah draped around his neck, covering the lower part of his face. His right thigh was heavily bandaged with duct tape — a common way to secure a pressure dressing in the field — and the injury made me smile. It was Deeta's final blow that had provided our ability to track the prick.

I could see only the thin long-barreled Ruger in a holster under his left arm, but I knew he had to have that big gun on him, as well. I didn't dare reposition my hands, for fear it would instantly devolve into a full-blown shootout. The problem was my nearest serious cover besides the couch was, unfortunately, Snaggletooth, a few yards back and to my left.

I squinted at the Hanner Brid, giving him my best Clint Eastwood scowl, and for the briefest of moments, I considered telling him to make my day. "Make this easy on yourself and give up now," I said instead.

Duma began to creep to his left, putting a hallway to his back. It wouldn't have been my choice, but then Duma and I rarely shared tactical preferences. The golden glint in the Hanner Brid's eyes shifted to follow Duma's movement then returned to me.

Damn, I need my own soundtrack.

"I tell you what," I said, taking a slight step forward to keep him on edge, "at least tell me what to call you, because frankly, Hanner Brid just sounds dumb."

"How'd you get in here?" Gracen asked with a faltering and unsteady voice.

"Gracen, shut up," Duma said.

"See? His name is Gracen; that's Duma," I said, taking another half step forward. "And my name is Diomedes." I glared at him as I said my name, hoping that it would strike fear into his heart. It didn't. I tilted my head in disappointment. "I can't keep calling you... what was it again? Hammer Head?" It was childish, but it was all I had at the moment.

Duma shifted again, turning so that he was facing the Hanner Brid in profile, with his left shoulder forward in order to present a slimmer target. We all stood there for a long few moments without anyone saying a word. If this were Hollywood, the scene where we'd all end up dead in deep pools of blood because someone accidentally stepped on a stick was about to happen. I could feel it.

"Why'd you come here?" Gracen asked, his voice still cracking. For some reason, he was trying to assert authority.

"Gracen, why don't you and the others clear out, so you don't get hurt," I said.

"Do as he says, Gracen. Just get everyone out of here," Duma said through clenched teeth. "Now!"

"You want to know why I came here?" the Hanner Brid replied in a smooth, even voice as if everything were happening exactly as he'd planned. "To protect *you*. From *him*." He motioned toward me with his chin, keeping his hands loose at his sides.

Confused, the five derelicts eyed each other, then me and Duma, then the Hanner Brid again.

"He's come to kill you *all*." His aura pulsed brightly for a split second.

A strong buzzing began inside my head, similar to the sensation I experienced back on that rooftop in Libya. I blinked hard twice and pushed the sensation back as everyone shifted around me. Knowing what he was trying to do, I became concerned about Duma.

"That's just dumb," Duma replied, his voice flush with confusion. "Why would he come here to kill me?" Without taking my eyes off the Hanner Brid, in my periphery, I could see Duma juddering his head in short violent jerks as if to clear it. The others in the room started to surround me.

"I'm only here for the Hanner Brid," I said, remaining still so as not to come off as threatening. "Duma, are you with me?"

I could see the flash of a smile through the shadow around the Hanner Brid's head and simultaneously sensed movement to my left. The female was floating a foot off the ground, a short sword in each hand, causing me to do a double take. I lost track of the Hanner Brid.

"Duma," I shouted as loudly as I could while he shook his head, "if you're with me, don't let him get away."

Gracen pointed a small handgun at me while his two lackeys each drew long knives. Somewhere back, to my right, the Hanner Brid laughed.

This is going to be all kinds of ugly.

The floating woman came at me like a whirling dervish, or more accurately, a helicopter blade, given the swords she wielded. Not wanting to kill her or any of the others unless I had no other choice, I grabbed the chair I had been sitting in and swung it at her as she closed in on me. The impact shattered it and sent her flying into one of the columns with a thud. She fell limply to the floor.

The second she hit the ground, an enraged Snaggletooth charged me with a deafening roar that echoed through the warehouse. Crazed, he awkwardly swung a massive arm in a wide arc that was easy to evade. I ducked and darted farther to my left, sliding past the mountainous creature. Once behind him, I jumped and hammered my fist down on the back of its massive skull with a blow that nearly broke every finger in my hand. I don't think Snaggletooth even noticed it. The lumbering hulk spun around, but he moved so predictably that it was like watching a film in slow motion. I pushed at him with my good hand as hard as I could, forcing the giant further off balance. He stumbled into the couch and fell, crushing the ratty piece of furniture beneath him.

At the moment I shoved the behemoth, three sharp pops rang out, followed by several minor impacts to my chest and abdomen. Back across the room, Gracen was unsteadily aiming his small pistol at me. The harsh report of the little gun startled Duma, who stood only feet away, still trying to clear his head, and he almost fell over.

"Duma, are you with me?" I said, shouting again.

Regaining his composure, Duma eyed me, blinked hard several times, then pulled his two kukri knives from their sheaths.

Holy hell.

"Duma, don't do this." I raised my hands in front of me. "It's me, Diomedes. I saved you and your brother from Rubezahl all those years ago."

He took a slow step forward, lowered his head, then charged, spinning so quickly that I barely had time to react. I was able to grab one hand as he spun, but he was too fast to stop. He brought the pommel of the knife in his free hand down on my left forearm. Wincing, I grasped my arm and stepped back. Duma faced me, holding both knives down at his sides. My arm wasn't broken, but it hurt.

Reluctantly, I pulled my swords. "Come on, Duma...dammit, it's me."

The others kept their distance as if waiting to see what happened between us. Duma was much faster than me, but I could overpower him easily. My only option in fighting him would be to get close – but not too close – and keep it that way.

Again, Duma charged, turning and slashing as he advanced. I parried his attacks as fast as I could, trying to use my longer swords to keep him from getting near enough to connect with his knives. Twice, he drew blood from my arms. Being on the defensive wasn't working, but I didn't want to attack him. On a calculated risk, I drew him in, narrowly avoiding a blow aimed at my neck. Sword still in hand, I slammed my fist into Duma's chin then heel-kicked him, pulling the kick and punch as much as I could. He fell awkwardly back into the wall as the thin wood shattered. He doubled over but didn't fall.

"Duma, snap out of it!" I screamed. "All of you."

With Duma down for the moment, I glanced quickly around the room, searching for the Hanner Brid. There were no signs of him anywhere. *I don't have time for this crap.*

I stepped toward the shorter of the two henchmen, putting away my swords, trying to impress upon him that I was not a threat. "I'm not here to hurt you, I swear," I said calmly. The problem was that the creatures were not fighters—but they were survivors. That made them desperate and unpredictable.

Unfortunately, the shorter of the two henchmen stepped toward me, his long, thin stiletto pointed in my direction but angled downward, his other hand extended for balance. He circled warily to his right, and I took a few more deliberate steps toward him to close the distance. I waved my hands around as I walked, making a show of the fact I was unarmed but keeping them ready just in case. Behind me, Snaggletooth had managed to drag himself back to his feet and snatched one of the wooden roof support columns loose with one hand to use as a club. The snapping wood freaked the knife-wielding henchman out enough that he lunged at me.

I was too far away, and his attack was sloppy and unfocused, which made it easy for me to sidestep him, slap his arm farther to my right, and kick him in the butt as he flew past. The little guy bounced off Snaggletooth's gut with a meaty smack then dropped to the ground in a daze. Snaggletooth roared again, wielding the wooden beam like a baseball bat as he stepped over the prostrate henchman.

Luckily his combined size and the length of the club made swinging it nearly impossible, so the infuriated creature attempted to charge me instead. Given enough distance to build up momentum, that kind of an attack would have been frightening to see, but in the tight confines of the building, it ended up resembling a toddler taking his first steps before a face-plant. I slid the rickety wooden table into the giant's path, further entangling his ungainly gait. He crashed into a pile of trash and through a wooden wall, rattling the warehouse and probably every one nearby as well.

Duma slowly regained his composure but continued to shake his head violently. Gracen had closed the distance between them as if hoping the Peri might offer protection from me. Gracen watched Duma for a moment then reluctantly raised his little pistol at me again as I faced him. Without warning, Duma dropped one knife and chopped his open hand into Gracen's throat. Continuing the motion fluidly, the Peri spun to face the tallest of Gracen's henchmen, stopping with the giant curved blade of his knife resting on the henchman's throat. Duma had pinned him before Gracen finished falling to his knees.

With Snaggletooth out of the way, Duma—back in control of

himself—kept the kukri's blade pressed against the tall henchman's throat. Gracen was on his butt, legs splayed, sucking in air audibly while clutching at his throat. I quickly glanced around the rest of the room but found no sign of the Hanner Brid anywhere. The entire damn thing had taken less than a minute, and he was gone.

"Duma, are you with me now?" I asked cautiously, ready to grab my swords again if he didn't answer.

"Yeah, I'm good," he said hoarsely.

Relieved, I dropped my arms to my sides and began searching the room. "Where the hell could he have gone?"

"I don't think I even saw him move," Duma replied, finally removing the knife from the henchman's throat, returning it to its sheath.

The guy quickly backed into the wall then scooted along it away from Duma. Ignoring him, Duma bent down and helped Gracen back to his feet. Beyond the bumps and bruises, everyone was acting more subdued as they gathered themselves. Though they all eyed me, it was more out of apprehension than aggression. I was hopeful that the influence had waned with the absence of the Hanner Brid.

"Dammit!" I bolted as fast as I could to Gracen, who was still struggling to breathe normally. "I *told* you we weren't here to hurt you guys. That was the bastard we were after." I waved my hands in the direction the Hanner Brid had been standing, then threw them up in exasperation, lolled my head back, and stared at the ceiling.

"Sorry about... you know..." Duma said, rolling one hand but looking me square in the eye this time.

"Can you find him again?" I asked, dismissing his comment. I knew he wasn't acting of his own accord. Besides, I was far more upset that the fucker had gotten away. *Again.*

"It's going to take some time." Duma walked through one of the many doors that lined the edges of the warehouse's interior and closed it behind him. I assumed the doors led to individual rooms or storage areas, but given my luck recently, they probably led directly to the gates of hell.

CHAPTER 21

I STARED AT THE FLOOR IN silence for a minute while everyone else in the room began to pick themselves back up and collect their wits. All of them gave me a wide berth. Gracen began to gather up the smaller pieces of smashed furniture and toss them into the trash piles against the walls. His henchmen followed suit.

The taller of the two hooded goons brushed his hood back as he and the smaller one dragged the flattened couch off to a corner. I found myself confused as I watched him. Understandably, he refused to make eye contact with me.

"His mother was an Elf," said the female whirling dervish from behind me. She had apparently noticed I was staring. I tried to pretend I wasn't, but it was hard not to.

"That makes sense," I replied quietly. "His eyes are distinctly Elvish." Their size and dark solid color had caught my attention the minute he'd pushed his hood back. They also revealed an alert intelligence and a shiftiness I didn't like. "But the rest of him..." He had large pointed ears, massive jagged teeth, high cheekbones, a beak of a nose, and skin the hue of someone who was recently deceased.

"His father, a Goblin, raped her. She died giving birth to him." She grimaced, rubbing at her upper arm. "I told you, we are all half-breeds here. Even Gracen. Outcasts, each and every one."

I shook my head, watching her swing her arm as if testing it. "I apologize. I meant you no harm, I swear. But how did he get in here without you guys knowing it? I watched your reactions. You guys clearly didn't know he was here. Duma made it sound like getting in here was like breaking into Fort Knox."

"I don't know about the others, but I certainly had no idea that anyone other than the five of us and you two were here. And I have no idea how he would have gotten past the two door guards."

"There are no other ways in or out?" I asked.

"Not unless you go through the walls, floor, or ceiling. And good luck with that." She raised her arm and winced.

Gracen threw down a broken table leg. "The only way in or out is the way you came. I paid for some serious enchantments to protect this place, and they're all still intact."

I could still see the magical energy that covered this place. Frustrated, I started to grab some of the broken furniture in an effort to appear friendly and cooperative, but I was still mostly focused on what I should do next. Duma was taking an awful long time in that room. Every minute that passed was an eternity, letting the Hanner Brid get farther and farther away.

"Hey, someone give me a hand," a voice called from near the entrance. "The Doormen are destroyed."

"Dammit." Gracen coughed as he headed over.

I followed. At the entryway, parts of two humanoid figures lay on the floor among metal debris and clods of dirt. I'd known the one being in the entry wasn't flesh and blood when I'd first encountered it, but I hadn't even seen the second. "Golems?" I asked.

"Yeah." Gracen knelt beside one of the carcasses, sifting through fragments. "Both inset with bronze armor and skeletons. Shit."

Golems were rare and very expensive automatons, so I understood why Gracen was ticked off. It also explained the magic around the being in the entryway. I knelt over one of the heads and noted that it had a bullet hole in its forehead right at the end of a word formed into the clay.

I prodded the bullet hole. "The bullet to the head alone wouldn't be enough to kill this thing, but what the bullet obliterated was."

Gracen nodded. "Yeah, these golems were directly inscribed to bring them to life. I thought it would be stronger than hanging their animating enchantment on them."

"Few know that removing that inscription would disable it, and fewer still could survive doing it," I said.

The Hanner Brid had shot both of the constructs precisely in very specific parts of their inscriptions, changing the Hebrew word *emet*, meaning truth, to *met*, meaning death. Obliterating the letter "aleph" had utterly destroyed them.

I stood up, shaking my head in disbelief. "You're lucky it was only

Igg and Ook, here, and not one of you," I said, returning to what was left of the seating area.

Several hours later, I was becoming concerned that Duma still hadn't come out of that room, but since finding the Hanner Brid involved all that touchy-feely energy manipulation magic-y stuff and tracking movement through the Ways, I decided I'd probably better wait. In the meantime, I continued to help pick up the mess that I was forced to create. Over the *next* several hours of cleaning, the woman insisted on talking to me despite my efforts to ignore her. My patience was gone, and I wasn't in the mood to socialize.

"My name is Aislin, and I'm half-human, half-Nephele Vila," she said.

"Really? A cloud nymph," I replied, surprised and impressed, having never seen one before. I realized that despite her half-human ancestry, she was exactly how I'd pictured a cloud nymph. My surprise stemmed from the fact that all types of Vila were rare because they were one of the three most notorious races of the Anseelie Fae. Both Fae Courts branded them—along with the Peri, Blud, and a few other extinct races—as traitors and hunted them mercilessly. I hadn't seen any kind of Vila in over a thousand years, and the Hanner Brid was the first Blud I'd ever encountered. If I were on a Fae scavenger hunt, I would have been in the lead for sure.

"My friend Tolfin there"—she pointed at her giant companion, who was struggling to pick up the remnants of the table with his massive fingers—"is half troll and half ogre."

That has to be the worst combination ever.

"He's big, clumsy, and unfortunately, mute, but he's incredibly intelligent. In fact, he has an aptitude for complex computational mathematics, which he can do in his head—something that is way beyond human capabilities."

I grunted. "He also obviously likes you."

"We watch out for each other." She shrugged one shoulder. "Gracen is half Peri and half Sidhe. He owns this place and runs it with the help of his two buddies, the Goblin-Elf and the little guy. Nobody knows much about the little guy, except that he has pitch-black skin, but the rumors are the three of them have traveled together for centuries. Those two never speak to anyone but Gracen."

I had assumed Duma and Abraxos were the last of their kind,

though the fact they weren't didn't surprise me. They were secretive by nature and necessity, and in the scheme of things, they had no reason to tell me about some other Anseelie fae in hiding. On the other hand, that no one knew *anything* about the little black-skinned guy bothered me. Even more troublesome was that I hadn't seen the little guy since before we found the destroyed golems. It just added to my growing unease.

I decided I'd waited long enough for Duma. Before I could kick in his door, he opened it, gaunt and exhausted, which for him was saying something.

"It ain't good," he replied, exhaling heavily.

"Good or bad, I'm after him. Just tell me where he ended up."

"Well, I knew he would most likely head to the park to get back to the same nexus point we used, so I had to give him time to get there and then get to a final destination, or it would have been like playing geographic bingo." He found a functional chair and flopped into it.

Duma was dragging out his explanation, and the delay tactic was not lost on me. "Okay, fine, so where is he now?"

"Well, the blood we have is drying up, so it's starting to become harder to get a solid fix on him." He closed his eyes, rolling his shoulders.

I threw my hands up, stared at the ceiling for a second and then back to Duma, tapping my foot. "Fine, I get it. It's hard work. Now where the hell *is* he?"

Duma hung his head. "Laszlovara."

"Good, let's... wait..." The name sank in. "You mean the Coronini Commune? In Romania?" I couldn't help but cringe.

The slaughterhouses of the Chicago Stockyards during the late nineteenth century were a playground on a pleasant spring day compared to Coronini.

"Yeah," he replied.

Everyone in the room eyed us without saying a word. All eyes were wide except Aislin's; her face was scrunched in confusion.

I dropped my head in frustration. *Shit.*

CHAPTER 22

"**W**HAT'S THE BIG DEAL ABOUT Laszlovara?" Aislin asked, breaking the cemetery-like silence in the room.

"You will have to forgive her," Gracen replied. "She's young."

"It's an utter nightmare is what it is," Duma said, pushing himself to his feet to pace.

"I gathered as much by all of your reactions," Aislin said. "But that doesn't explain *why*."

"Vampires," I said without facing her. "Laszlovara is the region's historic name. Everyone knows it now as Coronini—a working commune that lies right on the banks of the Danube in Romania, right across the river from Serbia. And it's the home of the Liuntika Strigoi—the oldest and most powerful vampire coven in existence."

"Not to mention it's probably also Lilith's—the freakin' Mother of all Strigoi—refuge," Duma said.

"And there's that," I replied. "You're positive about the location?"

"Very," Duma said. "He hasn't moved significantly in the last hour. I checked several times to make *damn* sure."

Wonderful. I recalled my first foray into the area in the late ninth century, when I fought with the Magyars against the Bulgarians and Emperor Simeon I, mostly because Simeon made a pact with the vampires of the region to grant them protection and land within his realm. We won the first battle, but I barely escaped after I publicly killed a vampire envoy that had enthralled my commander. Unfortunately, in the battle that followed, the vampires pushed the Magyars back to what is now Csepel Island in Budapest, where King Arpad finally built a fortress to hold them back.

The vampires, rumored to be led by Lilith herself, eventually retreated south along the Danube to an area that became known as

Laszlovara. The early Hungarians fought many wars with these Strigoi over the area, which was famous for its gold and iron mines, and eventually even erected a stronghold there named after one of their greatest kings and warriors — and vampire killers — Saint Ladislaus. The provisional human outpost and their control over the area did not last. And we still had no human, or even nonhuman, allies in the area we could count on to help us find the Hanner Brid.

"Vampires are a human problem, not ours," Gracen said. "Besides, if that's where the Demon Fae went, then I say good riddance. They'll kill him the moment he trespasses on their land. They don't tolerate outsiders."

"Possibly," I replied. "I don't know how many vampires are there, but there are about two thousand human inhabitants living in that commune, and all of them — including the slave traders and smugglers that use the area as a base — are thralls working for and protecting the Strigoi living in the nearby caverns and mines. The thralls won't stand a chance against this guy."

Of all the creatures and beings I'd dealt with in my long life, I despised vampires the most. All of them — from the immortal Strigoi that live off human blood to the mortal Moroi that live off human energy — were parasites and perversions of humanity. And they all deserved to die. While other creatures and beings try to use humans or even twist us to their wills, vampires simply used us for food, and that I couldn't abide. *And I get to head into their capital city to chase an even bigger proctological nuisance. Yay!*

"You think they'll give us permission to search for this prick on their land?" I asked Duma, already knowing the answer.

"Not likely," he replied with a derisive snort. "We don't even have time to ask, and I can't even imagine trying to sneak into the place, either. No one steps foot on their land without their knowing it."

"So if this Half Breed is there, then they know it. And maybe they even allowed it." I didn't like the implications of that.

Duma stopped in his tracks, his face stern. "What? You think he's working for them?"

"Well, Athena mentioned that several smaller Strigoi covens have been attacked in recent days. It's possible. Depressing, but possible," I replied. "Why else would he go there? Like Gracen said, I don't care how good he is, there is no way he could attack them by himself and survive. And like you said, there's no way to even sneak into that place without them knowing. He could be doing wet work for them covertly while Lilith and her vampires remain under the radar. Her usual MO isn't subtle, but I wouldn't put it past her."

"Maybe he's trying to throw you off his trail. Or maybe this Demon Fae is going to attack them..." the half goblin replied.

"It's possible, but would *you* flee through Bouvet, much less attack the very Seat of the Unseelie Court, while *you* were being pursued?" I hoped my statement about the island stronghold of the Unseelie Court, the likely site of Queen Mab's throne, would make my point to a Fae.

Someone grunted, but no one said anything.

"Exactly. No one would be that crazy," I said turning to face Duma. "He's working with them. He's got to be."

"Speaking of Bouvet..." said a familiar female voice.

Everyone froze, staring past me. I suddenly got chills and an odd sense of déjà vu.

I spun around to see Belphoebe and three other cloaked figures standing inside the doorway. All armed with long swords, the cloaked beings were significantly larger than the huntress. Then the smallest of Gracen's entourage—the little black-skinned guy—stepped out from behind them. *And the hits just keep on coming.*

"Hi, Pheebs," I said.

"Did you really think I wouldn't find you?" she replied, glancing around the room rather than at me. She absently touched a chair then rubbed her fingers in disgust.

"To be honest, yeah, I was kinda hoping. At least long enough for me to find the sonofabitch that framed me," I replied.

"So are you going to go the easy way or the hard way?" She grinned wolfishly. "Please say hard. *Please.*"

"Oh, you have no idea how hard..." I dropped to one knee and drew both my Sig and Glock, aiming at the two henchmen closest to Belphoebe. I put two rounds into one's head, dropping him instantly, and at least three out of four rounds into the upper chest and head of the other. He stumbled to the side and fell across Gracen's little helper, who let out a sound somewhere between a whimper and a moan as they hit the floor.

I brought the guns to bear on the third cloaked figure while

Belphoebe was already diving to her left. In a single fluid motion, she rolled behind one of the structural supports and came up with her bow in hand. I fired three more times into the third cloaked figure, hitting him center mass. A familiar dull *thwap* accompanied each impact. *Body armor.* Nevertheless, the shots caused the figure to stagger.

A cold breeze built behind me, then Aislin whirled past me, blades flashing in a cloudy mist, straight toward Belphoebe. Before I could say anything, Belphoebe drew down on the half-cloud nymph and fired two arrows in the blink of an eye. Aislin deflected one of the arrows and sent it ricocheting into the far wall with a woody *thock*, but the other arrow hit home and knocked Aislin from her spin, dropping her in a tangled heap. Across the room, Tolfin roared and flew into a rage.

Shit. Aislin and the rest of the motley crew were merely trying to survive in a world where they didn't fit in, and I'd brought the Huntress from one of the most serious threats to their existence to their doorstep. If any of them died, it would be my fault. Except that little black-skinned guy.

Knives in hand, Duma shot past the last of the assailants at the door, leaving trails of yellow and green blood arcing behind. As Duma passed, the guard I'd shot got to his knees then toppled over, clutching his throat. Duma came to a sudden stop on one knee above Gracen's little snitch-henchman, one blade low and behind him. The blade above his head dripped thick black liquid. The inky-skinned lackey went still under the figure that had fallen on him, and a dark pool rapidly formed around him.

Back across the room, Tolfin thundered toward Belphoebe in a blind rage, a score of arrows protruding from his massive arms and shoulders. However, Belphoebe easily avoided the creature's ungainly lunge, and Tolfin flailed forward until he lost balance and went crashing into the far wall.

I tracked Belphoebe's movement with my guns, waiting for a clean shot, as she raced toward Gracen, who was now being held at knifepoint by the goblin-elf. Gracen's eyes were wide, and his face was tight with surprise and shock. I had both guns trained on Belphoebe when all the action came to an abrupt halt. She laughed as if she were genuinely enjoying herself.

"Stop where you are, traitorous scum, or your brethren die," the

Unseelie Huntress said to Duma, her eyes flashing briefly from me to somewhere behind me. I didn't budge—not that I intended to take my eyes off her for even a second. "You, too, Diomedes—both of you drop your weapons. All of them, or *he* dies."

I could feel myself sneer in response. Negotiations with psychopaths, especially psychopathic fae, rarely lead anywhere productive. Belphoebe was standing far enough away from Gracen that I wasn't concerned about hitting him if I fired at her. I knew Duma was also too accurate to miss a target in these tight quarters. And I was sure the half goblin would release Gracen the moment I took out Belphoebe.

I dropped the gun in my left hand as a distraction then dove to my left, tucked into a roll, and came up on one knee as I fired three times into Belphoebe's chest. I knew she was wearing armor, but I couldn't risk firing at her head and missing after my tricky maneuver. Killing her would cause me even greater problems. I had to go center mass and hope for the best.

The shots caught Belphoebe in her ribs under her right arm as she drew her bow. She faltered as she aimed at me, and the nocked arrow clattered to the ground. The force didn't penetrate her cuirass, but it did drive the air from her lungs, causing her to double over and stagger back. She fell to one knee right as a long-bladed knife struck the half goblin in his nose, causing his eyes to roll back in his head as he collapsed to the ground like a boned fish, emitting a raspy gurgle as he fell. Gracen remained stock-still, only his fingers trembled as a small puddle grew at his feet.

"Now that's just nasty." I picked up my other gun then walked toward Belphoebe.

With one arm wrapped around her chest, breathing in rapid, shallow gasps, she mumbled something that sounded like "cheater."

"Maybe, but at least you aren't dead." I popped her on the back of her head and neck with the butt of my gun hard enough to knock her out and hopefully leave a nasty bruise that would remain for longer than an hour.

"We should kill her now," Duma said from behind me. "You know that."

"It's the smart thing to do tactically, yes, but politically, it'd be the start of a shit storm of epic proportions and all but nail my coffin shut for these other deaths. Against my personal inclination, we'll tie her up and leave her here."

Duma glanced at the puddle at Gracen's feet and shook his head. "You know we can't leave her here with Gracen and the others injured like this," he said in a whisper. "Belphoebe will escape and kill anyone still around — especially this lot, which I will guarantee she would see as a mercy killing."

"Well, we certainly can't take her with us. And since his buddies showed her where this place is, they probably shouldn't stick around here anyway. Frankly, I'd burn the place down."

"I don't understand..." Gracen said stammering. "Burn it down?"

"Duma, check on Aislin and Tolfin," I said, motioning behind me with my head as I kicked Belphoebe's bow well out of her reach. "And, Gracen" — I clapped my hands to get his attention — "get me some rope."

I secured Belphoebe using some of my best mariner's knots for good measure. Even after taking extra time, I didn't expect her to remain tied up forever, but I hoped a few hours' head start would be more than enough for our *idiotic* next move.

Meanwhile, Duma made sure Aislin and Tolfin were okay. Aislin had taken the arrow to her midsection, roughly where a human's kidney would have been, but I had no idea what, if anything, it hit in her. She seemed okay enough, though she did pass out when Duma broke the shaft of the arrow and pulled it through.

Tolfin pulled the arrows from his body with little reaction. Once Aislin passed out, he carried her to the remains of the couch, laid her down gently, then sat at her side like an elephant-sized watchdog. I checked on them both then wrote Will "Geek" Elmsmore's contact information on a scrap of paper, which I gave to Tolfin. He took it clumsily in his massive hand, his small eyes watery as he eyed Aislin, and I patted him on his shoulder.

"You should get her out of here as soon as possible. Contact the person on that paper when you can," I said to him. "He'll help you, and I think you can help him, too. He's a computer genius, and he knows about our kind. I trust him."

I hoped that Geek could use Tolfin's skills somehow, maybe with codes or programming. As the current head of cybersecurity and the electronics expert for the Metis Foundation, if anyone could use and understand Tolfin's skills, it would be Geek.

The henchmen who had entered with Belphoebe were dressed like the guards I encountered on Poveglia, which I had assumed to be Dreaichbard. I had little doubt that Belphoebe had additional soldiers with her covering the area as backup, and we needed to get moving anyway. I stuck my tongue out at her bound form even though she was still unconscious. I didn't care if she couldn't see it; it made me feel better.

"What was that all about?" Duma asked me as he walked up.

"What was what?"

"Never mind," he said, lolling his head. "Tell me what you need for this *invasion* of Coronini, and I'll get it for you by the time we arrive. Of course, I'll have to use your phone to make the call."

"My phone... aw crap!" I hadn't switched my phone on since we left Atlanta.

I fumbled through the pockets on my vest to find it and switched it on. *Twenty-three messages.*

They started with Sarah telling me she may have found something useful then rapidly progressed into panicked messages about being unable to reach me. It was nice to have someone worry about me, but given what I did for a living, that could preoccupy a professional team on a daily basis. Putting Sarah through that wasn't fair of me. I sighed then handed the phone to Duma.

"Make your call," I said, shaking my head.

"What's up?"

"Nothing. Sarah's been trying to contact me. She's worried. I'll call her as soon as I can, but we don't have much time here. Pheebs has to have backup waiting for us outside. They won't wait long before coming in to check."

"Oooh, Sarah's worried, is she?" He wiggled his hips to mock me.

"Shut up and focus, dammit. We'll need more ammo, a couple of LAR-5 or -6s, or even LAV-7 rebreathers and dry suits. Oh, and a fast boat to meet us someplace like Kostolac across the river in Serbia. And a good map of Coronini, too."

"Man, that's the Danube you want to swim in. It's cold and, well, yuck." Duma stuck out his tongue, retching.

"I'm well aware." Sarah's many panicked messages had left me in no mood to jockey with him. "Just do it. We got a little time once we get there, though. No way in hell I'm putting a foot on that land at night. No way, no how."

"Whatever..." He sighed. "Day or night, you know we're probably going to end up dying there."

"What about me? What should I do?" Gracen asked in a shaky voice.

"I'm really sorry about destroying your place, but I have no idea," I said, making sure all my gear was properly stowed in my vest. "Duma and I will leave first and draw any of Belphoebe's men with us, so you guys should be clear. But I'd be gone before *she* wakes up and gets herself free."

"But this place was all I had," Gracen whined. "Duma, you know I don't have anything else. I wasn't raised like you and Ab—"

"Dammit, Gracen," Duma said, his brow deeply furrowed. "Listen, get somewhere and lay low. I'll contact you as soon as I can. That's the best I can do. For now."

Duma cocked up one corner of his mouth in a partial grimace as he began to dial the phone. "Family..." he said, cocking his head.

CHAPTER 23

O NCE DUMA MADE HIS CALLS, we left. I would have been disappointed if Belphoebe didn't have additional thugs waiting for us outside. I would love to have been disappointed. The first pair of her Dreaichbard Goon Squad were standing across the street inside the shadow line of an alleyway.

I signaled my observation to Duma, and he reached for one of his kukri knives then eyed me quizzically with his eyebrows raised. I didn't stop him. Being armed was definitely a good idea. There were undoubtedly more that we didn't see. Time was critical, though, and a prolonged battle would only slow us down.

I grabbed Duma's shoulder and pointed up then southeast, toward our exit in the park. Duma tracked my gesture then nodded that he understood I intended to travel in as straight a line as possible to the Ways. I tapped Duma's other kukri, still in its sheath. He pulled it with a wicked grin. The boy enjoyed violence a little too much.

Waiting for the goons to turn, I jumped up to grab the edge of the two-story warehouse at the roofline then pulled myself up the rest of the way, rolling onto the roof. As I began lizard-crawling, Duma landed next to me in a crouch without the slightest crunch of gravel on the hot tar. We crept across the roof, moving toward the park and our exit.

At the edge of the building, I pulled myself up to get a view of the direction we wanted to go. Our path was clear. Part of me wanted to believe that it could be true, but the more pragmatic part quickly kicked those happy notions aside. I had to expect the worst—that was how I'd managed to stay alive for so long.

Lowering myself below the knee wall, I signaled to Duma to wait five seconds before following me to the next building, about thirty feet across an alley. I crawled back to the center of the roof, got into a runner's starting crouch, then took off. I tucked into a roll as I landed, trying to maintain as low a profile as possible. While I'm sure the jump would have earned me nines and above from all but the Russian judge, my landing was loud and ungainly. Duma followed with a maneuver that would have made Nadia Comaneci jealous.

"Showoff," I muttered, getting to my feet.

Duma's grin quickly became a scowl as he took off past me, knives in hand. I reached for my swords.

On the opposite end of the roof, the last of four cloaked figures landed in an easy manner similar to Duma's. Like the ones who accompanied Belphoebe into Gracen's building, these soldiers were dressed in black hide greatcoats that covered them from shoulder to ankle with a high collar that covered the lower part of their faces. They were all bald. Two of them were armed with massive two-handed greatswords, and one carried a poleaxe. The last pulled out an enormous recurved hunting bow.

Dreaichbard were the Unseelie's most elite soldiers, chosen from the strongest of the Sidhe families and trained from the day they were old enough to carry a weapon. In all my years, I'd never fought one. *Of course, I shot the ones back at Gracen's place.*

In the split second it took Duma to close the distance, the lead Dreaichbard took several steps forward and braced himself on one knee to intercept Duma, holding the seven-foot-long two-handed sword low to the ground. The large sword appeared unwieldy, but in the hands of someone skilled with such a weapon, it could be devastating. The guy quivered like a spring ready to be released.

Duma's blur made a sharp turn then launch over the kneeling swordsman before he could react. Using the kneeling guard's shoulder as a springboard, he propelled himself straight at the bowman at the back of the group. Duma hit the archer with both kukri knives in the upper chest. The head of the swordsman Duma had vaulted over fell at a funny angle, then his body toppled limply, the giant sword clanging to the tar-covered roof. The Peri pulled the knives free of the archer's chest, sending the bowman backward over the roof's edge. Wearing a wild, predatory expression, Duma then attacked the remaining two guards from behind.

The speed and ferocity of Duma's attack left the two remaining Dreaichbard in shock that quickly devolved into panic as they both tried to turn to face him, disregarding me completely. *Bad idea.* Trying not to take it personally, I closed the distance as fast as I could. I severed the pikeman's extended arms with a downward slash of my sword and spun to my right, bringing the sword in my right hand around in a full arc, removing his head easily, continuing to advance as I spun.

The final guard regained enough composure to take up a defensive stance, keeping Duma to his left and me to his right. In true warrior fashion, the swordsman took the offensive, even though he was outnumbered.

The Sidhe, easily seven feet tall, moved with a grace and speed that belied his size. He lunged at me, using the sword's impressive reach to his advantage. I easily parried the straightforward attack, but the Dreaichbard deftly turned the lengthy blade's momentum back to his open left flank to fend off Duma. The Peri barely managed to jump back far enough to avoid being cut in half by the lengthy blade.

Given the guard's height and the reach of his blade, he kept us easily eight feet away. I feigned an advance, attempting to draw the swordsman's attention, while Duma stepped back and threw one of his kukris. The Dreaichbard shifted attention so quickly, it was as if he knew what was going to happen. He dropped the point of his sword, tucked into a roll, and came up directly between Duma and me, swinging the long sword in a massive arc.

I followed his attack and blocked the swing with one sword while I brought the other down on his blade, snapping it cleanly. From behind, Duma closed in and plunged his remaining knife into the Sidhe's back, causing him to fall to his knees and drop the broken sword. Duma growled something in the Dreaichbard's ear through clenched teeth, then he jerked the knife free and kicked the guard to the ground.

"Do I need to ask what that was about?" I asked, pretty sure it had something to do with grudges long past.

Duma stooped to pick up the knife he'd thrown. "Let's go."

The rest of our trip went quickly until we hit the outskirts of the park we'd come through. It was dark, and because of the gate to the Ways' presence, Belphoebe's entourage would have the entire park covered. We managed to sneak past all but the pair left to guard the portal through the Ways itself then dispatched them as quietly as we could.

We traveled through the Ways to someplace cold and wet, like the rainforests of the Pacific Northwest, first, followed by a small outpost-like town that was colder than the ninth level of hell. As an exciting change of pace, Duma walked us into an unbelievably arid area that was hotter than the sun before we finally exited in a wooded area near a small farming town Duma said was Dubravica, Serbia.

Duma had arranged for our transport to meet us at the mouth of the Great Morava River near its confluence with the Danube, about a half mile from our landing. From there, we would cover the remaining sixty miles or so to Coronini by water while Duma used a map of the town to locate the Hanner Brid within it. I was hopeful the blood we had was still useful for tracking him, because there was no way we would have enough time to wander around the village checking door to door for him. That would be reserved for Plan Z.

Plan A was to enter the river upstream of the commune, go ashore at first light, and get to the Hanner Brid as quickly as possible. If all went well, we would get the guy and make it back to our pick-up boat before the vampires could get to us. Our exfil plan was a bit more loosey-goosey, mostly because neither of us expected to actually survive to that point.

The only thing I wanted to do before we left for Coronini was call Sarah back. She answered before the first ring finished.

"Where the hell are you?" she asked, her voice a mixture of fear and anger.

"You're better off not knowing. I'm still with Duma, and we're both okay."

"Fine. But I'm still seeing bulletins with your description on them, along with reports that you're working with Libyan extremists and even Al Qaeda," she said. "The latest said you were in Seville, Spain, but that you were on the run, traveling with another known terrorist. I'm starting to get questions from superiors about why I'm keeping up with those terrorist bulletins at all, and an hour ago, one of our ballistics experts asked me what case those bullets you gave me were connected to. To make matters worse, I can't ever get in touch with you. So I'm starting to wonder why I'm even putting my career on the line to help at all."

"Sarah, trust me when I say things are complicated," I replied.

"Things are always complicated with you, but you don't even have the decency to apologize or thank me. Our personal stuff aside, my career is on the line here, Steve."

After a long, silent pause, I said, "I'm sorry. For the way I've ignored you, for endangering your job. Sorry I keep dragging you into my world. But right now, I'm neck deep in a pile of shit. We've found the guy, Sarah, but he's slippery. And he's fae."

"Seriously? He's a fairy?"

"Well, half fae and half demon," I said. "Technically, he's a cambion."

"You mean like Merlin?" she said, as if it were common terminology.

"How do you know that?" I asked, impressed. It was little wonder I liked her, even if I had no idea how to show her. I smiled.

"I told you that day at your house before we went after Medea that I was a geek as a kid. I loved all the stuff I used to think was just stories and mythology."

"Okay, then yeah, like Merlin, only half Blud Fae and half Succubus and with training similar to mine," I said. "He has no issues with using a gun, and according to Duma, he's also a fae boogeyman of sorts, believed to be a spook-story. Apparently, he's been creating mayhem among the Paran community as well as the human one for eons." The tension in my shoulders and neck relaxed as the conversation steered toward more comfortable subjects.

"Well, I can't be positive, but I think I've found a few incidents that haven't been linked together yet but might also be this guy. Given what you told me about weapons and previous attacks, I think he might be responsible for the deaths of people or, well, *not* people, in Saarbrucken and Bremen in Germany, Prague, Vilnius in Russia, outside Yellowknife and Southern Louisiana near Breaux Bridge. Some of the remains *appear* human, but the DNA gathered from the scenes all came back inconclusive. Part of the reason these attacks haven't been linked to anything is that it's assumed that the evidence is contaminated."

"How recent are these attacks?" I asked.

"All within the last few months." I could hear her flipping pages as she talked. "None older than July of this year."

"That's probably him. He's hit werewolf clans, vampire covens, various human splinter groups of wizards and witches, you name it. Not to mention somehow having a hand in the destabilization of Libya. Probably Egypt, too."

"Interesting you mention those places, because the CIA has reports of a single highly skilled assassin working with both of those governments in recent months." She flipped more papers. "From what I can tell, lots of assassinations, bombings, and other terrorist activities that can't be solved or attributed to others tend to get thrown into this one file. The one connection is the precision and skill with which the jobs were carried out. One theory is that it's one man with a base of operations somewhere in Eastern Europe."

"That fits with what we know, as well." I stared out into the trees while I rubbed at my forehead. "Anything about those bullets?"

"The .22LR is worthless." She shuffled papers again. "Too common to be useful. And the .338 was likely homemade. But it had to be by someone who really knows his stuff. Our guys are still fawning over its properties. The alloy created for it is unique. That's why they want to know where I got it. The only thing I can tell you with any certainty is that some of the metal used to form it carries isotope signatures from the Banat region of Western Romania. Specifically, in mines from an area near—"

"Coronini," I said.

"How'd you... is that where you are now?"

"Like I said, better you not know." I closed my eyes at the realization that the Hanner Brid had clearly been operating in conjunction with Lilith for some time, but to what end?

"Hey, kissy-kissy later, D. We gotta go meet the boat," Duma said, more loudly than he needed to from right next to me.

"Was that Duma?" Sarah asked.

I could feel myself blushing. "Ah, you heard that?" I kicked at the ground then winced.

"Yeah." She exhaled heavily. "Is there any way I can help? I mean really help? Tell me where you are, and I'll be there as soon as possible." Her tone was flat and serious.

I knew she would be, and frankly, she would probably be a big help in Coronini, but there was no way I was dragging her into a hornet's nest. It was going to be hard enough getting into that place, and while I didn't need to watch out for her, I wouldn't be able to help myself — and that would cause more trouble than her skills could offset, especially in Vampire Central. Besides, I had already caused her enough trouble.

"No, it's better if you stay outta this. Trust me, please. I'll get back in touch in a few days on a new number." I tried to sound as though I believed it. "We've talked too long on this one."

"Okay, but please be safe." Her voice softened ever so faintly.

"I'll do my best. And Duma's got my back."

CHAPTER 24

DUMA AND I HIGHTAILED IT a few hundred yards through the woods to the confluence of the Great Morava River and the Danube, then we waited inside the tree line along the banks. I could smell the wood smoke from nearby chimneys and see rooftops off in the distance both north and south of us. The area was largely rural with a low population and favored by smugglers as a result.

Twenty minutes later, a sleek forty-foot-long boat pulled into the mouth of the narrow tributary and beached along its eastern shore less than a hundred yards down from where we were hiding. A boat as long as this one with the engines to push it should have been easy to hear as it approached, but it barely produced a sound beyond a low thrumming vibration.

Duma headed toward the vessel without hesitation, but on instinct, I followed at a distance. Duma was entirely too laid-back about the whole idea of meeting a boat on a river that was home to smugglers of all kinds, driven by who knew who, en route to one of the largest and oldest vampire dens on Earth. He hopped on the boat and smiled at the scruffy, mustachioed captain, who simply nodded back. The skipper, wearing a heavy peacoat with a wool watch cap on his head to fight the chill of the river, was definitely human and alone on the boat. Grudgingly, I jumped aboard and quickly bowed my head. The small, thin man, at least half a foot shorter than me, acknowledged my presence with little more than a sideways glare.

The boat had the lines of an open-ocean racer, but once on board, I could see that the deck was entirely open and dotted with metal tie-down rings and only a small galley-way forward. This boat was clearly designed for smuggling, but my purview didn't include enforcing human laws.

"*Aveti hartile?*" Duma said to the captain. I had no idea what he'd said.

I felt like I was in the Eastern European version of *Key Largo.*

He reached into a cabinet under his seat and tossed Duma a small waterproof duffle. "*Restul este mai jos,*" he replied in the same guttural language Duma used.

Has to be either Romanian or Hungarian.

"He says the rest is down below." Duma pointed to the forward galley-way then began withdrawing maps from the duffle.

I cautiously poked my head into the small dark space, half expecting to find the Hanner Brid staring back at me. I glanced back at the little man, who noted my apprehension and flipped a switch on the console in front of him. A red light snapped on inside the galley-way, illuminating the small storage area in the bow. I went below and took my time checking the gear. Everything, down to the LAR-5 UBA rebreathers, was in order. Even the dry suits were brand-new. I was two percent more comfortable with my insane plan.

Satisfied with the gear, I emerged to find Duma and the captain leaning over a chart and chatting in the same guttural language. Duma probably didn't even know he was speaking a different language. After a moment, he waved me over.

"Gheorghe says the closest safe insertion point is here." He pointed at a map of the river lit by a small flashlight with a red filter.

"*Da,*" Gheorghe said, nodding vigorously.

The spot put us about two miles upriver from Coronini, under a bridge. Gheorghe spoke in his native language, glancing back and forth from Duma to the map, indicating several locations.

"He says that the current runs swiftly in the center, but it's shallow and calmer along the edges through here. We can come ashore here, where there's a small drainage canal," Duma said, translating and pointing slightly downstream from the bridge. "He says it runs through a dense stand of trees that spread right to the shore. He'll pick us up here, on the shore at Golubac Fortress. If we're not there by nightfall, though, we're on our own."

"I don't blame him," I said. Since Golubac, the remnants of a medieval fortress, was across the river and downstream of Coronini, it made sense, assuming we survived. I checked my watch. "Let's get going."

Sunrise was about four hours away. After we got underway, the boat had to be running nearly seventy miles an hour, and I heard little more than the wind whipping past my ears. *Smugglers and that mother of all invention: necessity.*

Meanwhile, Duma hunkered down on the foredeck in the lee of the bow, scrying to locate the Demon Fae. Every few minutes, he shifted, rolled his shoulders and head, then appeared to restart. Maybe it was the rocking boat, the deteriorating blood, or both, but things were not going well. I left him to it.

After about twenty minutes in isolation on the foredeck, Duma finally came over to me with the satellite image he was using as a map, his face drawn and dark rings under his eyes. A circle marked one building in a field at the edge of town. It was only about half a mile from our insertion point, but according to the image, we would have to cross an open field next to a major thoroughfare for most of that distance.

He leaned heavily against the gunwale next to me. "You know we should have killed Belphoebe back there," Duma shouted over the wind. "She's a real balloon knot, and *if* we survive *this*, she's gonna end up biting us in the ass again."

"What the hell is a balloon knot?"

"An asshole," he replied. "Tie a knot in a balloon. When you look at the end, it's all puckered, like an—"

"I get it." I held up my hand. "Couldn't you just say asshole?"

"It's more colorful." He smiled, despite the weariness still evident in his face.

"You're probably right."

"Of course I am. It's hipper, too," he said.

"No, I mean about Belphoebe. Hopefully, we can wrap this whole thing up here and do it fast."

"That's the one quirky thing about you that I've never understood, D," Duma said. "You have the capacity for great violence. I've seen you kill scores of beings, humans among them, without batting an eyelash. And yet, there are so many times you choose to avoid it, even when it may be prudent. Mark my words, she will come back to bite you in the ass—and not in a good way, my friend."

I glanced at him then stared at the deck. "Duma, I choose to look past your predilection for bloodshed because you are my friend and because you are not human and I know you see the world in a different way. That's okay. But you have always known that I don't fight for myself. I fight for my kind to be able to exist in a world where you, as bloodthirsty as you can be, aren't even close to the most dangerous thing out there. Compared to most Parans and especially the Old Ones, humans are easy prey. As a species, we are weak, but I am not. So I fight—and I kill. I would gladly put down the weapons and armor and walk away if the conflicts ended today. Killing and violence have to serve a purpose, not *be* the purpose. And maybe you're right about Belphoebe—you probably are—but maybe this time she'll see sparing her life as compassion rather than weakness. Or maybe, given her limited range of emotions, she'll simply see it as the prudent thing and realize that death only leads to more death, not to peace. I've been a soldier for over three thousand years, and the one thing I can tell you for sure is that the only ones who see the end of war are the ones who die. I may be good at it, but I don't seek it out."

"Nice speech." Duma waggled his head back and forth as if weighing what I'd said. "But you don't need to seek it out. It always seems to know exactly where you are. And I will always be a firm believer that the best deterrent is a brutal show of force. Something you humans have taken to heart."

"Yeah, well, the day Parans and Old Ones back off and decide to let us humans kill ourselves off without their interference, I will retire." I clapped him on the shoulder. "And I promise you, I will not miss it one bit."

"The hell you won't."

Duma smiled at me, and we both walked to the galley-way. We sat silently, half-dressed in our dry suits so we didn't overheat as we waited for the captain to tell us it was okay to slide into the water.

"How did you get this stuff so fast?" I asked. "I mean, this stuff is top-shelf. Even these old LAR-5s are pristine."

"Connections, my friend. It's all about who you know in this part of the world. I've worked with this guy before, lots of times." He gestured toward the captain. "Best in the area. But he ain't cheap. This little boat ride is gonna cost you..." he said, rubbing his fingers and thumb together.

"Are you kidding me? How much?"

Standing at the helm, the captain hooked his thumb overboard and slowed the boat until he was merely holding ground against the rapid current.

"Now ain't the time, D. Cappy says time for froggies to get wet."

I suited up and walked over to the starboard corner, where I put on my fins and rolled backward off the cap rail. Swimming hard against the current, I tried to locate Duma in the dark, cold water. I flashed a red-filtered light at the captain to let him know I was okay, and Duma did likewise. We ducked underwater as the boat pulled away.

The current swept us quickly downstream as we made our way to the calmer shallow flats along the banks. Once we cleared the swifter water, we continued slowly and deliberately, working our way shallower as we neared the ditch. I kept an eye on the GPS, remembering when I had to navigate by compass. By the time the dull green screen of the GPS indicated we were a hundred yards from our target, we were in less than three feet of water. In the ditch, I slowly rose from the water until I could see. Nothing moved as the first rays of the sun rose over the hills in front of us. The small farming village about a half mile to our right was quiet. Behind me, across the black surface of the Danube, I could see the shadow of the ruins of Golubac almost directly across the river from the village. Duma surfaced next to me, and I raised my hand out of the water to motion for him to continue forward.

We came ashore silently then took cover in the stand of trees marked on the satellite image. After stashing our diving gear, we cut off our dry suits. I hated to ruin them, but they were too difficult to remove quickly and even harder to put back on in a hurry.

Once we were set, we waded farther up the length of the drainage canal within the stand of trees then paused to check the satellite image of the town. Right in front of us, the DN57 Highway ran roughly parallel to the shore, leading straight through town. It was entirely deserted, and not because it was oh-dark-thirty. *No one comes through this town unless they absolutely have no other choice.*

Across an open field sat the structure in which Duma said the Demon Fae was hiding. If we headed straight from our current position, we would pass too close to the houses, and every human in the village worked for the Liuntika Strigoi in some capacity. Our only safe option was to head beyond the houses and well into the fields for an additional half mile or so before heading toward our target.

171

We covered the open ground cautiously, but within twenty minutes, the first streaks of sunlight illuminated the wooden roof of our target—a large, rustic, well-used two-story barn—dead ahead. The structure had no windows at all.

Roosters from the large farmhouse near the barn began crowing at the dawn, and the soft, indistinct noises of people beginning to start their day spread from the buildings to our right. As we approached our target, Duma veered to the left while I circled around the barn to the right. I kept my gun ready to fire upon contact.

I crept painfully slowly down the building's flank, examining every hole, crack, and crevasse I ran across. All I could see inside was a large, open space. At the front of the barn, I quickly popped my head around and saw Duma kneeling at the opposite corner, waiting for me. He shook his head then waved his hand in front of his face, wrinkling his nose as if he smelled something rank.

Along the front of the structure, a large sliding door took up most of the wall. A normal-sized door stood between it and Duma. The doors had no windows and no visible locks. In fact, the handle on the door was a dowel rod attached to a piece of rope that ran through a hole in the wood. There were no other means of entry.

We met at the smaller door, and I held up three fingers. I ticked them off, then he jerked the door open without so much as a squeak. The fact that the door had opened without a sound was very odd.

From my kneeling position, I peeked around the corner. *Nothing.* I stepped inside, and instantly, the overwhelming sickly sweet metallic smell of blood assaulted my nose. I swept the gun from left to right as I scanned the large, open space for movement and potential targets. The entire structure, including the stall, was devoid of any sign of animals, hay, or even tools. Duma stepped inside and closed the door, holding the back of one hand under his nose. His kukri knives were out and ready. Blood, at least several days old, stained the wooden floor.

"Vampires…" Duma said quietly, his face distorted in disgust.

A wooden walkway, ten feet off the ground, circled the entire building, leading to a substantial hayloft. A collection of bloody chains and shackles hung to the right of the barn door, and a rail-and-pulley system ran along the rafters down the center of the building. I scowled at Duma for talking then motioned for him to jump to the floor above.

We could both make the jump, but he would do so far more quietly than I could. He sprang upward and landed on the wooden walkway without as much as a creak.

After a moment, Duma peered down at me and shook his head, indicating he observed nothing up top. Then he pointed at a metal grate in the center of the first floor. Cautiously, I crept to the edge of the grate, and Duma jumped down, landing near me in a low crouch without even an audible exhale on impact. I shook my head while he grinned.

I peeked down. The inside was completely dark, but the rancid odor emanating from it was almost overwhelming. I jerked back, jamming a hand under my nose.

If Duma tracked the Hanner Brid to this location and he was wildcatting ammunition using materials from the area, then he had to be working alongside the vampires. Even if he wasn't employed by them, he could be a guest. I scrunched up my face, disgusted by our only option. Expressionless, Duma pointed down at the grate. It was our only path.

"Let's make sure we give this place a solid once-over before we head down," I whispered.

Nodding, he jumped back up to the walkway.

The sunlight filtering through the cracks between the barn's wooden slats offered a little comfort, even though the interior remained mostly dank and dark. Unfortunately, while sunlight wouldn't kill the vampires like it did in the movies, it could hurt them, so they should all have taken cover already. Since the barn appeared largely unused recently, I wasn't worried about townsfolk showing up, either.

I circled clockwise around the space, checking the stalls. In the last stall, I found a scrap of bloody cloth and a necklace with a heart-shaped pendant. Inside the pendant was a tiny photo of a light-haired young man and a red-haired woman. For some reason, I stuffed the necklace into my pocket. I continued around the rest of the space but found nothing at all. Duma hopped down next to me and shook his head. We both stared at the heavy grate, and my stomach instantly soured.

CHAPTER 25

STANDING OVER THE GRATE, BREATHING through my mouth — which didn't help — I contemplated using the overhead pulley system to lift the heavy metal grid. Worried it might take too long and make too much noise, I grabbed the grate, jerked it loose, and laid it aside. It wasn't as heavy as I'd expected, but its three-foot diameter made it awkward to lift.

We did a quick roshambo for the honor of being first down the hellhole. I threw rock, and Duma threw scissors. I pumped my fist in victory, and Duma flipped me off. He rubbed at the back of his neck, glanced at me, then dropped down the hole. A moment later, he flashed the filtered red light up at me to let me know it was clear for me to follow. *Yippee.*

The drop was only about fifteen feet, and the soft ground below made for an easy landing. I snapped on my light to get my bearings, but the stench of rot and offal overwhelmed me to the point of disorientation. Duma grabbed my shoulder, shined his light in my face, then slapped me lightly, which finally roused my attention. I took a second to clear my head as Duma pointed his light in front of us, revealing a large tunnel. I flashed my red-tinted light over the ground, which was muddy but solid. The tunnel ahead resembled a mineshaft, complete with wooden support beams. I had no idea how long I would be able to maintain effectiveness in the quagmire, but we needed to work fast anyway.

Still feeling light-headed, I decided that anything we ran into was going to be bad, so I raised my gun to an extended combat position, ready to fire at anything that popped up. I snapped my light into a mount on the gun, took point, and began sneaking down the passage. Frankly, the red light made everything that much more unnerving, but it was the most efficient color to maintain night vision and remain covert. All I could hear was my own breathing and the occasional water drip.

After an agonizing five minutes, the tunnel stopped at a T-junction. I applied all my years of training and my considerable skill to determine which way we should take. Finally, I chose to use Gandalf's logic: we went left because the air smelled slightly less foul in that direction. I figured that the Half Breed would be as overwhelmed by the smell as we were.

With my first step to the left, a noise that sounded like a whimper came from down the tunnel to the right. *Crap.*

I stopped for a second to convince myself it was the right decision, trap or not, then waved my hand at Duma in a chopping motion back down to the right. He fell in behind me, knives ready. We made it about ten feet before the whimper echoed down the tunnel again, definitely coming from somewhere right in front of us. We eventually came to a passageway leading off to our left, where the air was rife with the smell of fresh blood.

I poked my head around the corner just enough to see that it was some sort of cell with metal bars stretched across the opening. I signaled to Duma that he should keep watch, then I snuck into the doorway, which offered enough space between the cage-like door and the main passageway for me to stand unseen. I shined the red light around the tiny cell, revealing a woman curled up in a ball next to a prone figure with its arms and legs twisted at odd angles, covered by a dark, shiny substance I assumed to be blood.

"Psst, hey," I whispered hoarsely, trying to get the woman's attention without waking up every vampire in the hole. Even if she didn't speak English, I expected her at least to acknowledge me, but she didn't.

"Hey, miss, are you okay?" I asked as loudly as I dared. Still nothing. She was either in shock, injured, or both. Or maybe deaf.

I examined the crude locking mechanism on the door. It was old and simple. Hell, it probably took one of those big old-fashioned keys with the long shaft. I sucked at picking locks, so I pulled one sword free and placed the tip against the rusted metal where it met the stone wall, roughly where I assumed the bolt engaged the strike plate. As quietly as possible, I shoved as hard and fast as I could, forcing the blade through the ancient metal with a slight screech. I froze and winced as the door swung open a fraction.

Opening the door quietly the rest of the way proved impossible. Rather than prolong the metallic screeching, which would likely make fingernails on a chalkboard sound pleasant by comparison, I simply shouldered it, ramming the door fully open. Thankfully, the resultant thud was considerably quieter. The woman never reacted.

I entered the cell and grabbed her shoulder to turn her. Doing so took considerable effort—far more than I'd expected for such a frail woman. She suddenly spun with a hiss, revealing longer, sharper teeth than she should have had, in a mouth far too wide. Up close, her skin was blotchy and sickly, as if stretched far too tightly across her skull, and clumps of her greasy hair was missing. She glared at me with milky, dead eyes and hissed again.

A lesser man would have peed his pants. Given that I was tough and had seen things that would give a devil nightmares, I snatched my hand away and hopped back. She flung herself over the body of the dead man, sobbing and mumbling incoherently. She was in the initial stages of becoming a Strigoi.

It was hard to repress the knowledge of what would happen to her. First, the parasites would infect her, then her body would begin changing, going through a physiological metamorphosis. Most of her organs and tissues would die, and others would transform completely to store blood. Teeth would break and appear to lengthen as her gums receded, her jaw would distend, and all the living tissue would begin to decay. Her hands would become clawlike as the body lost its natural fluids, making the nails look like talons. Her skin would lose its suppleness and at first become greasy, but then it would turn leathery as it dried out and would lose its ability to protect itself from sunlight. While not blind, her eyes would become nearly useless, and she would rely mostly on her sense of smell and taste like a cat or dog.

What was left would resemble a bloated corpse stuck in a constant state of decay, kept alive only through ingesting and storing fresh human blood. Along the way, some aspect of the prion-like infection would cause her bones to become denser and her rangy muscles to increase greatly in strength. The infection would warp her joints, as well, making normal human-type movement nearly impossible, until she became powerful. She might end up moving like a lizard or a monkey walking upright, or maybe even become partially lame, losing the use of one or more limbs altogether. I recalled the first time I witnessed the process, finding a comrade in a similar stage during the vampire wars while fighting with the Magyars against Simeon in 896, not far from our location. His body had become so twisted that he could only move like a crab with his limbs splayed out to his sides.

"Hey, D, come on. We gotta go," Duma whispered from outside the cell as the woman continued to sob over the corpse.

Anger welled up inside me as I thought about her transformation. The first feeding would be the worst: ravenous, sloppy, and merciless. Until the first feeding, she would retain her faculties, and she could fight it or give in willingly. Those who fight eventually succumb to the primal urge to feed, breaking the mind in the process, leaving a creature driven solely by instinct. Those who feed willingly somehow maintain a semblance of their sanity. Either way, nothing is left of the person who was, except a twisted visage that bears a superficial resemblance. Twelve hundred years ago, I locked my friend up on Csepel Island with the intention of protecting and hopefully saving him by not allowing him to feed. I unknowingly changed him into a mindless monster that I was forced to kill. The process took weeks, and the memory made me shiver.

The woman was gone—her mind was shattered, and she was well on her way to full-fledged vampirism. I did the most merciful thing I could and removed her head. The body flailed on the stone floor, spraying blood as it writhed until I pinned her to the ground with a sword through her back. Her severed head came to rest next to the dead man's broken body, and despite the anguish and terror frozen on his face and the monstrousness that ravaged the woman's, they were familiar. *The locket I found upstairs. This was them.*

I pulled the sword free from the now-quiet body and headed out. The creatures had likely infected her and placed her in the cell with the man as her first feed. She may have resisted for days while the man, probably desperate to save them both, ultimately died gruesomely at her hands.

I'd burn them all if I could.

I dropped the locket next to them and emerged, shaking my head in disgust as I returned my sword to its sheath on my back. I left the cell and continued down the path we'd chosen initially. Duma fell in silently behind me, predictably not the least bit inquisitive about what I'd found. I pulled the SCAR back to an extended combat position and crept slowly down the tunnel.

The farther we traveled down the passage, the clearer the air became, driven by a light, fresh breeze that filled the tunnel. The air wasn't clean, but rather a lot less foul and stale. Along with the idea of what happened to that poor couple, the air focused my drive to a laser-like intensity. We continued for several dozen yards before I finally noticed that the passageway lacked support beams. While the walls were still rough-hewn, they were cleaner and more refined. The floor was smoother, level, and less muddy, too.

After about a hundred yards, the tunnel made an abrupt right turn, where an elaborate, heavy wooden door was set in the wall at the corner. And it was ajar.

Duma grabbed my shoulder, stopping me, then pushed past me to approach the door. He sniffed the air like a dog then placed a few fingers on the door and shoved. The door swung open silently, revealing a small room partially lit by a smoldering fire in a container that resembled a big gumbo pot in the corner.

I followed Duma in, turning around to make sure our six was clear. No one was present, but someone had been maybe moments ago. The glowing embers gave off enough illumination that I could tell the room was comfortably furnished, with a narrow bed along one wall and a wooden table and chairs along another. Everything from axes and swords to modern rifles and explosives hung on the walls, covering every square inch of space, sitting in racks and on shelves. A heavily modified sniper rifle caught my eye. Next to it, on a shelf, were a few dozen racks of wildcatted .338 Lapua Magnum rounds, along with several metal ingots, smelting tools, scales, and a press to make them. *This space was definitely used by the Hanner Brid.*

I continued to explore the room, but when I got to the table, I stopped dead. The entire surface was covered with maps, photos, schematics, and design plans for buildings, trains, cars, equipment— all kinds of things. Some of the photos were of people, and most of those had been dog-eared.

I quickly began sorting through them and found an incredibly detailed geological survey and satellite photos of Kholat Syakhl in Russia, maps of Vanuatu, a thermal satellite image of Mount Gharat, and even a schedule of movements of several Third Order members of the Hermetic Order of the Golden Dawn. Future dates and times were written on detailed maps of the railroad system in North Korea, as well as schematics for a special train. Paperclips held a series of maps and photos of Sirte and a few other cities in Libya to a list of names. A handful were circled. I also found intricate blueprints of the Tishreen Palace in Syria showing underground passages leading into the structure.

"D," Duma whispered behind me. He was standing next to the giant pot filled with burning embers, holding up a charred piece of partially melted duct tape—likely the stuff used by the Hanner Brid to bind his wounds back in Libya. Reaching for the duct tape, I sensed another presence, then out of the corner of my eye, I glimpsed something long and skinny emerge through the barely open doorway: the barrel of a gun. I heard two *tinks* then felt a light impact to my rib cage. The barrel began to shift toward Duma, and I lurched, taking another shot cleanly to the back while another other went through the deltoid of my left shoulder. I crashed into Duma, knocking him down, but Duma's speed and reflexes allowed him to catch me so that we didn't end up on the ground in a heap.

The blow to my shoulder, while painful, wasn't that bad, but by the time I gathered my wits and got moving, all hell was breaking loose down the tunnel. Screeching, shrieking, and slapping on the stone walls echoed throughout the shaft system, followed by the raucous and primordial sound of the entire mine coming to life.

"After him!" I screamed at Duma. "That was the prick!"

He bolted into the darkness and back up the passage we'd come down, but I stopped long enough to grab a few things off the table, along with the modified sniper rifle and a handful of the special .338 Lapua Magnum shells. I shoved the shells into one of the pockets on my vest, jammed the papers under the vest, then swung the rifle over my shoulder and took off after Duma. The burning pain in my shoulder helped me focus as I ran.

I scrambled down the passageway as fast as I could go, pulling my swords. A cacophony of gruff noises grew rapidly from every direction as I approached the path that led out of the catacombs. I couldn't see Duma, but I knew I wouldn't hear him or even catch up to him unless something happened.

Frantic, I practically ran past the entryway, but managed to make the sudden turn. Smashing my left shoulder into the rock wall to stop my momentum, I rounded the corner. When my cuirass dug into the back of my arm upon impact, my vision narrowed for a moment.

From very close behind, I could hear chaotic scrabbling and slapping footfalls on rock. Unwilling to slow down to see what was behind me, I kept running. Once past the first wooden beam supports, I got an idea. I began dragging my swords along the rock walls at about chest level, trailing sparks as I went, slicing through the wooden supports every few yards or so. After I cut through four of them without caving in the shaft, I decided I had to do something more drastic. *Not to mention crazy.*

At the next set of support beams, I stopped, hacked through the side supports, then sliced through the cross-member overhead. Gnomes must have dug the damn mines, because nothing happened. In panicked frustration, I rammed one sword into the rock ceiling above the beam and began using it as a pry bar.

The first few Strigoi scrambled at me like roaches running from light. Several of the unnaturally pale-skinned and hairless creatures skittered across the ground while one ran along a wall and another on the ceiling like freakish four-legged insects. *That has to be hell on a manicure.* They came to an abrupt halt just outside of my sword's reach, twisting their heads around like dogs hearing a sharp sound, trying to understand what I was up to, but smart enough to know the weapon could do them harm. They were definitely not the mindless rabble of the vampire world. Fortunately, they weren't the cognoscenti, either.

I could feel the rock start to give way when an unearthly howl erupted from down the tunnel as a pair of Strigoi came bounding up in a mad rush, running over those that had stopped outside my range. *These are the mindless rabble.*

I used my free sword to stab at the first one, sticking the blade into its ashen, distorted face, instantly causing it to retreat clumsily and noisily, disrupting the momentum of the second one. I swung backhanded across the tunnel to catch the waylaid one across its chest and bloated abdomen. The contents of its blood-pouch, located where its stomach used to be, spewed everywhere while it fell to the ground, twisting and writhing like a fish on land.

It gave me enough time for one final overhead heave. A few

bowling-ball-sized rocks fell from the ceiling, causing the original rank of vampires to jump back. I jerked hard on the sword to wrench it free then turned and ran. I made it only a few yards before the entire roof of the shaft began falling in larger and larger chunks, while smaller rocks pelted me as I ran. Behind me, the shockwave grew as the entire tunnel began to collapse on itself with a deafening roar, which drowned out the high-pitched shrieking of the Strigoi. I covered my head with my arms and swords and kept running, assuming Duma was on the heels of the damned Demon Fae sonofabitch.

At the entrance grate, I jumped and barely landed on my feet at the rear of the barn, facing a gaping hole in what used to be the back wall of the structure. A crowd of people stood gawking through it, surprised by my sudden appearance. Behind me, one of the Strigoi managed to escape the cave-in, scrabbling out of the hole as the floor above the tunnel and part of the upper walkway around the barn connected to the hayloft collapsed. I squared off, swords in hand, ready to attack the vampire before it could gain its footing, but the creature forgot about me the instant it encountered the sunlight flooding in through the breach in the barn's rear wall. The scared Strigoi skittered backward into one of the stalls, wailing like an injured child. The barn began creaking and rumbling as if a freight train were running through it.

I backed up quickly toward the shattered wall while the Strigoi frantically pressed back farther into the stall for protection from the light. With no other option, I stepped out of the barn backward, keeping an eye on the retreating vampire, only to get smacked hard across the back. It jarred me, knocking me forward onto one knee. The blow didn't hurt, but it did startle the hell out of me. When I turned around, the crowd — thralls of the vampires and townspeople — surrounded me.

CHAPTER 26

U NDER NO REAL INFLUENCE OF the vampires beyond fear or some twisted sense of generational loyalty, the townsfolk of Coronini had been guarding the Liuntika Strigoi for hundreds of years. But thralls or not, they were still human, and I didn't want to hurt them if I didn't have to.

I took a few quick steps forward, pushing the unsteady crowd farther into the field. Once we were far enough away from the building, the villagers completely encircled me, armed with a variety of farming implements and a few old shotguns. I was disappointed that there were no pitchforks or burning torches, but I still had a pretty good feeling how Frankenstein's monster felt.

One of the men with a shotgun finally racked a shell, and I attacked. Roaring, I stepped fast and hard to my right then planted an elbow into the face of a man armed with a hoe. Spinning to my left, I planted the pommel of my sword into the gut of the next and continued circling. I hacked through the next villager's rake and heel-kicked him about three yards.

Startled by my roar and sudden attack, most of the townspeople remained frozen, but a few stumbled backward. I pressed my advantage and quickly crossed the circle toward another man armed with a shotgun. His eyes grew wide as I threw both swords into the ground. I jumped straight at him, grabbed the barrel of the gun, and forced it up before it went off. Ramming the gun back down at the man, I smashed its butt into his chin. He let go of the gun and fell to the ground, grasping his face. I swung the gun like a bat, hitting the nearest man across the neck and head, then threw the gun at another man, who was caught completely off guard. The instant I let the gun go, I drew both of my sidearms and pointed them at two random people of the five that were still standing. The remaining crowd absolutely froze.

"What we have here," I said, "is a failure to communicate..."

Clearly, no one else spoke English, because no one laughed. No one said anything or even moved until one guy, for some reason beyond my comprehension, suddenly tried to reach for my swords stuck in the ground about five feet away from me.

"Ah, ah, ah," I said, chiding the young man. "No touchy." I covered the five feet toward my swords fast enough to beat the kid easily then brought one of my guns down on his head lightly with a dull thud. The kid collapsed. *Damn.* I holstered the Glock as I knelt by his prone form to see if he was still alive. He wasn't breathing, and I could find no sign of a pulse. Before I could even stand, the remaining four villagers screamed and attacked me as a group, swinging at me with fists and broken handles. One guy even grabbed one of my swords. *That's it. I'm done being Mr. Nice Guy.*

I grabbed one attacker by his shirt and threw him aside then shot the villager holding my sword as he raised the blade above his head. I stood and brought my elbow around, catching another person square in the face. Hard. He fell to the ground motionless, and the loud report of the gun stopped the remaining attacker in mid swing. From around the corner of the barn, two more villagers appeared carrying AK-47s.

"That's enough!" I screamed. *I do not have time for this.*

Everyone jerked with a start at my shout, but the two new gunmen kept approaching. One began shouting in a language I didn't understand. The more he shouted, the louder and more insistent he became, inciting the others to become more aggressive again, as well. Still, their hands quivered as they inched closer.

Part of me wanted to make a break for it and leave the simple but deluded people alive. With AK-47s in the mix, I'd probably end up taking a few errant rounds in the legs or arms, maybe even my head as I ran. Even if I made it, they would probably chase me. Though they couldn't keep up with me, I didn't need to watch my back as I tried to catch up with Duma and the Hanner Brid—who were who knew how far ahead of me.

I quickly fired three rounds, center mass, at the verbal gunman. At least one hit him in the upper chest while one splintered the wooden shoulder stock of his rifle. As the second gunman turned toward his wounded companion, I put two rounds into his thigh and pulled my Sig. He twisted as he fell, inadvertently firing as he screamed in pain. His errant volley hit the last upright attacker in the back, killing him instantly. The villager I'd thrown aside rolled onto his back and raised his empty hands in surrender. For a second, I contemplated shooting him.

I put away my guns and sheathed my swords as the wounded villagers writhed on the ground around me. Then the barn collapsed. I took off sprinting as fast as I could.

Way across the field, on the other side of the ditch we'd used as an entry point, was a blur I assumed to be Duma. The low scrub blocked my view, but I kept running, pulling the sniper rifle I took from the Half Breed's arsenal off my shoulder to get it ready. Even at full speed, which I couldn't maintain for long, I would never come close to catching up with Duma or the Half Breed, but if I stood any chance of following them, I had to clear that ditch — fast.

I recalled that the map we'd used to plan our assault showed clear fields for several miles to the north, but there was also a heavily forested area in the hills to the east. The idea of losing them in the forest caused me to bear down and push myself harder.

I charged through the scrub brush and small trees around the ditch without slowing and took several nasty scrapes to the face from errant branches for the effort. Emerging from the other side of the thicket, I saw several figures standing in a loose group about a thousand yards ahead of me, but I was too far out to make out any details of what was happening.

Confused, I threw myself into a straight-leg slide. I skidded along the grass and dirt, fishing in a vest pocket to grab one of the modified shells I'd taken for the rifle, unsure if it had a full magazine in it or not. The group was too focused on whatever was going on within it to notice me. The moment I came to a stop, I opened the bolt, slid the cartridge in, and closed it. I pulled myself up to sit cross-legged, resting the back of my elbows on the front part of my raised knees to steady my aim as I peered through the riflescope.

The Hanner Brid's distinctive brown aura flashed around him along one side of the group. The rest of the group, including Duma, faced the Half Breed. Duma's back was to me. The Hanner Brid was roughly six feet tall, and based on his size through the scope, I judged the distance at roughly nine hundred yards. Given the distance and the fact that I had no idea about windage, a shot at that distance would be tough, to say the least. But that didn't bother me nearly as much as what I was seeing.

Five of the other figures were dressed in the familiar long dark coats of the Dreaichbard. Spread out loosely, they faced the Half Breed, who was using someone as a shield. Duma stood between the Hanner Brid and me, blocking my view of the hostage. Everyone was still. For the first time, I could see that the Hanner Brid shared Duma's pale coloration, though his hair was significantly shorter and more golden than white.

After a moment, the Hanner Brid's aura pulsed again, and the Dreaichbard dropped their weapons and stepped back. Duma shook his head as if clearing cobwebs. Giving up his weapons under any conditions was against his nature, and I hoped his previous experiences might help him resist.

Finally, the Hanner Brid backed up just far enough that I could see he had Belphoebe by the throat. He also had the silenced .22 aimed at Duma. With that gun, he'd have to hit Duma in the head to kill him instantly, but I had little doubt he could do that with the short distance between them.

Everything I'd learned working with snipers over the years flooded into my head at once. *The only sure kill shot is one to the head — especially in a hostage situation. A person can still move for as long as ten seconds after a shot directly to the heart. A sniper's target on a head is a line that goes roughly from ear to ear, which is about seven inches on a person. However, the sweet spot is dead in the middle of that line, right behind the eyes. So seven inches actually becomes two inches, and that makes a functional head shot downright impossible beyond about two hundred yards.* At my range, without a good wind reading and a hostage covering most of my target, I would be lucky not to hit Belphoebe — and killing her wouldn't help my case even if I handed them the real culprit.

I had one chance. If I could make it to the tree line less than two hundred yards behind them without being seen, I could get close enough to take the shot. The forest lay about three hundred yards to my right. I only hoped that Duma could keep things cool and focused on him while I closed the distance.

I crouched and ran. Staying low, I covered ground far more slowly than I would have liked. The crossing seemed to take forever, but I made it in under two minutes, and nothing changed with the standoff. Duma still had his knives in hand, shaking his head like a wet dog, and the Hanner Brid still clutched Belphoebe. The Dreaichbard, however, were all kneeling. I couldn't see her face from my position behind them, but I could only imagine that she was either furious or unconscious.

I made my way through the forest until I was as close to directly behind the psychotic asshole as I could get. I knelt, leaning against a tree, and brought the rifle up to my shoulder. I was three hundred yards out.

Despite the shorter distance, a definite head shot would still be a struggle, so I aimed at the largest target: the Hanner Brid's mid-upper back. I hoped Duma could duck out of the bastard's line of fire fast enough. Given a choice between Duma and Belphoebe, I wasn't as concerned about her — consequences or no. I flipped the rifle's safety off, took a few slow deep breaths, and then squeezed the trigger.

Through the scope, I watched the Hanner Brid lurch forward and Duma suddenly jerk upright then fall over. I threw the rifle aside and ran toward them as fast as I could move my already-weary legs. The Dreaichbard began getting to their feet until an incoherent bellow arose from the group followed by the same odd aura flash enveloping the assassin. My heart almost stopped when the Demon Fae not only didn't collapse but barely even faltered.

The guardsmen quickly reassumed their kneeling positions, and the Hanner Brid righted himself, still clutching Belphoebe by her neck. *Holy Hell.* Once upright, he threw Belphoebe over his shoulder like a rag doll into a fireman's carry. After shooting me a glare, his face contorted into an expression of pain and fury, he glanced back toward the village of Coronini then took off running away from the town. I headed straight for Duma and the kneeling Dreaichbard while an angry mob of people crossed into the field from Coronini. In addition, two large old Soviet-era six-wheeled trucks loaded with even more people were barreling up the DN57, in our direction.

By the time I made it to Duma, he was struggling to get to his feet, clutching at his chest near his left arm. He appeared more stunned than injured.

"Come on, get up," I said, grabbing his uninjured arm. "We gotta get outta here, and I mean now."

Duma grunted, then he noticed the coming onslaught. "Holy shit! The villagers are really pissed off! Screw the Hanner Brid — we gotta get outta here."

He snagged his knives, and we took off for the river, a few hundred yards in front of us. I had no doubt the villagers were after Duma and me rather than the Hanner Brid, and there was no way we could pursue him with the villagers on our tail. Our best shot was to escape then somehow head him off.

"What did you do?"

"Shot some of them, destroyed that barn, shit like that," I said to Duma as I ran. "Move it, guys, or you're never gonna see Pheebs again," I said as we sprinted past the befuddled Dreaichbard. I could only imagine he'd taken her as added insurance against the Dreaichbard and me taking potshots at him as he ran. Several of the guardsmen were still on their knees, while others were stumbling to their feet like newborn babies. All of them glanced around stiffly, as if they were unsure what to do. *Elite guards, my ass.* For a half a heartbeat, I contemplated helping them then came to my senses. There was no way I was going to get myself killed helping *those* guys out.

I wasn't as worried about the people on foot as I was about the trucks. The vehicles were big and had a top speed of about forty miles an hour, but even at that speed, it was going to be damn close for us. Automatic gunfire erupted from the throng of villagers behind us, though we were still well out of their range. We raced across the DN57 and headed toward a boat dock with a building on it. Over my shoulder, I could see that the Dreaichbard were closing on us quickly.

Probably need to rethink that last notion about them. In front of us, three people came out of the small structure at the base of the dock. And they were armed with rifles.

"Split up!" I yelled to Duma, who clutched at his arm and wasn't running as fast as he usually did.

He veered to the left, and I went right as we neared the dock. One of the three gunmen began firing at Duma while the other two targeted me. A few bullets whizzed by, but none struck home. Luckily, we ran fast enough to make an unskilled marksman's job all but impossible.

Once we hit the edge of the clearing around the dock, Duma

changed directions back toward the building. I ran straight at the nearest gunman firing at me. The guy panicked, dropped his weapon, stumbled, then collided with the other gunman shooting at me, taking them both out. Duma hit the third gunman, trailing a spray of crimson behind him as the man collapsed. I didn't have time to protest, nor did I care to at that point.

Legs aching, I pushed myself to the dock. A few yards downstream, Duma dove in. I did the same then swam hard. Onshore, all hell broke loose, but I wasn't about to stop to look. Working my arms and kicking my booted feet, I felt the full effect of my exhaustion. The weight of my gear made treading water in the rapidly increasing current much harder. I ditched the SCAR-H near the main channel, where the current picked us up and swept us toward our meeting point near the ruined fortress.

I had flashbacks of "drownproofing" while I was in Basic Underwater Demolition/SEAL training: the instructors wrestling with us, trying to pull us under while our hands were tied. I'd spent hours treading water while holding heavy weights, learning to keep my head above water no matter what. I relaxed and focused only on keeping my face above the water, using my arms only occasionally like flippers to raise my head enough to breathe as I drifted. Before long, I recognized the ruined fortifications on the banks above the river.

Apparently, our escapades had taken us far enough upstream that the current carried us almost right up to Golubac across the river. I dragged myself onto the shallow flats along the Danube's western edge, underneath the walls of the fortress. As Duma and I sat in the shallows, both too exhausted to speak and numb from the cold, I could feel the rumble of boat engines vibrating through the water before I could hear them.

When Gheorghe pulled up, I flopped onto the deck like a bag of rice then lay there with my eyes closed until Duma pressed a cold plastic bottle into my hand. I sat up, crossing my arms over my knees, as Duma collapsed next to me with a groan.

"Where's the nearest gate through the Ways?" I asked, feeling battered but elated to have survived our jaunt into vampire central.

"Ow! Damn," Duma said, clutching his shoulder. "The spot upriver where we met Gheorghe, which is exactly where *I* would head if I were him. There's no way he can beat us there by land, so we've got him unless he has a boat somewhere."

"Excellent, have Gheorghe get us there as fast as he can." I pointed the bottle at Duma's shoulder. "You okay?"

"Through and through. Will be in a few days."

"We're going to catch this fucker," I said then cracked open the bottle of water and chugged it.

Trying to put myself in the Hanner Brid's position, I could only imagine he would dump Belphoebe's added weight as soon as he assumed he was clear. Keeping her longer than that made no tactical sense. If we were lucky, we would intercept him, with or without Belphoebe, at the Ways. Otherwise, I hoped something in the papers I'd taken from his hidey-hole would give us another place to search for him.

Duma said something to Gheorghe, then the smuggler brought us a pair of blankets and a small paper sack before heading back to the helm, where he gunned the engines. The Peri dug into the bag and pulled out a couple of candy bars and several apples. I took the candy; he ate the apples.

Rule Number One when on an operation of any kind is always eat and sleep whenever possible. I had a little time, so I rested. It wasn't really optional, especially when combined with the resonant thrum of the engines below deck. The sound was positively hypnotic even though I could have slept directly on the engines without any problem. It probably would have been warmer.

CHAPTER 27

WOKE UP WITH A START. Duma was standing next to Gheorghe at the helm, munching on another apple. Still wrapped in the blanket, I walked over.

"Not that I expected it, but no sign of him so far," Duma shouted over the wind. "We got another hour or so to go yet, though."

I went down into the galley and dug out a few more candy bars, an apple, an energy drink, and a box of crackers. When I approached the helm, Duma and Gheorghe stared at me and my armful of food.

"What? I haven't eaten much in the last few days. Besides, it's all you got."

I sat down against the port gunnel and started eating, and Duma joined me, trying to fold up a map so that he could hold it against the wind.

"Gheorghe says we're about here." He pointed to a spot on the Danube. "And unless the Hanner Brid has a faster boat, his likely route over land would be the DN57 north to the 115 west to the 24 south and then over to Ŝalinac." He traced the route with his finger.

The overland route was easily several hundred miles long over rural highways, but if he was driving one of Duma's type of cars, he might be able to make it almost as fast as we could by river. Still, the boat was our only real option. Duma grimaced when he used his left arm to put away the map then reach for my crackers.

"Getting shot hurts, don't it?" I asked, yielding the package of crackers.

"Yeah, but not that bad. I don't know what kind of gun that was, but it barely made a noise, and it startled me more than hurt."

"The guy's got to be in pain, as well," I said. "I hit him square in the back with one of his .338 rounds from a few hundred yards out. He had to be wearing some serious body armor, but at that range and with a round that big, I must have broken some of his ribs at the least. I mean, assuming he has ribs."

"I don't know, but I don't think he was wearing heavy body armor, D. I can tell you for sure the bullet didn't pass through him. All I know is that when he jerked, I jumped. Apparently, not fast enough."

I laughed. "Fast enough that he didn't shoot you in the head."

"Yeah, I guess you're right."

"How the hell did he get Pheebs?" I asked.

"It all happened pretty fast. I was on his ass, less than ten yards back and gaining, when I see Belphoebe and her Dreaich charging directly at him and me from across the field. I slowed, but that nutcase kept going, full tilt. The archers stopped to ready arrows, but the other three Dreaich and Belphoebe kept charging toward me until the wacko screamed *halt* in a voice that vibrated my entire skull and made me want to stop, too. I almost did. Belphoebe and her guards *did* stop — dead in their tracks. He hit her like a runaway freight train, she went limp, and he grabbed her. That's when the Dreaich snapped back to attention and I closed in."

"Why would taking her hostage stop *you* from attacking?" I asked, trying to picture the scene.

"I'm not sure..." He shook his head. "I had that same weird feeling like back in Sirte and Seville, only not as intense this time. Once I got close to him, I could hear him tell the Dreaich to keep their distance, and I *believed* he meant me, too. When he told us to drop our weapons, for some reason, I just couldn't bring myself to do it. It didn't make sense even though he *asked* me to. I can't explain the feeling — the confusion. Dunno. All I *knew* was that if I dropped my knives, he'd have me at a major disadvantage. His suggestion rubbed me the wrong way. I couldn't have cared less about Belphoebe."

"So, wait, those weren't Dreaich*bard*, then?" I asked.

"Ah, heck no. Just Dreaich." Laughing, he held up his hand dismissively. "You think they'd send the royal *elite* guard after a human? Even a Guardian? Ha! The Courts don't see you guys as that big of a threat."

"Well, I assumed..."

"Sorry, D, you only rate Dreaich. They wouldn't send the *Bard* out unless it was all-out war with the Seelie Court itself or Mab showed up personally. Those guys were good, but they're cannon fodder by comparison."

"I guess that makes sense, because they didn't seem that tough to me," I said, actually a little insulted and disappointed.

"Oh, they're capable." Duma smiled wickedly then elbowed me in my injured shoulder. "It's just that we're much better."

I laughed and cringed at the same time. "Any chance you can try to track him?" I asked, knowing the answer.

Duma appeared as fatigued as I've ever seen him. "Blood's going to be way too degraded. I might end up forcing an inaccurate reading. It's not worth it."

I leaned back against the gunnel. "No worries. We *are* going to get this guy."

Staring out over the cold, muddy water, I contemplated my situation and Belphoebe. I didn't like what we had to do, and I knew Duma was going to like it even less. I jerked my head back against the bulkhead in frustration then sighed.

"You know, as much as I'd like to kill her myself, we have to try to get Pheebs back *alive* if at all possible," I said. "It would go a long way to helping me make amends once we catch this guy."

Duma glanced up into the air for a second, probably daydreaming about strangling her, then he rolled his head toward me. "Hey, if anyone can do this, it's us. Remember... *we're that good.*" He slapped my injured shoulder again with the back of his hand.

"There is that," I replied, trying to force a smile past the wince.

When we pulled up to the spot where we planned to catch the boat at the mouth of the Great Morava River, I grabbed a Hungarian-made AMD-65 assault rifle and a couple spare magazines from Gheorghe's stores below deck and jumped out. Since it was still daylight, I began examining the marshy ground along the riverbank for footprints when Duma landed right where I was looking. I glared at him and briefly considered breaking his knee as he walked off smugly.

"Don't worry, I won't mess up any tracks. I don't leave footprints," he said over his shoulder. "By the way, I doubt he does, either."

Just great.

We jogged quickly along the river's edge, taking advantage of the forest for cover in the midday sun. Once we got back to the portal through the Telluric Pathways, Duma circled the spot for several minutes, staring into the area, with his forehead deeply furrowed and his eyes narrowed to slits. I could see the portal's energy signature, but to me, it was nothing more than something resembling heat waves rising off pavement.

After a few minutes, he said, "I'm pretty sure no one's been through here since us."

I took his statement to mean we'd beat the Hanner Brid to the portal.

"The likely overland route is to approach from there." I pointed toward the road across the river from us. "But he's got to know we're after him. So if he thinks he beat us here, he might come as directly as he can. But... if it were me, I'd pass that area and swim it from the Danube because it would be more unexpected."

Duma shook his head. "But if he still has Belphoebe, he wouldn't swim it dragging a hostage."

"Still, you watch the approach from the road across the river from those trees." I nodded to the forest on the west side of the clearing. "I'll keep an eye on the water from over here," I said, hooking my thumb to the opposite end of the glade. "We need to get him between us if we can. And remember—"

He held up his hands. "I know, I know: try to save Belphoebe if we can."

"I don't care how we take him," I replied.

The sun was high overhead, working its way westward in a cloudless sky. Tactically, if I were trying to escape, I wouldn't have gone anywhere near the clearing while people were chasing me unless I had no other choice. This portal through the Ways was the most expedient and obvious of the Hanner Brid's few options.

Unfortunately, for my part, all the places to lay an ambush from were obvious, as well. Ideally, I would have taken up a position *in* the river a little farther upstream, within the cover of overhanging trees. In the cold water, I would need a dry suit or at least a heavy wet suit. Without those, I chose to reinforce a dense stand of brush at the edge of the clearing to create a blind for myself. I quickly cut branches from trees well into the forest and dragged them back, covering my tracks. Satisfied with my camouflage, I took up position and waited, expecting him to show any time. Duma hid somewhere in the trees across the clearing from me.

Our plan was simple: When the Half Breed showed up, we would pin him. I would step in from the rear and keep him from retreating across the river, while Duma would cover him from the front and prevent him from going through the Ways. With luck, we'd get Belphoebe back and kill the bastard. Even if he stayed halfway between Duma and me in this small clearing, I had little doubt about being able to expose his brains to the light of day with the AMD-65. While I didn't mention it to Duma, I also figured if the Hanner Brid tried to control him again, the cambion bastard would have to risk turning away from me to do so.

Call that Plan A. While I sat in my blind, I worked on Plans B through Q. I tried to run every possible variation of what could happen through my mind—everything from him not showing to him showing up with a small army. *Failing to plan is planning to fail.*

If everything went sideways, my escape route was the river. I didn't know what Duma would do, but he and I had been through so many similar situations that I knew he had his escape route figured as well. We would meet back up when it was safe.

We waited for several hours. The sun had almost set, and as part of me started to worry we had guessed wrong about his exit strategy, an indistinct engine noise carried through the evening air from across the river. I focused all my attention on listening rather than trying to see in the fading light. After several more minutes, something that sounded like an abruptly ended muffled scream broke the silence. It was hard to tell for sure, but it *sounded* as though it had come from the other side of the river. I had to force myself to be patient and not jump the gun. The guy was too slippery.

I carefully pulled the clunky AMD-65 up to a seated firing position then scanned the water's edge, watching for movement rather than a specific shape, and listened. After a painful few minutes of watching into the final glow of the setting sun combined with the reflections off the water and low light levels around the river, I had to blink hard a few times to verify I did actually see a series of small ripples hit the bank in front of me. Then came the corroborating soft sounds of the water lapping against the bank.

The ripples continued but struck me as being too small to be caused by something roughly as large as I was, not to mention something large carrying something else sizable. I knew the fae rarely left a mark on any surface they traversed, but I found it hard to believe even a fae could defy the physics of fluid dynamics. *If this sonofabitch walks on water, I give up here and now.*

I slowly flexed my legs to make sure the muscles were ready for action. I was stretching my left leg when a distinct splashing sound came from the river, like an alligator sliding in from a bank. Then a series of larger ripples grew into small waves as they hit the bank near my position. It was exactly the type of disturbance I expected, and I seriously doubted there were any alligators on the Danube.

I slowly shifted from a seated position to kneeling, still supporting the submachine gun by resting my right elbow on my thigh as I watched the flattest part of the shoreline. A soft grunt was followed by another splash, and it dawned on me that normally, that would be the ideal time to spring the ambush. *This guy is neck deep in the water, maybe carrying a listless body — how much more helpless could he be?*

Of course, I still couldn't see him to verify if it even was him. For all I knew, it was a cow taking an evening swim. That was unlikely but possible, and I couldn't afford to take the chance. I needed as clean a shot as I could get.

After another half minute that felt more like an eternity, I finally began to make out a dark mass in the water. The silhouette increased in size as it approached the bank, and the form began to take shape. Unless the Hanner Brid had a big hump and more appendages than an octopus, he was still carrying Pheebs across his shoulders.

Once he emerged from the river, he dropped into a kneeling position only a few yards from me. Belphoebe's limp form blocked any shot I had at his head. I'd already shot the prick in the back with a massive round, and I wasn't going to make the same mistake twice. Plus, I couldn't risk accidentally hitting Pheebs. I had to keep telling myself I couldn't, hoping that eventually I'd believe it.

He got back to his feet after a moment and took a few tentative steps closer to the gate. He took a few more cautious steps then started to trot. That was my cue.

I got to my feet and pushed through the blind, moving carefully and purposefully, keeping him in my sights. Both eyes wide open, I pressed the gun's stock tight to my shoulder while my cheek rested along it. My only shot at his head from this vantage point was through Pheebs, so I couldn't take it yet. Duma emerged from the trees along the other side of the clearing off to my right, giving me a clear zone of fire in front of me the moment he dropped her.

"Freeze, dickless," I said, almost shouting.

He stopped but not in such a way that let me think we'd actually surprised him. Duma continued to close the distance between them, and I could see the moonlight glinting off his knives as he swung them around. I approached to within thirty feet then stopped. Duma did the same.

"Let Belphoebe go, now," I said.

"Or what, Diomedes?"

"Or... I promise you I will leave you alive," I replied.

He let out a snort that sounded more as if he'd choked.

"You won't like it, but you'll be *alive*," I said. "A vegetable, maybe. Possibly quadriplegic. I don't know yet, but I'll figure it out. It won't be pleasant. Drooling and diapers will be involved, so I suggest you put her down. Gently."

"Duma, why would you consort with this bruchad? You're better than that. Your family was better than that. Your father was—"

"Don't you dare mention my family. You have no right!" Duma said, snarling like a rabid animal.

"Maybe not. After all, it was *me* that betrayed your family to the Dreaichbard all those years ago," the Half Breed replied, amusement in his tone. I was surprised by the revelation but too focused to respond to it.

Duma, on the other hand, reacted like a snapped rubber band. He moved so quickly, he simply disappeared from where he stood. The Hanner Brid stepped sideways and backhanded Duma across his already-injured shoulder as he passed. Duma dropped to his knees at the blow. The Hanner Brid instantly shifted his weight and faced me in a deep crouch. Before I could pull the trigger at his exposed head, he threw Belphoebe's limp form directly at me as if she were no more than a sack of laundry. My instinct was to duck, though I managed to fire one uncontrolled burst in the process. The shot went wide as I dropped to the ground to avoid the impact. *All my freakin' contingencies, and not a damn one included this guy throwing Belphoebe at me.*

In the seconds it took me to get back to my feet, the Half Breed had the Ways open and was halfway through. I followed without thinking.

CHAPTER 28

MANAGED TO GET THROUGH THE portal into the Ways before it closed and blindly followed the Hanner Brid's trail. Once inside the confines of the Telluric Paths, I felt a nearly overwhelming combination of smug superiority, rage and, surprisingly, fear. I emerged into bright sunlight, heat, and humidity so thick it was like a sauna on the surface of the sun.

I threw my hand over my eyes until they could adjust to the intense light, acutely aware that I was defenseless for the moment. When something heavy hit me across the chest, I half expected it, so I went limp and rolled with the blow. My cuirass took the brunt of the impact, but my head snapped back into the ground in the fall.

When I came to, someone was standing over me, saying, "Vo cyst ah kay." I reflexively swung my leg fast and wide along the ground, sweeping the feet out from under the figure, sending it tumbling over.

I gathered my wits and got my feet back under me. The guy I had knocked over was lying spread eagle on the ground—and definitely wasn't the Half Breed, who was nowhere to be seen. Instead, a few tan-skinned, dark-haired people were standing around, screaming and gesturing wildly at me while others helped the poor guy I'd waylaid back to his feet. I didn't understand a word they said, but I finally recognized the language as Portuguese, which likely meant I was in Brazil.

For an instant, I remembered that I left Duma back in the clearing with Belphoebe and hoped one of them wouldn't kill the other. *Maybe they'll help each other. Ha!* Either way, there was no way I was letting this guy get away from me again.

Ignoring the people, who, despite my weapons, became increasingly irate, I located the only way out of the small cement paddock in which I stood. Structurally questionable buildings all but surrounded what apparently passed for a parking lot here, with a few cars sitting haphazardly in the open space. Outside the passageway to the street, a Jitney bus that smelled like gasoline, oil, and sweat and sounded like a carnival on a tugboat went by as people on bikes and mopeds randomly sped past in both directions. I pushed through the small crowd gathered around me and ran out to the street in the hopes of getting a better idea of my location and maybe to catch a glimpse of the Hanner Brid.

Colorful multistory shanties of all sizes and shapes surrounded me in every direction. An empty lot across the street and the road itself formed the only open areas. Massive bundles of electrical wires stretched between structures and across the street like heavy nets. I had to be in one of the Favelas outside of Rio or Sao Paulo.

I'm screwed.

Favelas consisted of hundreds of thousands of apartments and buildings built and rebuilt on, around, over, and under each other. The structures formed a constantly changing warren that only local residents could navigate with any real success.

Other than the road I was standing on, dodging motorcycles and scooters, I couldn't see a single obvious route to take. My head pounded, and my vision kept blurring, but I wandered up the street trying to formulate a plan of action, quickly weaving among pedestrians along the road. Up ahead, a group of frazzled and perturbed people stared, pointing at rooftops. Several people within the crowd were helping others up from the ground, while a few picked up things off the streets. One man in front of a four-story structure cursed and yelled as he stooped to pick up the scattered contents of a box. *The half-demon bastard had to have gone through here and up onto the roofs.*

The building's roofline was the lowest one in the area, but it was still out of my vertical-leaping range. Luckily, I saw a makeshift balcony that was little more than wooden framework that someone had somehow levered out through a large opening in the third-floor façade. I could reach it—I only hoped it didn't collapse when I grabbed on to it. Making the superhuman jump would draw attention, but I didn't have time to worry about the audience.

Running as fast as I could, I leaped and grabbed the balcony, ripping it partly loose from its supports and sending a homemade grill made from an old oil drum cascading to the street below, along with all its ashes. My ungainly gymnastics gave the passersby even more to squawk at as they scrambled to avoid the falling debris. The metal cooking grate barely missed the old man picking up his items, but he got a full shower of ash.

"Sorry!" I screamed as I pulled myself onto the rickety wooden deck. The last thing I wanted to do was accidentally kill someone while I was trying to save them from the balloon knot.

I ducked inside the opening and into a dark room, searching for a door and a way up. Frantic, high-pitched screams met me as I walked through the dank, hot room. Some were directed at me, and some came from outside and farther above, giving me hope I wasn't far behind the Hanner Brid. I found my way through an open door to an even darker passageway lined with garbage, debris, and numerous other doorways—some covered with sheets rather than actual doors. Overhead, a huge bundle of hundreds of wires and cables, many spliced together haphazardly, ran along the ceiling. Everything and anything from belts to string held the dangerous collection in place, and some of the cables crackled and buzzed with electricity.

The hallway, for lack of a better term, was lit by only a few random dim bulbs hanging from the wires overhead. The place reeked of an odd combination of human waste, rotting garbage, sweat, pungent cooking smells, and other scents that I couldn't identify.

If I followed the overhead bundle, I might eventually find a way out or up. Arbitrarily, I chose to head to the right. I kept pushing through the building as fast as I could, narrowly avoiding collisions with residents and several small children playing, eliciting random angry shouts as I dodged around them.

After several more turns, I finally came to a hole in a wall that opened onto a courtyard of sorts, letting in light from above and allowing people to dump dirty water and trash onto the space below. Screams and angry shouts echoed from the other side of the courtyard. The overhead bundle of wires joined an even larger mass of lines spreading across the vertical space, forming a web of wires and cables that would have made a spider jealous. Old, dried-out paper and trash was draped over them, garbage that hadn't made the full drop.

I had time to contemplate neither hygiene nor the safety of using wires of questionable integrity as a support, so I jumped up, grabbed the heaviest wires, pulled myself through them to the next level, then jumped to grab the edge of the lowest roof above. Cables parted as I pushed off, sending sparks everywhere. I managed to avoid getting shocked, although I could feel my hair stand on end.

I pulled myself up on the roof and quickly spun around, hoping for a glimpse of something — anything. Almost immediately, a figure jumped down to a lower level a hundred yards to my right. I would never catch him in a foot race, especially not across questionable corrugated metal and suspect wooden roofs. Scanning the adjacent roofs, I saw that my circuitous path through the building behind me had actually paralleled the street below.

I ran back across the building toward the edge overlooking the street and watched the Hanner Brid jump back up to a roof even with mine then continue running at a breakneck pace less than two hundred yards in front of me. For some reason, he was also following the road below.

I glanced up and down the street, searching for some sort of vehicle. If he was paralleling the road along the rooftops, then maybe I could chase him from down there on something that was faster than I was. Below, someone was riding an ancient racing dirt bike that had seen better days while a young kid duck-walked one of those mopeds that had to be pedaled before it would start. *Tough choice.*

I jumped down into a bundle of wires that connected to what probably served as one of the original poles strung by the local power company eons ago. Thousands of wires from every floor of the surrounding buildings met at the pole, and when I hit them, a small jolt of electricity passed through me as some of the smaller wires ripped free, sending sparks flying. Thankfully, dangling like that, I wasn't grounded, so other than shocks and singed arm hair, I wasn't at risk for electrocution. That was what I kept telling myself until the motorcyclist came up the street.

The kid approached faster than I'd expected, but right as I was about to drop the last fifteen feet to the street, a loud buzzing began above me. Then a massive electrical shock surged through my arms when a large number of the wires I clung to ripped free from the pole. I let go before hitting the ground with a thud then stumbled into a flop onto my keister.

I was alert enough to roll into the middle of the street to avoid the falling wires — most of which were so enmeshed with others at the pole that they never made it to the ground. Sparks rained down, arcing everywhere like a blinding fireworks display. I covered my head, got to my feet, and ran at the guy approaching on the motorbike. My hands and arms alternated between feeling tingly and burning.

The motorcyclist skidded to a halt, and once again, I found myself feeling bad about throwing some poor guy off his bike. Shoving the kid off without much resistance, I hopped on then popped the clutch and shot off down the street as fast as the old dirt bike could go. If it helped me catch the Hanner Brid, I would buy the kid an expensive motorcycle to replace it.

I whipped down the crowded street, weaving around people, bicycles, and other motorcycles, keeping my eye on the roofline, hoping to catch sight of the Hanner Brid. I nearly crashed into a pile of garbage and a derelict car left haphazardly in the street, but I kept pushing the old bike until thick, oily black smoke started pouring out from between my legs and the engine began sputtering. I hit the brakes, dumped the bike, and started running, trying to find the quickest way back up to the roof.

When I spied a two-story building among the taller structures, I jumped. Landing hard in a sloppy crouch on all fours on its roof, I thought the wobbly roof might actually collapse, but rather than wait to find out, I charged for another roofline one story higher right in front of me. I executed the jump better and used an opening in the wall to vault myself up to the next floor. Pulling myself up onto my stomach, I swung my leg up. Pushing to my feet, out of the corner of my eye, I saw the Hanner Brid come to an abrupt halt as he watched me emerge less than fifty feet in front of him. A second later, he changed directions and angled to his left.

I pulled the Glock off my hip and jumped the space between the buildings through which I had just climbed. I was no more than twenty yards behind him, but he was still much faster than I was, and I was already weary. With no other options, I kept charging ahead when he jumped down to a lower level. I made it to the edge of the building as he untucked from his landing roll — then I saw my chance.

"Freeze!" I screamed between deep, ragged breaths. "I swear, if you make me chase you any longer, I'm gonna dump honey all over your head and jam it into the biggest ant pile I can find *after* I'm through with you."

He actually stopped less than fifty feet away and slowly raised his hands. "You really think you can catch me?" he shouted over his shoulder. I could even hear his mirthless laugh.

"You bet, Hopalong," I replied. "Take one more step, and we'll see what your brain thinks of all this sunshine."

I reluctantly took my eyes off him for half a second to see what the easiest way down might be. It was a gravity special—straight down about fifteen feet onto a corrugated metal roof. Quick but far from ideal. The moment I focused on him again, his body tensed up ever so slightly, telling me he was about to bolt again. I aimed at his head and fired. *Twice.* He toppled forward in a heap, and I jumped down, paying closer attention to him than where I was going to land.

I crashed right through the corrugated roof, hit the floor below, and smashed through that one, as well, before eventually stopping with a bone-jarring thud an untold number of floors below.

At first, all I could do was breathe—painfully—but finally, I willed my fingers and toes into action then checked my arms and legs. All of my limbs were functional, though I hurt everywhere—including my eyelashes. Once I'd opened my eyes, it took me a few seconds to realize I wasn't staring up at a dark ceiling, but gazing at the night sky.

"Sonofabitch," I moaned, trying to pull myself into a seated position.

Something warm trickled down my forehead, and I reached up to find a tender area that stung when I touched it. My hand came back covered in blood. *Nice.*

Tinny voices were screaming from every direction, muted by the metal sheeting that had formed a bit of a cocoon around me as I'd fallen. With the realization that I was okay, my concern shifted to the people who lived in the building. *Were they shouting because of what happened or because the collapse had trapped or injured people?*

Examining the destruction I'd created, I was only slightly surprised to see it had spread farther than expected. The first hole up on the roof level was much larger than the second and the third, but the collapsed roofing and floor joists from above all but clogged everything around me. Debris and home furnishings teetered at the edge of the ruined floors above, forming a kind of enclosed pit with me at the bottom.

The only way out was straight up, and I couldn't have made that jump even on my best day.

I tried to think of a creative way to escape before human rescuers or gang enforcers showed up to save me and ask questions I really didn't want to answer or maybe simply tried to shoot me. In my slight stupor, I grasped the fact that my gun was still in my hand, then my mind flashed to the Hanner Brid. What a clusterfuck that would be if people found his body with two bullet holes in his head back up on the roof. *I should be so lucky.*

I lay back, exhausted. A featureless face in the darkness above was peering down at me from the edge of the hole in the roof. I blinked hard several times, assuming I had a concussion that was causing me to hallucinate. People began pounding on the metal roofing surrounding me, shouting in Portuguese. I had no idea if it was help or an angry mob. I glanced back up and found the featureless head still staring down at me. I couldn't fathom who it was. *Duma? Rescuers? Nightmare above all nightmares — the Hanner Brid himself?*

"Do you require some assistance?" asked a clear, crisp, and familiar male voice.

"Elegast?" I asked, straining hard trying to identify features on the face glaring at me from the darkness three stories up.

"At your service." He saluted. "Shall I lower a rope? Perhaps a harness? Or do you feel capable of making the distance in a jump? Whatever your choice, I suggest you make it with haste."

"Rope," I said, my voice cracking. *Perfect. Out of the frying pan, into the fire.*

A rope dropped down next to me. I grabbed the bitter end, formed a simple loop using a sheepshank, put it around me so it wrapped under my arms, then tugged on it to indicate my readiness. My head pounded for the effort, and I felt like a marlin being boated. The feeling sucked.

Though I expected to see Belphoebe and a host of Dreaich guards on the roof, I was too tired to care. To my complete surprise, the Elf was alone, hoisting me easily. Once I was near the roof, he reached out his hand to me with a wide, easy smile on his *perfect* face — entirely devoid of any injuries at all. It was dark, but given what I'd done to him at Poveglia, I'd expected him to at least have a bruise somewhere. *It's not fair how fast fae heal.*

"You, uh, look pretty good," I said as he pulled me out of the hole.

He was dressed in a khaki safari outfit, minus the pith helmet, and resembled Stewart Granger in one of those old movies about Africa, down to his perfectly coifed blond hair. He had a knife on his belt and a sword strapped to his back.

"How kind," he replied. "I wish I could return the compliment, but you look, well, rather like dung. And frankly, we should go." He glanced down into the crater. "Between the myriad of people heading our way and the acres of metal up here, my comfort level is quite low. Shall we?" He bowed slightly and ushered me with a flourish of his hand.

"Where's the body?" I asked, trying to locate the Hanner Brid. "Did you already dispose of it?"

"What body?"

CHAPTER 29

I BENT OVER THE AREA WHERE I swore I'd shot the Hanner Brid. *Twice.* In the head. There was absolutely no blood anywhere. I absently rubbed at my forehead, which brought tears to my eyes, and I cringed at the pounding pain in my head.

"Dammit! He was *right here*," I said, gritting my teeth. "I shot him twice. I *might* have missed once, but I got him at least once in the head, for sure. I was only right there." I gestured up at the rooftop behind us, no more than fifty feet away. "There's no way I missed."

"I assure you there was no body here when I arrived a short time ago. I really must insist that we leave. Now," Elegast said.

I followed Elegast for the better part of an hour in a fog, vacillating between notions of making a run for it and contemplating what had happened on the roof. Since I couldn't wrap my head around the latter issue, I focused on the former. I decided not to run only because everything hurt way too much and Elegast just didn't seem to be *capturing* me. After all, he let me follow rather than prodding me along like a prisoner.

Our long, circuitous path led us across rooftops, along streets, and through buildings to end up eventually back in the parking lot where I'd come through the Ways. I was tired, and my head hurt. Actually, everything hurt, but the pain in my head stood out. I didn't know if it was from an injury or the incomprehension. *I shot the sonofabitch at least once in the head.* I didn't even find blood, let alone his cold, dead body. Hell, I would have been thrilled with tepid and partly alive. With this guy, I wasn't going to be picky. Something else bothered me, too.

"How did you find me?" I asked.

"You were the last one through that portal, and it led me here," Elegast replied like it was common knowledge that the Ways worked like that. "Then I simply followed the sounds of catastrophe, which led me to you."

"Right. Hey, I know you gotta take me back and all, but that fucker is still out there," I said, rubbing gingerly at my head and picking the dried blood out of my hair. "The Hanner Brid, you know... the assassin we talked about."

Elegast smiled at me with a grin so wide that his annoyingly perfect teeth showed. "We should go," he said, opening a path through the Ways with a vertical slash of his hand.

I followed him back into the field near Ŝalinac. Going from hot and humid to cold in a matter of a few steps was a shock, and the sudden climate change didn't help my head or my mood at all. I saw a dozen Dreaich standing in the field, with two more kneeling at Belphoebe's side, tending to her as she sat on the ground. I had mixed feelings about her being okay. The guardsmen all watched us, and me in particular, but none of them really reacted. I felt like a mouse walking through a room full of cats. Half expecting the Dreaich to jump me at any moment, I raised my hands in submission. To my surprise, they ignored me and simply watched their brethren help Belphoebe, leaving me standing there like an idiot with my hands up. I lowered my hands. *Did I miss something?*

"It's okay," Elegast said with a smirk and a slap on the shoulder. "We aren't here to take you back to Poveglia." His chuck on the shoulder was an overdone imitation of human sentiment that mostly served to jar me and make me wince. "Get this man some first aid for his head. He saved your mistress from certain death," Elegast told the nearest of the guard then continued over to check on Belphoebe.

For a few moments, I stood dumbfounded, my hands on my hips. Although I could feel my eyes shift around, I didn't actually see anything while it all sank in. It took me a moment longer to realize I could walk. I took a single step and decided it would probably be best if I sat down. I saw neither hide nor hair of Duma in the clearing, which knowing him, meant he was alive somewhere and probably avoiding this crowd like the plague.

One of the Dreaich came over and grabbed my head roughly. I jerked away, and he mumbled something in a mellifluous language I didn't understand. He could have called me an asshole for all I knew, but it sounded nice. When I determined he was actually tending my wounds, I let him examine my head despite the fact he treated it as if it was a bowling ball.

While the guardsman tended my injuries, Belphoebe got to her feet, walked over, and sat down heavily next to me. Even in the darkness of the wee hours of the night, I could see she was weary — a first in my experience. I always imagined she would be dead for a year before she even appeared sickly.

"You look like I feel." I laughed.

She attempted a smile that brought to mind a lion lifting its lip to reveal the teeth it would have liked to sink into its prey. "I suppose decorum dictates that I... thank you," she said softly as if not wanting to be overheard.

"Well, I'll be honest, the Hanner Brid actually threw you at me. I mostly ducked," I said.

"No, I wasn't unconscious. He told me not to move, so I didn't. I heard what you said when we came out of the river over there. You could have shot through me to get to him, but you didn't. For that and your concern he release me, I thank you."

"Whoa, that had to have been hard to say," I replied, jerking back a little. She was being serious. Not just *serious*, but *fae serious*, and that meant my normal mordant acceptance of her modest attempt at gratitude was inappropriate. Ingenuous acceptance of appreciation had led to wars among the Fae, so I quickly changed my tone. "You are welcome," I replied again, putting my hand over my heart and bowing my pounding head.

"And..." She coughed, staring down at the ground, "Thank the... *Peri*... for me, as well." She spat the word out as if it were acidic. "I'm not sure where he disappeared to after you followed that half-breed through the Ways."

I had to fight suddenly snorting in shock, but I did manage to compose myself quickly enough to smile and nod. Duma would have laughed himself sick to hear her say that in person, decorum be damned. "I will," I said, rubbing my face to hide my amusement at her uneasiness.

"The appearance of this Hanner Brid, comments he made while I was in his custody, and Elegast's elucidation of the matter as he sees it have convinced me of your potential innocence. He and I will lobby on your behalf to our respective Courts regarding the —" She paused to find the right word. "Possible *mistake* that may have been made regarding your presumptive persecution for these acts."

"Good to know." Something told me this wasn't a good time for I-told-you-sos.

"But" — she met my gaze, her face an emotionless mask but her voice becoming harsh and cold as usual — "this Hanner Brid must be caught for you to be found completely innocent. And this does not mean we are on friendly terms. Should we meet on the field of battle again, I will face you as mine enemy."

"Aw heck, Pheebs, I wouldn't have it any other way." I smiled at her then winked, figuring if she could revert, then so could I.

Elegast joined us without sitting, preferring to tower over us. "So the Hanner Brid *actually* exists," he said, his eyebrows raised and a slight lilt in his voice that might have indicated amusement. His standing over us had to be some kind of Fae pissing contest because Belphoebe refused to gaze *up* at him.

"Well, at least someone fitting that bill exists," I said, straining my neck to see him then glance back at Pheebs. "I shot the guy several times, and he still ain't dead. Apparently, he's a cambion, Blud Fae father with a Succubus for a mother. He's also clearly had similar human military training to me, and he *definitely* doesn't have a problem with using guns. He's also got some sort of relationship with the Liuntika Strigoi. That's where I found these." I pulled the pile of soggy papers I grabbed in the Hanner Brid's room out from inside my vest. Elegast reached down to take them, then I fished in my vest pocket for one of the wildcatted .338 rounds. "It's a modified bullet designed for greater distances and accuracy. I would bet it's a match for the one that killed Indronivay. I pulled a similar one out of a simargl outside his stronghold."

Both of them eyed the large round, and Belphoebe took it in her gloved hand. "Well, I will attest that he certainly carries the Blud ability to cloud a mind. I knew the ability would affect lesser fae, but I had no idea it would work that well on one of the Sidhe, however. He held all my men *and me* at bay with a suggestion. I've never felt so powerless." She shook her head, in either disgust or incredulity.

I did not miss the fact that Pheebs clearly directed her comment about *lesser* fae at Elegast — a mere Elf and not a Sidhe. Then I began to wonder how Duma had managed to ignore the Hanner Brid's suggestions the last few times.

"Unfortunately, it sounds as though he also inherited some characteristics from his maternal lineage, as well. You say you shot him several times to no avail?" Elegast asked, examining the papers with interest.

"Yeah, a few times in Sirte and once in Coronini with a high-powered rifle at a few hundred yards, but he was wearing a vest. I shot him twice back in that favela with a forty-five at less than fifty feet—once definitely in the head. By all accounts, he should be dead. Why?"

"His mother is a Succubus," he replied, flourishing his hand.

"Yeah, so?"

"They are of a race that does not exactly originate from this world..." He dragged it out slowly as if talking to a child.

I dropped my head, feeling a bit slow on the uptake. I should have made the connection after seeing his crazy damned aura. *Demons, or fallen angels, like most Old Ones, were almost impervious to small-arms fire.* It's reasonable, in that case, that even a point-blank shot with my Glock would leave no more than a nasty bruise. However, I couldn't help but think that a close-range shot from a fifty caliber would do some damage and that armor-piercing rounds might cause serious injury. I was even willing to bet those wildcatted .338 rounds would do some damage if fired from close enough. While I relished the idea of testing those theories, a good blade had always proven effective at hacking bulletproof monsters to pieces. At least I knew better than to pull a gun on the prick the next time we met.

"He's still out there," I said, craning my neck to see Elegast.

"Indeed," he replied. "What, pray tell, do you intend to do about it?"

"Me?"

"After Elegast and I affirm this story and all of these revelations, you will be able to pursue him without reprisal from either Court," Belphoebe added. "And we will lift the warrants issued through human channels on our behalf, as well."

"Wow, that's mighty nice of you," I said, unable to stop myself from snorting.

"Naturally, we will," she responded, completely missing my indignation.

"Would a little help be too much to ask?" I replied, getting to my feet and glaring at them both. "After all, the bastard did kill members of both Courts, too." I folded my arms.

"Of course both Courts want nothing more than to see justice done and vengeance meted out against the one responsible for the death of our kith and kin," Elegast replied, suddenly resembling a politician on the campaign trail. "But think of how grateful both Courts would be to the individual, or individuals, who carried out this justice."

Elegast, ever the statesman.

"Diomedes, *we* are the ones that would hunt this wretch," Belphoebe said, rising to her feet and pointing from herself to Elegast. "But more pressingly for you, we are also the ones who will plead your case, no? Besides, I would think the great human Guardian Diomedes ought to easily manage taking down a lone cambion miscreant."

Of course. Pheebs was Sidhe, and they never do anything straightforward. I narrowed my eyes at both of them. I couldn't help but feel as though I'd been volunteered as shark bait.

Then I comprehended what was happening, and I had to look away and take a few deep breaths: being fae, they expected me to bargain with them for their help. Despite the obvious gain they would get out of capturing the Hanner Brid, they knew I would pursue him no matter what, so they gained nothing by helping freely. Paranoid or not, I'd dealt with the fae enough to know that I couldn't trust any of them when there was something to be gained or lost. I glared at both of them then let my eyes fall to the ground, and put my hands on my hips. I left my affinity for dealing with political crap with Agamemnon and Nestor at Troy. I was done with games.

"Pheebs, don't play coy with me. You admit that Duma and I saved your ass from that so-called '*miscreant*.' *You* owe *me*. And you both know I'm going after this guy with or without your help. This piece of shit is as much a pain in my ass as he is yours, so if I need help of any kind, just give it to me for once."

"Things are never as simple as they appear to you humans." Belphoebe narrowed her eyes.

My pointing out to her that she owed me for saving her life no doubt royally pissed her off. Elegast, on the other hand, nodded almost imperceptibly.

"We should all be on our respective ways," Elegast said, placing a hand on Belphoebe's shoulder. "There is much to do on all our parts, and time is pressing, is it not?"

"Yeah, it is." I scratched at my head, trying not to irritate the cuts and bruises that covered it as I tried to control my temper.

I walked to the game trail that led toward the confluence of the Great Morava and the Danube. Irritated at both Pheebs and Elegast, I trudged halfway before I remembered I had no need to head there since the boat would be long gone and that Duma and I were supposed to meet up at the portal through the Ways back in the clearing. *Where the hell is he?*

By the time I got back to the glade, the Dreaich and Belphoebe had already left, and Elegast was standing in front of the opening about to step through himself. He stopped and faced me, placing one hand on the pommel of his knife, holding out the Hanner Brid's papers in the other.

"Most of this is ruined, but what isn't details events and happenings within the human realm, not Fae. They are of more concern to you than us. There does appear to be some actionable intelligence in there, however. And tell the Peri that I will be in Calanchi. If you have need, have him contact me there." He said the last a little louder than was probably necessary.

Elegast stepped into the portal, and suddenly everything was quiet again. And dark. As I stood alone in silence, finally recognizing what I was going up against, the depth of my fatigue hit me. Not only at chasing the Hanner Brid, but three thousand years of politics and mayhem while being an underdog. I started to think about Sarah and all the what-ifs and tried to imagine what "normal" was like. It made me feel like the giant Tolfin at a high school prom. Normal and I didn't fit in the same sentence — probably not even the same book.

Rather than search for Duma, I sat down and decided to wait for him to show himself. Finding a hidden fae in the dark in unfamiliar terrain was tantamount to finding an Action Comics Number One Superman comic at a yard sale, and I wasn't about to waste my time. Instead, I began examining the sheaf of papers I'd grabbed.

Elegast was right. The wad of papers, maps, and documents were melded into a warm wet lump that proved useless to me, with two notable exceptions. Mixed into the molten mass of indistinguishable paper pulp were two maps. Like most military-grade charts, they were waterproof and still completely legible. I knew from my glimpse at them back in the underground room that they were highly detailed topographic maps of railroads in North Korea. I couldn't make out much in the moonlight, but I could still see the handwritten notations at several points along the map where the graphite glinted in the limited ambient light. *Is there any way these are related to an assassination attempt that hasn't happened yet? Could I be that lucky?*

I found myself smiling. The sudden realization that I might actually know when and where the Hanner Brid would be brought me instantly to my feet. I had to find Duma. *Now.*

"'Bout time those jackasses left," Duma said from my right in a tone that suggested both relief and irritation. "Based on that shit-eating grin on your face, please tell me you got something good, D. After the last few days, I could use some good news."

"Maybe. Get us someplace safe."

CHAPTER 30

I COULD TELL WHERE WE WERE even before Duma opened the gateway back into the world. The heat and humidity pressed in on us inside the Ways, but it also became electric. I had an overwhelming sense of mangroves, suntan lotion, and the tropical scent of coconuts, garlic, cumin, and pork. Miami.

We emerged in the dark into a sandy stand of sea grape, gumbo-limbo, and palm trees. I could hear, but not see, the surf as well as traffic, very close by, coming from opposite directions. I could also make out the faint sounds of heavy electronic thumping of club music somewhere farther up the beach. *Of course Duma would bring us to South Beach.* We hurried toward the traffic, pushed through the trees, and hopped over a short wall onto the boardwalk along Ocean Drive.

"I got a place a few blocks up Ocean," Duma said without slowing or even concerning himself with the fact he appeared to be a refugee from a renaissance fair and I was dressed like a cosplayer at a *Call of Duty* convention. "C'mon." Despite his injuries, he definitely was faring far better than I was. My body ached everywhere, and I was ready to fall over and sleep for a month.

Bombarded by the thumping noises emanating from hotel bars and cars painted garish colors, I passed an endless line of pink, light-blue and pale-yellow art deco hotels trimmed in matching neon, all surrounded by throngs of people dressed in everything from the tiniest bikinis to formal wear. As we walked along the boardwalk, we just didn't stand out. *Hell, compared to the guy on roller skates wearing a plastic pink flamingo as a hat, with rainbow suspenders holding up his Speedo, we are downright boring.*

Duma strolled along as if he made the trip on a regular basis, and every so often, women waved at him as if they knew him.

"Keep a low profile here, do you?" I asked.

"No such thing as low profile here. I fit right in."

We continued without garnering so much as a disinterested double take before stopping directly across the street from an unremarkable and almost subdued pastel-pink five-story building with light-blue trim. We jogged through the mostly stopped traffic to cross the street then walked past the hostess station set in a row of square blue umbrellas that read "Clevelander."

I followed Duma straight toward the building's lobby, where a full chorus of "Good evening, Mr. Fermini," greeted him as we strolled through the crowd waiting to be seated. Duma gave a friendly but dismissive wave and kept walking.

We walked through the funky art deco showroom of a lobby to the front desk. The space was a combination of open marble floors ranging from dark brown to white and pea green, and brown-checkered carpet completed the seating area. It was like something from the Mad Hatter's acid trip. As we approached the desk, the young woman behind it smiled at Duma, offered a cheery greeting, and held out an RFID key card. He wordlessly snatched it without really acknowledging her. I felt like a donkey stomping along behind him, clearly out of place.

I couldn't help but stare at the remarkably bizarre chairs as we passed through the lobby. The seats varied from brown to red and took shapes from buckets to slides, while some even resembled plush park benches. I distractedly followed Duma to the elevators, where he swiped the card then pressed a button for the top floor. We got off and headed down the hall to a room at the front of the hotel that would almost certainly have a view out over the ocean. Despite the crowds, or maybe because of them, I actually felt safe. Now that I didn't have to keep watching over my shoulder for either Fairy Court, a huge weight had been lifted off my shoulders. The governmental agencies still after us didn't bother me as much. I'd been avoiding human authorities forever. Besides, South Beach was full of human fugitives of one kind or another, so a few more wouldn't raise an eyebrow. In addition, while I may not have seen his security measures, I knew Duma would never have brought us somewhere that wasn't secure.

Once inside the austere guest room, decorated with cold white marble floors and light-beige and white furniture, the bank of jalousie windows with an unobstructed view of the Atlantic drew my eye. I could barely hear over the music booming up from the pool area below, but I could still hear the ocean, which made me relax a bit, and I sat down.

"Whoa, ah, ah, ah. Get your grimy ass off my furniture," Duma said, animatedly shooing me off the couch.

"Nice view," I said, jumping back up and walking over to the window.

"Yeah, no kidding." Duma stood at the windows overlooking the pool area. "Damn, will you look at the ass on that one..."

"Duma, hey... Duma!" I shouted, snapping my fingers. "Hey, pool boy, can you get us some food while I clean up so we can start figuring out what we need to do next?"

"Anything you want," he said without breaking his focus on the activity around the pool below.

I picked a pillow up off the bed and threw it at him. "Yo! Food, plan, catch bad guy... remember..." I said, raising my voice even louder.

"Oh, yeah," he replied, finally facing me. "Food, sure. Got it." He grabbed the phone on a table next to the couch while I went into the bathroom to clean up.

After showering, I headed back out into the suite with a towel wrapped around my waist, noticing that the room itself reminded me of the bathroom — and not in a good way. Nothing about the room said or even suggested comfort, but it was the kind of place people paid big money for.

Duma was nowhere to be found, but two carts loaded with covered plates and a champagne bucket filled with ice and tiny bottles of water were waiting near the only table in the room. I grabbed a bottle of water, pulled the maps from my vest, and spread them on the curving chrome-and-wood monstrosity of a table that was more artsy than functional. The piece of furniture was low, too, but it matched the height of the ridiculously rigid white leather sofa. The whole place made my skin crawl.

I began to study the maps. I guessed the region as North Korea because I recognized the name of one of the cities on one of the maps — Ch'ongjin, along the country's northern coast. A region approximately forty miles south of Ch'ongjin running west from the coast, almost to the border with China, was circled in red. The second map was a smaller-scale topographic survey of a railroad line passing through a valley running roughly southeast-northwest. Key geographical features proved that the second one was, in fact, a more detailed map of the region circled on the larger one.

Although my exhilarating dip in the Danube had destroyed them, I recalled that some of the documents I'd grabbed along with the maps detailed the North Korean *presidential* railway system and even included some blueprints of a special train. A series of times and dates were listed neatly along the eastern and western edges of the smaller-scale map and next to four points marked with Xs along the floor of the valley. One notation, which read *12/17/11* with an arrow pointing west, was written at the eastern edge of the valley, while *12/24/11* with an arrow pointing east was printed on the western side. Whatever it was for, it was going to happen either on December seventeenth or the twenty-fourth, less than six weeks out.

Given Elegast's assessment and my assumption about the maps, I guessed that the dates and times were a schedule for the presidential train. The only reason the Hanner Brid would have them was because he intended to kill, or at the very least attack, the only human of political consequence in the entire country — Kim Jong-Il. To really stir things up, however, he would have to make it appear as if a Western power, most likely the United States, had carried out the attack. Equally frightening was the recollection of another set of blueprints among those now-useless papers I'd taken for a tunnel system beneath the Tishreen Palace in Syria. And if what I'd been told so far was at all correct, the Hanner Brid had a hand in what was *already* happening in both Libya and Egypt. That certainly would explain the chaotic and unorganized fighting we'd encountered in Sirte. He was trying to cause further destabilization in already-unstable regions. That could send the human world into war. *But how would that benefit him?* What really scared me was the realization that he was a mercenary, not a mastermind. *So who's pulling his strings?*

Since I no longer had usable information on Syria, I would have to make the most of the North Korean intel I did have. If I couldn't catch the bastard, I could at least stop him.

While I was making sense of what I had, Duma walked in, barefooted, wearing a plush white robe, and his long blond hair slicked back and wet. He stopped, glanced at me on the couch, strolled to the bathroom, grabbed a robe off a shelf, and threw it to me.

"This may be South Beach, but cover up, D," he said as he flopped down with an audible sigh of contentment into a white leather chair that resembled a teacup open along one side.

"Sorry, I needed to see what we had to work with here," I said, pulling on the robe.

It took me less than ten minutes to fill him in on what I'd figured out so far as we ate. "Based on other documents we found in Coronini, this is part of the Presidential Railway System, and I can only imagine that his intention is to somehow attack it," I said.

"So you think this is where we'll find him then?"

"Well, even if we don't, I have no intention of letting him kill Kim Jong-Il," I said.

"Isn't that guy some sort of major jerk? Why not just let him do it? Your world would be better off without him, wouldn't it?"

"Yeah, he's a first-class *balloon knot*, but his death could cause all kinds of trouble if it appears as if the West did it."

Duma smiled at me when I used his term.

"Supposedly, the Hanner Brid has already had a hand in furthering the discord throughout the Middle East and North Africa. We can't let him start up trouble with an unstable *nuclear* power. Whatever his plan, we can't let him succeed, and if this" — I pointed to the maps — "gives me a chance to stop or kill him, then I'm going to take it."

"Assuming he'll still go through with it now that we have these maps."

"Trust me, the same thing occurred to me, but right now, this is the only actionable intelligence we have," I said.

"Whatever," Duma said, sitting back in his chair again. "Count me in. When do we leave?"

"The dates listed here aren't for a few weeks, but we'll need to gather our own eyes-on intelligence before the target dates, and I need to find out as much about the North Korean Presidential Rail System as possible before we leave."

"So I have some time." He waggled his eyebrows at me and walked back over to the window above the bar and pool, surveying his kingdom from on high. "And if it's a few weeks out, Ab should be able to join us. Me-ow..." he said, once again focused on the activities below.

CHAPTER 31

I LET DUMA HAVE HIS FUN while I got some much-needed sleep—or at least some rest. The constant thump of music and dancing coming from outside my window combined with the fact the bed was only marginally softer than the marble floor made sleeping nearly impossible. And waiting it out proved useless. South Beach went from dusk till dawn and back to dusk again. Still, I was tired enough that I managed to sleep most of the night.

A day later, Duma got us new burner cell phones, and we began contacting sources that might have useful information about anything in North Korea. My first call was to the Metis Foundation. Before the phone rang three times on my end, there was a knock at the hotel room door, and a familiar tingle surged up my spine and into my skull. I wasn't even remotely surprised Athena had chosen to show up.

"Just trying to call..." I said, holding up the phone as I answered the door. "But seeing as you've come all this way, please come in."

"You seem none the worse for wear, Diomedes," she said in a concerned tone while remaining otherwise completely stoic.

As usual, she was dressed in a well-tailored linen suit with a tight skirt cut right above the knee, only instead of her usual charcoal-gray pinstripe, the suit was cream colored. She wore her fiery-red hair pulled back into a heavy double braid. The light-colored suit somehow made her normally pale skin appear slightly less wan. Even without makeup, she would put the women of South Beach to shame if she ever decided to reveal her true form to any human but me and a few others. Unlike her Protogenoi brethren, she never cared about her appearance and never dallied with anyone or anything in our world. She took pride in her virgin goddess reputation, but I'd seen men lay down their lives for her on the chance that she might deign to offer her favors. I'd also seen aspects of her countenance that were equally as disturbing as her striking beauty. Despite her present appearance, those were the ones that kept me focused.

Athena gave me an odd once-over as she entered. It finally dawned on me that I was still wearing the robe because my only apparel consisted of dirty fatigues, boots, a grimy T-shirt, and my vest.

"Don't look at me in that tone of voice," I said. "Everything I have is a bit ripe and covered in either blood, mud, or both."

She simply smiled in the same agreeable manner a mother uses when her child offers her a handful of tadpoles.

I sat down on the couch in front of the maps, and she eyed the funky chair opposite as if trying to determine the best way to lower herself into it. She chose to stand, arms crossed across her chest. Her mouth was little more than a soft slit across her face, but her eyes blazed intensely beneath the deep blue of her irises. That was my cue.

As usual, my debriefing with Athena was mostly perfunctory and a pragmatic exercise for my benefit. We were connected to such a degree that she knew not only where I was, but also what was going on in my mind at all times. She respected me enough, however, to stay out of my head. She sat and listened passively without batting an eyelash in response. After I told her everything I knew, she brought me up to date on everything I *didn't know* in the same mechanical way she'd listened to me.

As if she were reading a grocery list, she told me the current situation in North Africa had escalated, leading to the murder of Gaddafi within the last few days, and that the underpinnings of an uprising had begun in Syria. Apparently, she and the Metis Foundation also had their hands full trying to assuage increasing tensions in the Gaza Strip and Iran.

A bounty had been placed on my head by the leader of the Hacky Yacky Barracuda thingy back in Japan, and the Liuntika Strigoi were grumbling about my recent uninvited visit. And while I was still wanted by the US government for acts of terrorism, the bounties offered by the Seelie and Unseelie Courts had been officially suspended. *The small things in life make us feel special.*

The only thing she told me that actually surprised me was that Belphoebe had orchestrated the blackout of most of Southern California that had complicated my original flight from the Cu Sith in order to make her pursuit of me through San Diego easier. City and county officials were blaming the power failure on simple human error, though locals weren't buying it. It was kind of flattering that she'd found it necessary to go to such extremes. Apparently, rumors about green dogs and bears running around San Diego were rampant, along with conspiracy theories about the sonic booms that were heard across the city. Typical of videos of such nature, they all showed the glamoured Cu Sith as little more than an out-of-focus indistinguishable green quadruped of indeterminate size and shape, and were the butt of jokes and ridicule on morning radio and across the Internet. Unfortunately, there was still a BOLO out for someone sort of fitting my description with regards to attacking and kidnapping police and stealing a patrol car the night of the blackout.

After spending the better part of the morning debriefing, Athena left, promising to get me everything she could on North Korea while I figured out the best way to stop the Hanner Brid from attacking that train or, at the very least, keep him from killing Kim Jong-Il. Duma returned sometime after sunset with clothes, food, and a laptop, and I sat down to research North Korea.

There was damn little out there on North Korea. I did pull up satellite maps of the area south of Ch'ongjin but found next to nothing on the Presidential Railway System except rumors and speculation. There was one BBC news report of an explosion along the railroad near Ryongchon on the southern border with China back in 2004. According to the report, the disaster had led to extreme paranoia regarding presidential safety and prompted increased security measures around the train. Increased from *what*, I couldn't tell.

Despite my best efforts and hours of searching, I found nothing of any real value, but on a lark, I pulled up weather conditions for December in that part of North Korea and practically froze while I read. Snow. Cold and snow. Really cold and lots of snow. Everything I read said it was a freaking winter wonderland—way up in the mountains, isolated, covered in snow, and perhaps as cold as ten below during the day.

Hoo-fuckin'-yah.

After another meal and another fitful night's sleep, I was starting to feel somewhat normal though still dismayed about the dearth of information. I was back to searching when the room phone rang. No one except Duma and Athena knew where I was. On edge, I picked it up to find it was the receptionist at the front desk. I unclenched a bit.

"There is a courier here with a package for you," said the desk clerk.

"Sure, send them up." I hung up then pulled the Sig from my vest still lying in a smelly heap on the floor outside the bathroom.

I went into the bathroom to watch the door from a safe vantage point. *In my line of work, it pays to wear a tinfoil hat sometimes.*

I could hear footsteps echoing outside in the marble-floored hallway, followed by several sharp raps at the door.

"Leave it at the door, please." I dropped to one knee, aiming about a foot above the doorknob.

"Steve!" a familiar female voice replied.

I stood up, holding the gun down at my side. "Um... Sarah?"

"Steve, yes. It's me, Sarah," she replied hoarsely. She didn't come across as surprised at all.

Agent Sarah Wright of the Department of Homeland Security, at my hotel hidey-hole door in Miami. *What the hell is she doing here? How did she know where to find me? What am I supposed to say to her?* After our last brief meeting and our recent phone conversations, maybe I would be better off jumping out the window instead of answering the door. My stomach started to flop, and my hands got all sweaty. As I wiped my hands off on my shorts, the sight of my gun shifted my thoughts from Sarah and me to the situation with the Hanner Brid again. Things were complicated, to say the least.

"Steve... Diomedes," Sarah said again in a hoarse whisper, knocking a little more insistently. "Let me in."

After what felt like an eternity, I finally discovered I could move again. "Uh, yeah," I said, my voice cracking. "Hold on."

As I reached to open the door, the paranoid part of me kicked back in. Medea, a particularly nasty witch, had used Sarah to try to kill me by sending her unexpectedly to my home in San Diego. The Hanner Brid had the ability to do the same thing. I avoided peering through the peephole because a skilled attacker would know exactly where I was when the light through the hole darkened as I blocked it. Instead, I stood as far to the side of the door as I could, unlatched it, then leaned back, ready to fire.

"Diomedes," Sarah whispered as the door opened a bit. Then the door opened all the way, and she walked into the room, carrying a large banker's box. Her eyes quickly darted around to take stock of the situation.

Unlike the last time she'd showed unexpectedly, nothing about her suggested she was under a spell or the influence of someone else, so I relaxed a bit against the wall and lowered my gun. The subtle movement drew Sarah's attention, and she dropped the box and jumped with a start.

"You son of a bitch!" she screamed, hands on hips, trying to catch her breath. As soon as I was close enough, she hit me in the shoulder—the same one I'd been shot in. "Why'd you scare me like that? And what the hell is going on?"

The shock of the impact on my sore shoulder almost made me drop my gun. Grasping the wound, I put the gun back on safety and walked toward the couch, relieved it was really Sarah.

"Did you just *safety* that gun?" She slammed the door behind her, jarring the windows, and me, sending my maps and papers flying with the breeze.

"Well, after the last time you showed up unexpectedly, I thought it might be wise." I dropped onto the couch with a sigh, followed by a loud grunt as my spine experienced the equivalent of a car crash. I dropped the gun next to me then set about gathering the errant maps and papers.

Sarah picked up the box, and I motioned at the chair across from me. She crossed to the table and dropped the heavy box onto it with a thud that sent the rest of the papers flying. She folded her arms and glowered at me with such force that I had to sit back.

Even in her agitated state, she was attractive. Her black pantsuit and white shirt were disheveled, from travel and probably irritation. Her brown ponytail was starting to come apart, and her gray eyes, while at the moment coldly boring into my skull, also offered an odd comfort and provided a fleeting instant of exhilaration as our eyes met. Her expression softened a bit when she saw the fresh bruises and injuries. It only lasted a second, though.

"What the hell have you gotten into now? You look like hell. And what's up with this... place?" She gestured around at the room. "I was under the impression that you and Duma were laying low. And don't tell me it's a long story." After a second of stark silence, she continued in a quieter voice. "No kidding." She glanced around the room then down at the box and papers I'd placed back on the table.

"I'm sorry," I said. My mind was a total blank except for her. And I suddenly found myself out of my depth. I had almost a hundred sixty generations of grandchildren, though none past my own children ever knew I existed, thanks to Aphrodite. I hadn't allowed myself to care for, let alone have a relationship with, anyone in nearly two centuries. Personal relationships, romantic or otherwise, didn't fit in very well with my job. But despite my immortality, I refused to give up my humanity, and that part of me craved contact no matter how much I denied it or tried to avoid it.

Her frown disappeared, and she let her arms fall to her side as if she knew what was going on in my head. And then things became awkward again. I didn't even know *how* to say what was on my mind, and she probably was afraid to say anything for fear I would shoot her down.

The silence between us was palpable, and I suddenly couldn't look at her. I was embarrassed. Not only because I was awkward at personal relationships, but because I had treated her unfairly over the past few months. She deserved better. I prided myself on being an honorable man, yet I reacted toward her like a confused teenager.

I was about to say something when the door opened, and Duma entered in grand style, dressed as if he were going out for the night. Or, more likely, just coming back.

"Well, I'll be," he said, taking off his sunglasses and spreading his arms as he recognized Sarah. "If it ain't Sarah, Warrior Princess! Still a hottie, I see."

Sarah smiled at him and gave him a friendly, girlish wave with both hands, but then her expression turned dour again.

"Aw, come on," he said, glancing between us. "Things would be a whole lot easier for me if you two would hop in the sack and get it over with already. This whole denial-avoidance thing is getting old." He waved his hands around randomly as he spoke.

Sarah stared down and scratched absently at her neck. I could feel myself flush as I cleared my throat and sat up, pretending to focus on the maps in front of me. While Duma had no problems with casual relationships, they weren't my style.

"No? Oh, well—suit yourselves." He somehow managed to sit in the artsy chair without appearing ungainly, then put his sunglasses back on. "I can do every bit as weird as you guys can."

After a few more minutes of pregnant silence, Duma finally spoke up again. "Wow, you two really are freaks. So, Sarah... how in the hell did you find us here?"

"Oh, uh, I got a message from the Metis Foundation to forward this" — she pointed at the box on the table — "to this address and room number. When the request came from them, I thought Diomed... you guys might need my help, so I took some emergency leave from work and flew down with it."

"Oh, goodies from Lady High and Mighty. What's in it?"

When I didn't reply, Duma clapped his hands and called my name.

"I assume it's information on North Korea," I said, gathering myself.

"North Korea?" Sarah replied. "Are you kidding me?"

"Yeah, North Korea." Opening it, I told myself I had to focus and that Sarah's presence was exactly the kind of distraction I didn't need.

The box held multiple file folders, each stuffed with pages of documents, papers, charts, maps, pictures, and even some hand-drawn sketches. There were also two discs in paper envelopes. I spread photos across the table and started to sort the contents into similar piles, mostly to give the impression I was suddenly busy. Much of it appeared to be reports on possible recent missile tests and suspected weapons programs, but there were also multiple files on state-run transportation, including the railway, and the country's geography.

"This appears to be some sort of special train and railway." Sarah picked up one image and pointed at a few others. "This isn't Kim Jong-Il's train, is it?" she asked, her voice raised and agitated.

"Balloon knot!" Duma said enthusiastically. "I've decided every time someone says that name, I'm gonna shout 'balloon knot.' Ooh, better yet, I'll get a few bottles of tequila, and we can take shots instead."

I glowered at him. "Would you be serious, Duma."

"Balloon knot?" Sarah asked. "Do I want to know?"

"Means asshole," I said. "We got work to do."

"D, you gotta lighten up, man." Duma shook his head, slapping his thighs. "Tell you what — I'm gonna go down to the pool for a bit. You two figure things out. Beat each other up, play a game, or, ah, whatever. I'll be back in an hour, then we'll get to work." He hopped up and left without making a sound on the hard floor.

Agitated, I stood up, and Sarah dropped the photo back onto the table.

"Look—" Sarah said.

"Sarah, the last thing I want is to 'get things out of the way,' as Duma suggests, but I'm not interested in just hopping into bed. We really do need to talk about us, but now isn't the right time."

"There never is a *right* time," she said, meeting my gaze. "I understand something serious is going on with you right now. Hell, I have the terrorist watch list bulletin with a sketch that is the spitting image of you sitting on my desk." She walked over and took my hand in hers. "But I don't have a clue what's going on between us, or even if there is an us. But I'll tell you that not knowing is driving me crazy. I don't know if I'm just helping you or if there really is something here."

"I—"

"I'm not finished. I understand the situation better than you think. Now is *not* the time to figure things out, but when this is done, we need to—I need us to—figure it out, okay?"

"I promise," I said through a closed-up throat then squeezed her hand.

Smiling, she returned the gesture. I suddenly realized the prospect of figuring out what, if any, future we had, buoyed my spirits.

"Good. I'll hold you to it this time, but right now we've got work to do."

No sooner did she finish her statement than the door opened and Duma walked back in.

"Not what I was hoping for, but what did I expect from you two?" Duma shook his head. "Yeah, I was listening at the door. Get over it. You humans: as short as your lives are, well, most of your lives"—he glanced at me then back at Sarah—"you'd think you wouldn't dillydally so much. Tch."

CHAPTER 32

WE SPENT MOST OF THE rest of the day going over the documents that Sarah had brought, and even with my tactical background, Sarah's past experience on the FBI's counterterrorism Fly Team, and Duma's knack for stealth and infiltration, the general assessment was not a positive one. To make things worse, Duma's contacts proved entirely unhelpful. On the upside, I recognized some of the classified documents Sarah had brought because I had seen copies in the Hanner Brid's collection back in Coronini. She'd obtained the secret documents through government channels with the help of Athena, and that was scary enough. I didn't even want to think about how the Hanner Brid got them.

"According to these intelligence reports, the area circled"—I pointed to the smaller-scale map—"is a valley through which the Paektusan Ch'ŏngnyŏn rail line runs. And it's the only east-west rail connector in the northern state of Yanggang-do. Three of the four marks on that map coincide with rail tunnels along the line, while the remaining spot marks a railway trestle. The entire area lies anywhere from eight to thirty miles out from the nearest reasonably sized town."

"According to this geological survey, that entire valley is deep, mountainous, and altogether inhospitable—and very isolated," Duma replied. "All things considered, this particular valley would make an excellent kill box from a tactical point of view."

"You're assuming that's what this shows?" Sarah asked. "This is this guy's planned area to attack Kim Jong-Il's train? Because, according to these documents, these buildings are military industrial complexes, and that"—she pointed to several areas around the circled area—"is presumed to be an active nuclear testing area. And those are airbases. The area is crawling with military. It doesn't sound so logical to me."

"Well, logical, tactical or not, even if the Hanner Brid knows where Kim will be and when, there's still an issue with the train," I said. "Or should I say trains. Because the paranoid SOB has a fleet of six of them—two sets of three heavily armored ninety-car trains. One train travels in front to check rail safety and security, the middle train transports Kim, while the third train carries security, support staff, and communications equipment. It's insane."

Duma laughed. "That fits 'cause the Hanner Brid's clearly crazy. If you're right and these maps detail where and when he's going to attack this balloon knot, then sane or not, we have to figure out how and stop him, right?"

Sarah stared down at the maps, arms crossed over her chest. "Maybe he intends to blow up the trains?"

"I doubt it," I replied, digging at a few papers and passing them across the table toward her. "Kim's extremely paranoid after a potential bombing back in 2004. Those indicate there is a time gap of twenty minutes between the first and second train and an hour between the second and third train. People are sent ahead with the first train specifically to sweep the tracks for safety. I'm guessing—given the time lag between trains—that he intends to isolate the middle train by blowing one or more of the tunnels and the trestle and stage an assault on it while it's trapped."

"That is crazy," Sarah said. "Where does that leave us? We can't stage an assault on an assault."

"Of course not. The Hanner Brid is far too good for that. Besides, we don't have the manpower to pull that off," I said. "And the last thing we need is a full-scale incursion and battle within the borders of the most closed-off country on the planet. I'm going to get on Kim's train and stop the Hanner Brid when he comes for him."

"Okay, I take it back," Duma said with a sarcastic laugh. "*That* plan is insane."

"How on earth do you plan on sneaking aboard the top-secret, heavily armored train of one of the most paranoid dictators the world has ever seen?" Sarah dropped her hands to her hips, and the scowl on her face reminded me of Athena's warrior countenance.

"I'm not entirely sure. Yet." I shuffled through more papers, searching for something. "But there are special train stations that only

Kim uses. I can wait for him at one of those and sneak onboard while he's there."

"You mean the nineteen stations that US, South Korean, and Japanese intelligence agencies *think* exist but have only successfully identified four?" Sarah asked. "And those four are all on the other side of the area we're talking about."

"Yeah," I said. "But if this area is heavily militarized and is also the location for ongoing nuclear testing, then there has to be a station nearby, right? We just need to find it."

"So assuming we find it, your plan is to, what? *Sneak* aboard what is probably the most secure train in the known world?" Sarah asked.

"Yeah, Mr. Stealthy, you just gonna tiptoe over to it and hop on?" Duma smiled broadly, more amused than upset. "At least you're not planning on pulling a Butch and Sundance."

Duma was right. Getting aboard that train surreptitiously was his thing, not mine, but given the mind-control issues, Duma was not my best option. It had to be me onboard that train. "I'm fucked." I slammed a pencil down on the table, scattering papers, pens, and other objects.

Sarah jumped a bit but quickly recovered and went back to examining a handful of papers.

Duma watched me quizzically, his brow heavily knitted. "Wrong." He leaned forward in his seat. "*We're* fucked, unless you can turn invisible."

Sarah said nothing while she continued to read. Suddenly, I felt claustrophobic—hemmed in by the ugly table, couch, Duma and Sarah—not to mention seriously irritated at the possibility of losing this bastard. *Again.* I pounded my fist down on the table so hard, the wood broke and the marble floor beneath it cracked. Duma and Sarah both jerked back.

"If that prick figured out some way to pull this off, then I can damn well figure a way onto that train to stop him," I said, practically roaring.

"D, calm the hell down," Duma said, sitting forward again and holding up his hands. "Don't break the room! And besides, it won't help to get pissed."

"We have to rethink it," Sarah said calmly, picking up papers and maps. "Maybe we should focus on those tunnels and bridges marked on the map."

I growled dismissively and stormed off toward the oceanfront window. I could hear papers being shuffled and Duma mumbling about the floor and table.

Out the window, the running lights of a boat bobbed in the darkness. The boat made its way north against the winds until the little red light suddenly vanished. The disappearance caught my attention, but the light suddenly popped up again a short distance farther north. The boat must have passed behind *something* I couldn't see in the blackness, which momentarily obscured it from view. And Duma's words hit me: *Invisible.*

"Invisible," I said, turning back to Duma and Sarah. "I need to be invisible."

I moved with blinding speed back to Sarah, pulled her close, and kissed her — not a romantic kiss, but a joyous one. My action caught us both completely by surprise. Sarah stiffened and stood wide-eyed, glancing between Duma and me.

"Uh, sorry," I said, quickly letting her go before turning to Duma, who was prying at the broken marble tiles on the floor. "Duma..."

"What?" he said, agitatedly picking at the broken pieces.

"*Invisible,*" I replied, noticing that Sarah was smiling, which almost made me forget my point. "Oh, come on, Duma, forget the floor. Surely this can't be the first time one of these rooms has been trashed. Besides, I think I figured it out. Maybe."

Duma stood up, hands on his hips, and sighed heavily. "Okay, I know. *Invisibility.* So? You know where the Ring of Gyges is or something? And if you do, are you sure you want to go down *that* road? I mean, *I* would, but then you know I don't have your moral compass."

His comment stopped me for a second. I couldn't risk the consequences even if I did know where the ring was. Most items that allow the user to cloak themselves, like the Ring of Gyges, exacted a huge price. Even that simple gold ring found by a shepherd named Gyges of Lydia several thousand years ago caused the wearer to become increasingly morally corrupted each time he wore it.

"What about some other object that has similar powers?" I asked. "There have to be others."

"The only other thing I know like the ring is Cassivellaunus's cloak, and it has the same issues for you humans—your morals and all that. Plus, good luck finding it," Duma replied.

"No, it's destroyed," I said. "I stole it from him and burned it back about 50 BC. He obtained it under questionable circumstances and used it to his advantage over other kings. I couldn't allow that to continue."

Sarah stared at us, eyes wide and mouth agape, as if we were speaking some foreign language. Magical items probably were a little farfetched to a mundane person, but after all she'd been through, I didn't think she would be so taken aback.

And then she spoke up. "What about Athena's helm?"

"Well, technically, it's not hers. It's Hades's cap, and it's not likely he'll loan it to me like he did Perseus," I replied, suddenly staring hard at her. "He had pull since he was one of Zeus's sons after all." I continued staring.

"Don't act so shocked," she said. "I told you I was a geek."

"Geek! That's it," I said, clapping and then pointing at both Sarah and Duma at the same time. "The military has been working on cloaking technology for a while. If it exists, Geek will know about it. Once again, thanks, Sarah. You're a genius."

William "Geek" Elmsmore—computer dork and technological wizard—had impressed Athena with his prowess with electronics so much that she'd hired him as a consultant for the Metis Foundation. The former Royal Marine and one-time member of the British Navy's Special Boat Service, handpicked to help found its Squadron X, had to know if *any* branch of *any* military in *any* country were developing something like that. I grabbed my cell phone, punched in the number for the Metis Foundation, and asked for Will Elmsmore.

"Elmsmore," Geek said in a terse tone. I'd likely interrupted at least one of many projects he was probably working on simultaneously.

"Geek, it's me, Steve Dore, you know... Diomedes."

"Steve! Hang on a sec, mate," he said, suddenly excited. I could hear electronic clicking through the phone, followed by a low static hum that wouldn't go away. "There, that should do it," Geek said finally after a moment of silence. "Sorry, Steve, just want to make sure we're secure, mate. Good to hear your voice!"

"Good to talk to you, too. Listen, what can you tell me about cloaking technology? Is anyone close to developing a working device?" I asked, pushing the button to put him on speaker.

"You mean metamaterial cloaking?" Geek replied in a tone reminiscent of a child describing Christmas morning. "Fascinating field."

I sensed a lecture coming. It was like I was standing, stuck, at the bottom of a mountain as an avalanche barreled down at me at a hundred fifty miles per hour. *This is gonna hurt.*

Geek took a deep breath, then he began. "The whole idea is to control the way the light passes through some sort of manmade material. Has to be manmade 'cause nothing natural can be manipulated efficiently enough. The device wouldn't actually cause you to disappear as much as create a blind spot by deflecting the light spectrum through the metamaterial and *around* you. Think of the metamaterial like a sheet made up of a massive group of crystals lined up in a specific relationship, passing light around you, yeah?"

I suspected he was waiting for me to respond, but I'd already zoned out, so I mumbled affirmatively.

"The problem with natural crystals is they can only bend specific wavelengths of light in a single direction, and it can't be controlled well. If we want to use it as a cloaking device, it needs to be able to bend *all* wavelengths of light in *various* directions so that it can transmit light no matter where the next crystal is in relation to it. So they've been working on so-called metamaterials to do the work of the crystal. The metamaterials have a broader and controllable response range. Plus these manmade materials, unlike natural crystals, allow for a negative refractive index or even a zero RI or any fraction therein. Most importantly, they can deliver any response you want *at will.*"

He paused as if I were supposed to be impressed, but at that point, I was numb.

"Ah, Geek, forgive me, but I really don't have the time," I said. "I don't care how it works, I simply need to know if anyone has it working yet."

I could almost hear Geek deflate over the phone. "Well," he said, sighing heavily, "not really, though reports suggest that DARPA isn't far out from a working prototype. Maybe another few years or so. Sorry, mate."

"Damn, that's what I was afraid of."

"Isn't there some sort of, you know, *object* you can use, like, say, Harry Potter or Frodo?" Geek's voice became barely louder than a whisper. "Or some kind of magic or glamour?"

"Glamours and spells require the caster to be present, and I'm trying to keep this thing small. As for objects, we've already been down that road. There might be one object out there, but it's too risky to use and would take me too long to track down anyway. Thanks for your help, though, Geek. I'll try to stay in better touch. Oh, and if some... *one* named Tolfin contacts you, be nice, please. For my sake."

"Anytime, mate. Ah, should I be concerned about this Tolfin?"

"Nah, you guys will get along like two peas in a pod." I hung up and tossed the phone on the couch. "Well, damn."

I'm gonna stop this prick, even if I have to wear a tree costume and hide in the freakin' forest.

We were quiet for quite some time. I was deep in deliberation and assumed the others were, as well, but for all I knew, they were daydreaming about pancakes. I was stumped. Even at my most stealthy, there was no way to sneak on a train that would be that heavily guarded while underway, let alone while housed at a special train station built because the guy was so paranoid about such things happening.

The Hanner Brid had the easy part—there was no reason he would be covert when he hit the train. He needed a spectacle the world would see. Otherwise, what would be the point of an attack like this in such an isolated country?

"Dvalinn," Duma said.

"Huh?" I replied, initially caught off guard. "Oh, you mean the Dvergar smith?"

"Dvergar, Svartálfars, freaky underground metalheads, whatever you want to call them," Duma said with a shiver and an expression as though he'd eaten a sour apple. "Yeah. I remember hearing something a very long time ago that he created something that could make you disappear. Some stories say it was a helmet, others a cloak. But if anybody could pull it off..."

"I know him," I said. "And I know where he is. He made my knives and greaves. And some of his people work for Athena."

Sarah's vacant and mildly stunned expression suggested our conversation was beyond her.

"Dvalinn is the leader of what was left of the Dvergar, sometimes called Svartálfars or Dökkálfars, but are best known to humans as dwarves," I explained. "I don't know why, except that there are some archaic Germanic words for 'dwarf' that sound similar to 'dvergar.' They are also mistakenly called black or dark elves, too, though they are not elves and not even fae, for that matter. And they are no shorter than the average human. While they all don't have beards, they all share a love of smithing and technology, they live exclusively underground — to an individual — and they're creepy and very greedy. Including Dvalinn, who is probably the finest smith ever to walk this planet and makes metal items of such fine quality that some think they are magical in nature. Some of the objects he created thousands of years ago with his kinsman Durinn are even coveted by the Old Ones."

"Wow. Dvalinn, Durinn, sounds like the *Hobbit*," Sarah replied.

"They were definitely the inspiration for those dwarves," I said, smiling. "I don't know about the helm-cloak thing, but if something like this exists, then he'd be the one who made it."

Sarah's eyes grew larger, and she sat down heavily as if overwhelmed.

Maybe Duma was on to something. "You think he's still in Iceland?" I asked Duma.

"I've never met the guy, but probably," he replied, sucking at his teeth dismissively. "Just like that freak Goibniu, where the hell else is a smith gonna build his forge but in a volcano?"

"Then we need to get to Iceland right now," I said. "The southern coastline near Vik. And Sarah, no offense" — I pointed at her — "but I'm not dragging you into this one any farther. Until this gets cleared up, I'm still a fugitive, and that could cause you serious professional problems."

She opened her mouth as if to protest, but then I could see her thinking it through as her brow knitted heavily at first then relaxed. She pursed her lips and barely nodded a single time.

"Great, another damned volcano," Duma grumbled.

The last place I'd met with Dvalinn some two hundred forty years ago was at his forge located under a massive ice sheet with a name that sounded like "Vatnayokel" and covered one of the most active volcano fields in the world. A quick check with Athena via text message confirmed that according to the Svartálfars who worked with her, that was still his primary location.

Despite my desire to get moving fast, Duma moaned and groaned for another half an hour about how long it would take him to set things up to get us around Iceland. Apparently, the only gateway through the Telluric Pathways into Iceland was near another volcano named Askja, practically in the dead center of the country. And because it was the end of October, the conditions would be cold and icy.

The highway system in Iceland was limited to say the least, and the snow and ice of near winter would make some roads altogether impassable. It wasn't going to be a picnic, but Duma had resources I didn't, at least not at the drop of a hat—and especially since Athena needed to stay out of this beyond providing some intel.

Duma disappeared into another guest room down the hall, leaving Sarah and me alone. I tried to gather my gear, but it was all lying in the same pile it had been for the last few days. After that brilliant maneuver, I stood there, trying to think of what to do next to avoid having to explain the excited kiss or talk about our awkward relationship.

"Um—" I cleared my throat, staring at the floor.

"Oh, for the love of..." In one surreal moment, Sarah closed the distance between us, grabbed my face with both hands, and kissed me. *Hard.*

My first reaction was total surprise, but I acquiesced quickly and kissed her back. Feelings I had locked up for decades began pouring out in the form of passion. And then Duma walked back in, and Sarah and I quickly and clumsily tried to part and act as if nothing was happening. His gaping mouth and wide eyes said otherwise.

"*Now!*" he screamed. "Now! You two idiots choose now! I give you guys time before, even encourage it, but you'd rather wait until two minutes before we're supposed to leave. And you damn well better believe we're leaving in two minutes after all the crap I just went through."

He walked in and closed the door behind him, shaking his head, mumbling to himself while Sarah and I tried to act casual. I'm sure our performance came off more like a couple of teenagers trying to deny everything after being caught making out behind the library. As Duma went by, he smacked me in the back of my head.

"Get your fucking gear together, would you?" he said, trying to feign irritation, but I could see the smile creeping into his stern expression.

I hopped into motion. I smiled at Sarah as I grabbed my vest, then clumsily dropped my gun. I could feel my face flush.

"Uh, we need to go. I guess we'll... talk later," I said.

"Yeah, later," she replied, smiling back, pushing her hair behind her ear.

She appeared to be a hell of a lot less uncomfortable than I was at that moment. I was lucky I didn't trip over a chair. I followed Duma out of the room and watched as Sarah closed the door behind us. I waved like a toddler when his mom leaves. As soon as the door closed, I realized I must have come off like a freaking idiot, and I bumped into Duma. He was standing with his hands on his hips, meeting my gaze intently with consternation.

"What?" I replied weakly. I was out of my depth. Duma knew it, too.

"After what I walked in on, that's how you leave her?" he said through clenched teeth, keeping his voice low. "Are you serious?"

I stared at him, feeling stupid and confused.

"Your idiocy is not endearing, D." Lightening up a bit, he pushed my shoulder to turn me around and then pointed at the door. "Go, show her you're not a complete dork, you dork. Give her a proper good-bye. But make it fast, Romeo."

I dropped my vest with a muffled clunk, walked back down to the door, and knocked. Sarah answered, and her eyes suddenly widened. I grabbed her around the waist and kissed her — not softly but not urgently, either. I kept it brief.

"I, uh, wanted to say bye properly," I said without letting her go.

"That was better than just letting me close the door," she replied, smiling and touching my face. "Now you can go."

CHAPTER 33

WE MADE OUR WAY DOWN South Beach in the early evening, passed through the Ways, and emerged into a moonscape. Surprisingly, I didn't see any snow or ice, only a barren, rocky, alien terrain. The freezing but humid wind cut into me like a knife, howling through the frigid night air. Next to me, Duma was searching for something on the horizon, using his hand to shield his eyes from the blistering wind. He was entirely unfazed by the temperature. *Just once, I'd like to see him shiver or complain about sweating.* I was cursing his fae blood under my breath when he suddenly smiled and pointed at something behind me.

I huddled up and stomped my feet, trying to maintain my warmth, but failed miserably. Shivering, I saw a few blinking lights in the black sky, accompanied by the familiar roar of helicopter blades beating the air. Then a sunflower-yellow chopper that resembled a bulky pollywog came into view. I didn't exactly feel warmer, but the sight buoyed my spirits—until the rotor wash hit me. *I didn't think I could get any colder.*

The chopper set down on a flat area about fifty yards downwind of us, and we ducked and ran toward it. Once inside, Duma showed our destination to the copilot, who said something then began fiddling with the helicopter's navigational instruments.

"He said that they may not be able to land exactly where we want them to on the glacier, but that they'd get us as close as they could," Duma said, leaning forward in his seat, elbows on knees. "And they'll only wait around an hour because we don't have the permits to legally land on the ice sheet. I had to offer them an extra six hundred and fifty thousand kronurs for that."

"Six hundred and fifty thousand?"

"Relax, it's only five grand US," he replied, sitting back and closing his eyes again.

"Five grand?"

"*That's* what bothers you?" Duma asked. "Money? You should be more concerned about what Dvalinn might want in return for a magic cloak *if* he even has one."

I hadn't gotten beyond the possibility that Dvalinn might have something that would cloak me, but Dvalinn *was* a greedy bastard. At least he was up front with his greed and straightforward with his prices, unlike the Fae.

For my knives and greaves, he'd required that I kill and bring him the dragon of Wawel Hill outside Krakow in Poland. Even though I'd accomplished the task, Dvalinn almost reneged because he wasn't thrilled with the condition of the dragon. Fortunately, my connection to an Old One and Dvalinn's fear of losing some of his best customers held him to the bargain. I could not even imagine what the Lord of the Forge would want for something that could cloak me, but I was prepared to pay whatever he wanted to stop the Hanner Brid.

The rest of the flight to the glacier took less than an hour, and we touched down a little after midnight local time. The lights of the chopper turned the snow into a blindingly brilliant field of white in the stark black night. The pilot told Duma that he'd brought us within a kilometer of the spot I'd pointed out. They said they couldn't get closer because the instruments start behaving oddly closer to the exact position. *Figures.*

Duma and I scrambled out then pillaged the gear bags in the cargo bay before heading off. I hadn't been there in nearly two and a half centuries, but I recalled the entrance would be along a line that transected the peak of Esjufjöll and the highest peak on the Skaftafell Glacier to the southeast. The peak's name was unpronounceable, but even in the dark, both summits were visible as the waning moon reflected off the massive ice sheet.

We traveled fast, trying to get into position between the two peaks, then headed toward the top of Esjufjöll. At our speed, even over the ice, I managed to locate the lava tube entrance I hoped would lead us to Dvalinn in less than fifteen minutes. I kicked off the crampons at the tunnel mouth, cracked a chemical light stick, and headed in at a steady jog. The lava tube was small—I could actually touch the walls on either side without stretching—but its diameter remained consistent.

We kept jogging along for at least ten minutes before I began to feel heat radiating up the tube. "You need to go back and hold that chopper here. It's going to take me longer than an hour, and it's nearly thirty miles to the nearest town," I said, stopping to grab Duma's shoulder. "If you have to, take off, and I'll pop a flare when I'm ready to go."

Duma slapped me on the shoulder and headed noiselessly back up the lava tube.

I continued down for another ten minutes until I ran into a sophisticated glamour that was supposed to make it appear as if the tube had collapsed. To me, it looked like a vaporous illusion, so I simply stepped past it, much to the surprise of five dvergar on the other side. Beyond the veil, the pale but persistent greenish glow from my light stick barely illuminated a small portion of what was a sizable open grotto that branched off into a dozen tunnels.

The dvergar that I could see wore heavy gloves and boots, as well as long, heavy blacksmith-like aprons made from some kind of skin. Their stout upper bodies were naked under the aprons, and while they were all shorter than me, it wasn't by much. None of them wore a beard. Their pale skin glowed in the illumination of my light stick, and several held up their hands to block the light while others pulled on dark goggles. The excited, insect-like chittering of their language quickly filled the chamber, though the conversations didn't sound particularly alarmed. After a minute, one of the begoggled dvergars approached me without apparent concern and in a gravelly voice said something I didn't understand. He repeated it twice.

I held up my hands. "I don't understand you."

"Who are you?" the dvergar asked slowly in a voice that sounded as if he were chewing on rocks.

"My name is Diomedes, Son of Tydeus, and Pallas Athena's champion. I wish to speak with Lord Dvalinn." I bowed my head out of respect then presented one of my knives to him. "He should recognize this."

The dvergar examined the knife then bowed his head sharply. "Wait here."

He walked over to one of the others, handed him the knife, and said something in their language. The dvergar with the knife disappeared down one of the tunnels. Then, one by one, all but the individual I'd spoken with left, leaving only the two of us in the cavern. I smiled politely and clasped my hands behind my back, and he returned the smile with a tilt of his head, never taking his eyes off me. Truthfully, I had no idea if the individual was male or female. It had no facial hair, but in the light of my glow stick, I could see the creature's build was substantial, no doubt from decades of smithing. *If it was female, human women bodybuilders would scream for drug tests. If it was male, he was a wiry, well-toned athlete.* As he watched me, he kept rapidly jerking around and twitching as if he were a small monkey eyeing a bug. Male or female, staring at me with those goggles glowing in the light of my cyalume stick with the spasmodic head movements creeped me out.

To get my mind off the creepiness, I began pacing and humming, smiling occasionally at the freaky androgynous creature, who simply smiled back. Ten minutes passed before another dvergar emerged from the darkness and spoke to my goggled companion before disappearing back into the inky blackness.

"Very well," my companion said. "The Lord of the Forge will see you. Please follow me."

Elated, I fell in step behind him, thankful that he did have pants on as he clomped down the tunnel in his heavy boots. The way dvergar walked always fascinated me. They moved as though they might fall over at any time, almost as if they would be more comfortable walking on all fours.

We passed through several chambers weakly lit only by bioluminescent growth along the walls, floors, and ceiling. After the initial cavern, none of the tunnels or chambers we passed were more than a few inches higher than my head, but every surface visible in the pale blue-green glow and the light from my chemical stick was unnaturally smooth. In fact, even the intersections between tunnels were crisp and clean.

The longer we walked, the noisier it became and warmer the air grew until, finally, I could see the faint orange flickering glow of fire down side passages. A sulfurous smell began stinging my nose, as well, bringing tears to my eyes. A cacophony of metallic clanks, occasional loud cracks, and heavy thuds and thunks mixed with the insect-like language. Eventually, we headed down a passageway, lit by an increasingly brighter glow, that funneled the noise, now augmented by a distinct roaring bellow that rumbled through the surrounding rock.

We emerged into a round firelit cavern bustling with movement of dozens of dvergar and blanketed by the nearly oppressive smell of molten metal, burning sulfur, and steam. *And it's freakin' hot.*

The clamor stopped almost instantly upon my entry into the room. There had to be thirty dvergar working at a variety of stations around the room, each dressed like my guide. All of them watched me through dark goggles. In the center of the room, an impressive masked figure stood over a massive anvil next to a blazing white-hot fire. He wasn't tall, but he was broad, and something about him made him appear bigger than his actual size. He tossed his hammer down on the anvil, pulled the welder-like mask up to the top of his head, and growled something to one of the creatures next to him. He grabbed the molten-hot piece of metal he was working with his bare hand, examined it, and tossed it back into the fire. Then he picked my knife up off a worktable to his left.

"Diomedes, the human champion of Pallas," he grumbled in a deep, resonant voice that sounded as though it came from a rock crusher. "Why do you wish to see me after all these years?"

He squinted at me, his mouth hidden by a massive and bushy ruddy beard, some of which was smoldering and smoking. The gleam in his eyes suggested he *knew* why I was there.

"Lord Dvalinn, it's good to see you after so many years. Lady Athena sends her regards, as well. As for my presence, I won't insult you, so I will simply tell you that I need your help."

"My help, say you," he replied, a warm, toothy smile appearing from within his beard. "Come, let us talk somewhere more comfortable." He motioned with one thick arm toward the only other exit from the cavern. His heavily calloused fingers resembled sausages, and I had visions of him crushing bowling balls like walnuts. He was exactly as I remembered.

I preceded him through the passage, which opened into a room about the size of a gymnasium, lit entirely by the same bioluminescent glow as the passageways. Whatever emitted the light completely covered the ceiling, yielding a pleasant but pale electric-blue light that illuminated everything in enough detail that I had no problem making my way around. Once inside, thankful to be out of that furnace, I stopped and waited for Dvalinn to lead the way.

He walked across the space to a massive rectangular table so polished that it reflected the light above, appearing to give off the light itself. Dvalinn sat in a massive and incredibly ornate metal chair at the head of the table made even more impressive by the way it so perfectly reflected the bluish light. He motioned to the rather mundane chair next to him and placed the knife on the table in front of it. I took my parka off and sat down as a dvergar servant placed two crystal goblets on the table between us. Dvalinn grabbed his and drank without waiting for me.

"I see you've put the knives to some use," he said, liquid dribbling through his beard, sizzling as it hit smoldering hair.

"More than you can imagine. They have served me well. Lord Dvalinn, I need to know if you can make a cloak that can cause me to appear invisible."

He laughed a deep belly laugh that would have made Santa Claus jealous and set his glass back down. "A cloak of invisibility, you ask?" He smiled broadly as he chuckled. "Like Harry Potter?" He laughed deeply again and slapped at the tabletop, causing it to rattle.

I was surprised that he knew who Harry Potter was, and my shock apparently showed.

"Don't be so surprised," he said, his grin wide to reveal his pointy teeth. "We have seen the projections of the boy who is supposed to be a wizard. I have even built a device to decode and emit your encoded picture discs containing these projections. We find them greatly entertaining."

"I apologize if my disbelief offended you," I said. "I was not surprised at your knowledge, only that you would find human entertainment... entertaining."

"Nonsense, you humans are very creative, though you waste your talents focusing too much on such dalliances rather than worthwhile endeavors. You create, but what you create serves no real purpose. Save maybe to destroy." He held out his glass for a servant to fill again. "Your race excels at destruction," he said, shaking his head.

"We do, but I am currently trying to stop a cambion Blud Fae-Succubus bent on causing even more destruction for my people. That is why I need the cloak. *If* you can make such a thing." I added the last part almost as a challenge.

He pushed himself back in his chair, his facial features sharpened, and the amusement in his eyes disappeared. "But I *have* made such a thing, though it has been repeatedly abused and not only by *your* race." He suddenly leaned on the great glowing armrest nearest to me.

Before I could rethink my idea to challenge him, a handful of cave crickets bounded across the table, stopping between us. I raised my hand to shoo them from the table, but in the blink of an eye, Dvalinn caught a pair of them in his hands and presented them to me.

I took them in hand, and to my astonishment, while one was a pale living insect, the other was actually made from a dull white metal. "A robot bug?"

"An automaton, yes, but even the real ones cannot tell the difference. It can do everything a living 'bug,' as you call it, can do, except breed. It even possesses a simple decision engine driving its behaviors."

"You built this?" I couldn't help but wonder about the implications such a thing might have in the human world and what he might actually have out there. Then I pictured Geek's reaction and had to stop myself from laughing.

"Of course, who else?" He rapped his knuckles on the table. "You humans are just arriving at the ability to make technology small enough to do this, but this particular creature is over a hundred years old and still requires no maintenance. The cloak you ask of was easy by comparison." He laughed deeply again. "You humans are struggling to develop crystalline solids to produce the effect of cloaking." His tone became condescending. "Natural crystals with such properties have *always* existed. You simply have no idea where to find them nor even how to use them if you did."

I sat quietly, afraid to defend humankind for fear of pissing him off since he possessed my only real option. Besides, he was apparently right.

He shook his head. "You are a young race, and your skills are growing rapidly. I only wish you had gained your knowledge in harmony *with* the earth, rather than in spite of it."

"I agree with you, mostly," I replied, putting the bugs back down on the table. "But I don't have the luxury of time for a philosophical debate on the destructive nature of my race, my lord. My time is short, and I need the cloak. If you're concerned about its misuse, I will return it to you as soon as I'm finished with it, but I don't think I can accomplish my goal of capturing this demon fae saboteur and assassin without it."

"The Hanner Brid?" He stroked his beard with a pensive but concerned expression. After a moment, he leaned back in his chair to speak to a dvergar who'd suddenly appeared next to him. They spoke quietly in their native insect language, then the attendant receded. "I know of the crimes you were accused of... *and* that your name has been cleared. You say this Half-Fae is guilty of these misconducts and that you intend to stop him?"

"Yes," I said, meeting his gaze.

"I am familiar with this being only by reputation," he said, staring back at me. "And I know you to be truthful and honorable, so I will help." As he spoke, another attendant showed up and placed two simple metal cases on the table. One resembled a thick briefcase; the other was more like a heavy-duty toolbox. My eyes traveled from the cases back to Dvalinn.

"I will provide you with the cloak under several conditions," he said, placing one big hand on the larger container. "First, you will return it to me upon your new year, no later. On this, I will not waver. Do you understand?"

I nodded. According to the information on the maps I had, that gave me several more weeks than I needed.

"Good. Second, in return for its use, you will arrange for an instrument of my design to be included as part of a low Earth or polar-orbit satellite. Several human nations are planning upcoming launches, including the territories of Bolivia, Belgium, and Austria. I do not care which."

I did a double take, and for a second, I thought I'd misheard him. I knew it was possible to buy space aboard research satellites, but I had no clue how much that would cost or even if it would be possible so close to the launch dates. And then I began to wonder about his intentions.

"This is the price I ask," he said, eyeing me intently.

I felt like a baby sea turtle trying to cross the beach with a hungry bird circling overhead. "If this thingamajig has any effect whatsoever on humans, I will have to refuse. Nor would I allow you to use it under any circumstances." I glared back. I wasn't sure what he could do, but if he could make a lifelike robotic bug, then I had no doubt he could figure out some way to worm into the global financial system or even invade human military infrastructure—which he clearly disliked.

"Rest assured, Guardian, that my intentions are only to aid my own people. Humans will suffer by neither its use nor the information it generates, I so swear," he said, his tone even and friendly.

I watched him fixedly for a moment, trying to decide if he was being truthful. The only thing I had going for me was that Dvergar were not deceitful like the Fae, and Dvalinn had always kept his word with me in the past. Then another issue dawned on me: *What if I arrange it and the damn thing won't plug in right or something?*

"Will it even be compatible with the technology these countries are using?" I asked.

"No need for apprehension regarding its congruity. The device is... *adaptive*, for lack of a better term. It will work with *any* human machinery."

My gut told me I could trust him, but it could have been my desire to hunt down the Hanner Brid at all costs. Either way, I decided to agree. "I will do my best—"

Dvalinn slammed his massive hand down on the table. "*No.* You will *succeed*. That is my price," he said, growling like a beast.

"Well, if you put it that way, then sure, I'll make sure it gets into space." I really didn't like being yelled at, and I could feel my resolve for decorum start to ebb away, but I *needed* that damn cloak.

"Good. Finally, I require one more thing." His tone became much more calm, almost jovial. "I would like a VIP pass to the upcoming Consumer Electronics Show to be held in your Los Angeles city."

"I'm sorry, did I hear you right? The big show where all the newest electronics, gear, and gadgets from around the world are unveiled for the coming year?"

I didn't know much about technology, but people made such a big deal out of the CES that even *I* knew about it. A wide, pointy-toothed grin split his bushy, smoldering beard again, and his eyes twinkled in the blue-green glow of the room.

"Okay, if that's what you want, no problem." Hell, I figured by

CHAOS UNBOUND

comparison to getting his doodad attached to a satellite, getting my hands on a VIP pass to the CES would be a cakewalk.

"Then we have an accord, Champion of Pallas Athena," he boomed in an affable tone as his grin broadened into a sharklike smile.

He flourished one meaty paw toward the two cases on the table then grabbed the briefcase-sized one and spun it to face me. He opened it to reveal a dark glittering mass that took up the entire interior of the container. He grasped the object, which appeared to flow like water as he lifted it, then draped it across an arm in front of him. Instantly, his torso, as well as part of the chair and table, disappeared. Then the same space became blurry and went completely black as he shook it out and dangled it from one hand with a clinking and chinking reminiscent of a crystal chandelier. Even with my gift of true sight, which allowed me to see through magic and glamours, the cloak completely blocked my view of what was behind it. *Amazing...*

"Alas, it cannot transmit light fast enough to cloak movements above a snail's pace, I am afraid, but it will shield you from every type of electromagnetic wave, including the infrared lengths of light. And, no, it is in no way magical," he said, his chest inflating as he talked. "I *built* it."

He threw it at me, and I was unprepared for its mass when it hit me. I expected the heft of a dense, thick garment—maybe fifteen pounds at most. But the thing weighed nearly a hundred pounds and hit me like a dead, boneless animal.

"Holy crap." I fumbled the cape as I caught it, making Dvalinn laugh deeply.

"Weighty, yes?" he said, beaming. "It's made from hundreds of thousands of special magmatic euhedral crystals that I grew myself, enmeshed within a special alloy then woven into the finest wool. Think of it as the weight of responsibility you carry when you use it. One last thing: to work, it must cover something generating an electrical field. That means it must be alive and have a mass of at least three or four stone."

"Got it. Alive and more than forty or so pounds." I briefly considered the cloak's limitations, but given it was my best option, I would make do.

I stood to fold the cloak back into the case, and Dvalinn got up with me.

"I look forward to our next meeting," he said then left unceremoniously.

Another dvergar approached me out of the darkness, carrying some sort of light-emitting device giving off the same blue-green light of the ceiling. As the attendant waited silently next to me, I closed the case, stowed my knife, and pulled on my parka before reaching for the other case. I expected it to be proportionally heavier, given its larger size. Again, I was surprised. It weighed hardly anything at all. In fact, it weighed less than I would have guessed the case itself should have.

"Please, if you will follow me, I will bring you to a passage that will bring you directly to your transport above," the attendant said.

CHAPTER 34

WE MADE IT BACK TO Duma's hotel on Miami Beach, and despite the fact it was four o'clock in the morning, we had to push our way through the still-writhing crowd. The room upstairs was empty. Sarah had gone. I deflated a bit and surprised myself by realizing I actually wanted to see her. She had left a note taped to the door that simply said, "Sorry, called to DHS business. Be careful. Looking forward to later."

Yeah, so am I.

"One last thing before we head out," I said down the hall to Duma as he unlocked the door to his room. "We're going to need some help on the ground once we get to North Korea. Elegast intimated that he would provide assistance if asked and to tell you that we could reach him at Calanchi."

"*What?* Figures, that prick," Duma said, suddenly shoving his door open.

"Oh, and we need to make this guy think we're still actively searching for him, so he doesn't spook off this thing in North Korea."

"Makes sense," he said from halfway into his room. "But who? We can't send humans."

"How about those guys from your cousin's halfway house?" I asked. "Sarah mentioned some unsolved incidents she found that sort of fit the Hanner Brid's style. We can have them poke into those older attacks and follow his trail."

He jerked back out the door so fast, it was surreal. "Seriously? Those guys aren't fighters. This guy'd kill them without batting an eyelash."

"I don't want them to confront him, but rather hound him from a distance. I want them to let him know someone is still chasing him, but not necessarily breathing down his neck. The events Sarah found are old enough that they should be safe. Hopefully, it'll appear like we lost him and had to go way back to try to pick up his trail again. Ask Elegast to help with that, too. Being pursued by several different groups flailing around that far behind him might feed his arrogance and make him feel secure about continuing with his plans in North Korea."

Duma's forehead creased deeply, his white eyes narrowed, and he cocked his head and eyed me sideways.

"I don't expect them to catch him. I'm hoping he'll think we're still searching for him while we lie in wait," I said. "Tell them to contact Geek at the Metis Foundation for help. I gave Tolfin his contact info." Part of me didn't like the idea of possibly putting those guys in danger, but I convinced myself they might find a sense of purpose if they could help.

Duma closed his door, and I went back to work checking out the maps yet again, trying to figure out what my options were for getting on a train at a top-secret station we hadn't found yet. After that, I only had to worry about figuring out what I was supposed to do once I was on the train no one knew anything about. The one thing I *did* know was that my guns were going to be all but useless, short of killing Kim's guards, and I wanted to avoid that at all costs. Despite their government's record of human rights abuses, they were still *human* and, therefore, under my protection. It wasn't my job to judge human behavior. Unfortunately, I also had no doubt the Hanner Brid would use humans as a means to an end.

As crazy as it sounded, though I was mostly in the dark about much of the ambush itself, the part that kept really giving me fits was getting *out* of North Korea *with* the Hanner Brid in tow—either dead or alive. I was giving myself a headache because I had no idea where the nearest path through the Ways would be, leaving our exfiltration a complete mystery. While the rest of the situation was far from concrete, at least I knew my goal was to sneak onto the train and wait for the attack, which theoretically would come somewhere in that valley in North Korea, bounded by those tunnels and the trestle, on December seventeenth.

Hell, I practically had the bastard in my hands.

Two days later, Duma walked into my room, agitatedly talking on a cell phone at two in the afternoon. I had slept until nearly one myself. Given what we were about to do for the next few weeks, I'd figured I should get as much rest as I could while I could get it.

Once he got off the phone, I wadded up a piece of paper with my required gear list on it and threw it at him. "Everything okay there?" I asked, wondering about his phone call. "Someone scratch one of your cars?"

His hand shot out in a blur and easily caught the scrunched-up ball. He straightened the wrinkled sheet, read it, then tilted his head.

"This is easy," he said, swatting at the list with his free hand. "What about that?" He pointed at the large case containing the satellite array.

"That's an Athena thing. I'll deal with that before we leave."

"Then you better hurry. And, yeah, everything is fine. That was Ab. His op went sideways. Lost most of his team, but he's okay. We need to meet up with him at one of our places." He crumpled the page, tossed it back at me, and left.

I caught it, too. It was obvious everything was other than fine, but it wasn't the time to push Duma.

I grabbed my phone and called Athena, who, as usual, answered before it even rang on my end. We spoke for a few minutes without revealing any major details about the plan in North Korea.

"I do not like this deal you have made with Dvalinn," Athena said. "I trust it was made of necessity, but Dvalinn is devious."

"I'm not sure what his intentions are, but I trust when he says that whatever this thing does, it will not impact humanity. I will admit that it may be worth keeping a closer eye on him. His technology is beyond what I expected, and far beyond human capabilities."

"Very well, perhaps I will have Mr. Elmsmore examine the device before we ship it off," she said. "Leave the suitcase in the room, and I will have Septimus pick it up shortly. It may well be time for a new accord with the Lord of the Forge, if for no other reason than to keep an eye on him." Then she hung up.

A moment later Duma came into my room. "Let's go. Ab is waiting for us."

We emerged from the Ways into a cold pastoral landscape where a paved road intersected with a dirt path near a massive, old, but well-built wooden building. I guessed we were outside a small town in Russia, based on the Cyrillic writing on the signs at the intersection.

We had exited at some point along a Pathway rather than at a nexus or terminus—something only fae or someone with intimate knowledge of the specific path could do with any certainty.

The building appeared to be some sort of long-abandoned military facility in the middle of farmland. We headed straight for the rear of the building and entered through an old, decaying door that was about to fall off its hinges. Inside, the old structure actually covered a much smaller ultramodern repository with a broad, heavy blast door that required both Ab and Duma to unlock simultaneously. Inside that structure, the incredibly brightly lit room stored half a dozen vehicles under tarps, a few unusual motorcycles on special jacks, and row upon row of racks of weaponry of every description. *What else would I expect from the Battle Brothers?* There were also explosive charges rigged in series around the room at the junction where the cement tarmac floor met the thick, reinforced walls. *Helluva security system.*

Completely opposite his brother in almost every way except complexion and their unusual fae failing of showing humanlike emotions, Ab met us as we entered. His normally close-cropped pale-blond hair was a tad longer than I remembered, but still high and tight. Dark circles under his eyes suggested something was weighing on him. Regardless, the moment he saw us, he smiled and gave me his usual bear-hug greeting. Duma and he acknowledged each other with a slight bob of their heads.

"Musclehead," Duma said without inflection.

"Runt," Ab replied.

Duma disappeared down the aisles between the weapon racks toward a small work area at the rear of the building. He went straight past the racks of clothing on the back wall to a black cabinet similar to a massive mechanic's tool chest and began opening drawer after drawer—removing bladed weapons of every description.

"Get what you need. I've got to make a few calls, and then we're done here," Duma said as he worked.

"That works for me," I replied, getting an idea of how the place was laid out. "The longer we have down range to gather intel, the better off we'll be. One last thing... where in the hell will we be landing in North Korea?"

"Baekdusan. Southeast face," he shouted back.

I began scouring through my pile of charts and maps. I found that Baekdusan was an active volcano along North Korea's border with China. *Yet another freakin' volcano.* Unfortunately, the most direct route to Kilju Town—the town nearest the military and nuclear testing sites and a likely area for a presidential train station in the region—from there passed too close to several major cities, including the provincial administrative center. It also passed over two mountain ranges. One way or another, we would get down the volcano and then follow a river south to the rail line, which we could then follow east to Kilju Town. If all went well, our exit path would be back up that same valley and back to Baekdusan. Knowing that, I felt loads better about our plan.

All I have to worry about now is everything else.

When I was finished prepping my gear, I pulled the cloak out of its case and threw it around me while I sat against the wall next to the table where all my gear was and waited. After about twenty minutes, Duma returned, shouting for me. Twice he walked within inches of me without as much as a flinch in my direction. He screamed to Ab, who joined in the search, defending his ignorance as to my whereabouts. I was going to let it go for a few minutes longer, but Duma stopped in front of the open case on the workbench.

"Very funny, D," he said, hands on his hips as he quickly glanced around. "We don't have time for this crap."

I began to shift my position to see if I could sneak out from in front of him.

"Not so fast," Duma said, stepping in front of me. "It worked great until you started to move. I could hear the thing jingle like a bag of broken glass, then the area around you went wonky. I still couldn't see you, but what I did see kept shifting ever so slightly. I suppose if they aren't staring directly at it or it was dark, people might not notice it, but the sound was still evident."

I couldn't help but laugh as I threw it off my head. Being able to hide like that was every kid's dream.

"That's freakin' awesome!" Ab said, grinning like a kid at a carnival.

"I guess it works," I said. "Maybe with the noises of a train under way, the sound won't be so obvious. I'll definitely have to limit my movements under this thing just in case." I asked Duma, "Did you get in touch with Gracen?"

"Yeah. He said they'd do it on one condition," he replied in a tone that implied frustration.

"What?"

Duma sighed. "Help finding and building a new place."

"Aw man, that's nothing. I'll help," I said.

"Wait..." Ab said. "Gracen? You mean *cousin* Gracen?" His voice rose in pitch as he said it. "Are you kidding me? That guy is helping us?" Ab threw his hands up. "Great. We're all dead."

At first, I was surprised at Ab's attitude, but families could be funny. "Well, he's not coming with us; he's only helping from afar," I replied, holding one hand up in an attempt to calm him down.

"Oh, well, maybe he'll only get himself killed then. Duma, you know better than to involve that guy in anything more complicated than carrying water. He's... he's... he's... weird," Ab said, shaking his head with a dismissive wave. "I still have nightmares from the time you tried to teach him to use a bow and arrow. And that was almost seven thousand years ago!"

"That's not even the worst part," Duma said, closely examining the edge of a particularly wicked knife.

"Lemme guess. Grandma's coming, too," Ab said from halfway up one row of racks. "She's dead, but we're going to go dig her up and drag her corpse along."

"Close. I had to contact Elegast for D," Duma said, staring at his knife.

"Wait, *that* pompous windbag is coming with us? Forget it. I'm out. No offense, D, but I'll kill the prick if he comes along." He turned from Duma to me, pointing at the ground in defiance.

"No, he's not coming," Duma said sternly, finally facing Ab. "We are meeting *Seelie* allies on Baekdusan, but it turns out that... Elegast took over Basilicata."

"What the *fuck*?" Ab dragged it out as if he'd been hit in the stomach.

"What the hell are you two talking about?" I asked.

"Basilicata is... *was*... the center of our family's holdings at one time. Our ancestors are interred in the catacombs below the Calanchi.

It's not bad enough you humans destroyed it by mining and drilling all over the hills, but now Elegast controls it," Duma said quietly.

I frowned. The Calanchi were the Italian badlands in a dirt-poor area that was almost devoid of people. I didn't know they were Ab and Duma's ancestral lands. I was finding out a lot about those two I didn't know. At first, I was a little ticked off, but then it dawned on me that as old I was, they had been around for eons before I was even born.

"Hey, don't feel too bad," I said. "My old kingdom of Argos is now basically one big ruin dotted with olive and lemon trees. And goats."

"Yeah, whatever. I'm tellin' you, if he's done anything to disturb the catacombs, I'll start the whole damn Schism over — even if it's just me against all a' them!" Ab said, contempt dripping from his words as he stormed off up the row of weapons.

"He'll be okay. It's got nothing to do with you or even this mess with the Hanner Brid," Duma said, turning toward me with a flat, unreadable expression. "He's mad at himself for the screwed-up op. Eleven of our guys died. I doubt he'd care if someone dug up our elders and put them on display in a museum as freaks. Gracen, however, is a different story." He let out a low whistle then went back to working on his knives.

"Ah. Maybe we should get going as soon as we can. Sitting around will only allow things to fester. Besides, we got a lot of ground to cover once we get there," I said.

CHAPTER 35

I COULD SENSE THE COLD, ISOLATED, and forbidding nature of our destination long before we emerged from the Ways onto the mountain. We exited at midday into a full-on gale-force wind blowing snow and ice right in our faces. I had to squint hard to see at all. We were on a small cliff overhanging a hundred-foot drop to a steep, snow-covered slope that appeared to stretch forever. Ab's poncho whipped in the wind as he dropped his heavy gear bag and started to pull out climbing gear.

As we waited for Ab to ready the ropes and pass out the climbing harnesses, a brief rain of snow and ice pelted us from above like a small-scale avalanche. The first time it happened, I figured it was simply a natural occurrence, but when it happened the second time, a shadow crept across our small ledge. I dropped to one knee and pulled the Glock from my hip, aiming along the ridge above us.

Duma put his hand on the gun and pushed down. "Relax, Dirty Harry. It's only the help Elegast arranged for us."

While I had no idea what type of help Elegast might provide us with, the creatures above us weren't even in the ballpark next to the ballpark I was thinking in. The four horned figures, one far larger than the others, crawled down the side of the mountain like spiders. They stopped less than fifty feet from us, and we began an uneasy standoff. Though they ranged greatly in size, each had a hideous conglomeration of facial features that would have given any child nightmares: horns, fangs, giant eyes, pug noses, massive lips, and ears stood out on their russet and mostly hairless heads. Finally, after a tense minute, the largest figure shifted its hand, sending a cascade of rocks, snow, ice, and debris down at us. Duma and I ducked in close to the rock wall, but Ab, still hunched over the gear bag, took the brunt of the snow and ice to his back. He roared, and the four figures above us laughed almost as loudly.

"What the..." Ab bellowed, shaking himself off.

In a blur of motion, Duma shot across the cliff, grabbed Ab's shoulder to stop him from going off, and glared back at me reproachfully, as if I'd done something to provoke the incident.

The four creatures scrambled down the slope until they were directly above us. The largest creature, closest to us on the mountainside above, jumped down and landed surefootedly without a sound in the snow and ice before standing upright to its full height. The imposing figure transitioned effortlessly from bulky quadruped to gargantuan biped.

Standing, it was humanoid in form, easily eight feet tall, and over five hundred pounds. It was dressed only in a ratty pair of black shorts with a bloodred sash tied around its waist. A dense growth of black hair started halfway back on its head, reaching the full length of its torso. Its face resembled a Japanese Hannya mask, including the fangs and horns, although its skin color was a dull ruddy brown, about the tone of dull copper.

The creature bowed its head and kept it ducked for a good ten seconds before assessing us. It finally settled on Ab and began to speak in a rapid, guttural language, very Asian-like in its nonstop flow and speed, but unlike any language with which I was familiar. Ab nodded along at several points. Finally, the creature stopped speaking, and Ab spoke—thankfully in English.

"I am Abraxos, and this is my brother, Duma. This is the human Guardian, Diomedes," he said, pointing from Duma to me. He then spoke quietly to me. "His name is Gun-jin, and he is the chieftain of the Sanbaek tribe of Dokkaebi. He apologized for dumping snow on us, but he found it funny at the time. He wishes to make it up to us by showing us an easier and faster way down the mountain."

"He didn't say anything about *easier*," Duma said, smirking. "Just faster."

Dokkaebi. Sure, why not.

"Gun-jin, thank you for your help. If the way is easier as well as faster, we'd be grateful. Your apology is accepted," I said to the chieftain.

He bowed his head curtly. "It is easy enough you will not require ropes and climbing equipment. Lord Elegast has said to afford you every courtesy in your efforts here, and so we shall, Lord Diomedes," Gun-jin said with an oddly soft voice that carried easily through the howling winds. Because he was fae, I knew he would be able to speak English if he wanted to. I could only guess that he hadn't because of his misunderstanding of our leadership and not because he meant to insult me. Fae were peculiar beings, and I wasn't about to take any offer of help for granted.

Gun-jin spoke to the three other Dokkaebi still peering down at us, and each creature extended an arm to help us up to the ridge above. Gun-jin hopped up the fifteen-foot icy cliff face to join us.

"Please, follow us exactly, lest you lose your footing," Gun-jin said then took off, once again on all fours, loping across the terrain like a cross between a gorilla and a horse. The other three, each dressed similarly to Gun-jin except for the color of the sash they wore, fell in line and followed.

Ab and Duma glanced at each other, smiled, then bowed at the waist in unison. "After you, your *lordship*," Duma said to me in a pinched, nasally twang with an elaborate flourish of his hand. "Elegast sent them to help *you*. Don't mean I trust them at all."

"You big baby." Shaking my head, I took off after them as fast as I was comfortable, taking care to stay within their pathway.

I didn't know much about Dokkaebi other than their appearance was the stuff of nightmares, although they were said to be benevolent. They reminded me a bit of goblins, though some human legends mistakenly said they were the transformed spirits of abandoned household objects. Their reputation as thieves and packrats who took anything they felt was abandoned was legendary. After they'd dumped snow on us, it was clear the stories of their penchant for pulling pranks was true, as well. I also remembered hearing they love ssireum — the Korean form of wrestling — and were all but unbeatable. Unfortunately, they smelled like sweaty kimchi. *Yummy.*

We traveled quickly and steadily down the mountain for about an hour until we finally got down to the tree line, where we stopped. The forest consisted mostly of a dense stand of pines and birch trees that mercifully blocked the biting wind and whirling snow. By my calculations, we were easily a full day's travel from Kilju Town.

"From here, travel is effortless. We have spoken to the leopardess that claims these hunting grounds, and she will bid us safe passage if we do not tarry. To proceed beyond these trees, I must inquire, however, as to our destination," Gun-jin said without even breathing heavily from our jaunt down the icy mountainside.

"Ultimately, we need to head toward Kilju Town then track along the railway between there and Hyesan," I said, trying not to huff and puff. "I also need to find the presidential rail station nearest to Kilju."

Gun-jin blinked his massive, heavily browed eyes exaggeratedly at me as I spoke. It was a little like being watched by a house cat. I couldn't tell if he found me to be an idiot or if he was simply thinking about the best route.

"Based on the only maps I have, my impression was that we should head toward Chinsadorigi Township and then follow the Sŏda-su River south..." I said, hoping he might say something and stop staring at me like he was trying to figure out if I was serious or not.

"The river lies more than thirteen leagues from here in that direction." Gun-jin pointed east. "Your course is reasonable, given that you are only human."

Duma and Ab laughed behind me. I reached around my shoulder as if to scratch an itch and flipped them off instead.

"Uh, yeah. Then I guess we'll follow you." I waved one hand at him, hanging my head as I tried to steady my breathing.

Gun-jin spoke briefly to his three companions before turning back to me. "I will send two to gather those that will aid us and meet us at the river's terminus if that is acceptable."

The pair, both roughly my size, though much more gangly, took off through the trees to the north at a full gallop.

I walked back to Duma and Ab, hands on my hips, still a little winded, and knelt as if checking my boots. "If he says anything other than what he tells me, let me know," I whispered through the side of my mouth.

They both nodded faintly.

"Shall we go?" Gun-jin asked politely, motioning quickly with one hand toward the east as he watched us. The air of distrust in the group was thick—we didn't trust them, and something about the way Gun-Jin watched us suggested he didn't trust us. Maybe it wasn't distrust, but rather my instincts reminding me that I didn't know them and they didn't know me. And there was one more wrinkle I couldn't smooth out in my head: I was traveling with two notorious traitorous Fae wanted by both Courts. Under the circumstances, I thought it better to be friendly but cautious.

We followed the Dokkaebi through forests and over forbidding terrain for hours until we came to a river. There, we waited until nightfall to make the rest of the journey to avoid issues with the small farming villages along the river. The terrain went from harsh to completely wild again as we headed back into the mountains. As soon as we crested the small range, the moonlight revealed a large valley stretching mostly east to west in front of us, and while I couldn't see it, I could hear running water below. The Paektusan Ch'ŏngnyŏn rail line would be down there, as well. It was nearly midnight, and I guessed we still had sixty or so more miles to cover before we got to Kilju Town. I needed another break — *badly*.

"We will wait here for the others to meet with us," Gun-jin said then sniffed the air. "They should join us within the hour."

Below us, I could barely make out the silhouette of a tiny village, silent and dark. To our right, farther up the valley, I was actually surprised to see light noise clouding the skyline.

"Below us is Sado, and Kilju Town is less than twenty leagues in that direction, straight as the arrow flies." Gun-jin pointed first at the village below us then off to the southeast.

Due to the possible presence of military bases and nuclear testing facilities in the region, we couldn't travel straight to Kilju even if we wanted to. I also needed to travel along the rail route to get a feel for its layout and the surrounding terrain.

True to Gun-jin's estimation, eight Dokkaebi showed up about forty-five minutes later. Some of the newcomers were built like Gun-jin, though none quite as massive. Most were lanky with long arms and around six feet tall. Each wore a sash of a different color or pattern, while two also had some sort of hats or caps tucked into them. One Dokkaebi was ancient and carried a long staff that glowed with magical energy. He was built like Gun-jin, only shorter, and he carried himself with a slight stoop to his shoulders, leaning on his staff as he stood. His hair was also unique in that it was a silver gray, including the thick tufts of hair sprouting from his ears and nose. His eyebrows must have been six inches long. Under the bushy mess, his eyes were still sharp and focused intently on us.

With everyone finally assembled, I laid out my plan. I asked for one of their tribe to accompany Ab and Duma on their patrol along the railway below, paying close attention to the tactical value of the tunnels and trestles. I also needed to know where any power substations in the area were because the local railways were still mostly electric, and a disruption of the power grid could shut down a major chunk of the line. While the information we'd recovered in Coronini didn't say anything specific about this tactic, it was still worth checking. Lastly, I told them I wanted to meet up again as soon as we found the train station but that I would leave the specific location at the discretion of the tribe.

Once Ab and Duma were underway, I explained to the rest of the tribe that my top priority was to find the nearest stop for the presidential rail line followed by figuring out some way of boarding the presidential train safely and unseen.

"The rail station you seek is more than two leagues south of Kilju-up," the old Dokkaebi said, speaking in a raspy voice. "The human leader's private fortress is not far beyond. I know the area."

"Excellent. We should head for it immediately," I replied.

"The leader is not there, however," he replied, blinking slowly under his overgrown eyebrows and leaning heavily on his staff.

"Not yet, but I have reason to believe he will be very soon," I said.

The old Dokkaebi nodded, and within moments, we left. As we departed, several of the Dokkaebi spoke quietly to each other, glancing back at me and mocking my awkward upright, bipedal gait over the rough terrain. I tried not to take it personally, but I felt about as welcome as a guppy in a shark tank. After a few minutes of the nattering, Gun-jin issued a stern warning to the gabby pair. The two abruptly bowed at the waist then pulled the caps from their sashes, draped them over their heads, and instantly shifted into a pale, colorless image of themselves as if they were made of smoke. They were invisible. I couldn't hide my surprise, which elicited smirks and muffled laughter from the group.

"Their head coverings afford them the ability to disappear upon donning them," Gun-jin said. "Such items are rare, but Bae and Jae-Hwa have inherited theirs. Unfortunately, we have lost the ability to make such things anymore."

"Such things are rare, indeed," I replied. "I know of only one who can still create things with the power to conceal, and I carry, with his permission, the only such garment he has ever produced. The fact that these two can also turn invisible will prove even more helpful."

Then I picked up a rock and softly tossed it at the closest of the invisible pair, hitting him squarely in the chest, though not hard enough to hurt him. What everyone witnessed was the rock's flight suddenly stop as it fell to the ground, followed by a noisy shuffle by something unseen in the pine straw on the ground. What *I* saw was the Dokkaebi that I'd hit react as if a bee had stung him. He suddenly jerked upright when the rock hit him, and his reaction made *me* laugh.

"It's almost as if they've completely disappeared." I smiled. "Almost... just not from me."

"We will do our best to aid you however you may need us." Gunjin bobbed his head a bit, and his eyes widened as he watched me.

He was reassessing me, which was exactly what I wanted. Now he knew I was more than I seemed and he couldn't take anything for granted. I smiled then pointed directly at the two invisible Dokkaebi.

With that, the Dokkaebi filed past me in a silent stampede, and following in their footsteps, we began covering ground more quickly. I knew I was holding them up, but there was no way I could keep up with any sort of fae in their native environment. They matched my slower pace without saying a word, though it was hard to miss the frequent surreptitious glances over shoulders, checking on me. Hell, I was slowing down Grandpa Dokkaebi — and he had to use a walking stick.

Skirting the valley, we passed along the peripheries of at least fifteen small workers' villages and several larger ones. Each struck me as desolate and lonely in the darkness, though some were no more than a few miles apart. The concept of an anthill kept popping into my head as we passed close to the villages. Every building was simple and stark in design, each identical, leaving no room for personal identity — everyone working for the good of the government. It had to be a bleak existence.

Eventually, we headed south, keeping to the foothills as we neared the largest town we'd come across so far. I guessed it was Kilju. We gave it a wide berth, left it behind us, and began following another nearly dry riverbed for what must have been a massive river during the summer. The rocky bed spread several hundred yards wide in some areas, but the mostly iced-over river flowed only through deeper channels.

As we traveled across a vast, spiderlike delta giving rise to multiple tributaries, the two invisible Dokkaebi suddenly reappeared in front of us, bringing the group to a halt. The delta was flat and open for miles in every direction with a few settlements along the various arms of the river. The horizon to our left was starting to brighten, and I knew sunrise wasn't far off.

"From here, the safest place for us to hide from the humans is in those hills." Gun-jin pointed to a gently sloping area southeast of us then swung his thick arm back to the west. "The rail station you seek is that way but not far. Bae and Jae-Hwa will accompany you to see it, but take caution because the sun will rise presently. They will bring you back to us, and we may return to meet your companions at dusk."

"Make haste and be wary," Grandpa said. "There is often a strong presence of soldiers in the village. Many men, heavily armed, especially around the fortress in the southern part of the hamlet."

"Let's move," I said to my two guides, both holding their caps in hand.

CHAPTER 36

W E ARRIVED IN THE PRESIDENTIAL town within an hour and crept slowly through the buildings along the outside of the rail station so I could get a feel for the layout of the rail yard and its surroundings. Without using the cloak, I snuck around the first structures I came to: two dozen cement-block buildings laid out in a single row parallel to the train tracks. Everything else sat on the opposite side of the railway, which meant I could quickly access the train and the station without having to make my way through town. As the sun began to light up the eastern sky, the blocky profiles of several much taller and larger buildings became visible a few hundred yards to the south. A small engine — likely a generator — fired up in the distance. Then a few lights winked on, indicating that the town definitely had a small group of residents, though the area around the train station sat empty and silent.

Poking around, I discovered that the structures outside the tracks were vacant dormitories and housing. From there, I slowly made my way across the tracks, which consisted of one main trunk rail line into the village that split into four feeders, up to a building that likely served as the stationhouse. The large square single-story brick building sat adjacent to a large cement tarmac at the terminus of a road through town.

My two Dokkaebi guides, wearing their caps, strolled around unconcerned nearby. They would be invisible to anyone not using thermal imaging. I ignored them and continued my reconnoiter.

Around the stationhouse were a series of small metal shedlike structures in good repair. The one closest to the stationhouse appeared to be an empty guard station. Each building's reinforced door was locked and shook little if at all within their frames. Overall, the construction of everything was solid. Despite definite signs of regular upkeep and recent human activity, there were no video cameras or even any signs of guards or sentries. The limited information I had suggested the towns were largely left unoccupied until right before a presidential visit, so I didn't expect any trouble sneaking about in the early hours without the cloak. Once the presidential contingent arrived, the place would be crawling with servants, workers, and soldiers twenty-four hours a day until after he left. I needed to do as much recon work as possible while the place was mostly empty.

Except for the rumbling of the lone generator, the town was eerily quiet until a rooster crowed somewhere farther into the settlement. Then cackling chickens and the sounds of a conversation echoed among the buildings. *That's my cue.* I picked up a small rock and nailed one of my Dokkaebi companions in the back to get his attention. My action nearly sent one of them tumbling into the large retractable door on the stationhouse before the other managed to catch him. Once they realized I had thrown the rock, I motioned it was time to leave. I followed as they grumbled and glowered at me over their shoulders as we traveled.

Back at the camp in the nearby hills, I spent the next few hours sketching out a plan for the town, or more specifically, the area around the train station—I didn't care about the rest of it. The invisibility brothers had been less than helpful on the recon, but I still believed they would prove useful when it actually came time to get me on board the train. Grandpa Dokkaebi was able to offer me some additional bits of information, though it was mostly about the larger buildings farther south, which he said were part of a presidential residence.

The next night, we met up with Duma and Ab in the hills outside one of the small workers' villages along the railroad tracks. They had explored the bridges and tunnels at the coordinates on the map and identified three power substations within the Hanner Brid's target area, none of which was heavily manned or even fortified.

Given that information and what I had seen in the presidential town, my plan was simple: Ab, Duma, and all but three Dokkaebi would take up watch along a specific stretch of railroad and wait for the attack while I snuck on board with the help of my small team and awaited the assault from on board the train. We had to let the attack happen before we acted. Averting it might save Kim, but it might not get us close enough to get the Hanner Brid.

I assumed that the Hanner Brid's intentions were to *kidnap* Kim rather than simply kill him. As one of the most closed-off countries in the world, the North Korean government would quickly cover up any incident that happened *inside* its borders and possibly not even react. To make a guaranteed impact on world relations, the Demon Fae would have to take Kim somewhere outside North Korea and kill him or at least demonstrate his abduction in a *very* public manner that would force North Korea to react. Since there was *absolutely* no way to fly over North Korean airspace, he would be entering and leaving the same way we'd gotten there. If he got past us at the train, we would have to stop him before he got to the Ways on Baekdusan.

The first train would be beyond the farthest tunnel by the time the president's personal train made it beyond the nearest tunnel, while the third train would yet to have left the station. This left the presidential train smack in the middle of a steep valley that could easily be blocked at both ends if those tunnels were collapsed. The other tunnels and the trestle were too far apart and made the potential area of attack even broader. Plus, any immediate *human* response to an attack on the train in between those two tunnels would be limited, which was also why I assumed he would choose the area.

Since I was the only human involved in the endeavor, I stressed to all that they were not to harm any other humans unless it was a matter of life and death. I reiterated that point to Duma several times before we broke into our groups and left for our positions until the train passed. Thankfully, no one acted put out by the request. Our groups split up, and I headed back to the presidential town and train station to wait with my small group.

From just after dusk until just before dawn for several nights, I wandered around the town, paying particular attention to everything within a hundred yards of the station. Many times, I heard people talking, but thanks to the acoustics of the hills along the western side of town, it was hard to pinpoint their origin at first. Finally, after several days of sneaking around, I was able to identify six people — four men and two women — who were apparently the town's only permanent residents. They all lived in one neat but small building made up of four separate residences on the far side of town, and they were easy to avoid.

Before dawn one morning, I finally chose a reasonable place to hide—a metal pole shed at the end of the rail line only a few yards outside the tracks. Based on scratches and gouges in the cement floor underneath it and the pulley rail system along its roof, I guessed it was likely some sort of staging area for supplies. I could easily hide along the beams or up on the flat roof under the cloak until it was time to sneak on board the train with the help of the invisibility brothers.

Unfortunately, the spot had several major downsides. Foremost was its proximity to the row of housing quarters or barracks on the outside of the tracks. Then there was the fact that it was likely part of the staging area. These things all meant that I would be in the middle of Grand Central Terminal at rush hour once the trains arrived, and I still had no idea when that might be.

After spending most of the next day and night on the top of the shed, I was startled awake early the next morning, when one of the male caretakers began sweeping directly under me in the shed. I was afraid to move at all for fear the heavy crystal-encrusted cloak would cause entirely too much noise on the metal roof. I couldn't even risk signaling the invisible brothers for a distraction. Lying there as the other caretakers began to open and clean the structures around the rail yard, I realized the shed actually vibrated softly as if it were alive. It was so subtle that it took me almost an hour to realize that the village's power plant had been started, though nothing in town was turned on yet.

I watched as the caretakers began making rounds to each of the two dozen residential buildings on the outside of the tracks, opening doors and checking to make sure everything inside was functional. The caretakers checked lights, fired up heating systems, and made sure the water was running in the cold pipes before returning to their normal chores through the rest of the town. From time to time, several of them would gather to chat below me as they worked at a glacial pace.

At one point during the middle of the day, I noticed something skulking around the edge of the buildings, creeping closer with a sense of urgency. Finally, after another half hour, the caretakers retreated across the village, and I jumped down from my roost and went to investigate what I'd seen. I quickly ran into the sentry I'd sent to keep watch down the line.

"A train carrying passengers has arrived at the rail station outside

Kilju Town and changed directions onto the cutoff back toward this village," he said with trepidation.

"Is it the first of the presidential trains?" I asked, unsure why he was so agitated.

The Dokkaebi shook his head. "It carries hundreds of passengers and soldiers," he said, glancing rapidly up the tracks and back at me. Then he pointed at a train off in the distance; its plume of white steam stood out in the cold, clear-blue midday sky.

I quickly pointed out my hiding spot to make it easier for him to warn me when the right train approached and told him to tell the invisible brothers to get ready to start playing their pranks, then we both returned to our posts. I knew there would be three ninety-car trains full of people flooding into the town, but it made sense that there would be at least one more train full of workers to support the government staff on the presidential trains.

From my elevated perch under the cloak, I could see a hundred-car train approach. In less than a half hour, the train pulled into the station on the line farthest from the stationhouse. Hundreds of people began filing out, many heading straight to the row of residences outside of the tracks, carrying luggage. The soldiers, on the other hand, broke into small squads of four men each and disappeared into the village. Over the course of the next few hours, people emerged from the apartment blocks and began opening other buildings around town. In short order, the town went from dead silent to a dull roar as people moved about, readying buildings and cleaning pathways.

At one point, several heavy diesel engines started up, then trucks and several other vehicles — all military and driven by soldiers — began to head through town on the village's limited roads. All but a few traveled toward a large multistory structure at the southern end of town. One ancient but pristine troop transport of some make right out of the Vietnam War era pulled up in front of the stationhouse's massive retractable door, and a dozen men poured out of the vehicle's covered bed. The soldiers opened the huge door, and though I couldn't see inside, I could hear what sounded like a series of smaller gas-powered engines start up. Before long, I could smell the exhaust, as well. It was some sort of motor pool, and they were prepping vehicles for more visitors. Kim was coming soon.

Late in the afternoon, a team of a dozen workers began to haul crates and boxes from one freight car and stack them up underneath the shed below me under the supervision of one of the four-man teams of soldiers. Twice, the soldiers screamed at the workers, and both times, I could hear savage beatings and anguished cries ensue. The second time, two of the workers had to carry a third into the nearby apartments outside the tracks. It was all I could do to stay out of it, knowing it was not my place to interfere in human conflicts, but I hated bullies — nonhuman or otherwise. I had to keep reminding myself of my mission.

As dusk approached, the hustle and bustle died down quickly, and workers began returning to the apartments. The only thing that didn't stop was the roar of the diesel engines on the big trucks as they roamed the village. Sentries, walking in two-man teams, appeared at regular intervals around the town, as well, particularly around the train station and workers' residences.

The town had come alive with not only sounds, but also smells: people, vehicles, and especially cooking. I'd been up on the cold metal roof for almost twenty-four hours, and the smells reminded me of how hungry I was. I needed a break, too. Even with the roaming sentries and the influx of residents, sneaking out of town and back to camp proved easy enough, and I found I actually had to stop myself from wanting to wander around among the residents unseen. *Damn side effects of the cloak.*

During the next few days, I made a point of going back to my roost at various times in order to find out how difficult it would be to sneak around while people were here. Thankfully, people, no matter where they are, always function as if everything was *normal.* And in the small village in the isolated country, where almost nothing extraordinary ever happened, the soldiers and people — clearly the presidential vanguard — were operating on autopilot. Bae and Jae-Hwa, the invisible brothers, began performing pranks on the townsfolk. I wanted everyone spooked and expectant of odd happenings, maybe even a bit frightened. When the time came, it would make my sneaking onto the train easier.

Most of their pranks were simple, like tools or objects disappearing and reappearing in different locations or unexplained noises. The brothers took particular delight in leading one four-man team into an alleyway between the apartments by creating soft scraping noises along the walls. Once the team was within the narrow confines of the space, Bae tripped the man at the rear of the group while Jae-Hwa pushed the man at the front, causing them to career into the middle two, collapsing them all into an awkward pile as the men screamed and shouted.

One afternoon, the four-man patrol that had beaten the worker a few days earlier stopped underneath the shed to have lunch. After convincing myself that beating them silly would be too risky, I settled for repeatedly whispering, "You will pay for what you've done," in Korean until the four became so spooked that they left in a rush, tripping over each other as they hurried off. At least that part of my plan was working.

That evening, feeling smug and secure in my invisibility, I snuck into the apartment of an old man after he'd finished up his chores for the day. I stood in his small apartment as he cooked, ate, and listened to the radio, never knowing I was five feet away. As he prepared for bed, a thunderous commotion out under the shed where I normally hid drew out the entire population of the barracks around the train tracks right before the generators cut out for the evening. I followed under cover of the cloak and the furor and found that at least half the boxes and crates under the structure had toppled over, some breaking open and spilling across the ground. Then something in the cold night air struck me, and I realized what I was doing. I quickly snuck to the edge of town and threw off the heavy cloak, suddenly drained. I was trying to refocus on the mission at hand as Bae and Jae-Hwa showed up, eyeing me suspiciously.

"We apologize for the severity of the distraction, but we lost track of you," Bae said. "We had been trying to inform you the other trains are on the way and should arrive after sunup."

The effects of the cloak were weighing on me more than I'd expected, but if the brothers were right, it would all be over soon.

CHAPTER 37

A T FIRST LIGHT, THINGS WERE once again different in the village. Several platoons of soldiers armed with metal detectors and other electronic equipment began walking up the train tracks, examining the rails, ties, and the surrounding ground like a gaggle of treasure hunters at the beach. Overall, the vibe was even more ramped up than it had been over the last few days, and I could feel my adrenaline build when I realized Kim had to be close.

Later that morning, from my roost on the shed, I watched the first of three trains approach and checked my watch to verify timing. Once the first dark-green ninety-car train arrived, hundreds of soldiers poured out and began swarming the town like locusts. Some went on foot back up the line, again checking the rails and ties for anything out of the ordinary. Others pulled five boxy, antiquated black limousines out of the stationhouse and lined them up next to the covered landing. The red, white, and pale-blue ensigns of the Democratic People's Republic of Korea along with the similarly colored Supreme Commander of the Korean People's Army flag adorned with a gold emblem flew from each of their fenders. The remaining troops—two full platoons of fifty soldiers each—formed up ranks for inspection at the railway station, and a team of people with bullhorns organized a throng of civilian workers into an orderly crowd. I remained stock-still under the cloak, waiting for my opportunity to sneak aboard the train.

In the near distance, a second massive green train approached. I eyed my watch under the cloak as the train pulled in: twenty-two minutes. Every soldier I could see stopped, stood at attention, and saluted while the gathered workers were encouraged to clap and cheer exuberantly. I watched the surprisingly diminutive form of Kim Jong-Il emerge from under the covered landing on the opposite side of the train. His bizarre spiky hair and short stature were hard to

269

miss among the cadre of taller, hat-wearing attendants and ministers traveling with him. Though I couldn't tell for sure from my vantage point, he seemed to exit from the third rail car at the rear of the train and entered the nearest limo, along with two other people dressed in uniform. Others climbed into the remaining limos in groups of four, and as soon as the last limo door closed, they took off with Kim's limo taking up the second position in the procession. The five-limousine procession headed toward the largest structure in the village—some sort of presidential residence. It appeared he was staying the night, which would give me plenty of time to sneak onboard.

The moment Kim left, the area around the trains became alive again with action, with more transport trucks pulling in where the limos had been. From over the hill behind the town, two massive old Mi-17 helicopters roared to a field north of town. One peeled off and landed, and the other headed straight for the train station before landing in the only open area among the apartments outside the tracks. Soldiers pulling handcarts and massive dollies swarmed it upon touchdown. They offloaded several dozen more crates of various sizes and pulled them straight under the shed below me. Suddenly so much was going on in the village that I couldn't safely follow Kim, but I was also sure that the level of activity would keep the Hanner Brid from attacking him in the city. Instead of worrying about that possibility, I chose to focus on getting aboard that train.

Fifty-five minutes later, the last of the three trains arrived, though no one stopped to acknowledge it. The people below spend the next four hours unloading crates and equipment from the train. With the town now fully alive, Bae and Jae-Hwa shifted into full prank mode, causing mischief everywhere and anywhere they could manage. Eventually the chaos around the train station died off, but even after things calmed down, I still counted no fewer than forty soldiers within fifty yards of the trains at all times, not including those still onboard.

As the sun was setting, the two helicopters took off toward the north, and once again, workers started to file back to their apartments. Things slowed considerably, but the number of men around the tracks remained constant.

While the engines stayed running continuously, the trains had few windows, so it was impossible to see what was going on inside them. Shadows from the lights of the covered landing suggested several more guards stood watch outside the third car where I'd seen Kim disembark.

After one particularly edgy patrol passed me, starting at every little noise and even for no apparent reason, I signaled the brothers and jumped down from my roost. Still draped in the cloak, I slowly made my way around the back of the trains, fighting the urge to be brazen about my approach. The cargo doors were open in the last two rail cars of Kim's train, but guards were stationed only outside a closed door in the third rail car. The last two carriages were apparently used for storage of some kind, and both were largely empty. I needed to get aboard one of those cars.

Bae and Jae-Hwa suddenly shoved the train, rocking it from side to side, causing the guards to quickly back away from their posts. After a moment, the startled guards crept around cautiously, guns at the ready, trying to figure out the cause. The pair of Dokkaebi even stomped around inside the two open rail cars, provoking shouts and pointing from the soldiers, who retreated to a nearby building, leaving the train completely unattended.

I jumped aboard the freight car closest to Kim's private car. Inside, I quickly found a narrow space between two stacks of crates already secured in place, pulled the cloak around me, and hunkered down. From my limited vantage point, I watched as the brothers continued their pranks — until all hell broke loose outside. Intensely bright security lights lit up the paddock around the trains as bright as day, and automatic gunfire erupted from somewhere beyond the train. Seconds later, the spooked soldiers ran past, guns pointed and firing randomly as they pursued something toward the outskirts of the village. Several of the soldiers wore thermal imaging equipment over their helmets. They had to be chasing the brothers, whose caps wouldn't shield them from that technology. For a few moments, I debated whether to help them, but before I could decide, another group of IR-goggle-clad soldiers entered my freight car. I held my breath while the soldiers quickly examined the space I occupied without a second glance and kept moving.

The gunfire died down quickly, and the soldiers all gathered outside my car to talk. As I hoped, they were frightened and on edge, and it was clear their leader didn't want to tell anyone else what was happening because of the odd nature of the events. The unit continued actively searching and examining every sound around the train the rest of the night. Despite their use of infrared equipment within feet of me multiple times, never once did they detect my presence.

Before the sun began to rise, the rail yard came to life again. Throngs of workers and soldiers flooded the train yard and began to board one of the other trains. *This is it.*

Around midmorning, the first presidential train left, and another security team began searching my car again. Instead of hiding at the back of the space, I found myself standing at the mouth of the narrow corridor between the stacks of crates as an overly curious young soldier shined a flashlight around in the darkness. Something caught his eye as he swept the beam over me, and my heart raced with excitement. Part of me dared him to find me. Sure enough, the guard pulled his sidearm and stepped down the narrow alley between the crates. Probing around with his gun, he brushed the cloak, making an odd tinkling sound that caused him to jerk back. Someone from outside the car called, and he turned to reply. Before he could utter a word, my hand shot out from under the cloak, striking him hard in the solar plexus. He doubled over, gasping for breath.

I threw the cloak partially aside, pulled the limp guard back to the end of the narrow space, and covered us with the cloak, keeping one hand pressed over his mouth. Fighting every urge to simply snap his neck, I instead choked him into unconsciousness. From my hidey-hole at the back of the space, with my heart pounding, I watched as another guard poked his head into the car and called out, searching for someone. Another voice from farther away called to him as the activity level around the train began to rise again. The guard turned and briefly argued with someone about having to secure the car, pointed back into the car, then suddenly stormed off, muttering to himself. Then the heavy doors of the freight car slid closed.

I could feel the vibrations and hear people boarding my train as I sat in the darkness of the closed-up freight car. Finally, the train lurched forward. I'd had enough waiting and skulking. I was ready to finally ditch the cloak and end the whole thing. If my calculations were correct, we would pass through the first tunnel within the hour.

CHAPTER 38

I TIED UP THE UNCONSCIOUS GUARD using his bootlaces, gagged him, then covered him with the cloak, keeping it and him hidden and out of the way during the fight. It was good to be out from under the damned thing on several levels, and I finally felt in control of myself again. In the darkness, I checked my knives and swords then chambered a round in my sidearms and secured the safeties, all by feel. I kept checking my watch. I forced myself to relax by controlling my breathing, rolling my shoulders, tilting my head around, and flexing my hands.

Forty minutes later, as I concentrated on breathing exercises, a commotion began to rise outside the train, followed by a raucous screech of the train's wheels on the tracks and an odd jerky movement of the car. A thunderous explosion behind my car rocked the train, and I braced myself against the crates as the train slammed to a violent stop. Crates and boxes went flying in the darkness, and seconds later, all hell broke loose outside. Based on timing, I knew we were definitely far enough along the track to be in the target zone.

Shouts and automatic gunfire became louder and more consistent as the train rocked side to side on the tracks. Over the muffled din of people yelling, a heavy metallic thunk rang out, followed by the hissing sound of a pressure seal engaging from the door between my car and Kim's private car. On the other side of the door, heavy automatic gunfire pelted the outside of the heavily armored freight car along both its flanks. Yelling quickly became screaming and frantic shouting.

I got to the windowless door between cars but found it locked. I jammed one of my swords into the area around the handle and pushed, depressurizing the locking mechanism. I shoved the door open to find the area between cars was an enclosed flexible gangway riddled with

273

bullet holes. I pressed into the recessed doorway on the next car and pried it open. The instant I stuck the sword into the door, a volley of bullets pelted the other side.

I wiggled the sword as it protruded through the door, drawing more automatic gunfire. Once I knew the door was loose in its track, I pulled my other sword, pushed the door open as fast as I could, and ducked back into the enclosed gangway between the cars. Dozens of rounds peppered the other car through the now-open doorway. The second the first spent magazine dropped, I stepped through the entryway, put a foot into the chest of a man on my left, and punched another to my right in the face, feeling his nose break. I spun back and brought the pommel of the sword in my left hand down on the helmet of the soldier I'd kicked, cracking his helmet and knocking him out.

I was in a small enclosed sentry post. On the other side of the tiny space was another windowless door. Though clad in wood, it was heavily armored underneath. Again, I pried open the door and ducked back to one side. Automatic gunfire ripped through the open door and into one of the guards I'd knocked unconscious. Staying in cover, I knelt and tried to pull the unfortunate soldier clear, but he'd already taken several rounds to the torso. I didn't have time to help him properly.

An explosion ripped through the hallway from the other end of the train, accompanied by screaming and a multitude of high-pitched shouts in Korean, followed by more automatic gunfire. The newest volley had a much different timbre — a small-caliber weapon, not the heavy rattle of the AK-47s and -74s the Koreans used. A significant explosion went off several cars behind me, rocking the train wildly. I assumed the small-arms fire was the Hanner Brid — or his team — as they breached the train while the explosion behind me was the rear engine car being destroyed.

Remaining low, I poked my head around the doorjamb to catch a glimpse into a smoke-filled long, dark wood-paneled hallway lit only by scattered emergency lighting. On the left, the two heavily armored outer doors into the car I had seen guarded at the station were both still intact. On the right, one of the doors had been ripped off its track. The transom entryway at the other end of the car was blown wide open, and the bodies of several Korean soldiers lay bloody and motionless along the hall. The smell of blood and the bitter sulfuric odor of gunpowder filled the corridor.

"Hey, dickhead!" I screamed, in an attempt to discern if the Hanner Brid was there and where he was exactly. "You really think I'm going to let you get away with this?"

A gunman appeared and sent a hail of bullets down the hallway. I ducked back behind the jamb of the sentry post. I couldn't tell for sure, but the gunman didn't appear to be a North Korean, reinforcing my notion that the Hanner Brid hadn't come alone. On the upside, the gunman definitely didn't have an odd or inhuman aura, so it wasn't the Hanner Brid or some other supernatural being. On the downside, that meant he was using humans.

I re-sheathed one sword, pulled the Glock, and knelt in the doorway. I took careful aim at the destroyed entryway down the hall.

"You missed," I shouted, ready for a gunman to appear.

As soon as a figure poked through the doorway, I fired twice, dropping him instantly. I stood and began advancing down the hallway, pressed tightly against the wooden interior wall. Any other gunman that came out of that ruined doorway would have to expose himself for a split second first to shoot me. It was a small tactical advantage, but with my speed, a second was more than I would need. I couldn't protect myself from anyone coming in through either transom door. Sure enough, gunfire from some position on the other side of the destroyed transom door at the far end of the car began tearing up the hall, leaving me no option but to slam through the middle sliding door in the hall. Fortunately, it buckled more easily than I'd expected.

I fell into a dimly lit room, tucking into a roll, and quickly got back to my feet, facing the doorway through which I'd crashed. The room had no windows, and the only light came from fluttering white emergency lighting along the ceiling and the outside wall. The space appeared to be a parlor or sitting area, with large, overly ornate furniture out of a seventeenth-century royal palace. Two soldiers cowered in a corner just inside the door. They never even attempted to stop me, so for a second I ignored them. Besides the outer one I'd crashed through, there were two other doors into the room: one forward and one to the rear, next to the supposed guards.

I faced the trembling soldiers still clinging to their guns. "Kim?" I screamed as I pointed at the forward door.

Nothing.

"Kim!" I screamed again, still pointing, when one of the guards shook his head while unsteadily pointing at the intact door behind them.

Some security these guys are.

Hopefully, that meant that Kim was behind me, through the door at the rear of the room—then the Hanner Brid would have to pass through me to get to his target. *Perfect.* I positioned myself closer to the destroyed exterior doorway to give me a better vantage point in case attackers came from either down the hallway or through the door at the front of the room.

No sooner did I move than a figure in winter camo stepped through the smoke from the next car up. I dropped flat and fired off two rounds at the figure, staggering it. The forward door inside the room exploded, flinging smoke, shrapnel, and shards of wood. Instinctively, I threw my hands over my head as bits of wood and metal ripped into my right arm and leg. Deafened but otherwise okay, I picked myself up to one knee and drew my gun around to focus on anything coming through the newly formed gaping hole. I felt more than heard a single shot and an impact to my chest against my cuirass near my left shoulder. I swung the gun back around to the hall where the shot had come from in time to see the figure I'd shot a moment ago standing shakily with a pistol in his hand. I could tell the shooter was human, but he left me no choice. I fired three times in rapid succession, dropping him again, and quickly refocused on the smoldering hole in the wall.

The car we were in rocked like a rowboat in a hurricane-tossed sea, nearly sending me sprawling, and a bullet tore past my head into the wall behind me. I dropped my Glock to steady myself and rolled toward the remnants of an overturned couch in the middle of the room. Then I pulled my other sword, waiting for a target to show through either entry point. As the car settled down from its lurch, four more shots rang out, followed by the dying gasps of the cowering guards behind me. Several more shots ripped into the couch, but the small-caliber rounds couldn't penetrate the sheer bulk of the heavy furniture.

"Are you still fighting, Diomedes?" came the Hanner Brid's far-too-casual voice from the other side of the ruined wall in front of me.

"Always," I growled.

"I figured those amateurs pursuing me the last few days couldn't have been you. So inept and clumsy. And that oaf Elegast — please. But not you, Diomedes, the Guardian of Bruchad... perhaps we can make a bargain?" he said, mocking me.

There's that damn word again... "Why? Want to give yourself up?"

"Not quite. But I'll make you a deal. Let me take the dictator, and I won't kill you. He's filth, even for a human, and you know I'd be doing your kind a service. You should be thanking me, not trying to stop me."

"Ah, no," I replied.

Two more rounds slammed into the couch. As the smoke cleared, I could see into the space — an opulent bar — but still couldn't see the Hanner Brid. Heavy automatic gunfire continued outside the train. Hopefully, Duma and Ab were keeping the North Koreans busy. Then those were the only noises I heard. For a brief moment, everything inside was still and quiet.

"Very well then. I suppose this was inevitable. Unstoppable force and immovable object and all that," he said, breaking the silence, then sent three more shots into the couch.

"Yeah, well, let me apply the brakes for you then." I vaulted the couch and charged at the wall that he was using for cover, throwing my arms up in front of my head as I hit the thin interior walls. I plowed right through, colliding with the son of a bitch on the other side, knocking the gun from his hand, and sending him flying into the bar room beyond. But when I hit the wall, something snapped in my left wrist, causing me to drop one of my swords.

We both scrambled to regain our footing, though it hurt like hell to move my left hand. The Hanner Brid, dressed similarly to me in a winter camo jumpsuit, got to his feet first and attacked. I couldn't turn fast enough to dodge the blow, so I went limp. He caught me around the midsection, smashing me back through the already-destroyed partition and into the couch I'd taken cover behind, sending my remaining sword flying. My cuirass saved me from a broken back as we hit the heavy piece of furniture. Impulsively, I drove my right fist into his head at the neck, causing him to roll off me.

I got to my feet before he did, and I watched as he climbed slowly to one knee then to his feet, shaking his head. My left hand was mostly useless, so I held the arm tucked alongside my chest, keeping my right hand up. I wanted him to attack first so I could assess his technique and develop a strategy now that I was one armed. I assumed his training was similar to mine, maybe even better, but I had no earthly clue how good he was in hand-to-hand combat.

He glared at me with golden-yellow eyes, and I sneered back.

"I bet that hurts," he said, glancing at my arm.

"Not that bad, actually."

He shot forward and swung his right arm in a wild roundhouse punch. I turned away from it and lowered my head, taking the blow largely on my back and to my cuirass. He followed with a body blow with his left that also connected with metal. Oddly, the blows weren't as fast as I'd expected from a half-demon, half-Blud Fae. Based on the speed of his first blow, I knew he was at least as fast as I was. *So why was his second attack so slow in coming?* I could have landed at least three or four more punches in the same timeframe—even injured.

Using my body, I drove my right elbow into his jaw. Though I couldn't get much force behind the blow so close in, the shot still knocked him back. I instantly closed, keeping the distance between us to a minimum. He ducked his head, put a leg between mine, and tried to shove me off balance, but I twisted entirely around to my right and brought my left elbow around to connect with the top of his ducked head, this time with much more force. It was another maneuver I shouldn't have been able to pull off against someone with his speed. While the blow staggered him, knocking him to his knee, the shock of pain that jolted through my left arm nearly blinded me for a second.

He swung his right fist toward my left knee, and I lifted my leg easily. The punch knocked me backward, and I landed awkwardly. At that point, I expected him to pounce—that was what I would have done. Instead, he got back to his feet and pulled a broad-bladed Bowie knife from his vest.

I rolled over to get up, but the Hanner Brid kicked me in the back, sending me flailing into the wall to Kim's room. Bouncing off the wall, I managed to spin in time to see him coming at me with the big knife pointed at me in his right hand, his left hand up near his throat and open. He was sneering like a predator with its prey cornered.

I pushed myself forward off the wall, and the Half Breed stabbed straight at my heart. The combined force of his blow and my speed caused the heavy blade to snap as it met my cuirass, *somehow* surprising him. I used my momentum to drive a head butt straight into his face with a gratifying crunch from his nose as a pale-yellow liquid spurted from it and his mouth. He staggered backward.

Keeping my hands low so as not to telegraph my intentions, I stepped forward. The moment I was in range, I jabbed at his throat with the span between the thumb and index finger of my right hand, followed by a blow to his head with my left elbow. Again, the pain was severe, but I didn't care. I followed with two more quick blows to his chest and stomach with my right hand then let him stagger backward.

In the back of my mind, one thing kept gnawing at me: why wasn't this guy *faster*? Then something occurred to me. Hand-to-hand combat in modern warfare was rare, and I was a relic who'd maintained and upgraded my skill set over the centuries. The Hanner Brid, on the other hand, was a world-class sniper who probably wasn't used to dealing face-to-face with targets, let alone with creatures of his own speed and strength—but I'd forced him into just such a situation. While he probably could easily overpower and outmaneuver any *normal* human target, even up close, and take out virtually *any* target at long range, when evenly matched for speed and strength, he wasn't prepared to go toe-to-toe. For my part, all I've *ever* done is face bigger, faster, and stronger creatures, and I *always* expect to be the underdog. It was a reasonable assumption, which if true, meant I needed to stay in close to him.

His sneer gone, the Hanner Brid wavered, barely able to stand, so I pressed the attack as he tried to catch his breath and regain his wits. I reached over, grabbed his head with my right hand, and pulled it down as hard and fast as I could. Bringing my knee up to meet his face, I felt something else crack. His legs buckled and gave way, causing him to fall straight down on his ass, pale-yellow blood pouring from his mouth and nose, his left cheek already swollen and misshapen. I could hear him wheeze as he tried to breathe through a damaged windpipe. "Unstoppable force, my ass," I said, standing over him.

I should have continued the fight, but instead, I tried to find one of my swords like an idiot. *Supernatural creatures like him don't go down as easily as humans do — ever.* Finding the sword I lost when we hit the couch, I picked it up, only to find the Hanner Brid standing, pointing my Glock at me with a crooked grin on his twisted, swollen face.

At this range he has me dead to rights — so why not go down fighting?

I bellowed at the top of my lungs and charged. His eyes widened, and without knowing if he fired or not, I tackled him about mid-chest and drove him back through the broken wall, across the next room, and into a massive marble-and-granite bar along the far wall. As we hit the bar, bones cracked inside the Hanner Brid's chest, and he fell completely limp as my left arm suddenly went from feeling as if it were on fire to completely numb, even at the break in my forearm.

I staggered back and nearly fell when I put pressure on my left leg and had to fight to keep myself upright. The Hanner Brid slid down to a seated position then fell to his right, coughing and spitting up yellow blood. His golden-yellow eyes darted back and forth. My left arm hung limply from the shoulder, and I knew I'd dislocated it as the feeling came back, giving way to intense pain. I also discovered that I'd been shot in my left thigh, and as I tried to cradle my useless left arm with my right, I became aware that I'd also taken a round to my left bicep, where blood stained my white suit. Neither wound was gushing, so I decided they weren't that bad.

I glared at the Hanner Brid, still lying in a pile on the floor, coughing and choking, eyes still unfocused and gun still clutched in his hand. I limped over and clumsily kicked the gun out of his hand, and he didn't resist. His body sat peculiarly on the ground, legs out at an odd angle, arms limp and akimbo. He tried to lift his head but couldn't manage it.

"I'd guess you have a broken back. I told you drooling and diapers would be involved if you made me chase you. Now this time, *don't* move. I'll be right back." My original intention had been to kill him, but seeing him like that, I wondered if I might be able to get some information out of him — maybe something to help Athena smooth things over or simply why this bastard did it. *Only now isn't the time.*

I shuffled through the car, trying to find my swords. I didn't care about the guns. Once I had them, I went to the only door still closed and on its hinges — the one the guards had said Kim was behind — and tried to open it. With all the strength I had left, I shoved one of my swords through the handle. The door swung open, and I staggered in.

A small form lay partly sprawled across a bed in the dull glow of the emergency lighting. The body, dressed in drab clothes, was unnaturally still, one arm dangling off the made bed while a pair of gaudy, large-framed eyeglasses sat on the floor beneath the head. I knew that it was Kim Jong-Il. It was also clear that he was dead. I dragged him fully onto the bed and found no wounds or injuries as I did so. Other than being dead, he appeared fine. Even his hair was — well, not normal, but in place. *Probably a heart attack, due to all the excitement of the attack outside.*

Great. Just great.

CHAPTER 39

I BEGAN TO LIMP OUT OF the bedchamber when voices speaking English carried through the car from behind me. One of them was Duma.

"Diomedes!" he shouted, then I heard him speaking rapidly in Korean.

"Down here," I said, trying to shout back, but it hurt too much.

I made it back to the overturned couch and leaned against it, noting that the Hanner Brid was partly on his stomach, trying to drag himself somewhere, legs still spread at a gruesome angle.

"Hey, dirt bag," I said to him. "You know you're done, right?"

He didn't, or couldn't, respond.

I nodded painfully to myself in satisfaction as the sounds of movement from farther down the train became closer. "You know, I don't even know your name. No one does. We keep calling you the Hanner Brid, which I guess means 'half breed' in some language or other," I said, again mostly to myself, but also in case he was listening. "And what the hell does *bruchad* really mean, dammit? It's been bothering me since Gracen said it in Seville."

I glanced up to see Duma appear out of the smoky hallway in the doorway. First, he spied the Hanner Brid, then me, and I laughed at his surprised expression—mouth open, eyes wide. Mostly the laugh was one of relief, though it was mixed with exhaustion and pain.

"Holy shit, D! You did it!"

"You sound surprised, but no, not *exactly*," I said, trying to keep myself upright against the couch and feeling more than a bit sheepish. "We apparently *scared* Kim to death." I hooked a thumb over my shoulder toward his bedchamber and nearly fell over without the support of my right arm.

I had no idea what the implications of his death would be, but I knew as long as we weren't there when they found the body, the highly insular government would likely cover it up. I had no doubt they would make underground inquiries to their limited allies as to who might have orchestrated the assault, but for them to publicly admit some government had snuck so far into their country and attacked their beloved leader would undermine the country's defiant bravado. *Hell, they probably won't even tell their own people what really happened. At least we avoided the conflicts that definitely would have resulted in a more public death.*

"Who cares? You got this fucker..." He did a double take when he noticed the Hanner Brid wasn't dead yet. "You want me to finish him?" He knelt next to him, pulling a long, wicked needlelike dagger called a miséricorde from his boot. It was a blade used to put dying knights out of their misery.

"No point," I replied. "If he dies, he dies. Either way, he's going back to Poveglia..." I tried to shrug in indifference, but it hurt too much. "Ow. Shit. Maybe this way, I can get a few answers out of him on the way."

"Well then, get your ass up. We only have a few minutes to get out of here before the choppers come or more soldiers show up," he said with renewed urgency.

Ab showed up behind Duma in the doorway. "Pick it up, D. We got incoming," the big Peri said, an intimidating automatic shotgun slung over his shoulder.

"Gotta get the cloak," I said, first trying to turn my head toward the storage car behind us, but settling for pointing due to the pain. "Just inside the next car back. Should be on the ground between some crates over a tied-up solider."

Ab headed back, and I pushed myself up and started hobbling forward. Ab returned with the cloak before I made it to the door, while Duma took off back up the train.

"Little help," I said to Ab, motioning down at the Hanner Brid with my head.

"Really? Do I gotta?"

"Well, I sure as hell can't," I replied. "And this bastard has a date with the Unseelie Court."

He reached down, grabbed the limp figure by one wrist, and began dragging him out. He could have easily picked him up, but I could see the disdain on his face for both the chore and the creature.

The Hanner Brid's face was too swollen and distorted to read, but he gagged and coughed up a gob of blood as Ab dragged him.

"Might be faster if we go out here," I said pointing at one of the still-intact reinforced bulkhead doors off the train.

Exasperated, Ab glared at me, dropped the Hanner Brid, mumbled something, then put his shoulder and all his strength into the door, rending it along one side as if it were hinged instead of on tracks. He shoved at it a few more times to make sure it was open wide enough. When he noticed me limping slowly toward him, his head lolled to one side, and he sighed.

"Fer cryin' out loud." He grabbed me with one arm and easily threw me into a fireman's carry over one shoulder with the cloak. It hurt, so I screamed, but not like a little girl or anything. He pulled the Hanner Brid under his right arm like a rag doll and headed out and around the train to meet up with the others. I bobbed along on Ab's shoulder.

Outside, I could see the train was in a very narrow part of the valley less than a hundred yards wide with a sheer wall along the southern edge. The engine car at the rear of the train was derailed and billowing black smoke. Several cars farther up the line were lying on their sides, but every car I could see was pockmarked with the impacts of small, and sometimes heavy, arms fire, though little of it appeared to have punctured the heavily armored outer shell of the cars. Thankfully, only a few bodies lay scattered around the rocky ground.

On the other side of the train, I was surprised to see the Dokkaebi surrounding a small group of winter-camouflaged men — all decidedly human, and very Western or European in complexion — on their knees with their hands over their heads.

"We need to get under cover, quickly," Gun-jin said, "back into the mountains."

"Go. Everyone," I said from my less-than-dignified perch on Ab's shoulder. Duma knew I was including the prisoners, whom I assumed were mercenaries brought by the Half Breed — and possibly not even voluntarily. There was no way I was leaving these men for the North Koreans to find at the foot of their dead leader. Plus, as prisoners, they would also add credibility to the country's inquiries about the perpetrator. Without them, the North Koreans would never have anything more than suspicions.

As we headed out, several of the Dokkaebi carried other figures dressed in winter camo across their shoulders in the same way Ab carried me. From my position, I managed to count seven mobile prisoners while the Dokkaebi carried another eight. I didn't see any injuries among the Dokkaebi, and Ab and Duma were also fine.

Ab was even slower than I had been, so he handed me off to one of the Dokkaebi to carry but continued to shoulder the Hanner Brid. We managed to clear the edge of the valley and head into the mountains before the helis swept in to help.

We traveled until nightfall and stayed under cover of the woods and in caves for three days. The unforgiving terrain of the country, the worsening winter weather, and efforts by the Dokkaebi to hide our trail hampered searches for us, but we had too many injured and wounded to remain hidden.

During our time hiding out in a massive cave system, one of the Dokkaebi offered to fix my dislocated shoulder and set my wrist, but they wanted nothing to do with my bullet wounds. I took them up on their offer and gritted through the pain like a real man, hardly losing consciousness at all. My shoulder instantly felt better, and the makeshift splint for my wrist helped tremendously. My bullet wounds, however, burned like hell. I knew Duma would help with those. In fact, he loved that kind of stuff. *Sometimes he can be a real ghoul.*

Presenting me with the Glock I'd left on the train before he dug out the bullets, Duma told me what happened from their end as he worked, explaining the entire assault had taken less than twelve minutes. "It went exactly like we figured. He collapsed the tunnels, but Ab and I also decided to take out two power substations in order to disrupt communications along the valley and give us more time. His team rappelled down the steep valley wall to the south and hit the engine cars with Javelin anti-tank missiles, then began their assault, blowing access doors with plastic explosives. We tried to slow them down, but we were on one side of the train, and they were on the other. It took a few minutes since we couldn't just kill everyone."

"I appreciate your restraint." I slowly got up to walk over to the group of mercenaries.

"It was funny as hell," Duma said with a laugh. "Ab's full auto shotgun scared the living daylights out of almost everybody when he fired it. He'd open up, and the North Korean soldiers ran for cover— they didn't know what the heck was happening."

Ab laughed as he leaned back against a rock next to the fire. Those two had a different view of the world, and I had long ago learned it was simply in their nature.

"You okay?" I asked a tall redheaded kid as I awkwardly lowered myself on my bad leg to sit down next to the surviving mercs.

"Got a splitting headache and no idea where I am or who you are, but otherwise, yeah, I'm okay," he said.

"Who are you guys?"

"Most of us are former Rangers," he said. "But those three were Marines. Force Recon." He pointed at the bodies of three young men with nearly shaved heads. "Far as I know, all of us were either homeless like Evans and Franklin over there, or having a real hard time making a go of things in the civilian world, like me. I don't know about the rest of these guys, but I responded to an ad on the Internet asking for private military contractors. Said you needed recent combat experience, but you'd get paid extra if you was special ops of some kind. I remember showing up to some shithole office then sitting around meeting these guys and talking about what we'd done in the military and stuff, and the next thing I remember is being surrounded by those funky-looking gorilla-bigfoot things back there in that valley. That's all I know." The other stories were similar—none of them remembered much after showing up at some office.

The team the Hanner Brid had assembled consisted of fifteen American men, dressed and equipped like soldiers in the US Army, down to the patches and emblems on their uniforms and dog tags. Two of the eight men had died by my hand inside the train; the rest had been killed by North Korean soldiers defending their leader. They were good guys who, like many soldiers who had seen combat, had a hard time readjusting to civilian life. I doubted the Hanner Brid intended for them to survive, so he could conveniently leave behind a smoking gun that would have pointed directly at the United States.

An idea hit me. I hobbled back over to Ab and sat down.

"I've got a suggestion. Most of these guys are former special operations guys," I said, keeping my voice low so it wouldn't carry in the cave.

"Yeah, so?" he replied, throwing a rock into the fire.

"Well, Duma mentioned you had an op go bad and you lost some guys before you joined us. Maybe these guys could fill some of those positions?" I figured if they were homeless and willing to follow the Hanner Brid—albeit unaware—they could earn a living working for Ab and Duma. At least with the Peris, these men would get the best equipment and support available.

Ab frowned and bobbled his head as if considering the idea. "I'll think about it. After we get the hell outta this country."

Ab was right. We had to get all of them and us the hell out of North Korea, and soon. And I needed to get the fairy-demon piece of trash to Poveglia to stand trial in my stead.

***

Before dawn, we prepared to make our exits. I thanked Gun-jin and his Dokkaebi for their help and told the chieftain I would personally report his tremendous efforts in achieving our goal to Elegast. I also offered my help in return if he should ever require it—assuming it didn't involve hurting or deceiving humans. Gun-jin was gracious but hard to read. I couldn't tell if he found our mission to be an imposition or an honorable task. Bae and Jae-Hwa thanked me profusely for giving them permission to wreak havoc on the presidential village and, in gratitude, presented me with a collection of native herbs and plants that they said would help with my healing and pain. It was clear they enjoyed their task. *Maybe a little too much.*

I asked the Dokkaebi to accompany Ab and the human prisoners directly to Baekdusan and the Ways. I told Ab to either bring the men to Central Park and release them or take them to his training facility and base camp if they agreed—his choice. Despite a myriad of curses and protestations, Duma agreed to help me take our prisoner back to Poveglia, under the condition that he himself wouldn't have to set foot anywhere near the island ever again.

CHAPTER 40

EVEN THOUGH I WAS FEELING better — thanks in no small part to the herbs Bae and Jae-Hwa had given me — it still took Duma and me four more days to make it to the portal through the Ways on Baekdu Mountain, dragging a trussed-up, but conscious, Hanner Brid with us. Normally, I wouldn't have had an issue carrying him, but I clearly didn't heal as fast as he did. In fact, I was seriously concerned that he appeared healthier with each passing day. Our slow progress wasn't only due to my condition. We purposely traveled by night and took a particularly difficult route back to ensure the North Koreans wouldn't be able to track us easily.

Sitting under a rocky outcropping to stay out of the snow before we began the final climb up the mountain, I decided it was as good a time as any to start questioning the Hanner Brid.

"Okay, truth is, all I really want to know is why?" I said to him, removing a gag from around his mouth. "What in the hell could you possibly stand to gain from all this — setting me up with both fairy courts, inciting further unrest in unstable human governments, going after members of other secret human groups, crap like that?"

Predictably, he said nothing and merely eyed me with seething hatred.

"You don't strike me as ambitious enough to be doing this on your own. I mean, you were hiding out in Coronini rather than some secret lair. Why? The whole thing comes across like you just wanted to cause chaos in the world."

"Maybe he's figured out that stuff Medea was doing back in that mountain in Iran — harnessing the power of chaos or something," Duma said, raising his eyebrows.

At the mention of Medea's name, the Hanner Brid's eyes shifted directly to Duma.

"Wait, do you know that name?" I asked. "You do know her, don't you? Were you working for her? *With* her? You know she's dead, right? I killed her."

"I honor my contracts," the Hanner Brid said, his voice cracking. "Besides, this world has always treated me as an outcast. What do I care if it tears itself apart?" He glanced first at Duma, then at me, then out into the snowy landscape beyond.

"How noble of you to follow through," I said. "But what's with the vampire thing?"

The Hanner Brid coughed until he spat up a thick gobbet of blood. "I'm done talking, bruchad. Take me to Poveglia, and let's get it over with."

"Okay, will someone tell me what the fuck *bruchad* means?" I asked, sitting up in a fair amount of pain to glower at Duma.

"It means *trash* in his language," the Hanner Brid said. "In fact, it's an insult specifically used to describe *humans*, isn't it?"

"Seriously," I said, painfully leaning in to backhand Duma's shoulder. "I knew it. You prick."

Duma cringed, feigning innocence.

I knew I didn't like that word. I would settle up with Duma about that one later.

Knowing that the Hanner Brid was involved with Medea worried me. I wondered how far her network to spread and create chaos extended. The psychotic witch was dead, and this guy was all but finished, too. In my experience, the Hanner Brid's attitude was an outlier. Loyalty to a cause was one thing, but it was uncommon among those with power—they commanded rather than obeyed it. Still, I would have to let Athena know the connection was worth following up. After that, no one spoke until we left.

After only two jumps from Baekdusan, we arrived in a wooded area on the island of Alberoni on the north side of Porto di Malamocco off Venice. Duma said it was the closest he would get to Poveglia, which lay a few miles north of us inside the Venetian Lagoon.

I gladly stripped off the winter camo jumpsuit, cut to hell and bloody as it was, while I babysat our prisoner so Duma could procure a boat. I was sore but healing, though I would definitely need to see a doctor as soon as I made it home and probably spend a month in hiding, which I judged I'd earned.

That evening, once activity slowed in the small waterfront town, I wrapped the Hanner Brid in the cloak to avoid prying eyes, and Duma and I carried him down to the boat. Unwilling to set foot on Poveglia again, the Peri stayed behind, so I headed across the lagoon to Spooky Island, not knowing if Duma would wait for me or not. I was leaning toward not, but after all he'd done for me over the past weeks, I was okay with that. Frankly, I really didn't know what would happen even if I presented the Unseelie Court with the real culprit behind the whole mess. They still might kill me anyway.

The run across the lagoon took me twenty minutes, and I docked and carried the demon-fae into the interior of the island. I could see and feel the cold, dark tendrils of energy from the island's genius loci envelop me as I walked. Before I made it a hundred yards, I found myself surrounded by Dreaich guards outside the shell of a building.

"Well, well, what do we have here?" said the singsong female voice I knew belonged to Belphoebe.

"I told you I'd find the prick." I dropped the body and rolled him out of the cloak to reveal the Hanner Brid's bruised and battered form.

I was exhausted down to my bones. Part of me was relieved, but the rest remained wary. I had no idea what would happen next. *At least this time I'm armed.*

Belphoebe was dressed in her formal dark-blue armor; the scales lining her long skirt glinted in the moonlight. Her eyes were equally as brilliant, and her dark hair was pulled into a tight braid down her back. She held her bow loosely in one hand as she walked out through a crumbling doorway toward us.

"Bring them both," she said with a smug air of satisfaction and a predatory smile.

The fae huntress and I walked a short distance surrounded by the Dreaich, who also, thankfully, dragged the Hanner Brid. We passed among the ruins of several other buildings, through the heavy overgrowth of trees and shrubs, and into a clearing, where the ground parted like elevator doors to reveal stairs. We headed down the earthen stairway as the entry closed above us, and the walls began to glow in the same eerie fashion I remembered from my lovely respite there. It gave me the chills. If any of them so much as picked their nose in an aggressive manner, I would start swinging.

The walk along the featureless subterranean hall lasted only a few minutes before we came to a dead end. Belphoebe raised her hand, and the Dreaich surrounding us dropped the Hanner Brid in a heap—which made me smile. The wall opened, allowing Belphoebe to pass through, then quickly closed again. I eyed the Dreaich and their exquisite black greatcoats. Actually, they looked cool, but there was no way in hell I'd ever admit it to them.

We waited for a good fifteen minutes in stark silence, broken only by the Hanner Brid's wheezing breaths, which given all I'd been through, were far too even and regular for my liking. Finally, the wall opened again.

"Lord Diomedes, son of Tydeus, Guardian protector of humankind and proctor of Lady Andunail," said the gray fairy who had translated for me during my last visit.

As he ushered me forth, the Dreaich in front of me parted, and I hobbled forward, followed by my retinue of not-quite elite royal guard dragging the Hanner Brid. We passed into the same massive, dimly lit chamber where I had been accused of killing Indronivay. Its creepy, cave-like feel hadn't improved with my situation in the least. I proceeded into the now-empty cavern, stood next to Belphoebe, then faced the tribunal. *Again.* This time, only a single figure sat at the bench upon the stage—the hooded form of Duchess Nicnevin. Despite my injuries, I bowed in deference to her authority and position as Mab's proctor.

"You may speak," Nicnevin said, her shrill voice penetrating my skull like a dentist's drill.

"Thank you, Duchess. I apologize for the misunderstanding that I may have caused on my previous... visit to this forum." I motioned at my surroundings, despite the lack of peanuts in the gallery.

Unexpectedly, I found my mind racing. I had to figure out a way to make it seem as if the whole situation were all my fault and paint Duchess Nicnevin and the Unseelie Court as blameless. Otherwise, I could start an entirely new conflict between us and them—or at least me and them. After all, I did escape and kill a few of their guys in the process. Even so, what I desperately *wanted* to say was, "Here, you old bat—I told you I didn't do this, but you wouldn't listen, you uptight, autocratic, overbearing, shriveled old bitch." I managed to corral my thoughts before I spoke, though. *Apparently, I do have a brain-mouth filter after all.*

"I... was fortunate enough to uncover the perpetrator of the... heinous and cowardly crime against Her Majesty, you, Lady Belphoebe, and indeed the entire Unseelie Court—namely the murder of Her Highness's Warmaster, Lord Indronivay. Given the skill and manner in which this crime was perpetrated, I am flattered that the Court might find me skilled enough to have accomplished the craven act. However, I respectfully submit the true culprit." I gestured at the trussed-up form of the Hanner Brid beside me. "A criminal not only to the Unseelie, but to all fae and indeed every race, including my own. A being so vile and cunning, he was believed to be mere myth and legend—a creature known as the Hanner Brid, a half-breed being partly of traitorous fae blood. He alone is responsible for the tragic death of Lord Indronivay, as well as Duke Goibniu of the Seelie Court and dozens, if not hundreds, of others over millennia."

"He speaks true, my lady," Belphoebe said. "Lord Elegast will attest to the same if you so deem it. While the Lord Guardian may indeed be guilty of many crimes against our people, Lord Indronivay's death is the responsibility of this creature. The Lord Guardian has done Her Majesty a service."

"Thank you, Lady Belphoebe," I said, trying to make sense of everything she'd said—including the backhanded comments. "I have risked my life to pursue and subdue him, and now I humbly present him to Your Grace as an apology to you and the Court for my requiring your attention, even coincidentally, to this matter. It is a small but heartfelt gesture to assuage your magnanimous nature."

I was really pushing it. Hell, I'd been harsher to that windbag Agamemnon, but with that, I bowed again and maintained it. I wasn't proud of the sycophantic bullshit I spouted, but it was appropriate under the circumstances. Next to me, Belphoebe snorted. *Someone really needs to spit in her soup.* My leg began to hurt and throb as I held the bow, but finally Nicnevin acknowledged me, and I struggled to right myself, trying not to wince.

"Son of Tydeus, Avatar of Lady Andunail, your gesture is deemed sufficient, and your apology is accepted." She got up, glanced down at the Hanner Brid, then at Belphoebe, and unceremoniously walked out, disappearing through an opening that appeared in the cavern wall and closed as quickly.

I stood there, relieved, surprised, and more than a little confused. I had no clue what I should do. Belphoebe promptly kicked the Hanner Brid's prone form and crouched down over him. Her face went from placid to predatory. She pulled a highly polished black-bladed knife from her boot and held it along the tied-up criminal's swollen face under his right eye.

"I owe you..." She growled in a manner so low, it sounded like the purr of a cat but without the contentment.

"Ah... Pheebs, should I be leaving now?" I asked in a hoarse whisper.

To be honest, I had a few things I wouldn't mind doing to the prick, either, but I got an uneasy feeling I really didn't want to know what Belphoebe and the Unseelie Court had in store for him. Given his apparent ability to heal and his inherent toughness, I foresaw years and years of torture ahead, and the notion made me shudder. *Me, they probably would have just killed.* Personally, I believed the guy deserved a fate far worse than death, and if that made me a bad person, so be it.

Luckily, before I had to watch Pheebs get to work, the gray fairy approached and led me off. As I left, the Dreaich filed out of the room, as well, leaving through openings on either side of the stage. The wall opened before me, and I gladly passed through, happy to be unescorted for once. Before the wall closed up behind me, I heard harsh, wet laughter coming from the Hanner Brid.

CHAPTER 41

FINALLY MADE IT BACK TO San Diego several months after my rendition of *The Fugitive*. It was days before Christmas, and I was sore, tired, and ready to lock myself in my house for a week. I didn't even care about my boat, mostly because I knew Ned would never allow anything to happen to it in my absence.

I walked from the terminus I always used through the Telluric Ways outside San Diego and meandered to the parking lot of the casino where I would normally leave my truck. Gazing across the parking lot full of cars, I remembered mine wouldn't be among them. *So close, yet so far.*

I would have to call the Metis Foundation to have them send a car for me, but it would be at least another hour of waiting after I made the damn call. Frankly, I wasn't in the mood to head into the casino to find a phone, either, so I stumbled to the first bench I found and plopped down. I kept my swords and remaining guns wrapped in Dvalinn's cloak. I planned to walk inside to make my call as soon as my head, my arm, or my leg stopped throbbing.

While I rested, a long, sleek black Mercedes Benz limousine pulled up and stopped, and a massive figure dressed in a long black coat and a chauffeur's hat got out and walked around to the passenger side of the rear compartment. I was so tired that at first, I didn't pay attention to the fact the limo had pulled right in front of me. The driver's insistent stare finally caught my attention, and I realized it was one of Athena's Spartoi. He opened the passenger door, and I blinked a few times then pushed to my feet. I ambled to the car, nearly too weary to climb into the back of a limo—even such a nice one—and mostly fell inside. The door closed behind me with a quiet and solid thump. In my weariness, I struggled to pull myself upright in the ridiculously soft leather seats until I felt Athena's presence. Then I gave up.

"Thanks for the ride home," I said, lying back in the seat.

"Of course," Athena replied from the seat across from me, "but we should talk before you rest."

"You talk; I'll listen. If I fall asleep, kick me..."

"You should know that North Korea has admitted to the world that Kim Jong-Il died of a heart attack while onboard his train. They make no mention of an assault against him of any kind, and while they have made a few covert inquiries into what really happened, they are content to leave it as such for the sake of their people. The new leader, Kim's son, Kim Jong-Un, will likely be worse than his father, though we can scarcely do anything about that."

I breathed a heavy sigh and chose to say nothing. A half victory was sometimes worse than a failure.

"Of course, we may never know what, if anything, transpired in Syria," she said, continuing to ruin my moment of Zen. "The situation within the entire Middle East remains highly unstable while Syria teeters on the brink of civil war because of Assad's increasingly irrational actions toward his people. Even his wife is acting outside of her norm. To date, all efforts by various governments and organizations, including the Metis Foundation, have been unsuccessful at defusing tensions. Civil war is all but inevitable. Either way, it is now a human conflict and outside of *our* realm to interfere." What she meant was her but, mostly, me. "The Metis Foundation will continue its efforts, of course."

"Party pooper," I replied, closing my eyes. "Oh, by the way, the Hanner Brid was working for Medea. Said he was trying to fulfill his contract for her, but it sounded like he had a personal grudge against the world, too. Probably wasn't hugged enough as a kid or something."

"That revelation makes more sense now," she said.

I didn't have a clue what she meant by that, nor did I care at the moment.

She had absolutely no information on what the Unseelie Court did with the Demon Fae. However, with the help of Artemis and Deeta's private collection of papers on various demons and fallen creatures, she did find a name for him: Nasi Ba'Urcalegon. Frankly, I liked Hanner Brid better. After that tidbit, Athena mercifully let me rest.

During the remainder of the drive back, all I could think about was climbing into bed for at least two days and the pleasure I would take in strangling anyone who dared disturb me. At one point, however, Sarah came to mind, and I found myself momentarily renewed by the conversation we'd had in Miami. I even found myself a little excited — and suddenly nervous as hell — as we arrived at my house on Point Loma.

I was lost in anticipation though a little queasy when I pulled myself from the comfy seat in the back of the limo, but before I could run into the house to get to the phone to call Sarah, Athena stepped between me and my front door, holding a brown file folder. Her normally intense blue eyes were a flat steely gray, and she pursed her lips and tilted her head as she watched me lumber along.

"In light of what you told me about this being's motives, you need to see this, and then we should talk. Get that wrist checked out and then get some rest, Diomedes. You really look like hell."

"Thanks, boss." I snatched the folder from her, unconcerned about what was in it. "Oh, and get this back to Dvalinn before New Year's Day. I'm busy." I dumped my weapons on my stoop then tossed the heavy garment to her.

Excitedly, I riffled through my keys a little more clumsily than normal to open the door, grabbed my swords, knives, and gun off the ground, and kicked open the door. Once inside, I shut the door with my hip, dropped my weapons, threw the folder on my counter, then grabbed the phone. I fumbled with the buttons because of my bad wrist and even hung up twice due to nerves before I finally finished dialing on my third try. I felt like a damned kid. I found myself both disappointed and somewhat relieved when she didn't answer. More disappointed, which actually made me smile at the realization.

Oddly, the fact I was as nervous as a schoolboy on a first date and excited about seeing Sarah again and prospects yet to come made me feel decidedly human for the first time in weeks. Not just human among nonhuman creatures, but human with simple, trivial, and *fantastic* human problems like dating.

I put the phone down and went back to the folder. It was thin, and when I opened it, there was nothing but a ripped and charred piece of paper with a list of names and countries on it. I got a wicked sense of déjà vu, leading to a sense of dread when I got to the bottom of the page: circled in blood was "rcalegon." *I'll be damned.* Athena had said his name was Nasi Ba'Urcalegon.

I'd recovered this list from Medea's chambers almost a year ago. On it was Assad of Syria, Mubarak of Egypt, Gaddafi of Libya, and *Kim of North Korea.* If only I'd known a year ago what the list meant.

A knock at the door accompanied by a familiar jovial voice jarred me. "You in there, boy?" Ned called out, followed by a barrage of dings from the doorbell. "I heard you're back, finally. Open up, I brought beer..."

I opened the door, and Ned greeted me with a big grin and a six-pack in both hands. The revelation from the contents of the folder still had me preoccupied, but seeing Ned's beaming grin and hideous pink-and-chartreuse shirt made me smile in return.

"Why the hell do *I* care if you brought beer?" I replied.

"You don't, but they're getting warm, and I want them *cold.* I didn't want to stand around out here all day. Besides, you got a package, too."

On my stoop at his feet was an unmarked brown box maybe ten inches cubed, secured with twine. Completely puzzled, I picked it up and invited Ned in. He promptly made a beeline for the fridge. I limped along behind him into the kitchen, set the box on the counter, and pulled a knife from one of the drawers. I cut the twine and found a smaller wooden box of exquisite craftsmanship inside. It was intricately carved with a fluid, winding design inlaid using a lighter-colored wood. I stared at Ned, even more confused. He swigged his beer, raised his eyebrows, and shrugged.

"Maybe walnut with mahogany inlays..." Ned said as I lifted it out and set it on the counter. "No sender on the box?"

"Nothing on the box at all."

"Well, open it. Maybe it's a thank-you gift from Mab!" Ned said sarcastically then burst into a fit of snorting laughter, dribbling beer down his bushy beard.

I lifted the fitted top off the wooden box, and a heavy metallic odor mixed with the scent of decay and rotting meat hit both of us like a fist. I covered my nose and mouth with my hand, but my eyes still watered at the putrid smell. Inside, something about the size of a baseball was wrapped in a piece of black cloth and bound by a black silk ribbon. When I picked it up, the smell became stronger, causing me to gag a bit as I placed it into the sink.

"Ugh. How long has this thing been sitting around?" I asked, not really expecting an answer.

"Wasn't there yesterday, I swear," Ned replied, grabbing the dishtowel from the front of the stove to cover his face.

"Wasn't there twenty minutes ago, either."

I put the package into the sink and cut the ribbon. A ghastly black-brown sludge poured out and down the drain. Once unwrapped, a gelatinous brown ball flopped out into the sink, oozing more sludge from a gash. All at once, I recognized what it was—*a heart*. Given its size, it could easily have been human, but given its state of decomposition, I couldn't tell for sure. My mind flashed instantly to Sarah. Right as I was about to panic, the phone rang, but I didn't answer it. I couldn't move. Finally, the ringing stopped, and the answering machine kicked in. Sarah's voice began leaving a message, snapping me back to reality, and I ran to pick up the phone, elated I was wrong.

"Sarah!" I said, mostly screaming into the phone, "I'm here. I'm here—"

"Oh, good. I was going to leave you a message. I'm on a call out, but I wanted to let you know I got your message, and I'm glad you're okay."

"Yeah, all good. Mostly, anyway," I said, staring back at Ned, who was standing over the sink. Then without thinking, I spoke. "Listen, why don't we meet up this weekend, maybe have dinner and talk?" I said, instantly horrified she might say no. *I've risked my neck for too long not to take chances like this one.*

"Sure, that would be great."

I could feel myself smile. "Okay... I'll call you later, and we can work out the details," I said, forgetting briefly about the nasty package on my counter.

"Looking forward to it."

We both hung up.

"You're making a date?" Ned asked, his eyes crinkled from a smile he hid under the dishtowel. "You got more important things to deal with right now. Sheesh. The smell is even makin' my beer taste bad, dude."

Leave it to Ned to boil any situation down to its most basic element.

"It's a heart," he said as I walked back into the kitchen and stared into the sink. He was poking at it with the knife. "Something else inside it, too."

I grabbed the knife from him and began prodding at the greasy hunk of meat. Something shiny and gold protruded from one of the severed vessels. I pulled another knife from a drawer and began cutting. While I hadn't thought it possible, the smell became worse, but I was so focused, it no longer bothered me.

From one of the chambers, I pulled a thin gold chain with a locket attached to it. I recognized it instantly from the caverns below Coronini and the woman in the cell. As it came free from the rotted meat, a small black metal object pulled free, as well. It was a small knife formed from a gothic-style ankh. I had no idea what it was beyond the Egyptian symbol for life.

"Damn," said Ned from behind me. "Vampires."

"Well, then, I'd guess Liuntika Strigoi. I may have killed a few of them and wrecked some of their caverns. And beat up some of their thralls. And killed a woman they were turning." I pointed at the locket. "That was hers."

"I'll bet the heart was hers, too. It's a threat. That little trinket there is a declaration of war. Looks like you pissed 'em off, dude."

I dropped the locket into the sink. "For the love of... can't I catch a damn break?"

"Trouble don't rest, dude," Ned said, toasting me with his beer. "What do you think that means for the troubleshooter?"

ACKNOWLEDGMENTS

I want to thank a number of people for helping me with *Chaos Unbound*. First and foremost, as always, I want to thank Teri and the rest of my family for their continued support and encouragement with this endeavor. I also want to thank my beta readers, Mary Cannon, Krissy Marie, and Colleen Poor, for their willingness to read early versions of this book and aid me in making it better. As always, there is no way I can thank my brilliant editors with Red Adept, Alyssa Hall and Stefanie Spangler Buswell, enough. Their hard work and efforts sharpen the story and my writing and give me the confidence to forge on. Lastly, I want to thank my readers. I have received lots of positive feedback, but more importantly, I love it when you guys feel strongly enough about something to comment on it to me directly — good or bad. Believe it or not, those comments help me make my stories better. So again, thank you.

And for those who asked for a glossary of characters, creatures, and objects, visit the wiki on my website, www.briansleon.com/wiki. It's way too large to include here!

ABOUT THE AUTHOR

 Brian S. Leon is truly a jack-of-all-trades and a master of none. He began writing in order to do something with all the useless degrees, knowledge, and skills–most of which have no practical application in civilized society–he accumulated over the years.

His varied interests include, most notably, mythology of all kinds and fishing, and he has spent time in jungles and museums all over the world, studying and oceans and seas across the globe chasing fish, sometimes even catching them. He has also spent time in various locations around the world doing other things that may or may not have ever happened.

Inspired by stories of classical masters like Homer and Jules Verne, as well as modern writers like J.R.R. Tolkien, David Morrell, and Jim Butcher, combined with an inordinate amount of free time, Mr. Leon finally decided to come up with tales of his own.

Brian currently resides in San Diego, California. You can visit his Web site at www.BrianSLeon.com.

www.ingramcontent.com/pod-product-compliance
Lightning Source LLC
Chambersburg PA
CBHW020228260626
47156CB00002B/595